Cast Down the Waters

A *Bosnia in Flames*

Cast Down the Waters

A Bosnia in Flames

A novel by

Clifford J. Moody

GoldenIsle Publishers, Inc.
Eastman, GA 31023

GoldenIsle Publishers, Inc.
2395 Hawkinsville Hwy
Eastman, GA 31023

Library of Congress Catalog Card Number: 99-95527

Clifford J. Moody, 1934-
    Cast Down the Waters; A Bosnia in Flames

ISBN 0-9666721-1-9

1. Suspense—sabotage. 2. Freedom fighters. 3. Romance
    4. War—political turmoil. Ethnic cleansing-Yugoslavia
        I. Title: Cast Down the Waters
        II. Subtitle:A Bosnia in Flames

Designed by Tena Ryals

Printed in the United States of America

First Edition

10 9 8 7 6 5 4 3 2 1

Part I

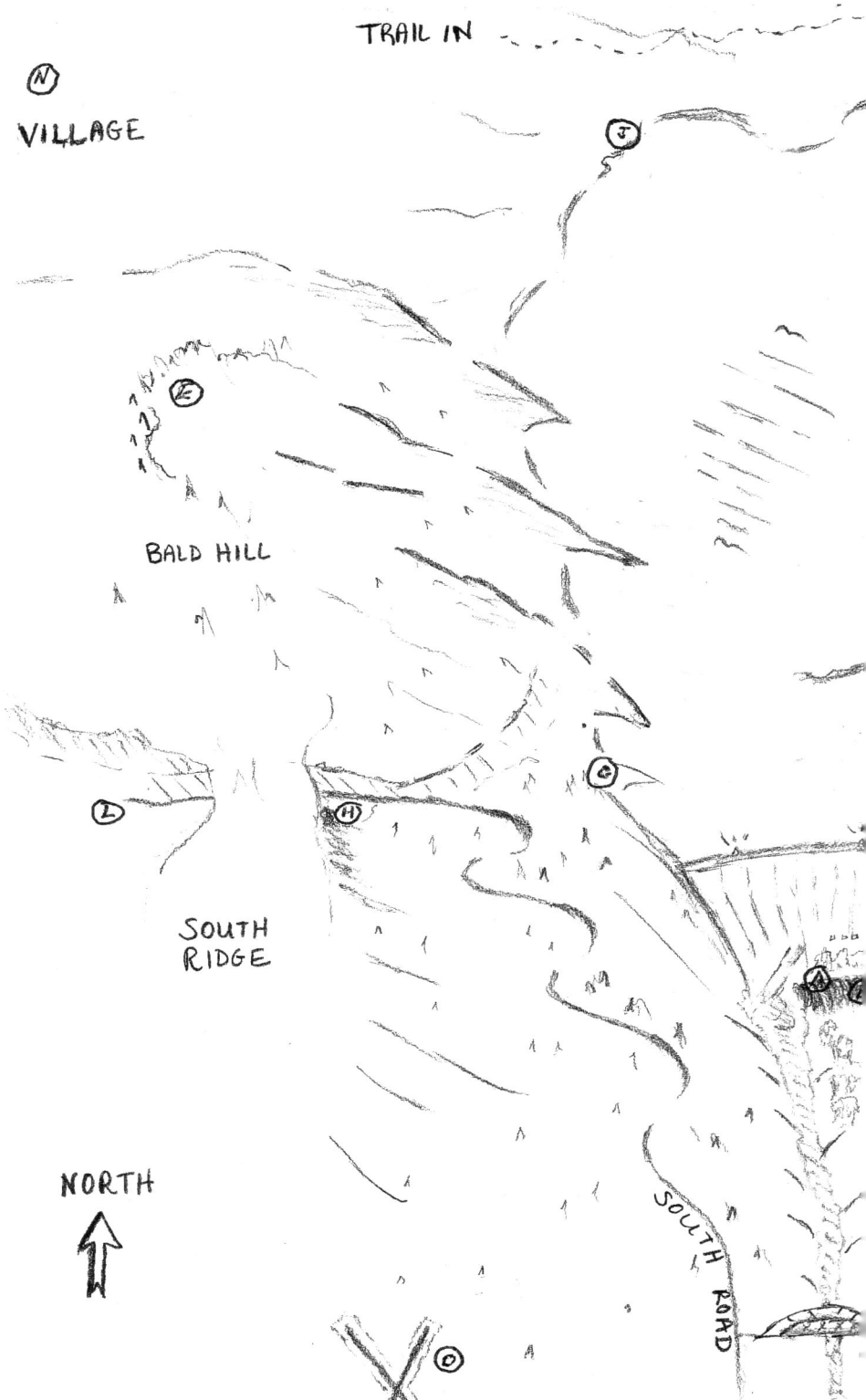

CASTLE MTN

SHAFT	A	STEEL BRIDGE	I
MOUND	B	MTG. WITH BAXTER	J
ABANDONED R.R.	C	RAFT	K
ESCAPE TUNNEL	D	WEST GUARD HUT	L
NEDO's CAMP	E	POWER STATION	M
RIVER CROSSING	F	ZELKO'S HOUSE	N
BATTLE — NEDO	G	ENEMY AIRSTRIP	O
FUEL TANKS	H	WATERFALL	P

Prologue

The book of time, large as creation itself, lay opened before the great circle of the globe. Not a single page had been turned since the era began at the end of the Second World War. Instead, peoples everywhere had shrunk wide-eyed before the stage where two Leviathans of the earth stood locked in mortal combat. So preoccupied was the world, in fact, that the fleecy bearded figure of Father Time went unobserved as he bent to his task, then paused to wet a pondering finger. It would be another blink in time before the page was finally turned to end the era. Yet, to the careful observer, already signs of the aftermath were coming into focus

THE YEAR 1992. The Iron Curtain had fallen, and the collapse of the Soviet Union been duly recorded for all to see. The time of speculation was over; now the world press found itself dealing with but the last scraps and remnants.

Twelve years earlier, Marshall Tito of Yugoslavia, symbol of defiance of the Soviet yoke and bulwark against Soviet expansion in the Balkans, had expired on his sick bed. Since, one by one, the disparate parts of that proud nation had fractured into warring factions, the bloodbath begun, opening a breach in the defenses along the southern flank of Central Europe which sent shivers down the corridors of Western power, reverberating from Bonn to London to Moscow, from the mirrored hallways of the Quai D'Orsay to the paneled offices at Foggy Bottom. But Father Time had yet to record the decisive blows of the real war.

1

Already rough hands had stripped her. Except for the boots on her feet and the gay red ribbon tied round her neck to mock her, she stood there, stark naked, lashed to a post in the village square. She stood with every shred of dignity stripped from her person, and yet she stood *tall*—chin uplifted, legs braced firmly apart, her gaze fixed on a distant point, to all outward appearances exhibiting all the noble assurance and grace of a white living Goddess, looking steadily beyond her tormentors.

From where Captain Lane Cil crouched, stunned and sweat-stained, at the far end of the wheat field, she may as well have been in a different world. He stared at her from across the field in that glassy-eyed way of a person who has just rushed to the hospital to discover a loved one slipping away. And now his eye caught a new threat. *"Oh, damn!"* The words came softly, as a gasp, and for a moment he had trouble controlling his breathing. He watched the soldier moving toward her with a rope.

The rumor, like the wind, had been sweeping through the Bosnian hill country for days, but gossip and rumors were the coin of the realm in this land; and tucked away in the mountains as this village was, the people had paid it no heed. So when the storm broke, it took them completely by surprise.

From where he watched, Cil counted five open-backed trucks in the military convoy pulled up before the village square. With so few invading soldiers, he wondered at the number of trucks. And now with the help of a blaring loud-speaker, the enemy soldiers began rounding up the villagers, roughly, dividing them into two groups, herding the women and children to where the naked Sonya stood on display at the corner of the square opposite where the trucks were parked. Across the way, the men of the village were being prodded at gunpoint to the edge of the wheat field.

But now Cil's focus shifted. He fixed in his mind the number and deployment of the soldiers, the position of the sun, the slant of the wooded hill that sprang up at a startling angle back of the square and the corner of the wheat field. He noted the fact that the late morning sun shown directly down on the square from the top of that hill.

All this his practiced eye took in at a glance. And now once again he thought of his orders. Well, orders or no orders, he had no doubt what he must do; it was only the question of time.

From his point of vantage, Cil could see that the soldiers for some reason were showing no sign of urgency, though a clear note of expectancy hung in the air.

A minute passed. A sleek staff car appeared on the road and pulled up at the square. The driver, a tall soldier, got out and moved around to the rear door where a second man, an officer clad in battle fatigues and the standard visored field cap of the Bosnian Serb Army, stepped to the ground. There was something about this burly man, the set of the head, the thrusting Mussolini chin; and even at this distance Cil at once recognized the officer from the newsreels.

The officer halted a good distance from where the naked Sonya stood on display. And Cil could see the way the huddle of village women shrank back at his approach as if sensing something faintly obscene about the officer's presence. On instinct, the women drew their children closer about them.

The officer seemed to stand in the role of an observer. At another's command, the workers in the field were forced to strip down to their shorts. They were handed long-handled spades, and the soldiers prodded them like cattle to a corner of the field beyond the view of the women. There, digging operations commenced.

In contrast, the famous officer appeared relaxed, even content. With studied nonchalance, he summoned a small boy from the huddle of women, and as the child timidly approached, the man went down on one knee, patting the child's cheek in a practiced, patronizing way, engaging him in a small game—almost as if to distance himself from the drama unfolding.

Not a quarter hour earlier, at first sight of the military convoy, a handful of men working the wheat field had broken and run for the woods. Cil and his companion, cutting back the stubble of last year's growth at the end of the field, had hidden at the fringe of the forest as a pursuing soldier crashed through the underbrush after the workers.

Cil turned to his companion. *"Peepo—The woods!* Keep an eye back there on the woods!" nodding toward the deeper cover of trees at their backs where the enemy soldier had disappeared. "Be ready! Soon he'll be back."

And now Cil's whole being seemed to take on new resolve. With swift, carefully gauged movements, he picked up the scythe with which he had fled the field, slipping its razor-sharp blade between a pair of poplar saplings. Applying steady pressure to the shaft, he snapped off the blade a foot from the end, then repeated the procedure. Roughly he tore the sleeve from his shirt and wrapped the cloth around the sharp blade. Holding the weapon as a dagger, he motioned to Peepo.

"Quick! Arm yourself. We've got to work fast." Once

similarly armed, upon whispered instructions, Peepo took up station behind the opposite tree.

From where Cil crouched waiting, concealed behind his own tree, he could only snatch glimpses of the scene by the square. He could see the stocky officer still idling before the small boy. But when Cil once again glimpsed Sonya, he winced and his mind drifted back.

Sometimes, perhaps once in a generation, is there born to a city the size of Zagreb, Yugoslavia, a child so sparklingly beautiful with charm and wits to match, and that certain mark of nobility which sets her apart from the world. As she approaches womanhood, she is lifted to the heights of legend. A person so other-worldly and flawless as to take her place in the imagination of men and women alike, and upon the basis of which folklore is born, and poems and songs are written and sung—such a woman was Sonya.

Granddaughter of a war hero beloved by the world, daughter of a European Countess, she was at once a throwback to the gay and frivolous elegance so characteristic of European capitals in the early century grandeur of Vienna and Paris. In addition, Sonya possessed that modern touch of the international jet-set one only reads about in the chic glossy tabloid magazines, and then mostly in photos, whirling at fancy-dress balls, cavorting on the French Riviera at Cannes and Nice and Saint Tropez.

Sonya's father, a great lion of a man, stood stiff and aloof, a holdover from the nineteenth century Hapsburg tradition of class and of empire, a military man raised in Zagreb, Croatia, under the harsh tutelage of his own father, the great warrior, legend to millions. The girl had inherited the good looks and quick wit of her father coupled with the air of nobility of her mother, The Countess.

Educated in the sheltered sanctuary of Swiss private schools, fluent in six languages, Sonya was a delicate, cultured creature, possessed of the voice of a hummingbird, a poise and acumen for dance that could turn every head in the royal ballroom. By the time she arrived at marriageable age, her beauty and wit were such as to intimidate all comers; and with the few prospective suitors of daring soon dispatched on their way, she found herself isolated and alone, admired and envied, yet despised and whispered about by those of lesser station. But the beautiful Sonya, at last tired of the social whirl and loving and cherishing her father above all others, under the weight of tradition and the family name, made her decision and set her cap to win her father's respect and unqualified favor. She determined to kick over the traces of privilege and use her gift for language in a useful, practical way.

By the time he chanced to meet the lovely Sonya—she in her twenty-seventh year, he seven years her senior—Cil had achieved the status of a coming-young-foreign operative with a reputation as a man cool under fire, capable, and as respected among his peers as by his superior officers. Perhaps that was part of her attraction to him. But by the time he had been afforded opportunity to observe her in training and learned that she had been assigned to his mission, it was already too late; he found himself already under her spell.

It was the Spring of 1992. The Administration in Washington, hopeful of reelection, had become increasingly mindful of rumblings in the press that a deliberate and systematic campaign of ethnic cleansing—possibly another holocaust—was underway in a remote European Republic called Bosnia. Believing itself vulnerable to lingering concerns: that during World War II, official Washington had turned its back while the Nazi holocaust progressed throughout a Europe plunged into war, the Department had been ordered to "discreetly dispatch" a pair of operatives to the mountains of Bosnia "to investigate and report back." As a fact-finding expedition, the Bosnian mission had not been considered unduly perilous, and it was the policy of the

Department, wherever possible, to assign male and female operatives to work in tandem, in part to render less conspicuous their presence behind enemy lines.

Once again Cil glanced back at the square. The soldier by Sonya was still toying with the length of rope at her back. And now Cil could see a second soldier move to her side—this one brandishing a knife. Though Cil could not see the crimson color from this distance, he could see the knife carving what looked to be a skin-deep cut along the ribcage beneath one firm, milk-white breast, apparently not to do mortal injury, but to taunt and strike terror in the hearts of the women of the village. Cil's face stiffened at the sight. His eyes squeezed to narrow slits.

A sudden warning from Peepo caused Cil to turn. The sound of one thrashing through brush emanated from the deeper woods at their backs. Cil crouched, compressing himself behind his own tree trunk, his senses assuming that state of silent readiness and anticipation—muscles quiet, yet roused and alert—the mark of the hunter. When the returning trooper advanced to a point between where Cil and his companion crouched hidden, Cil gave the signal.

Without hesitation and at point-blank range, Peepo stepped out in the open and showed himself. The trooper, startled, turned toward Peepo, raising his gun. Cil, at the trooper's back, took two running steps. By the time the trooper whirled to face him, Cil lunged. With all the strength and pent-up emotion at his command, Cil drove the crude dagger straight through the soft flesh of the trooper's throat. Another plunge of the knife and the job was done. The Serb trooper's body sagged to the ground without a sound, inert, folded into itself like a collapsible chair, the face wedged oddly askew against the rough bark of a tree.

Cil, snapping up the downed trooper's assault rifle from where it lay on the ground, scooped the extra loaded clip from the drooping cartridge pouch in a single effortless motion, then turned to Peepo.

"Come on—*fast!* To the construction shack! Follow close and stay low."

And now as Cil raced through the forest, crashing through the underbrush, the image of Sonya lashed to the post, stabbed at his mind—a woman trapped, yet wholly assured—even under torture?

This show of self-possession had not fooled Cil a bit; from the start he had read her brave exhibition for the lie that it was. Truth to tell, as time for the present mission had drawn near, Cil had found himself much too experienced and disciplined an operative not to observe in the training that Sonya, for all her good looks and noble air, was about as well suited to the rigors of savage human encounter as would be Princess Diana if dropped into the killing fields of Viet Nam. Yet, Cil's appeal to Headquarters had met with instant rebuke, and it was only after he had pressed for explanation to be greeted by one evasion after another that he began to comprehend how strong were the political strings pulled on her behalf.

Darting through the woods, Cil and Peepo had nearly reached the construction shed. Now in late May, the foliage of new growth was thickening into good cover, and Cil could feel the carpet of last year's fallen leaves soft and spongy underfoot. As he ran, it was with bitter irony that Cil reflected back on the earlier events of this day.

The day had broken clear and bright. And as Cil and Sonya had driven away in the first rays of sun from the village square, Cil had looked off to the left where an early morning gust drew furrows like fingers of wind through a field of wheat—the very field where in a couple of hours he would be laboring along with the men of the village. And coming closer, Cil had seen the wheat's tender stalks rippling peacefully and green in the morning sun.

And then the little car had roared on past the wheat field,

Cil nursing it gently up to speed, the engine wheezing at the strain as the road heaved into a narrow gut with forested ridges either side so thick they threatened to choke off the dirt track completely as it snaked along the mountain pass.

Then came the sound—the sharp crack of a single gunshot, clear and sharp in the mountain air.

"Down!" cried Cil. "Get your head down!"

At his command, Sonya dove, scrunching down crosswise in the passenger seat so that the back of her head rested against the warmth of his side as she faced the passenger door, knees updrawn, her head positioned so low that her eyes barely rose above the frame of the open passenger window. The snout of her automatic weapon stood poised on the sill, aimed at the woodlands rocketing past while Cil concentrated every fiber of his being upon the narrow roadway zigzagging before them. Cil's weapon rode in his lap, safety-off, ready for instant use, the barrel extended out the driver's side window. He could feel the rush of the wind and the constant slapping of tree branches against the car roof as it swept along the narrow dirt track.

At that moment the left front wheel snagged in a rut, twisting the car into a sideways lurch as a branch of leaves slapped against the windshield with a threatening blow.

"Laney!" gasped Sonya, raising up in her seat. "Slow down or you'll wreck us."

"Quick—get your head down!" He spat out the words through teeth tight-clenched, his foot stamping hard down on the gas as he reached forward, adjusting the rearview mirror and catching a glimpse of her image in the glass. "Easy now. We're a perfect target. At the first burst of fire, rake the whole hillside! In two or three minutes, we'll be outta range." But already she was staring ahead at a blind curve suddenly appearing.

"What if—what if another car is coming head on?"

"At this speed—another few minutes, that's all," he tried to assure, but already his thoughts were projecting forward, weighing the possibility of an ambush, planning ahead, figuring how to react. Though they had taken pains not to reveal their destination, anyone could have observed them departing the village and radioed ahead. Damn—these days, the Serbs—they were everywhere.

They went on this way, nerves taut as bowstrings, but Cil's eye was on the reflected image of Sonya in the glass, her features a picture of placid composure, yet he could feel her hand gripping the cuff of his pant leg for all it was worth; even through the thin cloth, he could feel the moistness of her palm. Swiftly, he moved to divert her attention from the danger.

"Come on," he challenged, now a lilt in his voice. "Let's sing."

"Sing?"

"Sure, sure; sing like we used to do."

She made no reply but flashed a brave grin.

"A Bosnian hill song."

"I, I don't know a Bosnian hill song."

"Sure you do." He ventured a grin while outside all hell was breaking loose; the little car seemed in the process of jouncing itself to pieces. "Come on now."

"When the red, red Robbin comes bob, bob, bobbin along—along." His free arm began waving with wild animation, like a band leader, breaking the tension. *"There'll be no more sobbin when he keeps throbbin his own—sweet song."*

"Wake up. Wake up, you sleepy head. Get up, get out of bed. Cheer up, the sun is red...."

He could see in the mirror the color begin to return to her cheeks, could feel her grip relax on his pant leg. *"Live, love, laugh and be happy!"*

They went on this way, stretching the nose of the reluctant jalopy through the cordon of danger until finally the two of them were shouting out the little ditty like school kids, so loud and raucously, in fact, that a score of enemy rounds piercing the hood of the car could scarcely have drawn their attention.

And now the little old car broke out into open country where the risks were far less. Cil sat back in his seat for a time, forcing himself to relax, clicking his rifle on safety, when abruptly he braked and skidded to avoid a rock in the roadway.

"Damn!" cried Sonya. "Can't we slow down now?" The tone of her voice caused him to smile.

"Well, Countess," he offered, aware that the immediate danger was past, his eyes sparkling as he eased back in his seat, slowing the car. "We can do even better than that! Ah, what do you say we stop for a minute—say, over there in those bushes? You know, now there's no one around." Here, without the rush of the wind, he inhaled the scent of her perfume and beamed like a schoolboy. "Just for a minute, you know; it wouldn't be long."

"What!" Now for the first time her indignation seemed to relax her. "You mean? Why, as I live and breath, *Captain*. Humph! The things that do spill out of that mouth of yours." But she did not move away. "And, damn it, don't call me Countess. My mother is the *Countess*."

"Just practicing. I never knew a Countess before." He braked again hard. "I'd rather practice something else."

"Oh you would, would you?" And now her proud chin had risen appreciably. "You know, with all that big talk of yours, Mister, a girl might just get the idea you're *afraid to marry above yourself.*" That remark earned his glance in the rear mirror, but his look was answered by that quick tossing of the head that she had whenever her pride was at stake. Then an impish twinkle reflected back at him, and he could feel the warmth of her love through the glass. Smiling, he promptly reached under the seat, drew something out, and placed it in her hand.

"Why, Laney, darling—wild flowers! Whenever did—and to think, at a time like this." She rose and swung around in the seat, a spontaneous, impulsive gesture; she covered his mouth with her own. "Oh Laney, you've got to be craa-zy—I do love you so."

"Well, they're—ah—not exactly a dozen red roses," he stumbled with the words, suddenly bashful at her sudden, overt display of affection.

"Oh, Laney, they're lovely."

They were approaching the outskirts of a town, and he frowned as his mind moved to the business at hand.

"You know, Sweetheart. I don't know about this interview stuff. After combing these village hamlets for nearly a month, what makes you think we'll hit the jackpot today?"

She paused, as if in thought, then gave a casual shrug. "Oh hell, Laney, I don't know. I've just got a feeling—call it women's intuition. But I'm sure of one thing—those damned Serbs; there's just got to be a plan." Head inclined, examining the small bouquet of flowers in her hand, she went on. "With the Muslims fleeing in droves, why, there simply has to be a deeper reason. I mean—not just the tensions, like those lazy, drunken irregulars shooting up the towns at night. That can't be the whole story, can't possibly account for the mass Muslim exodus." She shook her head. "No, it doesn't make sense; it's just got to be something else, something deeper. How do you say—subtle? Something they do to the people that's well thought out, you know, that's planned and systematic. Maybe blackmail or extortion. Some way to really get a grip on the fears of all those poor, wretched Muslims."

"OK, but how do you figure we'll do any better this time? By now we both know, these petty, local, Serb politicians—spouting nothing but a pack of lies at every question we put."

"No, no—listen." She gave that slight toss of the head. "You don't understand. This time I've got a line on a contact."

Yet, as quickly as the dingy factory buildings leapt into

view, Sonya's enthusiasm seemed suddenly to wane, her mood alter.

"You know," she said. An unmistakable sadness had crept into her voice as she peered down long and hard at the tiny bouquet tightly held in her hand, then back at the dingy factory buildings approaching. "This isn't exactly Monte Carlo, is it?"

Sensing her mood, his expression hardened. "No," he said. "Here, it's a different game of roulette."

It had taken far too much time for Cil and Peepo to reach the construction shack, snatch what they would need, then skirt through the woods back to the village. And now Cil could hear the breath sawing in his chest as he struggled unseen up the steep wooded slope behind the village square. He had given Peepo strict orders as to how to position himself, what to avoid, and how to proceed; the rest he would have to trust to luck. He trusted Peepo, having worked with him through scorching heat and drenching rains. Peepo, an ethnic Croat, Catholic, with sure hands and a quick eye for the girls which had earned him his nickname, had the month before lost two young sisters and his home to a street fight against gun-toting, beer-guzzling, Serb irregulars; he would not back away from a fight on this day.

But now Cil again thought of Sonya; he dared not imagine the worst of her plight, and he fought back his fears as he struggled on up the steep slant of the hill, rifle slung over his shoulder, a heavy box weighting his arms. He fixed his mind on Sonya's and his ride back from their interview this very morning in the neighboring village; he had to remind himself that after the warning they had received that the two of them had returned to the village without incident scarcely more than one hour ago. And now he reproached himself for his own indecisiveness. That earlier interview had produced a firm warning, and although Cil had insisted upon getting Sonya out now, she had shown that famous stubborn streak.

"Oh Laney, please; I've promised the children." And even now he could see in his mind just that imploring, delicate way she had of setting her face, her tone far braver, he knew, than she felt. "You let me stay just this once—and I don't throw you out of my earthly affections. A bargain? We came together; we leave together—tonight, if you say so." And then had come that sudden smile he always found himself powerless to resist. "You know, I promised I'd tend the kids while the women go on with the wood-splitting. Besides, I've yet to show the small ones that fancy new dance step."

Panting like a race horse, his arms made of lead, at last Cil arrived at the crest of the hill above the village square. His gaze raced to Sonya below. She was still standing upright. He placed down the heavy wooden box with a sigh of relief, unslung the dead soldier's automatic rifle, and leaned it in the pine boughs.

On the village side, the wooded hill was a solid limestone cliff thrusting two hundred feet straight up from the square and the near corner of the wheat field. Now here at the top, Cil stood in a cover of pines on a rim of ledge with the whole damned village scene spilling out below him. Almost directly below and to his left, at the edge of the wheat field, the half-naked village men under guard labored with shovels, digging a deep earthen trench, its location screened from the women by a band of trees. The village square with Sonya still lashed to the post lay below, slightly to Cil's right, her naked skin ivory in the noonday sun, her head still proud-set as before, but her posture less confident, less erect. The village women and children under guard huddled farther to Cil's right, in the center of the square. The Serb officer, standing directly in front of Cil and a good distance beyond Sonya, had given up his game with the small boy. He was watching the progress of events with evident pleasure. The convoy of trucks stood in a line across the square and far to Cil's right, parked before two high buildings housing the row of shopfronts at street level.

But now the picture had altered. A dozen or more soldiers scurried back and forth from the streets behind the square, lugging armfuls of freshly split firewood set up by the villagers to dry for the coming winter. Cil could see from the way they moved that these were hardly crack, disciplined troops, but uniformed rabble, scruffy-bearded and heavy-footed, piling the wood as if stacking cordwood—or constructing a funeral pyre close by Sonya's side.

And now Cil cursed aloud. The soldier with the knife was nowhere to be seen, but other mischief was afoot. While a pair of troopers knelt struggling to light sticks of green kindling at the base of the pile, the trooper with the rope stood fashioning a noose, arranging it about Sonya's neck, tightening, then loosening it in a threatening, goading way, much to the amusement of the rock-jawed Serbian officer.

Cil set about his task methodically, forcing himself not to rush. A slight breeze blew at his back. He opened the heavy wooden box and carefully arranged its contents in a small depression in the ground. He slipped a shiny Zippo lighter from his pocket and waited behind a screen of swaying pine boughs. He could feel his muscles tense. He waited for Peepo to move into position, hoping the young Croat still held all Cil's instructions in his head.

Below, Cil observed the Serb officer pacing back and forth, the step cocky, the man looking on curiously while Sonya's posture altered. Her head was still stoically erect as before, the loop of the rope at her throat, but the bulk of her form had now gone limp, her weight straining against the ropes that bound her. A dark serpent of blood crawled down her waist and curled down the outside of her leg. Cil could see that the post to which she was lashed stood perilously close to the thin spiral of smoke now pluming skyward from the base of the funeral pyre.

Cil stooped to light the first fuse, stifling his haste, sheltering the flame of the lighter with the cup of his hand. He paused in his labors only long enough to steal a look at the Serb officer. For only a second did Cil permit himself a secret smile, thin, wintry and fleeting, while clips from past newsreels whirled in his mind.

And now as the fuse sputtered and crackled to life, Cil signaled to his accomplice below and to his far right; he could see Peepo squatting behind a chimney on the rooftop above the shopfronts facing onto the square.

Cil waited. He knew this number of soldiers would not be easily frightened off by the acts of two men—especially with their commander present. No, the tactic had to be disciplined, precise, and convincing in order to produce just the proper effect. He waited for the fuse, crackling and sparking in his hand, to continue its burn-down. He paused to gauge the speed and direction of the wind.

With a toss of Cil's arm, the first stick of dynamite lofted into the air, queerly twisting and whirling to plummet quite silently through the hot noonday air. Cil could see that already one group of soldiers was beginning to herd the women and children toward the last of the five army trucks parked on the far side of the square, positioned far to his right, but directly below where Peepo crouched high on the roof above the shopfronts. Cil could hear the chorus of protest rise on the wind.

On instinct Cil ducked from the blast and concussion as the first explosion struck far to Cil's left, beyond the digging field workers, where three of the soldiers stood guard. The sheer force of the blast hurled the three soldiers into the air like so many matchsticks—to then descend in a waste of dust and debris.

Almost before the sound and concussion had reached Cil's ears, there came a second blast. To his far right, he could see Peepo on the steep rooftop with his hand still fully extended. Below, the windshield and cab of the second truck in the convoy dissolved in thin air. He could see the mob of women draw back, duck, then huddle low in a single fluid movement as if on some unspoken command. No sooner had Cil felt the ground at his feet heave from the second blast than he unleashed his own second stick, this one finely judged to strike the ground directly before him and halfway to the now cowering Serb commander.

Promptly two more sticks were released to land in a precise pattern, the progress of the blasts conveying the impression of an advancing mortar barrage. Now the scene below held just that terrifying smell and fog of battle he had witnessed so many times before. The stink of burnt explosive—that haze of swirling dust suspended in the air—the shouts of wounded men magnified by their closeness—that element of surprise and nerve-tingling confusion that clouded the mind in battle and syphoned away the nerve and the will.

And now Cil spotted the tall uniformed driver reach into the staff car, then turn, raising his rifle. He fired toward Peepo's position on the rooftop. Cil drew swiftly back within the cover of the pine boughs. Raising his own automatic rifle, the one he had captured, with care to keep his aim wide of the Serb officer, he sighted and squeezed off a single round. The shot caught the uniformed driver cleanly, the force of its impact flinging the soldier hard down on his back. From this distance, Cil could not see clearly the circle of blood and tissue bathing the fender of the staff car, but his mind conjured the oddly remembered image of just how fluffy and pink human brain tissue always appeared.

By now the huddle of women and young ones lay with faces pressed to the bare earth. The soldiers, surprised and bewildered and momentarily deafened by the force of the explosions, squinted upwards, protective hands encircling their heads. Blinded by the sun and haze of rising smoke, they fired into the air, wildly. At the stake Sonya slumped in her bonds, white in her nakedness. Her head drooped forward and lolled on her chest as if she had fallen into a faint.

By this time the half-naked field hands had ducked low as if in attempt to bury themselves in the deep slit-trench of their own making. The soldiers by the funeral pyre scrambled for the trucks. The lone officer, observing his driver down and pumping his lifeblood into the dust of the roadway, threw himself under the first truck in the convoy, seeking cover.

This action by the officer was immediately answered by an exploding missile dropped from the roof above the shopfronts. The sheer force of the blast propelled the concealed commander, spinning and rolling, out from under the truck like a ball of tumbling tumbleweed blown on the wind. The officer, now up on all fours, first shook his head, then, spying the staff car closeby and undamaged, crawled toward it in haste.

Within the space of a minute, the staff car had rounded the village square and vanished from sight. Within two minutes thereafter, the Serb rabble, noting the timely departure of their commander, too, abandoned the scene. All that remained were the wails of the women and a cloud of dust rising on the wind.

Cil's only thought as he bolted and scrambled down the hill was of Sonya. Even the dark recesses of his mind would not permit him to put the question.

2

Some say, from the instant of birth, Lane Cil was a person destined for a bad end. Others were openly rooting for it. It wasn't that he harbored such an overriding contempt for authority—at least, not at first—but that he enjoyed such an expansive, even insatiable appetite for life.

This phenomenon could be observed in him as early as the age of three when his family descended into its favorite meadow for a picnic celebration. Little Laney, his short legs scampering along to keep up with his mother, could be seen all the while holding her hand—that is, until his eye caught the glint of something shiny in the grass.

Releasing her hand, he suddenly bounded off.

"Oh, Laney—come back!" cried his mother, distress clouding her features.

The boy's father, walking close by the mother's side, reached out a reassuring arm to encircle her waist.

"It's all right, Beth, dear; we must let him go."

"But, Franklin, he's so young," she protested, watching her little son go. "And look how he's forever wandering off. And now, today—his birthday!"

"Please, dear." He tightened his grip on her waist. "We must give him room to discover the world on his own."

At the very idea, her eyes sprang wide.

"But, just look at him. He doesn't even want us."

"There, there, love; try to be patient. This one's a different child," nodding his head. "Believe me, I've watched. It's true, he sees about him the same beauty we see, but somehow he sees it bigger. It's almost as if 'The Powers' had put something special inside him." He eyed her with care. "Don't fret, dear; he's a sensitive child; he'll always be back."

By the age of seven, little Laney, in an attempt to expand his horizons of permissible activity, had developed such a colloquially schizophrenic personality, he would at one moment assume the prim and tactful role of the schoolmaster's son, the next, rush off to cavort with his chums in one piece of wild mischief or another.

By his fifth year in school, he had latched onto a foolproof scheme for relieving himself of the strictures of the household by begging permission to study at the town library. "All right, Laney," his mother would say, pausing to shake a cautioning finger. "But remember—you go straight to the library. And be sure to be quiet so others can study."

And, indeed, each time in keeping with his word, his little shoes would patter down and install themselves in that most Holy Mecca of study and learning, for a full five minutes, that is, just long enough to return a book, or greet a pal, before cavorting into the wider spaces of life which providence had laid at his feet.

By the time he had reached the first year of high school, his parents, fearful of his scholastic inattention and searching for a suitable incentive, had offered him a cool twenty dollars for each marking grade of "A" received in the more demanding subjects that would later pave the way for university admission. Cil accepted the challenge with a smile. But by the end of three straight marking periods, his father, screwing his features into an attitude of solemn rectitude befitting a high school principal, confronted his son with a scowl.

"Good Lord, young man—you're bankrupting the family!"

By his sophomore year in high school, Cil found that in a town where athletics was everything and an athlete a king, he could settle into a still broader *modus operandi*, expanding the clandestine third world of preferred existence with his friends by stretching the scope of parental license. Having fingered his father's athletic medals from an earlier day and aware of the preference of fathers everywhere to have their sons follow in their footsteps, Cil discovered that as long as he towed the line in school with sufficient results for his parents to harbor some hope of his "academic promise," display of prowess on the athletic field afforded him freedom to go on exploring his private fancies at will.

On occasion, however, the effects of this double life could be quite alarming. At the close of one nefarious frolic, a hard-partying evening if ever there was one, Cil had dropped off one of his buddies somewhat-the-worse-for-wear. The poor boy's mother took one look at her staggering progeny, clapped her hand to her mouth and exclaimed, "Oh Henry! Why can't you be like that nice principal's son?"

From the vantage of the surrounding hills, Cil's home-town, Hopedale, looked pretty much like any other small New England mill town, tucked away as it was in the forested ridges which marched along the banks of the Connecticut River dividing the State of New Hampshire from the State of Vermont. Only the stark white steeples of the Protestant churches could be seen standing firm and res-olute above the trees on one side of town while on the other stood the high rugged cross of the Sacred Heart Church; and beyond, the clutter of mill towers.

With a population of five thousand, including the cows, the townspeople were mostly hardworking, quiet-spoken, and friendly. The people themselves were about evenly divided along religious lines between the warm-hearted, large-familied, French-Canadian Catholics on one side of town (who had emigrated south from Quebec Province in search of steady mill jobs in the century since the industrial revolution), and the entrepreneurial Protestants on the other, who traced their roots back to the rigid, no-nonsense work ethic of the Puritans.

Aside from their iron-clad religious convictions, the focus of the townspeople and the glue that bound them together was the well-being of their children, and it was the overriding spirit of that concern, expressed through school sports teams, that somehow brought this otherwise ordinary mill town alive and lent poignant meaning to its rhythms.

Such a place was Hopedale. And to Cil, this town stood as his home, his roots, and the place to which he had always felt inexorably bound.

On this warm spring day, nearly three years after the suddenly aborted Bosnian Mission, Cil stood on the wide veranda of his parents' home in Hopedale. Out of nowhere, the image of Sonya leapt into his mind—and it required a supreme act of will to dislodge it.

At thirty-seven, Cil stood with a silent, almost lazy grace. Tall, lean, and granite-sure as the hill country he hailed from, he carried a sharp eye, an easy, trusting air, and a good proud New England chin that some said carried a penchant for sticking itself out once too often.

His shoulders and chest were still rock-solid while the hands, in contrast, were his mother's hands, the sensitive, sculpted hands of the artist or thinker, the hands running off to long slender finely tapered fingers—"Jesus's fingers,"

26

his old girlfriend used to call them. And on this day he wore a military-styled khaki shirt complete with shoulder epaulettes, which, incidentally, constituted the only items of his attire to hint of his profession. A pack of Marlboro cigarettes bulged from his left breast pocket. A braided, blue cloth belt encircled his waist above faded jeans while his feet snuggled into battered brown workboots—the better for hard use and wear.

Cil was happy to have changed out of his starched Sunday best. To mollify his parents, especially his mother—a devout Christian with a sincere, sensitive, and compassionate nature, a commitment to uncomplaining hard work and strict religious convention—he had consented to attendance at the ten o'clock Congregational service. One hour at the oratorical mercy of Parson Percy Twitchell invariably caused him to fidget and shift in his seat—and wonder how the Good Lord in his infinite wisdom could suffer to hire such long-winded help.

For some time, Cil had been keeping a weather eye on the sky, and now it came down in buckets. He hurried his step. He hated good-byes, had for that reason made them early. Now on the second trip down the porch steps, the first crash of thunder erupted like a cannon shot. As his head ducked against the sudden spatter of rain, Cil loped around to the driver's side door, tossing an affectionate grin at his parents huddled anxiously in the window; then, quite comfortably, he climbed in behind the wheel of Old Harry, his battered '52 Ford. A moment later, he twisted the key in the ignition and listened expectantly for the first full-throated rumble, then the sweet, familiar purr of that old V-8 engine.

In this part of the country, spring rains were common; but an April thunderstorm remained something of a rarity, and when the main body of the tempest had passed, a mood of melancholy descended under the leaden dome of the sky. As Cil pulled Old Harry into a slow turn around the village green with its neat, wrought-iron fence, he was eyeing the patter of rain spilling off the roof of the old bandstand to assault the last remnants of snow.

With a few minutes to kill, Cil figured on one last ride around town. After all, a little nostalgia never hurt anyone, and it offered a way to stave off immediate return to his military assignment.

The circle of the steering wheel felt warm and smooth in his hand as he made the right turn up Bank Street. And there it was. In its suit of weathered brick stood his old high school, stalwart and unbending against the low leaden sky. The old school on the hill was the junior high now, but it looked just the same, the high arched Colonial windows somehow lending the aged school that remembered touch of solemn dignity.

After high school, Cil had not followed his older brother to Dartmouth College though in miles it was just up the road. That had cut his father badly and disappointed his mother, but even in those days, Cil's convictions ran to bedrock when it came to the hard decisions of life. No, there had been no thought of leaving this, his town; the college life was not for him. Truth to tell—he had made other plans.

Cil hadn't a clue what caused Old Harry to suddenly veer and make the right turn up Shaw Street. The murmur of some inner voice? Or perhaps, some long delayed postscript to that old Bosnian mission at long last coaxing him back?

And now as the battered Ford ventured in under the ranks of ancient elms lining the street, sight of those spritely white, high-gabled houses, proud and unforgiving, scowling down through the foliage brought it all back. And even now, after all the years, vividly as a mirror image in a wellspring could he envision the planes of her face, recall the day April Fontaine had walked into his life.

April had lived right here on Shaw Street. As Cil approached her old house, Old Harry seemed to pull up and brake to a stop by itself. For some time did he sit silently, gravely staring across at that same old house with the veranda and the small flower plot out front, neatly boxed-in behind the white picket fence.

The sight of that prim old-maid house brought a smile to his lips as he recalled how, so long ago in the first rays of warming sun before school, he would step up on that very same front porch to pause, brush the dust from his shoe with a swipe of his pant cuff, smooth down his hair with the comb of his hand and then straighten his shoulders. And then, only when he was good and ready, would he step up, lift his hand, ánd deliver a sharp rap to the door.

And then, suddenly as the summer sun, there she would be, pert and smiling, just a fraction sassy, clad in a print summer dress that quietly showed off her figure, and always about her that fragrance, daisy-fresh as the smile on her face.

April had come from one of those rock-solid, French-Canadian Catholic families with half a dozen siblings. Her devotion to family, to duty, and above all, to her faith, was something that never ceased to fascinate and intrigue him.

Yes, that was his April, April Theresa—for Saint Theresa—Fontaine. And though only teenagers, they had become nearly inseparable. He had never seen it before, the longer the time, the more they became mystically bound—their thoughts, their plans, their hopes and their dreams; it somehow coalesced in a bewildering blend of elves. So delicately melded did they seem, in fact, that people on the street often mistook them for brother and sister. Cil had never thought seriously about, let alone believed in, mental telepathy—until those days.

Even now, after all these years, he could still sense the warmth, the shy, quiet way of her, the silent resolution that shone from within by the set of her features. Ever was there that changeful way about her: one moment, bashful, even painfully shy; the next—after he had teased or provoked her—the sudden summer storm bursting out on her face.

But always beneath it all, that constant, deep running current, the note of unspoken assurance, that no matter the hurdle, implicit in their bond lay the foreknowledge that somehow the strength of her faith and her love would see them through.

And he remembered how, all through that winter, they had come ever closer; and after the harsh winter winds finally softened to spring, they would hike together after school "up Hardy Hill way" to the sugaring-off grove he was working that spring with one of his pals. And there among the towering maples shorn of leaf, they would tramp, gaily, over the crusted snow, laboring shoulder to shoulder, collecting each weighted bucket of sap from the trees. It was hard work, but she was a sturdy and wholesome girl, no stranger to toil.

And when the hard work was done, they would wile away the late afternoon hours in the sugaring-off hut, amid the crackle of flame and the smell of the wood-smoke, peeking at one another through the swirl of steam rising from the boiling pans, planning out their life and their future right there in that town.

But the fierce winds of change had howled off the hill in that spring, and the fury of the gales forced both these young people to confront reality and grow up with a start. At the end of the school year, April's family, quite without warning, announced plans to move back to California.

And then, suddenly, she was gone. Who knows why? How life's plans could suddenly be blown astray by harsh winter winds? And then had come the real surprise, despite plans to join her promptly at the end of the school year, Cil received word from April that it was over.

Just as promptly—once the effect of her words had truly sunk in—Cil made applicaton for appointment to the US Military Academy at West Point.

Somewhere in the experience of many a young woman or man comes a turning point, a crucial juncture, a branching of the ways so swift, unexpected, and irrevocable as to alter the course and direction of one's life. So it was with Cil; and although some life experiences pass without trace, never would Lane Cil fully comprehend the true impact April Fontaine would have upon his life. And, while it is a well known historical fact that the military academy at West Point has often proven a means by which sons and daughters of families of modest means could acquire a first-rate college education, in Cil's case, the explanation may well have fallen more in line with a self-imposed penance.

In his first year on the plains at West Point, Cil acquired the institutional record for more conduct demerits than any single cadet since Dwight David Eisenhower, who, as a youth, had apparently exhibited a like aptitude for gridiron sport coupled with an aversion for petty regulations; he, too, had an irrepressible, devil-may-care turn of mind—if not, indeed, a kindred spirit..

Despite it all, during his tenure at The Point, Cil had been justly proud of one achievement. Convinced that it is language which lies at the heart of comprehending distant lands and distant peoples—and hence the future, he had buckled down, immersing himself in the nether, nether world of foreign languages, which, to some extent, came easy to him.

Upon graduation and receipt of his commission, Cil promptly volunteered for training with the 82nd Airborne Division, then won assignment to the vaunted Special Forces. Later, in recognition of his unusual blend of athletic and linguistic abilities combined with a "cool head in crisis," Cil had found himself assigned to Special Operations at Fort Rucker, Alabama, for advanced training in *the tactics of waging secret war,* in honing skills crucial to the conduct of guerilla operations behind enemy lines. And it was this track of events that had ultimately led to Sonya and the ill-fated Bosnian Mission.

Still seated quietly behind the wheel of Old Harry as he inspected April's house, Cil awoke from his reverie. Shaking his head to clear it, he reached down, restarted the engine and maneuvered away from the familiar streets of Hopedale, picking up the turnpike south toward Boston's Logan Airport and the special military flight that would flick him away, back to the far-off jungle base to which he had been assigned.

He thought of Sonya, his lovely Sonya, but the thought only served to burden his emotion. And then a fragment of memory leapt to his mind, something someone had said so long ago in comparing Sonya to one of her less fortunate cousins. Yes, yes—that old stable hand at the mountain retreat of Sonya's family. Now the image came to him clearly—of that knarled, old, hump-backed family retainer—of the odd way the old man had of putting things. . . .

"Hah! Listen to me, Cil-the-Capitan," snarled this ancient stable hand from the old country with the ear-splitting accent. "I tell you—is the biggest decision you make in the life—if you could—is who will be your parents!" Twisted and bent as an old apple tree, he stooped once again to lift a spadeful of manure from the stable floor with a thrust of his powerful arms, his eyes snapping with impatience. "Now take that cousin of Sonya. . . ."

And Cil recalled how the old man had painstakingly recounted the story of this poor-little-rich-girl, possessed at birth of all the talent and promise of Sonya herself, and how in the early years the family had made quite a competition between them, that is until the cousin's string of luck began to play out.

It seems that this cousin of Sonya's had been born to a wealthy landowner, possessed of vineyards in the south of France as far as the eye could see. And the girl's mother— sister of the colonel, Sonya's father, a strong and resolute if unlucky woman, tall of stature with a clear and steadying eye—had met with a tragic end. Even before the child reached the age of eight, the mother was lost to an accident as sudden as it was unexpected; and in consequence, the little girl's father, stricken with grief, had taken to the bottle. The way the old servant had phrased it, "The poor man with more tears than the grapes on his vines—almost to drown in his own despair." And of the aftermath, "Oh, Cil-the-Capitan, I tell you—that child? A leaf on the tide, shoved from one unwanting wave to the next. I do not know over the years how that precious child ever could she bear it!"

Still in his mind could Cil see the look of agitation stamped on that old man's lined and weathered face. And when Cil had inquired as to what had become of this unfortunate creature, the old man had lowered his head and spoken gravely. "Boarded out at that nose-in-the-air Swiss private school—same as Sonya. But, alas—that the big trouble. For wherever was this life to sweep her, always the cousin weighed in the shadow of Sonya—Sonya, the Dancer—Sonya, the Student. Ay! Ay! Sonya!—the eleegan-tae belle of the ball. I tell you, Capitan, what a cross was that child made to bear!"

"Yes; poor child—lost."

"Poor child! Lost, you say? Lost! Hah—that is the whole-very-big-story!" And Cil could still see the way the old man's cheeks puffed out with pride. "To our big, big surprise does this child conceal in that small breast a mountain of treasure. If I lie, God strike me dead!"

"Treasure?"

"Hah! Pig iron, I tell you—just like her dead grandpapa! And bye bye with the time, as she grow more old and more strong—ay! The more at that school do they maul her, the more do she raise up on her hind legs—and fight!"

"Fight?"

"Ah, Cil-the-Capitan—was a battle for the gods!"

As Cil proceeded down the highway, he weighed the plight of this poor luckless girl against his own bag of troubles. At the thought, he inhaled a deep breath, allowing the air to explode from his lungs.

His features sharpened; his hands tightened on the wheel. With a determined thrust of his boot, he shoved hard down on the accelerator—until the speedometer needle sprang up and settled on eighty.

3

Directly after the mission to Bosnia, Sonya simply disappeared. Though her wounds incurred in the mission had proven superficial, once she and Cil arrived back in the States and had undergone routine debriefing, she just plain vanished. Only after the fact had the grapevine informed Cil that her family, tired of her flirtation with the brutal world of undercover operations, had swept her away, had summoned her back within its shielding arms and the security which only great wealth and position can promise and assure.

At first, Cil had refused to believe it; then, when his gifts and letters were returned unopened, it began to sink in. As relieved as he was that she had opted out of this whole brutal business in time, still he missed her with all his heart and set about on his own to find her. He searched high and low; yet, despite his most determined and persistent efforts, he discovered all doors shut and bolted against him. In the end, he had picked himself up and gone on with his life.

In the intervening months, then years, not once had he forgotten or wavered in his devotion. Late at night as he lay in bed, she would come to him—or when he roused from sleep at the first blush of dawn. In his mind's eye and his heart, he had nurtured the memories, both the joy and the pain. In large things or small, he would summon up her image and consult her as if she were standing before him.

To Cil, perhaps part of his attraction to Sonya arose from the superficial resemblance which she bore to his beloved April—the sparkling freshness of countenance—the quick smile and easy way about her—but mostly, the simple kindnesses that never failed to touch him, that made him feel secure, feel needed. Whether the process was some kind of "psychological transference of affection," where all of his love for April and the faith and expectations he had stored and savored in his mind and his breast were suddenly lavished upon another, only an expert could say. Or maybe he found safety in the utter contrast with April, a sweet and wholesome down-to-earth girl with a sometimes timid, often bashful manner, yet the stubborn devotion and compassion of the angels, coupled with a dedication to duty and family and hard work, and above all, to her faith. For Sonya, on the other hand, knew little of work, and even less of faith and devotion, though possessed of a soaring spirit and thirst for life, for her range encompassed a world of opulence wholly foreign to Cil, and which she accepted as her birthright.

But the story had not ended there. In truth, the Administration in Washington, after catching one whiff of the content of Cil's report on the matter of "ethnic cleansing," had first worried itself sick, then worked itself into a frenzy. For, if this stark and vivid portrayal directly witnessed by two American foreign operatives in the field were in fact true—as quite clearly it was—then what did that portend? And what if it were discovered that they, the President's men, had, in full knowledge of the facts on the ground, failed to raise a finger to prevent these ongoing atrocities—as was the policy at the time? Now that the woman operative had vanished into thin air, what if the whole business were somehow leaked to the press? Or worse still, to the opposition party? And so the decision had quietly been made to "discredit the mission and the individuals involved."

Captain Cil's superiors lost no time in getting to the point. First, it was the firm policy of the Department that "fraternization between operatives was strictly forbidden," an edict to that effect had been circulated to all operatives; and violation of that edict was "punishable to the full extent of the law." Second, and most importantly, Sonya—technically a citizen of Romania, the country not of her birth, but that of her mother, the Countess—was a national of "a former iron curtain country," and her selection, assignment, and rank as a US operative had been as sudden and "officially unauthorized" as her mysterious departure after the mission.

To add to Cil's woes, the mission briefing and instructions had been both clear and precise. The Bosnian Mission was intended simply as a "fact-finding," not a combat mission against "the key Bosnian-Serb Commander," which might well have resulted in an international incident jeopardizing the posture of this government as a "neutral arbiter."

When Cil's intimate relationship with this "captivating woman" was linked to her sudden, unexplained, indeed, mysterious disappearance, all hell broke loose. In the absence of the woman co-operative, insufficient evidence existed to support a military court-martial. But Captain Cil—and he himself, of all things, a graduate of the Academy—soon found that he had acquired the status of an outcast, a pariah in official circles, with a notorious ring attached to his name.

Except for a few very close friends, fellow officers shunned him, and rank-conscious old comrades from the Point would cross the street to avoid his very presence, lest a particle of his tainted reputation should rub off and stain them.

When the pressure from Washington became intolerable, Cil, deciding that he had had enough, determined to make a clean and open breast of the whole matter, if necessary—publicly. And it was in response to notice of this stated intention that official Washington had, quite unaccountably, reversed itself, deciding "upon further examination" that Captain Cil did, indeed, deserve proper recognition. Cil found himself promptly promoted to the rank of major, and just as promptly, assigned to one hazardous mission after another.

Through it all, Cil had faced his travails with good cheer and without complaint, striving doggedly to prove himself anew and thereby clear his name, though at times he would ponder his future and take solace in the knowledge that even Dwight D. Eisenhower had himself languished for fifteen years between the great wars, stuck at the rank of major. But the steps of military life had only steepened, and it took no genius to realize that over time every new foreign mission diminished the odds of surviving another. And always in the background could he hear the incessant chop, chop, chopping sound of Congress wielding the budgetary ax to down-size the military.

Gradually, over a period of time, Cil had been forced to face facts, been compelled to take stock of himself and admit that realistic prospect of redeeming his name and salvaging his career was a long shot at best. Carefully he pondered the question, until at last, with full confidence in his own skills, he determined to chart a new course and make a new start; he would seek civilian employment. Yes, he would finish out his time and take normal retirement at the end of twenty years active service, which, counting his time at the Academy, would mean September 1, 1995.

When he had forthrightly announced this intention to his superiors, he had been greeted with an unexpected result. Headquarters had promptly assigned him as deputy commander to a guerilla training camp for his last eight months of active service.

As to his beloved Sonya, in spite of it all and though hope of her return had long since become a beggar's wish, he had attempted to remain true to her—if not without stumbling at times. But always had he carried a single memento, a symbol of their love.

4

The guerilla training camp was something to behold—
a hodgepodge of tents and dilapidated huts strewn
about a clearing, hacked out of the Central American jungle. The reason for the camp's location was the view of
defense planners that the lion's share of future conflicts
would arise in the emerging nations situated close to the
equator; this was an effort to simulate both conditions and
climate.

There were many problems with the camp beyond heat,
malaria, and the base commander, but the one that caused
the most apprehension was the honest-to-god civil war flaring just across the border—that and the propensity of rebel
pilots to overfly the border, and their inability to distinguish
one enemy camp from another; after all, one patch of jungle
looked pretty much like any other. On the day preceding
arrival of the new batch of foreign operatives for refresher
training, the camp had been strafed and bombed by rebel
pilots, mistaking it for a government stronghold.

Major Cil had no way to anticipate the pace of upcoming
events as he stepped from Headquarters Tent at the edge of
the clearing to inspect the recent arrivals standing before
him in neat military ranks. It was sweltering hot, and Cil

was not looking forward to the marksmanship evaluation slated to follow his standard orientation.

The undetected threat from afar came on in stages. At first, there was but a faint whirring sound in the distance, like the first warning buzz of a pesky mosquito, the sound soft, indistinct in the jungle so that no one reacted. By the time the sound took on true definition, there remained but time to react on instinct.

Out front, Major Cil, caught totally flat-footed, shouted, "Scatter!"

The sleek shark-nose of the approaching aircraft swooped in so low that the wings clipped the treetops, the slip-stream causing the palm fronds to thrash in its wake. The men bolted and scattered, scrambling for cover.

One solitary figure remained out there in the clearing. From behind his screen of cover, Major Cil and the others observed first with amazement, then with chilled fascination the manner in which that one lone figure left out on the exposed ground sank down on one knee with calm deliberation, then swung up the rifle, the motion agile and unhurried, rapid yet controlled, so that the butt-plate of the automatic weapon slapped into the shoulder as the barrel leveled and the marksman's head cocked to take aim.

There in the open, displaying the patience of Job, the lone figure waited, waited calmly, waited for the nose of the marauding plane to thrust within range.

When the time came to fire, the marksman, instead of spraying the oncoming aircraft with a blustering chain of fire, squeezed off a single round, the shot finely judged, then another and another, each carefully timed.

Like a diving meteor, the craft streaked overhead and shrank to a dot in the western sky. On the open ground, the solitary marksman revolved promptly but unhurriedly to meet the next challenge.

For a moment, the plane seemed to stand still, hovering low over the western horizon. And then slowly, ever so slowly, awkward as a pregnant goose, it banked and uncertainly started its climb. Abruptly, a pencil-thin line of angry black smoke commenced to stream from the plane's tail.

The lone marksman in the clearing—actually a *markswoman*—rested her weapon as her head lifted to watch. The plane limped higher, struggling for altitude, the feather of oily black smoke smearing the sky in its wake.

When the plane reached the apex of its climb, it seemed to stagger and lose power. Seconds passed. At once, a single cotton puff popped out softly and lightly against the high azure sky, then another. Men in small groups of two's and three's stumbled out of the jungle, heads upturned. As if leaves on a summer breeze, the silk umbrellas drifted earthward.

Cil, having already this day had one shock that should last a man a lifetime, was ill-prepared for the second. He had summoned the woman and was standing idly by his tent at the edge of the clearing when she stepped into view. As she drew closer, an audible gasp escaped his lips. She was easily the most striking woman Cil had ever seen—barring one, perhaps, the memory of whose image at this moment did not enter his mind. She was young, perhaps twenty-four, and as she strode smartly toward him, dense tresses of copper-blond hair tumbled out from beneath her soft visored cap, the hair glistening in the sun and bouncing sassily against delicate shoulders, or what could be seen of them under the lightweight camouflaged battle fatigues, clean and freshly creased. She was tall with overlong legs, and as he watched her stride toward him, the movement was graceful, the bearing assured.

She came to a disturbingly casual attention before him, a little too close, as some people will. She fixed her eyes directly and pleasantly upon his own, the eyes deep honey-brown pools that seemed to sparkle and dance as she stood there quietly, appraising him. And for a second he thought he detected in the depths of those eyes some half-hidden dare or call to adventure; he was immediately drawn to her.

"Your name, Miss?" he demanded.

"Michelle, *Monsieur*." She ignored his harsh tone and gave him the most radiant smile. "Michelle D'Orleans. So glad to make your acquaintance." There was about her a maddeningly innocent, non-military air, a disarming freshness, even a hint of flirtation. A mischievous quirk played at the corner of her mouth, only slightly mocking, which both aroused and infuriated him.

"Lady," he snapped. "I suppose you're aware that you just single-handedly shot down the base commander!"

This stunning figure of a woman standing uncomfortably close, now took a step closer. Chin proudly uplifted, she spoke again pleasantly. "Major," she declared firmly, "that plane was attacking."

"Attacking?" Her tone only served to heighten his pique. "That plane was simply buzzing-the-field!"

"That plane, *Monsieur*," she told him with undiminished aplomb, albeit politely, "was in an attacking mode—and this a military base on foreign soil." Her tone was entirely reasonable with that infuriating musical lilt, the words spilling out in the unmistakable accents of the French, the voice at once husky and supremely assured. "Only yesterday, as you know," she added firmly, "rebel planes staged an attack with strafing and bombs. And as you yourself saw, that aircraft was approaching from out of the sun." She flung her head back in a fashion that scratched at his memory; she lifted that lovely, elegant chin until it hovered a foot from his own. "Tell me, Major, are your troops not trained to react to clear provocation?"

"I gave the order to scatter."

"And did anyone, *Sir*, give the base commander the order to approach us with caution?" She was still smiling, but her chin as it led the fine, determined jawline was jutting defiantly. And angry as Cil found himself, he was clearly nonplused by the force of her candor—for not ten minutes earlier had he himself faced down the base commander with almost precisely the same words.

"That's none of your business," he said.

"True," she conceded gently; then again the mischievous grin. "But shouldn't it be yours?"

Then it struck him. It struck him fiercely. It struck with the force of first lightning crashing into his brain. He stared at her face.

Damn it all! He could feel his heart pounding. Something about her. And now he remembered, and he could feel the full weight of the memories from the long dead past surge back like a tide that threatened to swamp him. It disarmed him; he felt faint; for a second, he fell back a full step before able to gather himself.

And now as he stared at her, he could feel the rush of all that long held hurt and rage welling up from within.

"Lady!" he shrilled. "Consider yourself dismissed!" But as soon as the words left his mouth, he regretted their harshness. It was only after she left that he finally got hold of himself. With the rationalization of afterthought, he mumbled under his breath. "After all, damn it, discipline's important—early discipline essential."

He watched her go. Involuntarily he watched the long even stride and the pert swing of her buttocks until she vanished from sight. He felt more comfortable now that she was gone, but he was not happy she was gone. He snatched a cigarette from the breast pocket of his combat fatigues and swiftly lit up, but his throat felt parched, the taste repellent, so he flung down the unsmoked cigarette, grinding out the butt with the heel of his boot; only as an afterthought did he bend down and field-strip the butt out of old habit.

A familiar voice from behind roused him. It was Captain Claxson, the copilot of the ill-fated plane.

"Hey, Buddy!" came the easy, Georgia drawl. "So that's the one—my would-be assassin? Wow, what a fox!"

"Glad to see you taking it all in stride," came Cil's acid

response, content, nonetheless, for the diversion.

"Now I see why you went so far out on a limb with the Old Man." Captain Jim Claxson was tall and dark, and though nearly forty, still adolescently handsome; his eyes sparkled now with knowing candor and amusement.

"What?" retorted Cil hotly. "For your information, I never laid eyes on the woman before. She's one of the new batch."

"Oh sure, you didn't." Claxson struggling to stifle a grin. "That's why you put your damned head in a noose with the Old Man—because you don't know her." Then Claxson, reading the depth of his friend's discomforture, altered his train. "Ya know, Buddy, I've never seen the Old Man that pissed!"

Cil, his emotions still in turmoil, stood there staring at Claxson, at his expression of obvious concern, at the same Jim Claxson who had once been a crack fighter pilot with the ribbons to prove it. In recent years, however, he had gone pleasantly off to seed, reducing himself to little more than a flying cowboy, content in his waning years of service to go along riding shotgun for the brass. But now Claxson addressed him bluntly.

"By the time you got through, I thought the Old Man was gonna give you the damned court-martial."

"Well—I was right." Cil set his mouth stubbornly.

"Right, kite. You don't tell a bird colonel to his face he's a damned fool—even if he is one."

"Well, I didn't."

"The hell you didn't, Boy. Maybe not in so many words." And now Claxson was shaking his head in bewilderment. "And all over a girl? Damn, Cilley boy, you're losin' your touch."

"The woman's not the point—it's the principle. Besides, it serves the old bird right. Here we sit, surrounded by a sea of rebel troops, and there comes our esteemed base commander, hauling ass in that plane like some young stud in

46

heat."

"Hey! Let me tell you somethin', Cilley Boy." Claxson was standing his ground, wagging a warning finger like a reproachful schoolmarm. "Principle might be a damned fine thing back in seventh grade civics, but I wouldn't put too much stock in it out here in the boonies. And one thing more—if I were you, I'd forget about studs in heat and start mendin' my fences—and practicin' that ole salutin' arm, Boy, if you know what I mean. As it is, he's put the whole damned base 'On Report' fer the duration. Round here, that oughta give your little girl's place-in-the-ratings a real shot-in-the-arm."

Then in a pondering, gradual way, Claxson's face changed.

"Ya know somethin'," he said, raising one hand to scratch the back of his neck while a lascivious grin began flooding his features. "I was jes thinkin'—mebbee thet lil girl a yourn's got a hankerin' fer a expert shoulder to cry on. Boy, whadidya say her tent number was?"

"I didn't."

As much as Cil rankled at the Southern diminutive, he had to smile. While many a training officer looked down his nose at Claxson for his rumpled appearance and wisecracking manner, to Cil, the man had proven himself a good and trusted friend, who, on more than one occasion had, by sheer skill and grit alone at the controls of a fighter aircraft, saved Cil's skin.

Cil's thoughts raced back in time as he reflected upon his relationship with this smooth-drawling flyboy; his smile broadened. Captain Claxson was one of a kind, a fighter pilot with plenty of combat hours behind him—not all of them in the cockpit. He watched his old pal move away in the direction of Miss D'Orlean's tent; he watched Claxson lift one preening hand to smooth down the dark wavy locks peeking out from beneath the battered officer's cap tipped at a cocky angle. Claxson was a lady's man.

Next morning, training began in earnest. It was better to get a group like this, Cil was thinking. These were all seasoned agents from various walks—CIA, military types on TDY like Claxson and himself, even some mercenaries with a military background under contract with the Department who had undergone the training long before and just needed a refresher. As might be expected, they coasted a bit; but if at first glance, they looked a motley crew, then impressions were deceiving, for they were a clever, resourceful, and deadly assortment, smart enough, as their case histories attested, to remain in one piece after untold missions behind enemy lines. That is the reason they did not cheat this morning; the subject was hand-to-hand combat.

Cil called for each operative to choose a "buddy," and whoever was not chosen, well, then Cil himself would take the black sheep. He was not surprised when it turned out to be the woman. He sauntered over, concealing his reluctance behind a half smile.

"Guess you're stuck with me," he offered gamely, now that the shock of yesterday had somewhat abated, but she did not reply. Instead, she looked off with a certain expression, obviously chagrined at going unchosen after bringing the wrath of the base commander down on the men.

Cil excused himself to stand up at the front and get the men started. He gave each pair a number; their number was last. He demonstrated the holds and the throws with the first pair, admonishing that if in battle they failed to "neutralize" an attacking enemy soldier close-in within seven seconds of first physical contact, they likely never would. The point was not lost on the men. Then he rejoined Miss D'Orleans, and together they looked on as each pair in turn went through their paces, the assailant always with the knife. For some, it got pretty rough, and Cil had to remind them it was only the first day.

And now he looked at the woman and read her expression; he felt a twinge of sympathy for her. It was tough to be left out, especially piled on top of the other trouble she found herself in. He spoke in attempt to cheer her.

"Look," he said, "there's not a man here who hasn't been 'On Report' one time or another. So try to ease up, to put it behind you. And, ah—by the way, this training, I suppose you've been through it before?"

"Similar," she told him without expression, her attitude still downcast and sulky. And when she raised her head, she seemed to look right through him.

"Similar, but not this?" he queried, surprised, but she was watching the pair at the center.

"Not this, no—but similar."

Cil puzzled at the evasive response. If she had never had the training, why didn't she just come right out and say so? And yet, if that were the case, what was she doing in the refresher? He made a mental note to check her dossier when he returned to his tent.

When their turn came, Cil took the initiative and made the first moves. He was careful in throwing her. She was wielding the knife, and he threw her again, being always careful about the placing of the hands; she was light as a feather.

He started his last throw; then it would be her turn. He didn't want to be so obviously gentle the others would notice, so this time he employed a tad more force.

He swung her over his back, and in a single lithe motion, her body whipped to the ground, but this time with an earth-spanking *thud* clearly audible to the others standing around.

Slowly, uncertainly, she lifted herself from the ground, dazed, looking pale and unwell, not looking at him.

Cil, instantly taken aback, felt small and ashamed; he hadn't meant anything like this. A few catcalls and snickers of derision aimed at the woman echoed through the ranks.

"I'm sorry," he whispered as they began to circle again. This time it was his turn with the knife, hers to attempt a take-down. Her face held no expression, her reply a curt nod.

Cil felt even more guilty. He kept on with the slow, ritual circling, his arms extended like those of a wrestler, his eyes fixed on her own.

When it came, it came with such skill and lightning speed that he never saw it coming. To Cil, there was that first vague sensation of total weightlessness, followed on the instant by wide-eyed anticipation, as if he were suddenly glued to the spot, staring at an oncoming car careening straight at him. All this did Cil take in, in that last instant before the ground reached up and struck him.

He lay flat on his back, yet seemed still to be floating. From somewhere far away he could hear the wind exploding from his lungs, then the light following wheeze. The world went white—stark white—his head a hornet's nest of black swarming bees revolving in super slow-motion behind the closed lids of his eyes.

When he returned to his senses, looking about him, the woman appeared a menacing giant looming above him. He could see the determined set of her features, and for a split second he thought he read the hint of a sneer or grin on her face—or maybe he dreamed it.

Cil limped back to his tent with all the gathered aplomb of a half-revived prizefighter groping for sanctuary. He skipped the noon meal and launched into the endless toil of report writing to bury all thought of the woman and his past. He was working from the side of his cot when roused by a noise, a sound at the tent flap.

"Yes—what is it?"

At first, only silence; then, in a low voice, "Miss D'Orleans, *Monsieur*."

"Sorry—I'm busy."

The voice from without came soft and repentant. "I wish only to speak briefly, *Monsieur*."

Cil took a breath and released it. With cold resignation, he turned to Miss D'Orlean's step as she ducked through the tent flap and seated herself on the cot opposite, facing him. She did not say a word but, with almost the softness of a caress, placed her hand on his own.

At the touch, his hand withdrew—as if in contact with a red-hot stove.

"I come only to say I did not mean to do what you are thinking," she said simply, with a slight toss of her head. Yet, something in the movement triggered an old memory, firing up emotions that lanced at his soul. He vented his rage to repel them.

"Look, Lady!" he exploded. "I don't give a damn who you are—or who you think you are; kindly leave me in peace."

"But I...."

I don't give a...." He turned on her, his voice bitter, cutting. "Look, Miss. This is the business of killing and dying. And war is no place for a woman." He sucked in his breath to get hold of his nerves. "But since you're here, let me tell you something. Do you have the slightest idea why no one picked you today as a partner? Well, do you? Because, here, the men are serious, this training is serious—either they learn it here, or they don't learn it at all."

The young woman lowered her head. "I'm sorry," she said. She did not utter another word but slowly rose to her feet. Quietly she turned to leave. Still, the set of her shoulders retained an unruffled dignity.

When Michelle D'Orleans had left his tent, Cil struggled against both his temper and the basic sense of human decency which his parents had drilled into him since earliest childhood. He did poorly with both, cursed sharply under his breath, then pushed back into his work to ward off the ghosts.

What had gotten into him? It wasn't like him—he had railed against her like a damned beast. No—worse; he had taken it upon himself to laud it over her, this whole murky business of superior male strength. Sure, he believed it from training and instinct; why not? But who was he, a commander, to toy with her head, to shred every vestige of human dignity the poor girl possessed? And she a woman alone on this base. He shook his head, as if to clear it. Worse—he had fairly enjoyed it.

Sometime later he found himself unconsciously stroking the ancient broken sword hung on the canvas wall of his tent. He was thinking of Miss D'Orleans—of the softness of her touch—of the fragrance of her—of the tiny freckles strewn about the button nose—of the sturdy, marvelous set of the chin—and the fleshy, full lips with which she had mouthed her apology.

And now, startled, he thought of his beautiful Sonya, then glanced up guiltily at the stubby remnant of the sword where it hung there on the wall of his tent. In his mind, he could see his Sonya on that last night before the old Bosnian mission, could hear even the tone of her voice. "Take it as my gift," she had implored him. "This very sword was carried by my grandfather against the Nazis back in the great war. Please, carry it with the promise of our love—for surely it will save you."

Abruptly Cil thrust aside the half-completed report upon which he had been working—as he thrust away the impurity of his thoughts about this new trainee. His broad brow creased; he stepped to the file cabinet wedged against the back of the tent. Opening the second drawer from the top, impatiently his fingers flipped through the files until his hand fell upon that marked: D'ORLEANS. The dossier was very thin, only a few pages, and he returned to his cot and sat down to read. He had barely begun reading when the full weight of it struck him.

"No!" He leapt to his feet. "Sonya—and Michelle D'Orleans—*cousins*?" He trembled so that the papers in his hand shook as if he were a man in high fever. "No, it just couldn't be!" But there it was in black and white.

When he had had sufficient time to recover from the

shock, he read over the historical facts one at a time, though there was no need; he already knew the story by heart. But now as he thought, he was shaking his head.

Sonya's own cousin here? Impossible! Coincidence was one thing, but this was utterly out of the question. No, there had to be another explanation—and somehow he would find it.

Later, he was reading half aloud the part about her training. "Let's see—served a two-year stint with the Israeli Army—finished in April. Hmmm. Must have come straight here." He now focused on her prior training. Airborne maneuvers, commando tactics, specialist in small arms.

"No wonder she could throw me flat on my ass!" And he was recalling her reply to his query about earlier training. "What was it she had said? Something about—not the same training—'but similar.'"

Suddenly Cil's temper flared. "Similar—my left foot! Why, that smug...." He choked off the rest, forcing himself down on his cot. He reached under the bed for the half-empty bottle of Scotch he kept stashed there, then, twisting off the top, took a good slug. Any damned fool knew hand-to-hand combat training in the Israeli Army was second to none in the world.

Cil was studying her photograph with such fierce and single-minded concentration, wondering whether the world was ready for the second coming of Joan of Arc, that he failed to hear Captain Jim Claxson slip through the tent flap.

"Hey, Cilley Boy! Whadaya got there—a million dollar bill?"

"Nothing—reports," returned a startled Cil, discarding the photo as guiltily as a spy caught examining microfilm.

"Here—let me see that," cried a grinning Claxson, suddenly interested, seizing the photo from where Cil had placed it face down on the cot.

Cil, his cheeks flushed, faced his friend squarely. "You

didn't come here just to gape at photos."

"No." Captain Claxson's features sharpened. "It's the Old Man. He's sniffin' for a scapegoat. The most defenseless one he can dig up—the girl. Right now he's got his boys workin' up papers to wash her out—with a special censure addressed straight to Headquarters."

Cil drew himself up to his full-gathered height. Claxson watched him in silence. Cil was a tall man; he was standing there square-jawed and deathly still, his hands bunched into fists at his sides like a man going into a fight.

"Maybe," Cil spoke in measured tones, "the time has come to have a little chat with the base commander."

Reports of the evening "chat" between Major Cil and Alouysious Nutting III, Colonel Commanding, were at best sketchy and mysterious. The rumor mill failed to report how the colonel had not only refused to accept Cil's defense of the female recruit but insisted upon her immediate presence before him—that night. Nor had the usually reliable rumor mill reported the manner in which the colonel had chewed her up one side and down the other. And then his fatal mistake—the colonel had suddenly flown into a rage, striding forward and striking the female trainee a blow to the face. Then and only then had Major Cil stepped in.

In the days that followed, rumor had it that the "good colonel" had suddenly and unaccountably suffered "a flareup of an old and bothersome case of malaria." In truth, the colonel had not been seen leaving the infirmary tent for a week; and there was some loose talk among the orderlies about the Old Man's face. Apparently, in addition to the malarial affliction, the base commander had quite unaccountably "run square into a heavy door—several times."

And, too, the malarial attack must also have struck at the "Old Man's mind," for the letter of reprimand regarding Miss D'Orleans on the subject of dismissal had somehow "gotten bogged down in channels." Just as surprisingly, the camp had abruptly been taken "Off Report" with full privileges restored.

As the training cycle progressed, Major Cil went right on in his role as acting commander, becoming ever more concerned, however, by the attitude of the men toward what they had come to term, *"that Battling Bitch from Bordeaux."*

Women trainees of earlier cycles had been merely an irritant to the men for lack of physical prowess, but this lady was more—she was a competitor and apparently a person not to be toyed with. The more the male resentment reared its ugly head, the more it goaded her on. And word had it that Captain Claxson, ever the gallant savior, was waging a sturdy campaign to comfort the damsel in her travails—with some success, Cil had heard.

All in all, it was becoming an ugly business, the more so due to the excellent skills possessed by Miss D'Orleans. She was good—very good—and the men didn't know how to cope with it.

Cil was relieved when the mid-training break came around. Many of the trainees, including Miss D'Orleans, flew home for the week. Miss D'Orlean's home in the States meant her uncle's elegant estate in upstate New York—or so Claxson had advised him. Cil elected to stay in camp with the remaining handful of men; you could never be sure when rebel pilots across the border would get liquored up and go bombing again. And anyway, something he could not abide was leaving a heap of paperwork unattended.

But Cil did not sleep well. It was not the run-in with the base commander, nor the weeks of punishing training. It was the woman. He told himself it was due to the friction she caused in camp—though late at night, as he lay on his cot, he would wonder how she was getting along at her uncle's estate. He wondered if Claxson was there.

5

The force of the man's presence behind the huge polished desk was such as to compel some men to quake, to lower their eyes and go suddenly dry in the mouth, others to rail against the force and directness of his methods, and still others who knew the reach of the man, to nod in either admiration or envy. Even at age sixty-three, so broad were the shoulders, so booming the voice above the thick extended moustaches, so predatory and commanding the eyes of Mavro Anastasi that he more closely resembled a battle-scarred old lion of the jungle, at once fierce and uncompromising, than a retired colonel of the former Yugoslav National Army.

It was a lazy Sunday afternoon. Colonel Mavro Anastasia, seated at his desk in the den of the family estate tucked into the hills of upstate New York, was so absorbed by the printed words before him, he remained oblivious to the warmth of the hearth on the far side of the room or to the fact that his mearsham pipe had gone cold. A beam of light from the floor lamp at his back angled across the shoulder of his bright tweed blazer and streamed onto the pages of the Sunday *New York Times*, which he was studying intently; the flood of light seemed to bring the newsprint to life.

"So!" he growled, releasing the pages to flutter and drop to the desktop. Then he slapped the leather arm of his chair with such force that the resounding *smack* reverberated off the walls of the room. "Once again it begins!"

The loud noise was abruptly followed by a light knock at the door. A tall, statuesque, young woman stuck her head into the room, quite bashfully at first, then entered on silent, bare feet, lugging an armful of firewood.

"Did you wish something, Onkle?" she asked, employing the term of endearment used since a child. "Your cup of hot cocoa, perhaps? Brewed by an expert?" Her teasing voice came to him with the cheer and warmth of the fire in the hearth, its melodic lilt, soft on his ears; and in spite of his displeasure with her, his mouth softened—if only for an instant.

"My dear," he boomed. "Don't soft-soap me! A hundred times have I told you not to ride Le Grand. That damned horse—he's thrown more men than the Republicans have thrown national elections."

Her chin ascended with only a hint of defiance, and then a spark of mischief toyed with her mouth, but she made no reply, stooping instead to fill the woodbox.

"Oh, very well then," he roared. "Break that damn pretty neck, if you must. But don't come crying to me."

"What was that?" Though she spoke softly, her voice raised a challenge. "And when, Onkle Whiskers, was the last time that I ...."

"Figure of speech, my dear." Casting it off with a toss of the head. "Figure of speech, that's all," his voice crusty, harsh as his features, eyes burrowing from beneath the bush of his brows; he turned again to the paper.

"You see the news?" This time it was his turn to throw out a challenge. "Why, it's plastered all over the paper. 'Serb-Muslim cease-fire breaks down. Serbs once again on rampage in Bihac—scores feared dead—UN Peacekeepers surrounded.'"

"On, no," she cried. Even stacking the logs in the wood-box, she was unable to conceal the shock in her voice. "And you saw it coming."

"Listen to this," he declared, his thick fingers savagely drumming against the arm of the chair. "'Heavy armor spearheads attack.'" Then he stiffened. "'Rape and pillage! Relentless pattern of ethnic cleansing—Muslim villages ablaze.'"

"Oh! Bosnia burning—what does it mean?"

But before he could answer, a sound caused the young woman to start.

"A moment, Onkle—the phone." She ducked away down the hall as the den phone was set to activate strictly for business.

And now the colonel leaned heavily back in his chair, feeling the weight of his years, rubbing his eyes as he pondered, his mind reflecting back on the carnage of factional fighting he himself had witnessed as a young line officer in his native Yugoslavia; he shook his head knowingly. Like his father before him, Mavro Anastasi was one of those rare persons able to ride the tide of history, yet not be swamped by it. And now for a moment his fingers ran self-consciously over his bursitis-ridden shoulder. No, this time out, he would be taking no active role in the fighting.

"The call, it's for you. Voice sounds important," declared the young woman and left the room.

Irritably he flicked the switch to activate the phone on his desk, then jerked up the receiver.

"Anastasi here!"

"Good evening, Colonel." The cadence of the distant voice came brusque yet unhurried. "Lockwood, here at Defense. Sorry to break in on your Sunday, but.... It seems that something's come up since your discussions with our man Spruance. The Secretary has requested your presence here tomorrow by noon."

"Now, look here, Lockwood—that's pretty short notice," the colonel's voice sounding more as if addressing a buck private than the US Deputy Secretary of Defense. "You see, my niece...."

"Colonel—we all have nieces." Lockwood cut him off sharply. "This is urgent—the Secretary is sending his own military plane."

"Very well then," he grumbled, resigned. "Delighted to serve the Secretary in any way I can," but the depth of his sigh could scarcely have gone unnoticed over the wire.

"Till morning then—eight-thirty sharp—the usual airfield."

When the colonel had replaced the receiver, he sat for a moment, pondering. Strange, I told old Spruance only last week to be expecting the worst. Hmmm. What was it Lockwood had said? "....something's come up....this is urgent!" That didn't sound like Lockwood's boss, the indomitable Secretary of Defense. Rumor had it, the Secretary was a cool one. "Cold as a stone," was the way he had heard it phrased. He turned again to the paper before him. Headlines like this wouldn't scare him. Must be something really big.

The colonel took a moment to calm himself, to dampen his disappointment; he had so counted on spending these last few days with his favorite niece before her return to training. And now this.

And that was another thing—this training of hers. He could feel the old tide of emotion boiling up in his veins. Openly did he wonder if that damned banker brother-in-law of his, raising this child for so many years on his own, had gone soft in the head. Imagine! Allowing this spitfire of a girl a free rein. His fingers resumed their rhythmic drumming beat on the arm of the chair. He had hoped and expected that after completing her university studies at the Sorbonne in Paris, then the two-year stint with the Israeli Army—which he had opposed—the experience would have cured her of the whole damned silly notion. But, no—and now this business of guerilla training.

He cursed under his breath, for a moment fighting to repress memories of a similarly devastating episode a few years back involving his own daughter, Sonya.

And what was this business of the *letter?* He recalled the day when one of the maids, at his request, had brought him a resource book from Michelle's library—and how, strangely, a letter concealed between the pages had fallen out in his lap as he opened the book. Worse, this had not been just any letter, but an old love letter addressed to someone else. The whole matter had bothered him considerably at the time—it being so unlike Michelle.

Of course, it was true—in spite of a full six years in age separating these two talented cousins, always had Michelle felt a keen competition between herself and Sonya. Still, a bit of high-spirited rivalry was one thing, a gross and indiscreet interference in the other's private life, quite another. And now a shake of the head preceded his shrug.

Women! And to think how damned insistent Michelle had been upon being assigned to this one particular training unit.

He thought of his own past. What could it be—this fantasy legend, this ghost of the grandfather, his own father, whose hand could reach out of the grave to spread the infection across all the years—the great *Captain Louie.*

Damn! He swiped at the desktop with the flat of his hand. But after all, that was the very thing about legends, wasn't it? Legends don't die like ordinary mortals—so every red-blooded descendant has to be born under that same yoke of duty and fame. Fame was a *curse.*

But Michelle? War was horror enough for the toughest of men—but for a woman—for this girl? And this young lady scarcely more than a child! Again he found himself shaking his head. Damn it, why couldn't she just go find herself a husband—like any *normal* girl?

His mind ran back to that peaceful spring day so long ago, a day that would remain emblazoned upon his memory until the end of his years. It was in the gardens of Madam Jacque's School there on the Swiss lake front. Even now, after all the years, Colonel Anastasi could feel his breath sawing in his chest like a tired old lion at thought of that tragic day. Sitting here now, still he could recall the stark contrast: the hard, unvarnished truth—the fine warmth of the early spring sun as he waited, the sweet fragrance of jonquils wafting about him as he spied bunches of giddy schoolgirls in fetching blue uniforms shrieking in delight, spilling out of that staid old stone-faced building, cavorting over the lush green of the lawns. And then, there she was, that special bundle of joy, bursting forth, darting down the path to greet him, little arms outstretched, curls flying, voice bawling at the top of wee lungs: *"Onkle Whiskers! Onkle Whiskers!"* She could not have been past seven on that fateful day, and the task had fallen to him, yes, fallen to him—to break the news of her mother. At the memory, his stern mouth hardened to a firm, grim line.

And now Mavro Anastasi climbed to his feet. Before the wall mirror, he smoothed down his mustaches, made a show of clearing his throat, then marched solemnly down the broad marble hallway to the door of her room.

For a moment he paused, undetected in the open doorway, feasting his eyes on this favorite scene. He had observed the very phenomenon a hundred times before, but it never ceased to thrill and to warm him—the perfect counterpoint to the obsessive thoughts of that awful day. Yes, there was definitely something as natural and refreshing about this young woman as the return of the sun after a sudden spring rain, the sense of life and light and being alive which the girl seemed to exude and infect you with by the sheer force of her presence; the quality was nearly palpable, and he stood there entranced, drinking it in.

Michelle D'Orleans, clad in casual slacks and powder-blue cashmere sweater, sprawled contentedly on the floor, curled on the antelope rug with her nose buried in a book before the open hearth. The fire in mellow tones of browns and yellows and orangey reds reflected off the walls of the room and brought them alive; the embers crackled and sputtered; live sparks snapped and darted like fireflies, and the light flickering over the fiery highlights and rolling tresses of her hair. Gentle flecks of fireflight danced over the features of her face flushed by the heat of the fire, reflecting its warmth.

By her side cuddled Bobo, her Angora kitten, a tiny snowball furry as the sweater it rubbed against, the kitten purring softly, tiny teeth nibbling at the idle fingers of its mistress. Overhead, Kato, the sassy old parrot, chattered his noisy admonition: "Watch out for the cat! Watch out for the cat!" And the fire hissing its chuckled response. Next to the splashy burnt-orange cover draped over the bed stood an old stand-up Victrola, solid, stalwart, like some great ancient presence in the room, hand crank and all. And from the flute of its mouth spilled the soft soothing strains of Glenn Miller's *Moonglow*, a recording which the old man pridefully recognized as his own.

"Oh, Onkle Whiskers!" cried Michelle, unconsciously employing the mispronunciation she had used since childhood, her eyes startled open and soft as a fawn's. "Was it something important?"

"Someone at Defense," he said gruffly. "Are the servants about?"

"You've forgotten," she reminded gently. "It's Sunday night; they're off in the village." Closing the book on her thumb, she smiled up at him. "Can I help?"

"No, no; I'll have Marko drop me at the air base in the morning. What is it you're reading?"

"If they're sending a plane, it must be important. Clausewitz, on the evolution of tactics. How long will you be?"

"Drat the petty functionaries," he cursed, waving his hand about his head as if scaring off flies. "It's hard to say. Damn! Imagine the gall to drag me off on your very last days?"

"Only two days."

"Even so," he huffed possessively, and her quick eye instantly caught the barely perceptible slump of his shoulders. Lightly she jumped to her feet; then with her mouth pulled down and one curving brow lifted, she looked him straight in the eye.

"Forget our pills today, did we?" she reproved in the manner and tone of a stiff-necked old nursemaid.

His arm waved in protest, but she ignored it and drew out her sigh.

"Honnn-estly. Sometimes, I swear, you men all need a nursemaid." Then lithely she plucked at his sleeve and swung him around until his back faced the fire; she turned him with the sure, familiar hands of someone who had surely done this before. Gently, she slipped off his jacket and tossed it on the bed while she set to work on his bursitis-ridden shoulder. She worked like a practiced nurse, with soft kneading hands; he sighed with relief and contentment.

"I can drop you in the morning," she said. "Oh, and you don't mind if I take the Rolls?"

"What's that—the Rolls?" His ears perked up. "What's on your mind, young lady?" he demanded.

"You remember those friends of mine from Boston," she started vaguely. She had been flirting with the idea all week—but now with his leaving. "The ones that called the other day?" Rubbing his shoulder, she could feel his body stiffen.

"Not that rowdy *Harvard Crowd* of yours!"

"Oh, no," she laughed. "This one is a military crowd."

"A military *man*, you mean. What man?" But she could feel his shoulder beginning to relax now.

"Why, you know, the flyer I told you about. That flyboy

captain—the one I shot down."

"You be damned careful of those high-flying gigolos." His voice was a growl, the bite of his anger only pretense by half.

"Oh, is that sooo?"

"That's so. Because when *I* shoot a man down, young lady, he stays down. Is that understood?" He was shifting the painful shoulder just so, feeling the kneading action and the soothing effect of her hands.

"Oh *Onkle Whiskers—please*," she pleaded theatrically. "But this one is sooo handsome—and sexy." She was mocking him gaily. "Would you really be so cruuuel?" Her long dark lashes fluttered like soft feathers in the firelight.

This time the voice of Mavro Anastasi was a Howitzer. "You know damned well I would. . . and I will!" He wrenched his shoulder free. "Now where is that splendid damned cocoa I heard so much bragging about?"

She helped him with the jacket, then glided toward the door, at the last moment aiming a coy look back over her shoulder.

"And I suppose you'll even ask that I press your best Sunday suit," pretending to pout. "and then do your packing." Theatrically her hand flew to her breast and she issued a sigh. "Hon-nestly—you men. Didn't your mothers ever teach you anything?" She was already loping off down the hallway.

"What?" he bellowed at her disappearing back. "So you'd leave me for a *damned flyer!*"

When the sound of her footsteps returned, she stood by the doorway, one hand uplifted in that same theatrical fashion, but this time, like a classical Spanish dancer, her aspect proud, unapproachable, chin uplifted, a steaming mug of cocoa poised precariously over her head. And now she began to twirl in a flourish of pirouettes, her tall, willowy figure framed by the doorway, her bare feet pattering softly on the floor. And then while still on tiptoes, she raised her chin even higher, planting a kiss on the stiff, leathery cheek.

"But you know, Onkle Whiskers," she intoned in a sultry, fetching way, "Like Lady Guinevere, I have but one true love." But he ignored her.

"What name does this gallant captain—who can't afford a car—go by?"

"Claxson," she said. "Captain James Orville Claxson."

6

Dark-bellied low clouds threatening an imminent storm swept in over the Potomac River separating official Washington from the rolling hills of Virginia. The sleek black limousine raced down the exit ramp and swung up to the Pentagon entrance where a stone-faced lieutenant with clicking heels and a crisp salute escorted Colonel Mavro Anastasi up to the offices of rank. There, James Lockwood, the brusque, no-nonsense Deputy Secretary, a rough bull moose of a man, disheveled and in shirtsleeves, scowled the colonel into the inner sanctum of American military power.

The Office of the Secretary of Defense, at once regal and intimidating, made not the slightest impression upon the colonel, for he had spent the better part of a lifetime negotiating the minefields of Communist power at the very highest levels of government in the former Yugoslavia. His sole preoccupation was the business at hand.

As he entered, the windows on one wall of the room commanded an imperious view of official Washington. At the far end, in keeping with the size of the room, stood a huge mahogany desk, the desk flanked by a divan and pair of upholstered wing-backed chairs, all in such rich yet subdued gold and blue tones that ordinary outsiders would be instantly reminded where and in whose presence they found themselves. Twin flags on either side of the desk stood at rigid attention, one displaying the nation's colors; the other, the circular emblem of the Department of Defense. On the wall behind the writing desk hung a portrait of the current young President, staring down from on high.

The colonel strode briskly into the room. The great desk before him seemed to dwarf the man seated behind it—a bare wisp of a man, really, distinguished looking, yes, though astonishingly old, with features so severe they appeared chiseled from granite. A plain wooden plaque on the front of the desk announced without flourishes: ROBERT LEVITT, SECRETARY OF DEFENSE.

Upon Deputy Lockwood's brusque introduction, the tiny man behind the desk sprang lightly to his feet. Smiling graciously, he held out his hand.

"A distinct pleasure finally to meet you, Colonel," the little man stated, his manner warm and friendly, though Mavro Anastasi silently noted the watch-fires burning deep in those eyes.

Colonel Anastasi was plainly startled, startled at how truly petite the man was and how sprightly he carried himself for a man nearing eighty, the voice clipped and precise, the features sharp, eyes keen and alert. But pressing the small offered hand brought an immediate wince of pain that caused the gnarled fingers to withdraw themselves swiftly.

"Scourge of old age—that's all," chuckled the small man in apology, nodding toward one of the comfortable chairs facing the desk; and when both men were seated, the deputy standing, a somber-faced Secretary Levitt spoke forthrightly.

"I'm afraid, Colonel, we're up against the damnest riddle—a riddle, frankly, which has me stumped. But first...."

And as quickly as the smile had extinguished itself, it returned in full measure, this time the devilish grin of a schoolboy. Secretary Levitt, with a quick precise movement, ducked his hand into a side drawer of his desk to produce a sizable object. He proffered the ornate, wooden-topped jar filled with tobacco to his guest. "Not a pipe smoker myself," he allowed, "I cannot vouch for it personally, but I'm told—the stuff is a marvel."

One whiff and Mavro Anastasi instantly caught the aroma of superb Turkish tobacco, and while a disinterested Deputy Lockwood stood about stiffly, the colonel, without conscious thought, settled back in his chair, slipped his pipe from his pocket, extracted a pinch, and set about packing the rich fibers into the bowl of his pipe; he was wholly relaxed now.

"First off," declared the Secretary, "I've a slight confession to make." And for a moment his features clouded with memory. "At this late date, I suppose you'd have trouble believing, but at the outbreak of World War II, I was just one more junior foreign service officer stuck off in some lost outpost of the world. On the other hand," eyeing Colonel Anastasi, though addressing his deputy, "the father of the colonel here—well now, let me explain."

The Secretary pressed forward in his chair, his face suddenly lit with emotion.

"Every news flash carried word of his exploits—think of it—a mere handful of partisans hammering away behind enemy lines in a Europe overrun by the Axis." The old man was truly excited. "A fistful of rogue fighters tweaking the great Nazi tail!" His eyes burning coals in their sockets as the memories flooded back. "Why, I can see it as if it were only last week."

Now, suddenly, the little man leapt to his feet, theatrically, his silvery locks jouncing as he swung his arms wide and threw back his head. "Imagine—the shock of each new lightning move—and each succeeding move more daring than the last." His voice seemed to be gaining in strength as the drama unfolded, rising and falling in waves, and then finally, punctuating each new feat with a crashing crescendo.

"Think of it. The hijacking of a key ammunition train—the thunder and flash in the night as yet another munitions dump blew skyward, flames billowing up in the late night sky."

Suddenly breathless, carried away by the sheer force of his own presentation, the old man sank down in his chair, as if for the moment exhausted.

"Yes, Jim," nodding at his deputy. "This man to us, hah—Jesse James and Davy Crockett rolled into one, a beacon of hope in those early days of the war when the world lay in shadow, when one Allied defeat followed another like descending steps on a dark, endless staircase." He was pensive, remembering. "Why, in those days, I tell you, mere mention of the name—Captain Louie—evoked the image—visage of the man in white astride that great stallion—thundering over the night at the head of his men!"

The Secretary lay back, heaving a sigh that came straight from the soul. "What a man he was—and a deal of comfort to me, I can tell you." He was pulling hard on a cigarette unconsciously snatched from the desktop at the height of the drama, so engrossed had he been in his tale.

"Yes, Jim," he said, keen eyes steely, focused on the colonel, "I realize, for men of your generation, it's yesterday's news, but for us—us who were out there—why, this man's father and his countryman, Tito, battling the odds on sheer nerve alone? Make no mistake, their exploits were felt in every single theater of war."

But as soon as Secretary Levitt's voice subsided, Colonel Anastasi spoke up.

"You know, Mr. Secretary," observed the colonel dismissively, if not with a hint of irreverence. "That might be a slight exaggeration."

"Not on your life," the little man shot back, discarding

the half-spent cigarette, lighting another.

"Well, that's all well and good," the colonel intoned with a hint of impatience, perhaps feeling a bit patronized, and too, mindful of how arbitrarily he had been forced to part with his beloved niece. "But I doubt you called me all this way just to swap old war stories."

Deputy Lockwood, standing taut as a bowstring, was incensed at the imagined affront.

"The Secretary," he snapped, "will get to the point in his own time."

For response, Mavro Anastasi, with his arms perfectly relaxed and resting on the arms of his chair, merely cocked his head and stared up solemnly at Lockwood through the bush of his brows. The image of the colonel, seated comfortably, clad in a dark, finely pressed business suit, presented sharp contrast to the harried look of Deputy Lockwood, standing pinch-mouthed in shirtsleeves, his shirt hanging open at the collar with tie tugged askew.

"Well, Mr. Secretary?" prodded the colonel discreetly, nodding in his direction.

"Quite right," alertly agreed the man behind the desk, commencing to blow smoke rings, and quietly enjoying the drama.

When the volume of smoke from the colonel's pipe and the Secretary's own offerings converged at Lockwood's considerable height, the resulting fog of smoke seemed somehow to obscure the deputy and render his presence irrelevant.

"Jim." Secretary Levitt spoke to Deputy Lockwood, making a slight snap of the fingers. "I think that will be all for the moment—and if you'd hold my calls. And—oh yes—bring in the pictures." Something in the inflection of voice transformed a simple request to an unmistakable command, and the Secretary made a show of snuffing out his cigarette not to further embarrass his subordinate as the disheveled Lockwood retreated from the room.

Once alone, the little silver-haired man leaned far across the desk toward Colonel Anastasi, his tone conspiratorial.

"You know," he said with a wink, "I wasn't kidding about that partisan business—not to mention Captain Louie's assist all through the war in rescuing our downed flyers and OSS agents in those miserable black mountains of Bosnia." Then, as abruptly, his features straightened. "Nor am I one to forget a debt owed."

Secretary Levitt then proceeded to open a manila folder which lay before him on the desk; he scanned the first entries.

MAVRO ANASTASI, Colonel
Army of the former Yugoslavia—Retired.

Place of birth: Belgrade, Serbia, April 21, 1932. At the close of World War II when the country had gone Communist, and his father been assassinated at the hands of President Tito, at age 13 the boy was urgently removed from Yugoslavia by comrades-in-arms of his father for reasons of his personal safety.

> Father: Mavro Louie Anastasi, Serbian National
> Mother: Elsa Linsk, citizen of Slovenia
> Wife: Elena Hohenzollern, Countess of Moldavia
> One child: Sonya
> Higher Education: University of Zagreb, MS, Civil Engr.
> Graduate, Yugoslav Military Academy, Belgrade
> Military Service: Yugoslavia National Army
> Permanent rank: Colonel.
> NOTE: Imprisoned in Belgrade by Tito Regime: 1976-81 (Charge: anti-Communist activist).
>
> Yugoslav Govt Service: Ministry of Interior: 1981-90

Current status: Consultant—United States Dept of
Defense (Balkan Affairs).

Secretary Levitt looked up from his file, his voice a bare
whisper. "Six years in Tito's prison—that is no joke."

Colonel Anastasi nodded, though he made no reply.

"But later I see you served with the Yugoslav Ministry of
Interior—including public works?"

"Inspection and central planning."

"Roads, bridges, and dams?"

"All of that, yes," replied the colonel, puffing on his pipe,
nodding impatiently.

"So you are intimately familiar with Dalmatia on the
Adriatic coast and the mountains of the interior, the Dinaric
Alps, and the major projects north of Mostar?"

Anastasi, a great lion of a man, was stirring in his chair.
"Just what are you driving at?" he put in quickly, and just as
quickly attracted the sharp, steady gaze of Secretary Levitt
whose brow furrowed in impatience.

"The big dam," he snapped. "In Bosnia-Herzegovina—
above Mostar—do you know it?"

"I should know it," the colonel replied, cocking a furry,
inquiring brow. But before Secretary Levitt could follow
up, Lockwood re-entered the room.

"The photos, Mr. Secretary," declared Lockwood stiffly,
still smarting at his earlier dismissal, and handing a small
packet to the Defense Secretary with the care of one who
might well have been bestowing the Crown jewels. "Of
course, as you know, Mr. Secretary, the photos are highly
classified." He shot a condescending glance in Anastasi's
direction to emphasize the point, but the colonel ignored it.

The Secretary, as if a wily old trial lawyer displaying crucial exhibits to a jury, began arranging each photo in
sequence on the lip of the desk for the colonel's inspection.

As the colonel examined each one in turn, a silent alarm
began to tighten his features. Secretary Levitt, lighting yet

another cigarette, though one still smoldered in the ashtray, paused dramatically before he again spoke.

"Three days ago, Wednesday, May 31, one of our U-2 special reconnaissance aircraft overflying Bosnia-Herzegovina came up with these photos."

As Colonel Anastasi went on examining the photos, his mouth hardened even further. Finally, extracting the pipe from between his teeth, he gave a soft whistle.

"But—this is impossible!" he exclaimed. "That dam is not in Serb hands!"

"That's what I thought," returned the Secretary quietly. And it was at this point that a sound, the first rumble of distant thunder invaded the room. "But it is—now."

A stunned Anastasi carried the point forward. "Why—with this store of arms and equipment stockpiled in the basin below the dam—and that dam powering all life in the region?" He was incredulous. "Why, just look! Here are tanks—and troops—and heavy weapons—enough to mount an invasion—a full scale assault through the mountain passes in a thrust at Sarajevo. Worse—there's enough here to overrun the coastal plain and seal off the Adriatic ports—severing every vital supply line!" Forgetting himself in his excitement, he was speaking with open candor, for the immediate implications of massed weapons poised in this crucial pocket were not lost on the mind of a seasoned military tactician.

The Secretary offered only a somber nod.

"Has the Croatian High Command been alerted?" The question exploded from Anastasi's lips.

"No!" interjected the Deputy Lockwood with a pounce, suddenly belligerent. "And despite your Red past, you will not inform them!"

Taken aback by the outburst, the Secretary fell silent for a time; then came the same subtle snap of the fingers. Swiftly Deputy Lockwood made his retiring way from the room. Only when the door had firmly closed behind him did

Anastasi, still stunned by the revelations, turn to the small man behind the big desk.

"You have my word, Mr. Secretary. My lips are sealed. But at all costs, those combat units must not be allowed to break out."

"The President's and my sentiments precisely, responded the Secretary. But there are complications—grave ones, I'm afraid."

Secretary Levitt's statement was punctuated by a streak of lightning brightening the sky beyond the expanse of glass—then a close clap of thunder.

"Let's review what we're faced with," declared the Secretary. "Of primary concern is the United Nations arms embargo against all factions. As long as it remains in place, it serves only to deny arms to the Bosnian Muslims as well as the Croats, thereby tying the hands of all but the Serbs—who, incidentally, enjoy constant resupply from Belgrade."

Anastasi jumped in. "Worse, with the UN and NATO at each other's throats, and this whole crazy business of dual-key authority, only confusion of policy and action results. And now with all the belligerents shouting for removal of UNPROFOR and the Peacekeepers, the pot really boils. And meanwhile—in all deference, Sir—the great powers go on huffing-and-puffing, hopelessly snarled in the politics of upcoming elections while the Serbs go right on with their 'ethnic cleansing,' now even preparing to gobble up the so-called 'safe areas' of Srebrenica and Zepa, then finally Bihac and Sarajevo—and all with the full support of Belgrade."

"Precisely," agreed the Secretary. "From whence this armor and artillery almost certainly derives—unless, of course," on a more ominous note, "from the Serb's traditional patrons themselves—the Russians. And I can tell you one thing—Russia remains the real threat. Good Lord, with our ongoing efforts to disarm Russia herself as well as the other former soviet republics of nuclear, biological and chemical weapons, we daren't lift a finger—at least publicly." The small man threw back his head and blew a great smoke ring.

"You see," he went on, "we're damned if we do, and damned if we don't. Already the whole of north and east Bosnia is lost, the Serbs in their raping, plundering rein of terror have already grabbed off seventy per cent of the Bosnia-Herzegovina land area—and now they're reaching for more. And then with the Brits, French, and other allied peacekeepers in harms way on the ground and under constant Serb bombardment—and the ill-conceived endeavors of the UN to intervene—and the Contact Group in a crazy tight-rope act to walk the narrow, neutral line and work out a 'loaded' cease-fire, however well-intentioned. Well, it all sounds a familiar refrain—and all playing into the hands of the Serbs."

"Mr. Secretary, I don't have to tell you, with the Muslim enclave in Bihac surrounded, and the Krajina region seething with Serbs, a break-out toward the west and the coast would not only draw in the Slovens and Croats, but likely their patrons, the Germans. And in Dalmatia, the Italians as well. Nor can Albania, Macedonia, and Greece be far behind. And, as you say, we cannot count out the Great Russian Bear."

"To top off Serb tempers, Iran and the other Fundamentalist States are smuggling in arms and men in ever greater numbers to beef-up the Muslims."

"And now an imminent Serb drive through the mountains," chimed in the colonel. "Why, that could set up a crushing second front against Sarajevo."

At this, Secretary Levitt mashed out his last cigarette. He suddenly produced a small red rubber ball from the drawer of his desk. Swiveling his chair in a single agile movement, so that it faced the wall with his back to the colonel, the old Secretary commenced blithely bouncing the little red ball off the back wall—beneath a disapproving stare from the

President's portrait.

"Tell me," he ordered. "Tell me all you know about that dam. Is it impregnable?"

"Not to a well-placed torpedo or bomb."

"Like hell! No—that's out." The wisp of a man foreclosed him curtly. "Bombs and torpedoes are *positively* out. Why, our friends, the Russians, would enjoy nothing better than open provocation and an excuse to pile-on with the Serbs."

Abruptly he put down the ball. He revolved his chair to once again face Colonel Anastasi.

"The dam—the key is the dam. Show me the weakness," he demanded suddenly.

But Mavro Anastasi was not a man to be rushed. Of course, he knew the dam, had known every last detail of the structure when he had done the inspections for the Yugoslav Ministry of the Interior. Why, hadn't he even walked the grounds personally? But now he took his time going over the photographs, once again inspecting each one in turn, examining every minute detail with the care of the seasoned professional, verifying the accuracy of the depictions against his own memory. The little man went back to his game with the ball.

"Where are the satellite photos?" Anastasi inquired at length.

"We're awaiting a new batch."

Photos taken from directly overhead, whether by aircraft or satellite, were not all they were cracked up to be, this the colonel knew; they gave a distorted picture; while they would show the Serb compound well enough, they would most certainly fail to show the true vulnerability of the dam.

At last the colonel looked up. A rare twinkle showed in his eyes.

"Tell me," he said wryly. "They told me you were a sly one. Does bouncing that little damned ball really improve that arthritis—or did you just invent the device to force me to better examine these photos?"

There came but a slight chuckle from behind the great chair.

"And one thing more—I can see you never worked for a Communist regime," the colonel added.

"How's that?"

"The dam was originally a modest earthen dam, believe it or not—just an arm of land thrust out into the river from the base of the mountains. Enough of a dam to supply the power needs of the local inhabitants only. When Tito came to power, he approved the massive dam project to meet the needs of the towns and cities of the region—but there was a problem."

"Go on—go on." The little man's ears perked up.

"Controversy arose as to whether to raze the earthen dam completely, given the attendant danger of flooding the urban centers downriver—or to simply place the footings for the great dam through it, then construct the concrete gravity-arched dam, smaller but much like your own Hoover Dam, right over the top of the existing earthen structure. And that's exactly what they did."

"What's that? You say they went ahead and built one right on top of the other? Piggybacking a great, modern dam right on top of the original earthen dam? Sounds crazy as hell to me." The Secretary, his back to Colonel Anastasi, was still bouncing the ball in long, looping parabolas.

"Maybe not so crazy. Much of the base extending out from the foot of the opposing mountains was solid ledge, though a small section at the center is nothing but hard-packed ground."

"You don't say?"

"It gets better. When the high dam was completed and the lake formed behind, there was disconcerting leakage through the earthen dam at the location of the old spillway. Once the leaks were discovered, the builders, fearing reprisal and having no clue how to effect repairs once a million tons of concrete had already been poured, decided to make cosmetic repairs and pocket the savings."

"Yes, yes?"

"Further repair was attempted, but it remains a fiasco."

"A fiasco indeed."

"And a very dangerous one at that—if you consider the millions of tons of water backed up by that dam."

The thumping sounds on the wall behind ceased. Secretary Levitt snapped his chair around to face Colonel Mavro Anastasi—who was smiling.

"You mean?"

"Yes."

7

The ignominious departure of Base Commander Colonel Alouysious Nutting III for failure to adequately account for the loss of a "military fighter aircraft" had placed responsibility of command squarely upon the shoulders of Major Lane Cil and that is the reason he had seen little of Miss D'Orleans for the balance of the cycle. It was the "report" that brought him to the rifle range late this day, report of the soaring level of dissension between the men, and, in their own words, "that Battling Bitch from Bordeaux."

On the next to last day of training, an exercise had been scheduled that really caught the imagination of the men—a shooting competition. And, as nearly all of the trainees were experienced foreign operatives or combat veterans, marksmanship was one of their long suits. This was a one-on-one shoot-out with a series of heats; whoever took the final heat would be the overall winner, winner-take-all. The favorite, a skinny, sharp-eyed dude with a long Texas drawl named "Hawk-Eye" Colton, was a world class contestant, thrice Army Sharpshooter of the Year, who, rumor had it, had been robbed of an Olympic bronze medal by an overzealous Russian judge.

The object was to break down, field-strip, then re-assemble a foreign-made automatic weapon on the bare ground, blindfolded; as the blindfold was removed, the next step was to run through a set of moving targets; both speed and accuracy were important.

Emotion was running high at the twilight kick-off of the final heat as Major Cil reached the large circle of men surrounding the contestants, the men all hooting and bawling encouragement to their favorite. The odds were running 17-1 in favor of the man from Texas. The prize was a one-half share of the money bet, and since the wages of the men had accumulated here in the jungle, the stakes in the battered coffee can set between the contestants amounted to a small fortune.

Once having seen the "report," Cil was plainly worried. The tension had been building for weeks, and he knew these men, knew the coldness and savagery of which they were capable, for he had personally reviewed the written record of each in overseas operations. And he knew that their chosen representative, the Texan, was not playing for money, but in defense of their collective male honor.

Cil went over to the Texan where he sat in the grass, clad as he was in camouflaged jungle fatigues. He first checked the sharpshooter's blindfold, then set about shooing away his host of raucous admirers. Loud banter was directed at the other contestant—none of it complimentary.

And now Cil strode over to the woman similarly clad. He watched her cool detachment as he tightened her blindfold; he watched her hands folded together and noticed their icy calmness. Scrutinizing the attitude of the men and having some idea how much they had bet, Cil was suddenly afraid for her—and furious she was not afraid for herself. He wanted it over. Signaling for the competition to begin, it was with an anxious eye that he noted the weapon handed to each contestant.

Hawk-Eye Colton was issued a standard Czech weapon,

the woman an obscure and complicated piece manufactured by the Chinese for use by the North Koreans. The trick was to field-strip the weapon quickly, then clean and re-assemble it with care, paying strict attention to wipe or blow away the slightest particle of dust or dirt on each component of the weapon to avoid jamming later.

Now both weapons were in pieces, the woman falling behind in cleaning and re-assembly. Small wonder, thought Cil, given the unfamiliar characteristics and number of parts to her little known weapon. Hawk-Eye was the first to his feet. A wild cheer—almost a roar—went up for the Texan.

Miss D'Orleans was still seated, her fingers working slowly and carefully as the experienced Hawk-eye tore out onto the course, moving rapidly, his weapon spewing fire and barking from side to side as the targets sprang and skittered and dove. He was a quarter of the way through the course before the woman even got to her feet.

Cil could hear the sharp, even bursts as the sharpshooter sped along smoothly. Now the woman was on the course but moving more slowly, the gun-bursts cautious, ragged, as she struggled for rhythm.

The circle of men released a bellicose shout of approval as their man, Hawk-Eye, neared the finish line. Only a few targets remained.

And now Cil's attention turned to the woman. Although she was still far behind, she was not giving up.

Suddenly there was an alteration in the din of the guns. Cil craned his neck to see if the Texan had completed the course, but to his amazement, he discovered Hawk-Eye Colton just standing there, dead in his tracks, the expert marksman fumbling with his weapon, feverishly attempting to work the mechanism. The mechanism was jammed.

Cil's heart sank; he could see that the contest was over; the woman had only to finish the course to pick up the prize.

Swiftly Cil was on his feet, moving in long, deliberate strides toward Miss D'Orleans, intercepting her the moment her slim frame broke the tape at the finish line. By the time the true impact sank in and the uproar of the men exploded, Cil already had her at a safe distance, spiriting her away down a side trail.

"The moment we reach your tent in the clearing, pack up your gear," he growled. "And I'll expect to see your tent set up next to mine before the men have a chance to get back— is that clear?"

"But, *Cherie*—it is only one day until training is ended."

"Miss, that is an order."

Cil did not permit the woman to stray from his sight until she had carried out his instruction. He immediately assigned a bulldog of a sentry to remain at her side night and day.

Cil, nonetheless, had little time to contemplate the likely consequence of her actions, for he had a demanding demonstration to set up for the final day of training. He retired to the storage tent and threw himself into his task, for he knew from experience that this last exhibition carried with it real risk; it would require every ounce of his skill and training to minimize the danger.

Sometime later, while engrossed in his work at the back of the tent, Miss D'Orleans appeared.

"And what, this time?" he demanded. "And where is your escort?"

"Oh," she replied off-handedly, "I dismissed him."

"You *what*?"

Her laugh was nervous and short. "Oh, just for a brief call-of-nature. So tell me, what is it you do with those chutes?" she inquired, anxious to place her feet on firmer ground, and spying with interest both a packed main parachute and a reserve chute on the table behind.

"A demonstration," he told her, noting her somewhat excessive interest. "And that sentry of yours, he'd better be back by the time you leave this tent."

"But all that equipment; it must be something really big?"

Even in the dim light of the hurricane lantern, he could see that her face was pale, that she needed to talk, so he went right on with the game.

"Infiltration of an enemy coastline," he explained. "A freefall jump—not especially new—used sometimes by Special Operations units. But down here the tropics can complicate things. That's why, with the excessive humidity after yesterday's storm, I've repacked the chutes just to be safe." And it was then that he spotted her look of bemusement. "Miss D'Orleans, since your Israeli airborne experience, surely you're familiar with the procedure—you know—a HALO drop?"

"Oh, yes. A high altitude, low-opening, parachute jump? Oh, please—show me how it is done." He was fooled no more by her sudden affected curiosity than by her budding schoolgirl charm, but she was clearly a young lady with something on her mind, so, for the moment, he played along.

"Look, a plane sails in over the coastline on a moonless night, see—but high, at say, twenty-five, maybe thirty thousand feet—too high to be heard or easily spotted. It drops a special, airborne freefaller."

"Without oxygen? A chutist could barely survive at that altitude without oxygen," she pointed out.

"A special twenty-minute tank strapped to the belly; the fall takes only a four-minute supply," he told her. "He freefalls like a skydiver most of the way, controlling his flight...."

"Or *her* flight," she corrected.

"Or her flight," Cil repeated, annoyed, "by manipulating arms and legs until the chute opens at maybe five hundred feet, the chute release triggered by an automatic pressure device. Here, we do it over water—at night."

"But the danger," she exclaimed.

"The secret—slow and easy—is one step at a time. As your main chute opens, breaks your fall fast, your speed is reduced in a couple of seconds from well over a hundred to maybe fifteen miles an hour, not factoring in the wind. That gives just enough time if you stay alert. Then, in the last seconds before touchdown in the water, he—or she," the mocking smile, "first releases the unused reserve chute, then the waterproof equipment bag with weapon and ammo on the retaining line, like this one," pointing. "And finally, the main chute is jettisoned the instant before you hit the water. No good to find yourself tangled in a rolling sea with that suicide web down over your head."

"And if the agent is injured, say—wounded, or hopelessly separated from the main force?" she asked.

"We don't speak of hopeless, Miss. And aside from his GPS—Global Positioning System, the operative, like a downed pilot, carries a homing device which registers on a certain frequency of the special UHF satellite radio employed by the unit."

"But that won't provide coordinates to pinpoint position," she challenged.

"True enough; but the unit, utilizing the UHF radio, can communicate with a round-the-clock satellite surveillance facility which is just so equipped," he told her. "In fact, in a large operation, often an offshore surface ship stands by with just the equipment and skilled personnel."

"Could you show me?" Quite clearly she still didn't want to leave, and Cil, somewhat elated at her obvious interest, was beginning to enjoy himself. He moved to the back of the tent and retrieved a small pack containing the special UHF satellite radio. When he had led her step-by-step through the procedure, taking pains even to utilize the radio himself through a relay point to the appropriate satellite tracking station, she insisted on simulating the procedure herself, dragging out the process. Then finally she put the question.

"But who is to make such a dangerous jump?"

"Why, I am, of course."

"You?" A shadow of fear, sudden and swift, showed in the depths of her eyes. Once she had recovered, she paused, leaning over the makeshift table, cupping her chin in her hand, her nose twitching as it always did when she was deep in thought. "Please, tell me again in more detail just how it is done."

Little by little, he sketched out the procedure, explaining the valves and controls, the way, at the last minute, the parachute release mechanism worked, then the use of the scuba tanks.

But now a cloud of silence fell between them.

"What should I do with the money?" she suddenly asked with insistence, the words almost a plea.

For a second, he was taken aback.

"What? The money you won?" He frowned. "Didn't I warn you—didn't I tell you before not to rile the men?" A flush of quick anger rose to his cheeks as he followed her eyes to where the coffee tin stuffed with cash had been surreptitiously deposited the moment she entered the tent.

But now a great change had somehow transformed her; to his amazement, she was suddenly a little girl again.

"You will not believe." Her voice was small. "But I tried not to win."

"Yeah—so I saw."

"Please—what must I do?"

"Look, it's a little late for that. Now the money is yours."

"No, no—I must give it back."

"You can't."

"But you said it was my money."

"I tell you, you can't just give it back. On the other hand," his tone sardonic, "maybe one of your rich society friends has a favorite charity."

She fell silent; but after a while he could see that odd twitching of the nose once again.

And then, wholly without warning, she hastened to the coffee tin containing the cash. Instantly she was snatching up the fifty and hundred dollar bills, stuffing them unceremoniously down her shirtfront. As she made to leave, she turned to him.

"Thank you, *Cherie*," she said in a voice full of sweetness. And then she was gone.

Cil worked late into the night preparing the demonstration for the following day. At some point, he heard the roar of a plane overhead, but he was tired and preoccupied and paid it no heed.

Next morning it was as if a cyclone had struck him; he was weak; he felt faint, dizzy, his head throbbing as if someone had used it for a bass drum. He managed to rouse himself and stumble to the mess tent but was unable to keep anything down. Not a man to easily fall ill, Cil passed it off lightly; but by midafternoon, his condition had worsened.

When Miss D'Orleans arrived at his tent, she was a different person, suddenly cocksure and deliberate, brimming with confidence. Immediately she saw how sick he was, she insisted on taking his temperature. After reading it, she looked down upon him in a knowing, superior way.

"You cannot do the jump!" she clucked.

"I'll be the judge of that," he snapped at her brashness, though he was surprised at the feeble sound of his own voice.

"Major," displaying an imperious air. "You couldn't swim the length of this tent. So why not just lie still—like a good little boy?"

It had been a very long time since any woman had dared so to address him; and silently he vowed it would be a good deal longer before it happened again, but he stayed put.

Cil awoke with a start, the tent a vacuum of darkness. Blindly, he plucked up his wristwatch, squinting at the dial, then jerked himself upright. He had been out for hours. And then it struck him—he had failed to cancel the demonstration!

It was intuition and the revving of a jet engine on the airstrip that sent him yanking on his pants, disdaining his shoes, then to lunge headlong for the storage tent. The parachutes and equipment were gone.

Once again in the open, he could see that the camp was deserted; and by the time he noticed the jeep missing, the camp plane came on, streaking overhead. He felt suddenly weak; for a moment he sagged against a tree trunk.

"*The beach!* Damn, they're all at the beach." His throat all but swollen shut, his joints shrieking in protest, he took off at a run down the rutted dirt track toward the beach three miles distant.

He thought of the jump equipment missing from the tent—of the earlier cocksure demeanor of Miss D'Orleans. He quickened his pace.

A handful of stars pricked out of the heavens as he hobbled past the empty clearing. He could see the running lights of the camp jet overhead as it nosed into a climb.

On he staggered, past the dimly illuminated landing lights at the strip, but there was not a soul in sight.

It seemed forever before he reached the dark slope of the dunes back of the beach, the sand piled by the wind as high as a house. He still could not see the beach, and looking skyward, he could no longer detect the whine of the plane's jet engine nor pick out the intermittent flashing of its pink, running lights.

He plowed clumsily on, nearing the beach; the fresh scent of salt air, the pound of surf, invaded his senses.

Now looking off down the beach, he could see the line of breakers in their frothing phosphorescence, rolling in to crash in great following crescendos upon the wet sand. Further out, moonbeams reflected brightly off an angry, rolling sea.

For only an instant did Cil's mind dart back to the previous cycle of trainees—to the aide tent—to the shocking number of casualties after the night parachute drop gone haywire. But shoving that aside, his experienced eye was gauging the standing peaks of the breakers lashing the shore, the direction of wind and current, the glimmer of moonlight where the receding waters polished the dark sand of the beach.

"Tide's turning—and look at the run of that current!"

Far down the crescent line of the beach—maybe half a mile—he could see where his jeep stood with a host of men milling around, strung out down the shore. He raced for the men. He could feel his feet padding over the fluffy whiteness of the sand; he could hear the swishing sound of his every footfall, his breath sawing in his chest in short, panting gasps, the smell of the sea coming to him strongly.

He feared the worst. All the while, he charged on down the beach, waving his arms over his head like a wild man. "Crazy, spoiled brat!" But the sound of his shouting was drowned by the surf.

And then he saw a small gray moth the size of a silver dollar—the moth popping out against the ink-black sky.

"Oh, hell—too low!" A shudder of fear shot up his spine. She was falling like a rock. He shouted after the men.

But the men were just standing about, not moving, not seeing the girl, not hearing him over the crash of the surf. Finally someone must have heard—for two broke for the surf.

A good distance still from the jeep, Cil could feel himself stumble and fall; he felt weak, helpless; he was looking at the roll of the breakers—the smooth water farther out, shiny and black between the deep inky troughs.

He was back on his feet, again racing on and closing the distance when he spotted a tiny, heaving, black button amidst the huge inky rollers.

"There—*There!*" In the black silky water beyond the surf—in the grip of the current, being swept out to sea....

By the time Cil reached the jeep, there was not a man on shore. He could see half a dozen fanned out, bludgeoned by the breakers, yet helping her out. The rest—there must have been forty if there was one—all shouting and cheering and flailing their arms.

When all that possibly could, and then five more, had piled and crammed themselves onto the sagging old jeep, Cil in the back turned to Claxson.

"What the hell goes on here?" Cil's voice hoarse, dampened by the noise of the jeep jouncing along over the uneven sand.

"Ha, ya missed it, Boy. Ya missed it!"

"Missed what, you damned fool? Tell me."

"Why, the feed, Cilley Boy, the feed!"

"Are you drunk?"

"Her feed—ya missed it all. Every bit a *South-Geor-gia-County-Fair.*"

"Stop babbling and tell me what happened!" Fiercely did Cil seize the drunken Claxson's shirt front; but Claxson was in a world of his own.

"More booze than a damned battalion could drink," he was babbling. "Yes, sir—and food—why, ham and lobsters and steaks that thick!" Claxson attempted to demonstrate, but lost his balance in the process and nearly fell out of the jeep.

"From where?"

"Off the mail plane."

Now it dawned on Cil. "And I bet I can guess who manned the controls?" It was all Cil could do to hold back a punch.

"I tell you," Claxson blurted, eyes at once bleary, yet twinkly in the gay moonlight. "With all that money, we got us a good load, Cil Boy—a good load." He belched once loudly and grinned in surprise. "Cooked it all herself, by damn! All by herself, so whadaya think of that? Yep, that's our Lil Ole Michelly!"

As soon as the jeep reached the camp, Cil stepped gingerly to the ground, excused himself, and retired to his tent.

He was awakened sometime later by the swaying beam of a lamp.

"You must try to eat something." Michelle D'Orleans sat on the cot opposite, a spoonful of chicken gumbo soup in her hand, she looking as strict and determined as had ever an old mother hen.

"You could have been killed!"

"By the looks, *Cherie*, it is you who will be carried out sooner than I—open wide."

"I'm serious."

"So am I—open up."

They went on sparing this way for another five spoon-fuls, when at last he laid back on his cot, exhausted; but instead of clearing out, she puttered around, patting up his pillow, straightening the bedclothes, adjusting the old broken sword that hung on the wall.

Finally she worked up her courage and faced him.

"Ah—now, with tomorrow being the last day of training, and, well, ah—you see...." She was suddenly tongue-tied; he enjoyed it immensely.

"Yes?"

"Well, you see, Major—I was only wondering if...." And then she shot it straight from the shoulder. It was almost an order. "Will you come to my uncle's for just a few days?"

8

A cold rain spattered the pavement as the big car streaked away from the Capital toward Washington International Airport. In the back of the limousine, two men conferred in low tones.

"Seems as if I'm always apologizing, Colonel," Secretary Levitt told him. "But the truth is, events are on the march, and it takes good legs just to keep up." He paused. "You'd be amazed how many vital decisions these days are made in the back of this car."

"I see the Serbs are on the move again."

"Worse. It's the Russians. Yeltsin's in trouble. Failing health—once again losing his grip on power. With his disaster in Chechnia, he's losing support—both the people and the army."

"And desperate men are dangerous men," ventured the colonel.

"Been doing my damnest to keep the lid on Bosnia, but the word is out. Iran and the Islamic world still beefing up Muslim strength by smuggling in the *Mujahadeen*. The Russians are restless, convinced we've sanctioned the move, and know we're assisting the Croats. Now they're openly threatening to throw in with their old friends, the Serbs."

"Beyond political support for the sieges of Bihac, Srebrenica and Sarajevo—and pushing around the Blue Hats?"

Suddenly the Defense Secretary looked worried and drawn. For a moment, he peered out at the lightly falling rain.

"With Russian military advisors—care of Yeltsin."

"At the dam?"

"Worse. Word is, Yeltsin's sent in one of his cagiest line generals."

"Are you sure?"

"That makes it imperative that we knock out that dam immediately. Quickly and quietly, without a trace—so the world's never the wiser."

The colonel's jaw clamped shut; he made no response.

"Follow me on this, Colonel. We must force a cease-fire before things get totally out of hand. And that's out of the question unless there's some way to even things up on the ground over there. With the Serbs controlling 70% of Bosnia-Herzegovina, there's not a chance in hell of a cease-fire—let alone peace. The Muslims would never stand still for it."

"Unless?"

"Unless we authorize the Croat forces to open a whole new phase."

"Such as?" Colonel Anastasi held his breath, not daring to hope.

"Since the lightning assault to regain Western Slavonia and push the Serbs back south of the Sava has proven successful—as you assured it would—the President and I have agreed to go out on a limb—now—especially in light of this Russian thing. We've determined to give the green light to a lightning thrust by the Croats. Reconquest of that whole region of Croatia in the Bihac area occupied by the Serbs. That's right, the entire Krajina region—provided, of course, it can be accomplished in days."

The Secretary turned again to squint out the rain-streaked window. When he turned back to Anastasi, a wry smile played on his lips.

"Well, that's what you've been pushing for, isn't it, Colonel?" But the colonel only listened. "And if that lightning thrust is successful," the Secretary went on, "then we'll allow your coalition of Croat and Bosnian Moslem forces to attempt recapture of as much of their former territory in northern Bosnia as they can in the space of three weeks—all this running up to a cease-fire."

Secretary Levitt's voice hardened.

"And just for the record, Colonel—your assessment better be right."

The colonel nodded gravely, though in the shadows of the big car a tiny smile softened his lips.

"No," he said, but the smile was gone when he uttered the words. "Milosevic and the Yugoslav National Army will find no stomach to intervene—not this time."

"Well, that's the sticky wicket," rejoined the Secretary. "But if our luck holds, a bold move could force the Serb holdings in Bosnia down to manageable size, say, something like 50/50, the division already recommended by the Contact Group. If it's possible, that might just give the needed shot-in-the-arm that serious negotiations require." The Secretary was silent for a time; then his sigh was an audible thing. "I just hope that's enough. Those Muslims are stubborn as hell when they get a bone in their teeth." Then he cursed. "And it's our necks!"

"With the way you've beefed up their communications, then command and control structure," Colonel Anastasi assured, "present Croat forces should certainly be up to it—especially if NATO was to come in at just the right time with sustained air strikes—and put killing pressure on the Serbs in the Exclusion Zone around Sarajevo."

"That's enough," snapped the little man. "I can't afford Yeltsin jumping in with both feet."

"Sir—what can I do to help?"

"Well, there is one thing," returned the Secretary wryly. "You say, you still maintain contacts in the Serb Ministry of Interior."

Anastasi waited for the second shoe to drop.

"The dam construction blueprints—we've got to have 'em. Change Orders, Specs—the lot—and all record of repair of that old earthen dam."

"But those are in Belgrade."

"I know where they are, Colonel." The man's features remained chiseled in granite. "And your part in the operation—are your people ready to move?"

"I need a month," the colonel told him.

"You have three weeks. The Brits will ferry your people in. I'm told, they have a man—a real diamond in the rough, but a man of results. Explosives—combat engineer—that sort of thing."

He eyed the colonel. His gaze sharpened. "Lockwood tells me you're going with indigenous civilians. I tell you, I don't like it," he snapped. "To commit our people to civilians on a vital operation like this. It's out of the question."

"Indigenous irregulars, sir. Deniability."

"I don't like it," returned the Secretary tensely. "This nation can ill afford another Frances Gary Powers. Or a Bay of Pigs, for that matter. I want a top man in charge—cool under fire."

"I believe I have just such a man."

The Secretary appeared tense, peering out at the rain. "On this one," he said with finality, "I approve the man personally.

"And one thing more, Colonel—he has a right to know the odds."

9

The first leg of the trip back from training was crowded and hot, everyone bunched together and sweating in an old propeller-driven cargo plane designed for half the number. In Mexico City, all of that changed. Waiting to whisk Miss D'Orleans and "guest" away stood a sleek government jet while the balance of the trainees continued on by the same shabby means of conveyance. Cil deplored showiness and official fondling; he could see Michelle was embarrassed by it, too. He wondered who had arranged it, and how it was that those in authority so often felt the need to make a show of their station and privilege. He supposed it could be laid to the arrogance of class—or some more deep-seated insecurity satiated by feigned superiority; he had learned early in life not to trust prize winners.

At the thought, however, Cil felt a twinge of conscience, and for a moment he was forced to reproach himself, for he knew that his own motives on this day were not altogether pure. Yet, even that realization failed to dampen his spirits.

Cil permitted himself a contented smile when the plane set down at Westover Air Force Base in western Massachusetts. It was not until he noticed Michelle bubbling with excitement and waving out the window that the first pang of anxiety struck him. A late model Rolls Royce sat parked on the tarmac below the plane's window, its high-polished finish gleaming in the sun. Beside the car stood a big lion of a man waving up in Michelle's direction.

"Who's that?" Cil demanded quickly.

"Look, look; it is *Onkle*! Uncle Mavro come to meet us!"

"What?" Cil tensed. The very mention of the name fired a shock wave through his body. At first he froze where he sat, staring out the window past Michelle at the cocky appearance of the man. Then his brain kicked in. Shock transformed to anger, anger to loathing. So that's the man, is it? His eyes narrowed and flashed; when he had calmed, he sat glaring down at the man with a whole new expression—with the cold predatory eyes of the hunter.

The man, tall and broad-shouldered, stood militarily erect as a statue. His bearing alone left no doubt of his vocation. Judging by the hard eyes even while smiling, the heavy lines of the face, graying temples and mustache swept up at a jaunty angle, the man's countenance alone confirmed Cil's suspicions. He placed the man's age at no less than sixty. The man fitted out in khaki riding breeches, a tunic of military cut straight out of the Second World War, and the cavalry boots firmly planted on the tarmac carried the same high polish as the luxury sedan at his back. The dark beret cocked over one eye gave the large head an arrogant, almost comic appearance, and Cil could only think what a perfect damned fool the man looked, standing there pious and self-important as a peacock. Cil knew instantly who had ordered the plane.

As Cil hefted down the luggage, he stopped for a moment to pass a word, to convey his thanks to the young captain piloting the aircraft. Michelle, seeing her uncle, whirled, rushed down the steps, flung herself into the old man's arms, and hugged him affectionately; she was instantly the little girl again.

"Oh, Onkle Mavro, you must meet my very good friend,

Major Lane Cil," gushed Michelle with girlish delight, still in the colonel's arms as Cil descended to the tarmac. "I know you two will get along famously."

And it was with surprise that Cil received the old man's stiff salute, only then realizing that he himself was still in uniform, standard-issue, battle fatigues somewhat wrinkled from use. Cil passed back the same wary look offered by the colonel, forcing a grin as the big man gave a curt nod over the head of his niece.

"Cil?" The man seemed to ponder the name for a moment. "The name—can't seem to place it. Well, my boy, an honor to make your acquaintance."

No sign of recognition showed in the colonel's face though; to Cil, the cut of the man's voice sounded more of an indictment than greeting. Once again in his life he caught the clipped formal reserve and unapproachable aloofness of the European aristocracy.

Cil was relieved to excuse himself and stow the luggage, content, despite Michelle's protestations, to seat himself alone in the back seat of the Rolls while Colonel Mavro Anastasi took control of the wheel with Michelle chatting animatedly at his side. For Cil, it was a long drive into New York State, and he could see that the colonel, though his head remained militarily erect as before, paid less and less attention to the remarks of his niece; he appeared somehow preoccupied. The spring sun was already slanting down into the trees by the time the broad gate of the estate swung into view.

The rustic old estate stood on the high ground a quarter of a mile back from the main gate. It appeared smaller than its true dimensions, huddled as it was among tall pines and spruce. It was with a warm, almost giddy feeling in his chest that Cil inhaled the fragrance of the evergreen forest as a flood of old memories swept in upon him.

Cil could see that the rambling old structure capped

with a red-tiled roof had suffered little with the years. "Welcome back to Howard Johnson!" echoed a silent voice from the past, and his Sonya's quaint accent and irreverent laughter came back with a shock to his ears. The high-pitched roof above the stolid shoulders of the main house lent a certain stateliness to the rustic old building while sprawling wings covered in ivy ran gently off down the slope on either side. So, he thought with brittle irony—back to Shangri-La.

Michelle, as if a schoolgirl on the first day of summer vacation, seized Cil's hand as soon as the car pulled up. Bursting with glee, she led him into the main house. In a flurry of bubbling description, she showed him through the Spartan salon with its high ceiling of rough-hewn beams and its plain wooden walls. Its harshness was broken by the subtle warmth of indirect lighting, casting a pleasant hue over the rounded edges and warm autumn colors of the soft chairs and sofas and abundance of green plants tastefully arranged.

Above the mantle hung the portrait of a middle-aged woman—but not just any woman. The head was raised, set on the fluted neck in the stately fashion of an aristocrat, chin full and proud, the woman's skin clear and Magnolia-white, the skin of a child, like sometimes seen in women who have been pampered from childhood. A diamond tiara adorned her head as might befit a movie star or figure of royalty. The woman's high Slavic cheekbones and the noble set of the features bore a striking resemblance to Michelle, more so the hint of devilish mirth sprinkled at the corners of the mouth.

"And this is my dear aunt, The Countess," Michelle told him simply, standing at his side. He did not realize he was still holding her hand until he looked into the eyes of the woman in the portrait. It was as if he had received an electrical shock. Instantly he dropped her hand from his own. "One day you will come with me to meet her, I hope. Bucharest is so lovely this time of year."

It was the eyes that held him as they had so long ago—

great honey-brown pools, deep as well-springs, at once bewitching and beckoning. Yes, those were her eyes, almost forgotten; they seemed now to reach out and smile down only at him.

It was at that moment that another figure entered the room. As Colonel Anastasi turned at the sound, and Michelle flew to greet the newcomer, Cil stood as if his feet were nailed to the boards of the floor, having received his second shock within the space of one minute.

It was a toss-up as to which of them was the most astounded, Cil or the old family retainer, Marko, as he entered the room. The old man was seventy-five if a day, yet Cil read the instant recognition in those kindly, intense eyes, and signaled with his own. It was over in a second while Michelle held the floor.

"Oh, Major Cil, you must come and meet 'Our Marko,' the only man outside the family who has seen me as nature intended!"

The old eyes were calm and understanding. "And that was when you had but three years," the old man put in gently and smiled.

Except for the slight hunch of the back, the old man had not aged a day over the years. And for Cil, it was a fresh summer breeze to see his old ally and friend, the only friend beyond Sonya he had ever had in this family. As the stoop-shouldered, old man excused himself, he motioned with a glance in the direction of the stables, and Cil understood.

It was as Michelle led Cil down the long hallway to the room where he would stay that he turned to the door opposite and asked whose room it was. "Cousin Sonya's room. It is reserved for her when she comes," Michelle told him vaguely, but he detected a queer note in her voice and held his tongue; instead, he went to his room to change.

It was only after bathing and changing into casual sweater, slacks, and loafers, that Cil quietly inched open the door of his room. Satisfied that the hall was vacant, he tiptoed like a mischievous schoolboy, slowly, stealthily, twisting the knob of the door opposite his—but the door would not budge. It was locked.

When Cil re-entered the salon, intending to slip out to the stables, he found that the colonel had disappeared, and the very living room he had passed through only minutes before had been roughly altered, as if gripped by a cyclone. Glaring spotlights on great gawking necks hung from high and low. One of the sofas had been shoved in front of the huge stone fireplace where, above the mantle, hung the portrait of the Countess with the eyes smiling down.

In the far corner of the great room stood an earnest-faced Michelle, decked out in a smock with dried paint splotches trailing down her front as she busied herself, sorting her chalk and preparing her easel. She was all business, frowning in concentration.

"Now, that's right; just sit there," she declared, directing him onto the sofa, the request an instruction.

And if it was an imposition for Cil to put off his errand, it was doubly difficult for him to force himself to a sitting position, for he had always harbored an unreasoning aversion to such things, even to having his picture snapped. And now the glare of the lights shone in his eyes, and he blinked like a convict about to be grilled before strobe lights.

"You never told me you were an artist," he said offhandedly, really quite helpless.

"You never asked."

"But," he protested, "I thought a painter waited for the best morning light."

"If that were the case," she rejoined with a slightly superior air, "then all indoor art would be viewed with a flashlight. Now just sit still and don't fidget; it's only a charcoal sketch. My goodness, all you men behave like children."

Resigned to his fate, he sat, trying not to pose. And,

watching her, he was frankly amazed at how quickly and deftly she worked, each stroke of the charcoal keenly judged and precise, her hand as steady as that of a surgeon. Before he could feel the full wrath of the gaze stabbing down at him from the portrait above, Michelle turned to him gaily. "All right, Mr. Grump; it's done."

When he viewed the finished charcoal sketch, he could scarcely believe his eyes. A sketch within a sketch—that of himself larger and the bust of the Countess within the painting lesser in size and included as background, yet both cleverly embraced within the whole. Her talent for line and space was astounding, the likeness truer than he could imagine, and, too, she had captured an essence of inner sadness and turmoil which he had acted so long and so hard to conceal. It was at that moment that Cil came to the realization here was a person he had clearly misjudged, and, quite obviously, underestimated, for this woman possessed dimensions of talent and insight he had not dreamed of, much less set his sights to explore.

Later, Colonel Mavro Anastasi invited Michelle and Cil to join him for dinner, and as the three of them in semi-formal evening dress sat down at an elaborately set table, all sipping wine from Michelle's father's vineyards in the south of France, Michelle and the colonel carried on, speaking lightly of the day's activities, laughing and joking as the servants bustled about. The servants quietly served up the native seafood chowder of Dalmatia, then the customary multi-course dinner of fresh salmon charbroiled to perfection, baked cheese and vegetable casseroles exquisitely seasoned and served with fine sauces and the best vintage wines.

Yet, despite half-hearted attempts at easy banter between the men, a cloud as a pall hung over the table as Cil and the imperious and erudite Colonel Anastasi exchanged furtive glances.

When at last the servants left the room, the colonel turned

sharply to Cil.

"I see you do not like me much, Major," declared Colonel Anastasi.

"Onkle Mavro!" cried Michelle.

"No, my dear; it is all right," his harsh and steady gaze leveled at Cil. "That is true, is it not?"

Cil, taken aback by the sudden verbal assault, and not knowing just how to respond, said nothing.

"If I have said something—done something to offend you?" prodded the colonel, drumming his fingers on the table.

"*Please*, Onkle," she pleaded. "Major Cil is our guest. A quiet dinner—please."

"My dear, quiet is for the dead," declared the colonel, still staring at Cil. "Don't you agree, Major Cil?" the drumming of the fingers now more insistent.

In the silence that ensued, the sound of the grandfather clock in the corner was the beat of a drum. Cil held the colonel's gaze; he resolved not to back down, not to give an inch, not to give the man the satisfaction. And when Cil spoke, his voice came low and even and finely controlled.

"Now that you mentioned it," he said.

"Yes?" growled the broad-shouldered colonel.

"It was the *plane!*" blurted Michelle, reaching over and placing her hand on Cil's, as if to suddenly draw him within her field of protection. But Cil needed no savior. Thrusting forward in his chair, he met the colonel's accusing gaze.

"What Michelle says is true. I am not in a habit of accepting privileges not accorded my men."

"A laudable position, Major." The colonel smiled. "And?"

"Your old retainer Marko? I don't see him here at the table tonight."

The following silence was a real living thing, finally broken by the colonel.

"We all have our separate customs," was all he would say, but the drumming on the table had ceased, and by the colonel's change of expression, it was clear that the point had struck home. "And you're sure, young man, there is nothing else?"

"Now that you asked," spoke Cil. "Yes, perhaps there is one other thing. You see, in my country, people are a bit put off by the rich and famous, particularly foreign guests, making public exhibition of their station and wealth."

"I take your point," responded the colonel smoothly. "But there is little a man can do about his native country and station of birth." And then he paused, and when he resumed, a note of regret had crept into his voice. "On the other hand, sometimes a man is not always proud of his old habits, or his customs—or the mistakes he may have made in the past." Then a twinkle came into his eyes. "But, Major, can you yourself sit there and vouch for the purity of your every habit and thought?"

Cil looked at the colonel. There was something in the man's voice and manner which Cil had not before recognized, a tone of self-deprecation, yes, but also a good-natured warmth attached to his frankness and wit.

"At the least, Colonel," Cil said lightly, "I must applaud your directness and candor."

"And I yours, Major Cil. Here, here!" And they all lifted their glasses, nodded and drank. "You see, Major, I did not wish to make a scene, but this lady, well," and he reached over and patted Michelle's hand in a proprietary gesture, "she is important to me. I would not care to see her hurt. When we met, I detected a certain, let's say—distance. I would like it over and done with. I would hope, at the least, that we could come together in her interest—as she appears to have an interest in you."

At that, Cil again raised his glass; the colonel did likewise. Their glasses touched, and their eyes met, too. Michelle flushed crimson.

Dinner once concluded, proper amenities observed, Colonel Anastasi rose. He stepped to where Cil was standing and placed his arm about his shoulder in a kindly, almost fatherly fashion.

Asking Michelle to excuse them, he led Cil into his study where a warm and beckoning fire crackled on the hearth. And as they sipped clear Croatian plum brandy, and pulled on the best Havana cigars, Colonel Anastasi put a simple question.

"My country, do you know it?"

"Yugoslavia in general?" fended Cil.

"Croatia to the north and the west. South of the frontier with Austria, Hungary, and the Hapsburgs—that is my country."

"The Hapsburgs have been finished for eighty years," Cil corrected lightly, but his remark drew a quick, good-natured grin from the colonel.

"Not in my country, they haven't," chuckled the colonel. "Still their voices ring from every tower."

"Well, all right then," said Cil. "Yes, twice I have been there."

"You don't say."

Cil was wary; he still vividly remembered the old days, and he had little use for this arrogant foreign aristocrat of position and bearing. He wondered just how much the man knew—or remembered; and anyway, what he was driving at? If he didn't know already, he wondered how long it would be before the colonel discovered his true identity. But now he elected the bold approach.

"Yes, once I traveled by rail to your capital, Zagreb. I spent a few days at the Esplanade Hotel, and was frankly taken with the upper town, the Gothic cathedral set high on the hill. And by the blustery weather," he smiled, "the fog and the rain."

"Ha, yes—then you *have* been to visit my land. No man can forget that fog and rain."

At this juncture, the older man seemed to relax; he abandoned his cigar for a pipe, and his thick fingers set about packing the aromatic fibers of tobacco into the bowl of the pipe from an ornate glass jar on a side table, a transparent jar with a dark wooden top.

"And the second visit?" the colonel inquired.

"A mission." Cil hesitated. "I'm afraid that's all I'm at liberty to disclose. But I must tell you that what I found was shocking—the open wounds of the past—the hatreds." And it was with brutal irony that Cil pondered his own words, and his long smoldering antipathy toward this powerful stranger seated before him—though in many respects no stranger at all.

"You have served your country behind enemy lines for many years, have you not?" Colonel Anastasi asked suddenly, and at once Cil drew alert. Once again he wondered just how much this man knew, and how much he was likely to let on.

"What makes you think so?" he said.

"A man who has been there," the colonel declared simply and respectfully, "knows."

At that moment the two men were interrupted by a uniformed servant with a pot of coffee on a silver tray, the servant addressing the colonel in his own native language. When he spoke to Cil, Cil told him, cream and sugar with a dash of brandy, speaking fluently in the servant's native Serbo-Croatian tongue.

When the man was excused, the colonel's attitude seemed abruptly to alter. He was through with the fencing, and by the time Michelle joined them for coffee, the older man was fairly gushing with charm.

10

Next morning, Cil rose at first light. He washed up quietly, then slipped into casual, civilian clothes that gave him an odd, semi-naked feeling after weeks in uniform. Without a word, he made his way out to the stables in search of his old friend, the servant, Marko. As he approached, Cil heard a great commotion.

Upon rounding the corner of the barn, he found the old man cursing and tugging, struggling to maneuver a wild-eyed stallion into its stall. The horse reared up on its hind legs, bucking and snorting, its great arrogant mane rippling as the horse tossed its head and strained against the halter.

Cil leapt to the old man's aid. It required the combined strength of both men to force the frenzied horse back into its stall and bolt the door shut.

"That horse!" cried old Marko, still panting from the effort. "That is a mean one. I tell you, one day that horse—he strike a man dead!"

Cil paused to gather himself. A moment of awkward silence fell between the two men. Then, in a rush of pent-up emotion, the old man rushed to Cil and flung himself into Cil's arms. He greeted him as a father might greet a long lost son, grasping him in the vice of his powerful arms, fighting back tears, speaking in an accent that would fracture an egg. "I thought...." He stumbled with emotion. "I—I told her, Capitan, never more in our life do we two cross on the road." He was wiping his eyes with big callused hands.

"Tell me then, man. How is she?" Cil demanded, at once buoyant, intense. "I want to know everything!"

The old man, suddenly feeling Cil's own excitement, broke into a broad grin. "You never believe!" he cried lustily. "A little girl she have." Cil felt a stab of pain as the old man went on. "Hah, hair like the sun, the face of the angel. Elena, she calls her. I tell you, already is she that big." He slapped one hand against Cil's right leg between the knee and the hip. "And what a handful. Pretty, light-headed, and spoiled like her mama!"

"Well, speak, man, speak. Tell me of Sonya."

"Hah! Fresh as a daisy, wrapped in ermine and velvet. She is her mother all over again. She *is* the Countess!"

"Then you see her?"

Instantly the smile slipped from the old man's face. For a moment he faltered; his shoulders drooped. "I see her, yes," he said, "but...only in the homeland."

"What—you say she never comes here?" exclaimed Cil, astounded, frowning and rubbing his chin in disbelief. "Why, we always...."

"Not since...."

"But Michelle says she still keeps a room here." The old man looked away. "Never since that time does she set foot in this place. The colonel keep the room, yes; but never she come."

"But that is not my Sonya." Cil fumbled, confused.

The old man, the hunch in his back more pronounced, stared at the barn floor; at last, he lifted his gaze to Cil.

"The fear. The terror...." The old man broke off sadly. "Never do I ask what happen on that mission; maybe you know. But the fear—I do not know." He took a moment to compose himself. "But after that, no. Never is she the same Sonya again."

"But certainly...."

"No, no, my friend." Old Marko raised one hand to bar him. "I tell you, she is a woman different now. These days, like I say—she is the *Countess*. Paris in Spring, and then Monte Carlo. The rest in Vienna, or the great lands of her husband, the Count, on the grand River Danube near the city of Bucharest. No, Cil-the-Capitan. These days even you do not know her."

It was later in the heat of the day that Michelle, bubbling with youthful vigor and outfitted in form-fitting riding breeches, white, silk blouse, bright, polished boots, riding crop and all, took Cil's arm. "You must let me show you my favorite place in all the world," she chirped. "It is only a short ride on the way to 'the ledges.' Oh please, I know you will love it!"

Old Marko, apparently recalling what a poor horseman Cil was, selected his mount with care, saddling up a swift but gentle chestnut gelding. "I'll take Le Grand, dear Marko," Michelle declared boldly. When the old servant tried to warn her off, relating the stallion's wild fit of temper, and reminding of the colonel's strict orders, the irrepressible Miss D'Orleans shrugged off the danger with a toss of the head and a sassy flirtatious grin. "Oh Marko, my love, you are becoming such an old fussbudget! Next, you will come back from the old country announcing you've traded me in for another." And only then had old Marko grumblingly relented and with caution approached the great, white stallion, though the animal had calmed considerably since the ruckus earlier in the day.

Cil, the first to mount up, and himself now infected with Michelle's youthful exuberance, flung the reins over hard, dug in his heels, and shouted back at Michelle: "Come on, Old Lady. Let's see how you race!"

The big gelding wheeled on the instant and plunged off at

a gallop. Cil, some distance down the field, looked back to observe Michelle still on the ground, holding the stallion, Marko fussing about as an old man will, with a last minute adjustment.

Michelle, when it appeared she was out of the race, turned, slapped the rump of her mount, and in a sudden marvel of motion, took three loping strides and sprang up into the saddle, Indian-style. The feat was one thing, the ease and grace with which it was accomplished, quite another.

His mount pounding over the soft, sodden ground, its chestnut coat gleaming golden-bronze in the early sun, Cil hung on for dear life, both hands gripping the pommel, having all he could do to keep his body even arguably upright above the wildly rippling mane.

The wooden deck at the rear of the villa flew past in a blur. Cil could see the broad reach of the valley open before him, the lush meadow transforming a half mile ahead to gently rolling hills.

Off to his right, Cil observed a series of steeplechase jumps laid out on the floor of the meadow, the lowest farthest away, then each jump in turn higher and more closely spaced, the nearest hurdles being the highest, the last at a height of more than six feet, the final two jumps followed by a treacherous water barrier. A shower of rain during the night had left puddles of rain on the well-worn track preceding each hurdle.

In a hard-running gate, Cil's mount had stretched out a handsome lead. Glancing back, Cil could see Michelle gaining ground with each stride of the great white stallion. Only by the grace of God and old Marko's keen choice of steed was Cil able to reach the woods ahead by two lengths.

The sun at high noon burned down without mercy, and both riders as they dismounted, laughing and joking, found themselves gasping for breath. Cil, exhilarated at his own small triumph, led his mount up a narrow trail through the woods as Michelle followed behind, Michelle remarking to herself, "Now that's odd. *If* I didn't know better, I'd swear he'd been here before."

A quarter of an hour of climbing on a winding trail brought them to a grassy glade at the edge of a stream where the cooling shade of the trees offered refuge.

Michelle held up, but Cil, suddenly ill at ease, urged they push on. And only after a small argument did Cil finally relent.

"Isn't it lovely?" remarked Michelle as Cil seemed to pace the grass of the clearing. Quickly Michelle rummaged about, retrieving a pair of crystal goblets and a bottle of wine stored in her saddlebags. "Here, catch!" she cried, and Cil looked up in time to catch a flapping object, flying through the air.

"What's this?" he asked, surprised, examining a pearl-handled, dueling pistol and tugging it from the nest of its holster.

"Let's find a target," she said. "Since the training, I bet you a kiss I can beat you." But Cil in mild disgust shook his head and dropped the weapon in the grass by his side.

"Haven't we had enough of guns for a while?" he chided, still out of sorts, now perturbed, wiping the sweat from his brow; and then he sighed. "But a spot of wine for an old soldier might just hit the spot." And with no more encouragement, she flung herself down in the grass, tugging him down by her side.

"So you've had enough of this soldier business, have you, Mr. Major?" she suddenly reproached him, lying flat on her back, gazing up at the sky—but her voice had a serious ring.

"That's right," he said, opening the wine and charging the glasses. "Enough for a lifetime." But, in truth, his mind was a million miles away.

"Don't you just love this spot?" she asked gaily, changing her tack, but his lips had no answer.

And now as they lounged in the grass, sipping the wine,

he surveyed the clearing and let his mind take him back, Old Marko's words still echoing in his mind as he looked around the clearing.

Cil could see that over the gap of years nothing had changed. Nearly three years had passed; yet, here it all was, again, just as he remembered—the high open sky—the same sad, sagging limbs of the weeping willow by the stream—and high up in the tree that same song of a whip-poorwill calling him back. And the stream—still the same floating leaves in the current, the dance of the ripples, and the way the water tinkled over the rocks, sounding his name.

He recharged her glass, and she returned his smile warmly. She was lounging on her back, wholly relaxed, shading her eyes with one hand, and balancing the wine goblet precariously on the flat of her stomach. Silently she watched small floating wisps of cloud-like fairy schooners glide across the endless sky.

The combination of the heat and the hike made him thirsty; and that, added to his own discomfiture, caused him to pour out another, and another. And it was then that he spied a chipmunk skittering down a tree trunk, and the presence of the small animal at play seemed to place it all back in time.

So vividly did he recall the way on that long, lost afternoon when he and his Sonya had bustled about in this very clearing, collecting acorns, then lain quietly here in the grass, both half naked, slinging the acorns within easy reach of a pair of scampering, gray squirrels; and those squirrels had seemed so in love.

And now Cil looked at those dense tresses of golden blond hair spread wide and soft and so near in the grass, dazzling in the sun—and though the color was different, he saw Sonya's hair. He saw the chipmunk scamper about, and it was Sonya's squirrel. He tossed down another glass of wine, and he could hear the lilt of her voice in the call of the whippoorwill. And now he could see the same gentle curves of her face, if a trifle more serious, in the face of Michelle, the same hardly perceptible sheen of perspiration there on the upper lip, the quiet way of her, the undulating rise and fall of naked breasts under the thin, silken blouse, the inviting thrust of the nipples. So close beside him did she lie that he could smell that musky woman fragrance about her. And then as he reached for the bottle, he heard Michelle speak. "Laney, are you happy?" But it was her voice and her name for him, and suddenly she was calling.

It was then that he bent over and gently brushed her lips with his own. Slowly, with clear hesitation, she reached up her hand. Lightly, slim fingers in his hair, she drew his face down to close on his lips—tenderly, lingeringly.

"Oh, Sonya," he whispered.

"Sonya!"

Then came a moment of silence, stunned silence, filled with shock and confusion. What had he said—what had he done? He mumbled an apology and drew back abruptly. He was blinking his eyes, bewildered.

Michelle D'Orleans leapt to her feet. With a toss of the head, she shook out her hair—violently. Copper-blond tresses whipped and swirled to tumble and bounce off her shoulders—wildly. The indignation in her voice made the fiery highlights of her hair seem to hiss and crackle in the sun.

"Hah—so!" she hissed. "It is *Sonya*, is it?"

He was on his feet, cramming the holster and gun in his saddlebags.

"So it is true!" She was nodding knowingly. "And just as I was thinking—'If I didn't know better, I'd swear he had been here before.' Hah!"

Not knowing how to react and reacting on instinct to this stinging rebuke, he discarded the crystal goblet in the tall grass with a careless, almost negligent flick of the wrist.

"Back there," she accused, voice brittle with hurt. "You

think I could not see the way Old Marko was looking at you?"

He reached down to fetch up the near empty, wine bottle. He felt the whip of her tongue, and it brought out his rage over all the lost years.

Slowly, in almost a taunt, he tipped up the bottle and drained the last drop. With a single careless flick of his hand, he sent the bottle in disgust to crash in the trees.

She untied the white stallion.

"And just one more thing, Mr. Major! That old broken sword hung in your tent back at camp. Remember that sword? Well, I remember it, too. Once as a child—in my grandfather's attic in Zagreb, I would play with a sword broken just like that one! Funny, isn't it? Such a very special sword to me. And it was my favorite cousin who is older than I who would tell me how silly the games I loved to play with that sword—my cousin, Major. My cousin—Sonya."

Michelle, in sudden haste, first freed the white stallion from its tie in the trees, then leapt upon its back, tearing off down the trail through the woods toward home.

Slowly, too slowly, it dawned on Cil—the true weight of what he had done. He rushed to tear his own gelding's tie loose and mount up. Although no horseman, he gave chase, if clumsy in the attempt.

By the time he reached the low meadow, struggling constantly to right himself on his perch in the saddle, he could see the great stallion racing away over the knee-high grass at full gallop. Even at this distance, his eye fixed on Michelle, the ramrod back, the contemptuous tilt to her head; only one time did she turn back to glare in his direction.

She was flying away at a blistering pace; and in her turmoil and rage, she lent a taste of the whip to spur the horse onward.

Cil made every attempt to catch up, but the effort was

hopeless. And now he could see the great white stallion, at Michelle's direction, correct course and sweep down, lining up with the steeplechase hurdles. He could see the old colonel standing high on the wooden deck at the back of the house beyond.

Cil watched her take the first three jumps as if it were child's play. Before the fourth, her arm with the riding crop reached back and swatted the rump of the stallion for speed. The colonel stood on the deck, his arms upraised as if to warn her. She cleared the fourth and fifth jumps with room to spare. But before the great height and expanse of the sixth hurdle with the water hazard beyond, for a second the stallion seemed to lose rhythm and stumble.

Helpless, Cil watched as the sleek racing stallion, like an ill-fated race car, crashed head-on into the high wall of logs. But unlike the crash of a race car, no screeching of brakes nor squealing of tires preceded the crash—only the thunder of silence.

From a distance, Cil could see the huge beast thrashing about on the ground. After a moment, it attempted to rise, only to fall back. Then in a while, it struggled again, reaching out with its forelegs, shaking its mane, tossing its head in wild agitation.

Once it came upright, the spirited stallion started off over the meadow at a run, limping as it thundered along, snorting, blowing white mucus from wide flaring nostrils. Behind the bulk of the horse, Cil could see something dragging in its wake—like an elongated bundle of rags—or a flag with a long flowing banner unfurled, gold as the sun at its crest.

Cil's gelding gave chase. He could feel the great weight of it beneath him, pounding along at a wild galloping pace. And only when Cil gauged the time right did he yank back on the reins with such force that the bit in the animal's mouth pulled the gelding straight down on its haunches, hind legs splayed out, forward, braking along the green grass-covered ground.

Cil leapt from the horse. And now on solid ground, with precise, agile movements, he swiped the holster from the left saddlebag and went down on one knee in the high, blowing grass, extracting the pearl-handled revolver. As the hooves of the stallion resounded ever nearer, Cil could see one fevered jewel of an eye staring out, glaring madly in his direction.

Slowly, methodically, he slipped a single cartridge from the holster belt and slid the smooth round into the cylinder of the revolver. Out of the corner of his eye, he could see the colonel lumbering down the wooden steps from the deck, shouting and flailing his arms.

The white stallion, half mad and lurching as it ran, stampeded toward Cil at a furious pace—dragging its human cargo by one leg caught in the stirrup.

Still down on one knee, Cil raised the long-barreled pistol and aimed for a spot in back of the bright gleaming eye, just forward of the ear and the wildly rippling mane. He calculated just how much to lead him—he waited—he waited—he waited until the crippled stallion, coming in hard, began to veer right.

The moment Cil fired, the horse went down. It dropped in its tracks as if felled by an ax.

The momentum of the great beast and its direction of force acted to carry the weight of its fall away from the woman's body. Michelle D'Orleans lay on the ground with her thick golden hair spread on the grass like some Asian fan of death.

11

The big black letters on top of the building shouting
down—CHESTER COUNTY MEDICAL CEN-
TER—seemed more like a threat than a promise of care.

Once inside, the long corridor seemed somehow shut off
from the world by the white swinging doors marked,
EMERGENCY ROOM—STAFF ONLY. And the interior not
really white, but conveying the impression of a sullen looming cloud, gloomy as the thoughts of the men who sat on the
hard wooden bench, motionless, breathing in the odor of
hospital antiseptic, not speaking, each into his own private
thoughts, really trying not to think at all. Colonel Mavro
Anastasi and Major Cil had been seated that way for almost
a lifetime.

Both men started at the metallic click of a door latch
somewhere down the hall. Then came the rhythmic squeak-
ing of rubber-soled shoes from back of the white swinging
doors. By the time the doctor pushed through the doors,
both men stood at a rigid attention. The somber-faced doctor in hospital greens, clipboard in hand, came to a halt
before the two men; and now with professional reserve, he
offered a cautious smile.

"I'm happy to say she is finally coming around," allowed
Dr. Rutledge, a short, round-faced, middle-aged man with

hesitant eyes and the quiet, unhurried manner of a country doctor. "And a lucky young lady she is. It was the glancing blow that saved her." The doctor spoke slowly and sympathetically, the way good doctors do; and now again he smiled. "You see...."

"How is she?" Cil broke in.

"Conscious—but right now, there's little more I can say."

"No lasting injury?" demanded the colonel. "When can we see her?" The questions lashed out like a whip. The doctor stood patiently eyeing the battle-hardened features of the older of the two men standing before him, and though dressed in civilian clothes, it required little imagination for the doctor to envision the eagles of rank on the huge, hulking shoulders; the doctor's smile tightened.

"Vital signs stable. Breathing normal. And I detect no sensory dysfunction. As to the full extent of injury, well, we can better say in a day or two. But I can tell you this—I detect no skull fracture or paralysis, and the remaining question relates to the possibility of further intracranial hemorrhaging. You will simply have to be patient."

"You failed to answer my question." The colonel was bunching his fists, though his tone now showed surprising restraint.

"No promises. But if her improvement continues through the night," the doctor said, "then you can see her tomorrow—perhaps. But understand this: she remains a seriously injured patient in desperate need of rest."

"Of course, Doctor."

The return trip from the hospital felt more like a ride home from the graveside. At last the colonel at the wheel spoke, but his voice seemed to seep out from the depths of a tomb.

"I knew." And now he suddenly banged the wheel with such force that Cil felt the vibration. "I should have put away that horse the minute I knew!"

"There was standing water at the approach to the jump,"

explained Cil. "Horse must of lost footing."

But Colonel Anastasi went on as if alone in the car. "If I told her once, I—dammit, she could have been killed!"

By the time they reached the estate, darkness had fallen. While the colonel marched straight for his study, Cil made a bee-line for the stables. A single overhanging fixture bathed the stalls in a pale, uncertain light, and there Cil came upon Old Marko fidgeting where he waited.

"Tell me—is she—you bring her back home?"

Not to add to the old man's burden, Cil spoke gently, quietly. "She's come back to herself, old friend—and she is conscious. No cause to worry."

"Ay—but you do not bring her back home?" The old man seemed clearly in shock, clutching Cil's arm.

"Tomorrow. Tomorrow, we all can see her." Cil tried to assure, but as old Marko released the vice of his grip on Cil's arm, he spied the half stumble as the younger man shifted his weight.

"You are hurt, Cil-the-Capitan!"

"It's nothing," Cil said and changed the subject. "You took care of the gelding?"

Marko spoke harshly. "Sit yourself down—there on that stool—and no back talk. Now, pull up that pant leg." But when Cil tried to ignore him and moved to stroke the gelding mincing his hooves and poking his nose playfully out of the stall, Marko, suddenly angry, took Cil in tow, escorting him back to the main house.

"And the doctor, what he say of that leg, huh?" demanded Marko as he led Cil into the kitchen. And when no response was forthcoming, he clucked his scorn in a superior way. "As I suppose! Hah, Cil-the-Capitan, now even a major—but still no more smart than before. Sit you down there, in that chair, and stay put." And when the old man found he could not budge the pant leg for the swelling, he rummaged about the pantry like a possessive old rooster, returning in a few moments, waving a pair of shears and two bottles, one whiskey, one alcohol. He splashed whiskey into a glass and handed it to Cil.

"Take this," he ordered. "Hair on the chest!" And when Cil had complied, Marko, wielding the long shears, proceeded to cut the cloth, exposing a deep gash surrounded by puffy black-and-blue flesh.

The colonel, hearing the commotion, strode into the room.

"Damn, man!" he cried. "How did it happen?" But old Marko maintained the floor.

"What you think?" waving his arms. "When he leap from the horse!"

"Looks worse than it is," protested Cil.

"Nonsense," barked the colonel. "Call the physician."

Only when the colonel had been calmed was Cil able to convince both men that the wound could be attended to when they returned to the hospital next morning.

When, on the following day, the men were once again refused permission to see Michelle, Cil spirited the colonel back to the villa, then followed Marko out to the barn.

"I'll need a few things," he told the old man, and when, upon hearing the odd request, Marko bridled and asked how so and how soon, Cil had been quick to reply, if somewhat evasively. "I'll need every item by nightfall. Can you do it?"

During the afternoon, without identifying himself, Cil made a discreet call or two to the hospital, then another to Dr. Rutledge's office in his home, inquiring about evening office hours. When he was satisfied with the answers, he nodded and permitted himself a slow grin.

It was precisely 8:55 PM—five minutes before the nurses were due to change shift—when the tall lanky doctor, whistling a happy tune, entered the main entrance of the Chester County Medical Center. He strode down the corridor with a spring to his step and the carriage of a man who owned the place. He marched past the admission desk without so much as a nod. He was dressed in the same standard hospital greens as the other staff doctors; he wore protective shoe-coverings and the regulation cloth cap, also in green.

He did not slow down until he reached the third floor nurse's station, where he saw that the floor nurse was nowhere in sight. He paused only long enough before two gossiping young ladies to mouth a brusque order. The loquacious young ladies each sported a blue name tag encased in clear plastic, upon which was printed: Nurse's Aide.

"Miss D'Orlean's attending nurse, if you please," the doctor declared smoothly. "And kindly have her meet Doctor Hayes in Room 321 with Miss D'Orlean's chart. *Directly*—is that understood?"

At this striking young doctor, trim, broad-shouldered, well over six feet with a neat clean-cut look about him, and who gave each of the young ladies an engaging smile, they seemed more intent on tittering shyly at his back as he strode on than propounding impertinent questions. Besides, visiting doctors were often about, and they were on their way home in a minute anyway, so why bother?

Michelle D'Orleans was lying with her head slightly elevated in the faint illumination of the overhead night light attached to the frame of her bed. She was dozing when he entered. She only blinked awake after he extracted a bouquet of wild spring flowers from his doctor's bag and tucked them carefully under the white cover of her bed.

"Shhh!—Doctor Hayes. Come all the way from Albany; he's going to snap on your light."

"You!"

He snapped on the light, returning to take her wrist in his hand. "Your pulse, young lady. How are you feeling? And keep your voice down."

"Get the hell out of here!"

"Will you kiss me now?" he asked, smiling.

"You are disgusting!"

"It wouldn't do to be unkind to a specialist come all the way from Albany, now would it?" he asked expansively. But she hauled off and swatted him, though her lips looked moist and warm.

He had only just regained his aplomb when a very stern and determined-looking, middle-aged nurse pushed, scowling, through the door, chart-board in hand. But before she could speak, he gave the instruction.

"Nurse, could you help me? I need that head elevated at least another six inches, if you please." His tone carried authority, yes, but a note of kindness as well. "This is a very delicate head injury, and I'm sure a nurse of your experience recognizes the fact. I'll take that chart, thank you."

The nurse released the chart-board to him without protest. She was a plain-looking woman of fifty with pale cheeks, kind, motherly eyes, mousy-brown hair drawn up in a bun behind her nurse's cap. She jumped to carry out the doctor's order.

"But Doctor Rutledge gave strict instructions she was not to be disturbed," she blurted uncertainly.

"Yes, yes; it was 'Old Rut' himself who asked that I look in." He was examining the chart with care as the nurse promptly and methodically cranked up the head of the bed while Michelle D'Orleans, the covers yanked up to her chin, glared at the tall, smooth-talking doctor with stunning ferocity.

"The neural checks, Nurse Bracken." He had read her name tag and confirmed her findings by her initials at the base of the chart in his hand. "You've been taking them every four hours, I see. That's good. Your findings are absolutely normal?"

"Normal, Doctor, yes." Nurse Molly Bracken had been a nurse in this county hospital for thirty-one years, and she could not remember when she had seen a doctor come all the way down from Albany to examine one of her patients, certainly not a doctor of the renown of the famous neurosurgeon, Doctor Hayes of Albany, certainly not a doctor with the looks and assurance of this one. It was the end of her shift, but that fact had totally slipped her mind. She was a good nurse, had read the state medical journal each month religiously for more years than she cared to remember, and had known from the start that in a serious head injury case, the head must be properly elevated at all times; but Doctor Rutledge had scoffed at her suggestion. And now this kind, handsome specialist from the city had seen it instantly—just as she had.

"And the chart says there is no sign of pressure to indicate ongoing intracranial hemorrhaging, is that true, Nurse Bracken?"

"That is true, Doctor," she told him, and at sound of her name from the lips of this great man, she could not squelch a faint grin that would show off her best feature, her dimples. She had heard through the grapevine that this D'Orleans woman was a rich, foreign woman, and she could tell from her looks and demanding manner that it had to be true. And now with a doctor all the way down from University Hospital in Albany! Why, she had a sister in Albany, and she would gladly stay on through the third shift if he just gave the word; but now he was speaking again.

"And the Babinski sign. Has Doctor Rutledge obtained a positive Babinski sign? There is no indication on the chart. Well, never mind, I'll see to it myself."

Emma Bracken was fluffing up the patient's pillows to assure maximum head elevation as the doctor, at the foot of the bed, reached up under the covers, taking the patient's foot firmly in his hand. He commenced to stroke the under-surface of the foot as she herself had learned long ago—to check for sensation. And she could see from the patient's face as the toes began to wiggle involuntarily that the patient was eyeing the Doctor with contempt and hatred. But what could you expect of a high-born foreigner? Yes, she, Emma Bracken, was beginning to like this Doctor

Rutherford B. Hayes very much, thank you. Why, just look how distinguished the name on that name-tag. And, oh, look at the blue of those eyes! Why, if he smiled in her direction one more time—why—she just might blush like the peach she once had been, and still felt—sometimes.

12

It was the following day—May 11, 1995—when Colonel Mavro Anastasi, under rather mysterious circumstances, coaxed Cil into his study for an afternoon drink. The colonel was in a festive mood. His favorite niece was due to be released from the hospital the next day, and the colonel seemed prepared to make the most of the occasion. He had seated himself behind his desk with Cil lounging in a cushioned leather chair to the side; a warming fire crackled in the hearth.

Suddenly the phone rang. The colonel, apparently expecting the call, reached down and flicked a switch by the drawer of his desk.

"Anastasi here."

A second voice boomed out over the speaker phone, resounding off the walls of the room like an invading, full-bodied presence. **"Yes, Colonel. Lockwood at Defense."**

"Why, Lockwood. Delighted you called. I have someone here I'd like you to meet. Major Lane Cil, Mr. James Lockwood, Deputy Secretary of Defense."

"Good afternoon, Mr. Secretary," Cil heard himself saying, woodenly, speaking into thin air. Caught off guard, a prickle of alarm snaked up his spine. What was the meaning of this?

"A Pleasure to know you, Major," came the foreign voice, sailing into the room like a schooner on a gathering wind. **"Colonel Anastasi has mentioned your name with great interest."**

My name, puzzled Cil to himself—to the Deputy Secretary of Defense? Oh, hell! He could feel the muscles of his forearms begin to stiffen. What was this? Everybody knew that mere weeks separated him from his final release from the service.

"Colonel." This brusque stranger's voice seemed to hover in the room, stiff and precise. **"After due consideration, Secretary Levitt has granted your request to brief Major Cil on the details of the operation—in strictest confidence, of course."**

Cil took a healthy shot of his Scotch. What the hell goes on here? Some kind of sick joke after the little stunt I pulled at the hospital? Cil looked to the colonel, but the colonel was no help. And this invisible stranger, why, he was talking about Robert Levitt, the United States Secretary of Defense.

"Thank you, Mr. Secretary," Colonel Anastasi was saying. "And the security clearance?"

"No problem. On Secretary Levitt's explicit order, the major stands cleared at this moment for any operation the size of the one contemplated."

"Fine, Mr. Secretary," offered the colonel warmly. "And I thank you."

"Not at all. Good afternoon, Colonel. And you, Major Cil. Oh, and Major Cil—let's not have another performance like that one we all remember!"

The sound evaporated from the room, replaced by stony silence, interrupted only by the sputter and crackle of the fire at Cil's back. At these last words, Cil paled. Without hesitation he commandeered the bottle and poured himself a double shot as his mind dashed back to the earlier Bosnian mission.

So they knew! They knew it all. The bastards had found him out—even the Secretary of Defense! His hands were trembling.

And what was that business about clearance for a mission? What mission? And what did any of this have to do with him? Hadn't they heard? He was practically a civilian!"

"Major Cil—ah, Lane." The colonel was smiling at him fondly, tapping one thick forefinger against the desktop. "I have taken the liberty to have your security clearance determined for a number of reasons. Forgive my presumption; but after all, it is not every day one runs across a veteran special operations officer with a command of the Croatian-Serb language." He eyed the glass in Cil's hand which was again empty. "Care for a refill?"

Now with the initial shock past, Cil was thinking clearly and carefully; his eyes narrowed. This man across the desk with the phony smile had, after all, shared a very long history with him. He had abhorred and distrusted this man for years before they ever met. Imagine, right here before him, the very man who had brutally locked him out of Sonya's life, then barred the doors behind—and now this. He cursed himself roundly. The raw effrontery of the man, using his influence and contacts to bring him, Lane Cil, to the attention of the Secretary himself!

And now inwardly Cil tossed his head and squeezed off a sardonic smile. He fought to shrug off the whole thing. Very well, then; two could play at this game. In a matter of weeks, he would be a civilian. Then, he could laugh at them all.

Cil smiled at the colonel. "Believe I will have another drink, thank you."

"Why, that's just splendid," declared the colonel, clearly pleased with himself and reaching to pour the whiskey. "Then let me explain." He had the smile of a Cheshire cat, and for some reason Cil could hear an old Nat King Cole song welling up from the back of his mind. *"Ramblin rose—ramblin rose...."*

By the time Colonel Mavro Anastasi had finished his explanation of the details of the mission, Cil's inner chuckle had expanded to a gut-splitting guffaw. Lounging now almost pleasantly in the soft cushions of his chair, sipping his Scotch, it was all Cil could do to keep from spitting in the old bastard's face.

Imagine, crack enemy troops concealed behind a massive high dam. And the idea of sending in a ragtag band of crazies to root them out. Boy-oh-boy, even Disney couldn't unload this kind of manure without a magic shovel. And "partisans"? Why, the old boy was senile as hell; that term of reference had died fifty years back when Brother Tito had hood-winked the world, stolen the country of Yugoslavia, and turned it Communist right under the noses of the Western Powers. *"Ramblin rose—ramblin rose...."*

But the colonel was still holding forth, smiling contentedly, while Cil got down to some serious drinking; the tune was still in his head.

"Your President has made the decision that the dam must be destroyed, yet no US forces are to be employed."

"Ramblin rose—ramblin rose...." Cil could feel the cold intensity of the colonel's stare; he sounded so much like half a dozen other superior officers with squeaky-clean hands who had sent him off over the years on one grizzly mission or another.

"And there must, of course," the colonel was saying, "be complete deniability in case of failure."

"Why I want you, heaven knows...."

"You can understand that, can't you, Major?

"While I love you, with a love true, who can cling to—a rambling rose?"

"Well, speak up, man, speak up!"

"Look, Colonel, that's all well and good, but I really

don't see what this whole thing has to do with me." Only by force of will did he stifle a grin.

The colonel made no reply; he just sat staring at Cil.

"Maybe I just don't understand," added Cil, shaking a woozy head in disbelief. "Just whom would you get to lead such a mission?"

"I had hoped—you, Major Cil."

"Me?" Lane Cil could contain himself no longer. A belly-laugh exploded from his lungs of such magnitude that, for an instant, the whole room seemed to rock on its foundations. It was the look on the colonel's face that sobered him. "Colonel, in all seriousness," he recovered belatedly, "I bet you can find any number of qualified commanders better experienced in tactics than I, and who know a damned sight more about the people and the terrain."

Colonel Mavro Anastasi's gaze zeroed in on Cil like a laser shot from a cannon.

"No," he said quietly. "You are the man."

PART II

13

The day—Tuesday, August 1, 1995. The rush of damp night air clawed at the strands of his uncut hair as Major Lane Cil stood amidships next to the Royal Navy Leftenant manning the wheel of the fifty foot British motor patrol boat. The time—2:53 AM. The craft, stripped for speed, all but devoid of conventional armaments and camouflaged in zigzag stripes of drab pastels, knifed through the silvery sea on an easterly course, the speedometer needle skittering upwards of forty knots.

A wave of anticipation swept over Cil, rousing butterflies to flutter and swirl in his stomach. The roar of the Rolls Royce engine droned in his ears as he made his way to the stern to check on his second in command.

When he arrived in the stern, expecting her to be suffering his own pre-mission jitters, he could scarcely believe his eyes. Miss D'Orleans, lounging on a row of dewy cushions, sat strumming a guitar which could not be heard over the thunder of the engines; and as if half expecting his approach, she looked up, displaying a querulous smile, as if to mock him, long tresses streaming wildly out on the wind.

For only a second did he pause to stare in the flood of moonlight at this grinning image of an overgrown schoolgirl. Then, exhaling a sigh of disgust, he turned on his heel and retraced his steps up the rail. He was still shaking his head as he regained his position at the Brit Leftenant's side. Astern, as if reflecting his emotion, sharp propellers slashed at the sea, throwing out a wake of angry churning white foam.

Dead ahead lay the Dalmatian coast, that sliver of Western Croatia separating Bosnia-Herzegovina from the Adriatic Sea, separating the land of the condemned from the lands of the free. From where Cil stood at the rail, the ragged line of the coastal range thrust a thousand feet straight up out of the sea, a solid gray prison of rock in the dense murky light, implacable and forbidding. It was hard to believe that plush resorts once dotted this expanse of coastline, where, in happier days, royalty and movie stars cavorted beneath the hot Dalmatian sun.

For a moment a cloud hovered to darken the moonlit sea, and with it Cil's thoughts tumbled back over the kaleidoscope of events of the last hectic days. There had been long hours of heated, often bitter debate with Colonel Mavro Anastasi, until at last Washington's insistence and the pressure of time had won over Cil's reasoned skepticism of the haste, indeed the very efficacy, of the mission. True, Michelle's recovery had been prodigious—but was it complete? And what earthly business had she, though skilled, a relative greenhorn, on such a dangerous mission? Was it sheer cheek, or the force of the woman's charm and stubborn insistence that had carried the day? Or her uncle's undeniable weight in political circles? And then had come the fevered search for support and liaison.

"Where are we now?" shouted Cil into the ear of the patrol boat commander over the whistle of the wind.

"See there, Major—that continuous hump in the sea to starboard?" He was pointing with his chin. "That thin point of land protects the Dalmatian coast from the open sea. Soon we alter course for the three-mile limit. You'd best take her below, Sir, and make the change quickly."

Below, the two operatives, squeezed into cramped quarters, busied themselves donning their native costumes in pale infrared light. Michelle wore a plain black peasant dress with a white knitted shawl pulled over her shoulders, her hair swept back and arranged in a bun, covered by the customary native headscarf. Cil assumed the fisherman's costume of dark-weathered pants and pullover jersey, sturdy workboots, and a nondescript P-jacket with threadbare sleeves. In the heat of the engine room, it was roasting in the jacket.

Michelle now turned to gaze at Cil with undisguised contempt, eyeing the black beret cocked at an extravagant angle, so typical, she was thinking, of that haughty male chauvinism. Well, she had had a belly full of it, thank you, from the very instant her presence on the mission had been announced.

For his part, Cil, fumbling with the laces of his boot in the dim reddish light, threw a furtive glance at Michelle, who, suspecting his attention to her womanly features, gave him a wink and a lasciviously grin, then abruptly erased the grin and tugged her heavily knitted white shawl closer about her. To further clarify her position, she plunked herself down on an ammunition case, hoisted her bulging carrying bag, and placed the bag in her lap. The bag was packed with a second, more sturdy outfit, for climbing in the mountains, the outfit complete right down to woolen socks and hiking boots. She held her chin at an unapproachable angle; she was determined not to look his way and give him the satisfaction.

It was 3:12 AM Croatian time. The crew slipped the ancient wooden fishing skiff over the side, and its hull slipped silently into the dark murky waters of the Adriatic Sea. A billow of pre-dawn mist hovered over the sea where a good chop was running. The two operatives, each in turn, arms outstretched for balance, teetered for a moment beyond the rail of the British Motor Patrol Boat, then lunged for the heaving skiff; then they cast off. And moments later they sat in the small skiff, alone in the chill of the night, listening in the swirl of the mist as the rumble of heavy engines faded in the distance, then died away completely.

Only then did the full weight of the realization strike Michelle—of how truly alone they were, abandoned, discarded flotsam drifting on a hostile sea with nothing but oars, a patched fishing net, hunting knives, the clothes on their backs, the carrying bag tightly held in her lap, a pocket compass, and the keys to a second-hand car they had yet to lay eyes on.

The keel of the skiff had been slicing through lazy swells for some time now. An overcast, thick and murky, pressed down upon the blackness of the sea; and here closer to the coast, Cil, aided by an incoming tide, took care not to splash oars, not to risk unnecessary sound.

At last Michelle spied new colors through a break in the mist—red and green winking lights. "Yes, yes. See there—lights marking the mouth of the harbor!" And farther in, a string of lights—white glittering stars standing out on the line of the shore. And later, in the glow of the shore lights—a row of fishing smacks rocking at the quay. Fishermen, black ants at this distance, were ambling about on the quay, readying lines and nets for the day's catch—which she fervently hoped would not be them.

By the time the pair had reached shore, stowed the skiff, skirted the quay, then entered the sleeping village, Cil's watch read 4:27 AM. The fishermen, caught up in their toil, had paid the strangers in disguise small heed. And now the two operatives, setting aside their own private war and working as a team of professionals, threaded through a maze of shadowy alleys. Rows of squat stone buildings, sleeping ghosts in the night, emerged out of the darkness, crowding in over the cobblestones. The pair lightened their footsteps, now and again stumbling over a stray dog or tom-cat foraging among garbage cans lining the way. At a cor-ner of ways, Michelle whispered past the shield of her upraised hand.

"Where does it go?"

"Shhh, " he scolded. "This way."

At this hour, all lay silent as death. Advancing on tiptoe, holding their collective breath at each turn of the ways, they cut up a dark vine-covered lane.

"One block to go," he told her, more relaxed here in the stillness.

But then as the pair rounded the dark stone angle of a building, Cil in the lead pulled up short.

It was as if confronted by an apparition—not three steps ahead stood a policeman, his burly frame barring the way, his high-polished boots gleaming in the glow of a street lamp.

Shock and surprise froze Cil in place. Then, with light-ning quickness, he swung around to face a startled Michelle—his voice thundered in the stillness as he bel-lowed in her face..

"How! How could any stupid woman—forget the third net!" He fairly spat the words in his best native tongue. "Never should I listen to your fat brother—that you are so smart!" Swiftly he grabbed her arm, yanking her past the bewildered policeman. "And last night you blame me to be drunk on the wine!"

Glancing back, Cil caught a subtle movement, a faint shrug of the policeman's shoulders. What he could not see was the look of sympathetic disgust imprinted on the man's face as he patted the holster at his side and slowly sauntered off.

A minute later Cil lifted a vine at the face of a wall, jam-ming his finger hard down on the button. Both sets of eyes watched with relief the steady ascent of the overhead door.

Once inside the underground garage, Michelle, still stung

by the force of Cil's theatrics, turned on him.

"Tell me—are *all* ignorant American men savage and uncouth?" The force of her words betrayed the depth of her emotion, but already Cil's mind was racing ahead; he was worried; the wide open door of the garage had to loom large from the street—like the mouth of some great gaping under-sea monster.

Inside the ancient underground garage, all seemed gray and lifeless. Particles of fine choking dust hung in the air, spreading a thick woolly blanket over the cavernous interi-or, over the solemn rows of small European cars illuminat-ed by the faint light of a single bulb dangling on a wire from the high ceiling.

"Dark blue and small, with a stoved-up front end," whis-pered Cil.

"There—there in the corner." Michelle pointed in the gloom at a battered mini-sedan, the dilapidated little car peering out, wounded and hopeful, from where it stood all but hidden beneath the blanket of dust. Cil glanced at the plate number.

"That's the one," he said, again furtively eyeing the gap-ing entrance door that stood open to the street. "Quick—get a move on. Clear off the dust—check under the back seat."

Swiftly he fumbled in his pocket for the key; he opened the driver's side door, then the trunk, unscrewed the spare tire bracket, released the wheel, deflated the tire with a hiss, and removed just enough of the tire casing to get at the con-tents.

Within seconds, the tire re-inflated with a canister from the back, they huddled within the small car, taking stock of supplies and equipment: two unassembled automatic weapons of the M-16 type, silencers, a signaling rifle, clips, ammo and grenades, two canteens of water, a rough-sketched map, a fistful of currency, two packets of Yugoslav National Army C rations, papers for the car, folded field packs, a first-aid kit, night vision goggles, a special UHF radio pack, a pair of seven power artillery binoculars, a roll of duct tape, and a flask of "Slivovitz," the native plum brandy.

Cil looked to Michelle. "You're sure the papers are in order?" he said, eyes darting, his tone clipped and tense, gulping a swig of the clear native brandy.

"Go easy on that stuff!" she snapped. He offered but a fleeting glance for her trouble.

"Count the money and fill the packs while I assemble the weapons," he ordered.

"You're sure I'm up to it, *Cherie*?" she countered sourly.

"Hurry! See that garage door—you saw that cop on the street."

"The kuna and German marks are all there—forget the dinar; they're worthless," she said.

"Here." He shoved her the remaining parts of the second weapon. "Finish this one and hurry—then check the car papers. We've got to get a move on."

"The plan was to wait."

"Yeah—with that door yawning open?" Cil squinted at the map in the hopeless light as he fumbled again for the keys, his mind embroiled in a battle royal. Of course, it should have been safer to hole up here until rush hour as planned; after all, the Croats were supposed to be allies, but in this topsy turvy now-and-then war with the indigenous Croats hopelessly splintered into competing factions and commands, the HVO butchering their Muslim allies in the villages, and rogue bands of armed and drunken Croat irregulars prowling the streets and patrolling the highways, this was hardly the time to take unnecessary risks. No, Cil was thinking; they were stuck, and he knew it.

Once again he tossed a glance at the overhead door standing open like a whale's mouth with lighted tonsils. No, much too obvious, even for a few minutes. Attract that cop like a fish to a lure. Even if we knock out the light, a passing cop would spot that open door in a second and come sniffing around. He bit the inside of his lip and cursed Croatian contractors in general—in particular the consummate fool with no better sense than to install an overhead door and light with no inside switches.

"Got to make a break for it!" he told himself before turning to Michelle with his best imitation of rock-steady nerves.

"Ready?" he said.

Her nod was more swift than assured. "And here's your license and the other car papers." She mouthed the last with but a small pout, but he ignored the pout and shoved the papers into his pocket.

"That's right," he said. "Load the clips and attach the M-16 silencers. If we go down, we go down with a fight!"

She was looking up the ramp toward the street—warily. "Is the map as you thought?"

He shrugged. "If we make the mountains beyond Mostar, we've got a shot. He forced a smile and started the engine. It was 4:55 AM Croatian time.

The battered little car, clear victim of a life of privation, chugged noisily up the ramp, then, reaching the top and displaying the puzzled hesitation of a lost and neglected puppy, stretched the beams of its headlights timidly into the early morning gloom. At the edge of the roadway, it turned, slowly, bumping its tires down the cobblestone street with reluctance and caution. But when the little car saw that it had reached the main road unmolested, it took the broad lane in stride and speeded up with a vengeance, its tiny hood fairly swelling with pride.

"The guns and supplies?"

"Hidden—beneath the back seat," she said, not looking at him, still stung by his felt condescension.

They sped along through the night at good speed, following the road that snaked along the south bank of the Neretva River as it sliced through the limestone ledges of the coastal range, past Metkovic without incident and into the broader reaches of the river valley. At the Croatian frontier with Herzegovina, a flash of papers cleared them through the border checkpoint strung with barbed wire and blocked by tank traps and two large camouflaged tanks on alert in the trees.

Once past the checkpoint, Cil turned to Michelle. "Better recheck the weapons," he said. "And your carrying bag with the clothes—best to make your change now, OK."

There was a pause before she spoke. "Ah, the bag—well...." She faltered.

"Where?"

"In the trash—back at the garage," she confessed.

"But the hiking clothes?"

"Some I have in my pack," she said quickly.

"And your heavy boots?"

"No...."

"Forget it," he said, and once again forced a smile. "It's OK."

A silence fell between them, heavier than the gloom beyond the windshield, broken finally by Michelle.

"You know something?" she said lightly, apology coating her every word. "Here in Herzegovina—the village of Medugorje. The map shows it must be right over there. You remember—that's where the four school children first saw the Apparition of the Virgin Mary—on a hillside back in 1981. It was in all the papers. Anyway, they say she has appeared many times since, and only those four children can see her. And now there are pilgrims from all over the world—like so long ago at Lourdes in France. Did you see that movie, 'The Song of Bernadette?' Wasn't it lovely?"

With the darkness of night their only companion—with stealth and speed their only allies, the intruders pressed on, the little car charging through the curtain of blackness, the minutes streaming past without incident, the beams of the game little car's headlights probing forth into this hostile land. With each passing mile, their breathing eased. They had passed beyond the outskirts of Mostar without taking a sniper's bullet, finally locating the connector to the Sarajevo road, closed off by Serb forces since the start of the war. In the first soupy pre-dawn light, angry shell holes in the hulks of dead buildings showed up in the beams of the headlights where Serb heavy artillery had thundered down with impunity from the bald, rock-strewn hills rising up to their right.

Through the screen of penciled light, the little car sped along; they seemed to have the road all to themselves, the road broadening out below the cover of trees hugging the riverbank of the now swift-flowing Neretva below.

Suddenly out of nowhere came the shriek of an oncoming ambulance—dark, racing, convoyed by ghostly white armored personnel carriers, all gray in the poor light, eerie overhead lights speeding at the little car like great beetle-eyes out of the gloom—only at the last second to reveal the great black-painted block letters, UN, on the side of the high-backed beetle, at the same time proclaiming its right of passage.

Dawn broke. Through the mists that hung by the river just there to their left, they reached the great tunnels—huge—dark—hulking circles of darkness—one after the other—burrowing through steep-rising, bare, limestone ridges. Cil prodded the little car for speed, scant protection against prospect of a sniper's bullet loosed from high overhead at the end of each cavern of blackness.

Beyond the tunnels came the specter of war—blown bridges suddenly strewn to the side of their path—huge broken slabs, rectangles of white concrete sixty feet wide, a hundred feet long, half-submerged at the base of the gorge to their left as if interred in the depths of the river below. Now in the clearing light, the mist was rising from the great green river as it rose by the road, flowing wide and deep. And the gray-green opalescent color? It was almost as if one were looking into the heart of a freshly peeled grape.

The little car seemed tired now, struggling on, groaning with exertion, jouncing over stone cuts hastily scored into the slope of the ridge in order to detour past the lost bridges, a makeshift, scrub-board limestone track a half mile in length, cut by an army of bulldozers after blasting into the slope of the ridge overhanging the river.

Here with the first clear light came a new sight. Crouched on the steep-wooded slopes climbing away from the opposite bank of the river appeared a now and then Swiss alpine chalet, the same as seen in ski country, proud, spanking-clean structures crafted a half century earlier by skilled, sturdy hands.

But all that was before the war. Now, these neat white boxes with sloping roofs of Howard Johnson red-orange tile set among the trees displayed a queer aspect. Something was wrong, miserably wrong; but what? It was a little like staring into an open smiling face, only to suddenly discover upon closer inspection that the teeth were missing. Houses perfectly normal, yet—shorn of glass. And while stunning and vivid in all their whiteness and alpine grace, as they came on, their closeness answered the question.

Gutted hulks they were now, without laughter or life— solemn testament to what had come before. And then as the little car sped closer, the shell punctures pockmarking the white of the walls showed up clearly now in daylight. Telltale soot marks above window casings and under the eaves bore silent witness to the mortar shells which had been casually lobbed across the river from the safety of the high ridgeline, all in the service of ethnic cleansing.

The stench of charred timbers hung by the road: life without life; life drained away. The inhabitants, if lucky enough to cheat death, had long since stolen away on the mists to seek refuge in the hills.

At last, the little car found itself climbing, the road heaving over steep mountain passes as deserted as a graveyard, while above, solid green peaks above the green river seemed to squeeze in the roof of the sky.

Michelle and Cil found themselves snaking along high in the mountains, making good time, indeed talking quite pleasantly as they rounded a bend.

But around that bend, everything changed.

Looming dead ahead, they spied it. Moving in the same direction as they themselves, if at a snail's pace, they had suddenly come upon it—a truck caravan—clearly a convoy.

With the first rays of morning sun peaking over the ridgetop, instantly did Cil recognize the make and style of the trucks, the rear of each truck in line shrouded with canvas, carefully concealing the cargo.

Abruptly Cil backed off on the gas—slapped in the clutch—snapping down through the gears, thereby slowing the car and stretching the interval between themselves and the last truck in line.

"Keep your eye on that canvas flap," Cil nodding anxiously ahead at the canvas covering the rear of the last truck in line.

"Look!" cried Michelle.

The next gust of wind had ripped aside the corner of the flap, exposing a double row of helmeted troops in the body of the truck, the soldiers seated erect, stone-faced on hard wooden benches, facing one another, clad in full battle dress, each outfitted with field packs, every man armed with a shiny new AK-47 assault rifle positioned upright between his closed knees.

"Russian trucks," she gasped, already hastening to plot their position on the map in her lap.

"Serb trucks," he corrected. "Russian manufacture. And those are Serb troops!" And now, high up on the spine of the next ridge, Cil spied a pair of armed soldiers half hidden in the trees.

"But, but Uncle Mavro—he said the first signs of Serb troops would come much farther north!" A sudden touch of insecurity attached to her words.

"Then your uncle was mistaken," Cil offered gently.

Michelle's prior plotting on the map had told Cil they were now not far from the village they sought. Not anxious to remain so close to a secret the Serbs wanted so badly to keep, Cil further slackened speed, stretching the interval, awaiting his chance.

When abruptly the next road curve shielded the little car from the view of the last truck in line, Cil jerked the wheel left, swerving the little car to slam down a leafy embankment and crash through a low stand of pine, then careen down a narrow track, to finally brake to a stop in a tangle of brush.

"There have to be roadblocks," he told her, breathless. But to himself, he mused, "Not even the Devil himself could break through this enemy cordon in broad daylight."

14

Cil and Michelle, once out of the car with weapons drawn, found themselves stranded high up on the side of a steep forested ridge, the foliage lush, colored a deep Irish green. The time—7:15 AM. Cil could see from the banks of freshly turned sand on either side and recent tire tracks in the dirt that fate and the Serb convoy had catapulted them from the main road into a working gravel pit. Judging by the accumulated trash and debris farther in, where the land dropped off sharply, it had to be the local trash dump. Broken glass, rusted tin cans, and discarded tires abounded; the stink of garbage hung in the air like some great immovable thing; stinging flies hummed and swarmed.

"This'll do," Cil announced with satisfaction, surveying the sandpit, not noticing the accumulated moisture on his palms as his thoughts projected ahead. If this were the main access route for Serb troops and supplies, no doubt roadblocks lay ahead. Intelligence estimates during State-side planning warned of roadblocks, yes—but where?

"Secure weapons and ammo," he said, "while I take a quick look around—OK? And keep a sharp lookout."

"Hurry—I have a bad feeling." She was raising the trunk

lid, but her gaze remained fixed on the dirt track behind.

"A few minutes, that's all."

"Hurry."

Cil, clambering up the steep gravel embankment, crossed a gully and worked his way to a height from which he could get a feel for the terrain that lay ahead. One of the first lessons of survival training is not to over-rely on maps and charts; a map may be fine for distance, direction, and general proximity, but what it fails to reveal often proves more crucial than what it does. Slowly, methodically, Cil's gaze surveyed the lay-of-the-land, the obvious landmarks; he measured the terrain with a keen, experienced eye.

The landscape looked to be a picture postcard mailed from the Swiss Alps. Surrounding the ridge where he stood rose a circle of steep alpine peaks, lush and green, thrusting skyward, some still capped with snow. Removing his map from his pocket, Cil surveyed the characteristics of the land, carefully, comparing them against the contour lines, shadings, elevations, and distances shown on the topographical map. Right here, he calculated, they could be no more than eight to ten miles from the rendezvous point—at least as the crow flies. And the towering oaks blanketing these ridges should provide decent cover. Yes, this was close enough—they would hoof it from here.

He paused to sharpen his senses; even in these few minutes, he had detected a shift in the wind. Oddly, the scent of pine and the soft musical whisper of the wind brought a sense of momentary peace, of lingering serenity, and for only a few seconds did his mind trail back to childhood memories and the smell and feel of the woods of his native New England. But false signs they were, for now he spied a squadron of low scudding clouds closing in on the mountains—dark full-bellied clouds, laden with rain. Ten-to-one the rain would come soon. He scurried back over the rough terrain to where Michelle crouched waiting.

"We'll ditch the car here," he told her. "So burn every last identifying paper and document inside. Then bury the plates. I'll lug the rest of the stuff up that embankment."

By the time Cil had hauled the supplies and equipment to the top of the bank, Michelle had completed her tasks and returned to her look-out post by the road. As Cil approached her on silent feet, something odd caught his eye.

He stopped in his tracks. Her attention focused on the roadway; she failed to notice his approach—and for a few seconds he watched her, massaging her forehead with first one hand, then the other. When she detected his footsteps, her hand abruptly dropped to her side.

"Bet a penny you can't throw a pebble over that drop-off?" Cil challenged, for the moment ignoring what he had seen and nodding at a spot fifty paces beyond the car where the land dropped away sharply.

Promptly she picked up a handful of pebbles, and with a toss of the arm commenced to strike rocks and metal debris in the dump beyond with an audible ping.

"Good. Now look, we've got to get rid of this car. It'll take me awhile, so if there's the slightest movement up the road, let fly a stone to catch my attention. And whatever you do, unless it's your life, don't fire a shot."

In the space of two minutes, Cil had rolled the car to the rim of the drop-off, cramped the wheels, then shoved the little car over the lip to plunge down and come to rest on its side. With swift hands and a sturdy lug wrench, he removed the free-turning wheels and rolled them away, smashed out windshield and side panes, then scavenged an old discarded can of paint and spattered the overturned car until it resembled an abandoned wreck.

Having completed his task, he crawled back up the embankment and was raking the car tracks clean with an evergreen bough when he felt the sting of a pebble strike his back.

Wheeling, he spied Michelle, weapon at the ready in one hand, the other anxiously motioning him down.

Instantly he sprawled on all fours. With rapt anticipation, he eyed Michelle crouching in the brush, her weapon now leveled at something on the road.

Seconds passed. No noise of an engine came from the road. Flat down on the ground, he waited and watched. And then—he saw.

A farmer! A decrepit old farmer, the poor man bent half double with rheumatism and age, trudging up the road, driving before him two scrawny white goats.

Moments later Cil and Michelle crouched by a tree trunk on the high ground above, the map spread and flapping softly in the breeze. While the map revealed no major rivers between their present position and the rendezvous point, the terrain ran rough and jagged, the elevation ranging like a roller coaster, more so due to the fact that the Dalmatian Alps run north and south with the road hiking through the passes of the forested ridges. While Cil wore sturdy work clothes and walking boots, Michelle found herself clad only in the light dress, shawl and flat street shoes donned in the patrol boat, fine for cover in town, perhaps, but all but useless for the hard climbing ahead. And now, with what he had observed, Cil had an added worry. Silently he mulled an alternative plan, but she cut in on his thoughts as if reading his mind.

"Don't give it a thought!" she declared.

"Listen to me. On the map, sure, the distance may be eight to ten clicks, but look here." He pointed along the thin black line on the map, the line curling through the ridges and past a village on the way to the rendezvous point. "Staying wide of the road, why, over those ridges, you can double the distance; then, add a few miles for skirting the village." He raised his gaze to the sky. "You see those clouds, a storm blowing up, and you without boots and hiking clothes? No, no; you better stay here. I'll move on to the rendezvous point and pick you up later."

She was suddenly standing, very tall, her feet planted so

firmly apart that they seemed to be growing out of the ground—her assault rifle, thumb safety clicked off, aimed straight at his chest.

"Rough country like this, *Cherie*," she hissed, "demands two sets of eyes—and twice the fire power." The last erupted as nearly a boast.

"There'll be no talk of shooting," he snapped. "One shot, and we and the mission are history!"

"All right," she conceded swiftly. "But I go."

"How do you feel? Any headaches?" His tone betrayed his depth of concern.

"*Sacre Bleu!*" eyes once again blazing with that peculiar hauteur reserved to the French. "*Monsieur*, do I strike you as the invalid?"

Cil stood for a moment, silently eyeing her, though his eyes stared with a force that could bore through her soul. A slight spitting rain started out of the north.

Then, without so much as a word, he placed down his weapon, removed his P-Jacket, and quietly draped it over her shoulders. With a roll of duct tape snatched from his pack, he set about fashioning a sturdy makeshift cover, winding a triple layer of the sturdy tape round and over each of her street shoes, binding each shoe as if a miniature mummy, even a way up the legs.

"Come on," he said roughly. "Better hope this squall lasts; they don't make better cover." With that, they strapped on their knife sheaths, Cil's to his left thigh as he was left-handed, Michelle's to her right, under the flowing contours of the light cotton dress. Then, draping their weapons with the special neopreme covers to shield them from the wet, yet permit instant use, they set off through the rain under full combat pack. It was thirty seconds by his watch short of 8:00 AM.

The sweet fragrance of cool damp earth seemed to mingle with the elusive scent of things yet to come in this strange foreign land. The mountainous terrain rolled like waves on an endless sea as the two lone operatives tramped up one wooded slope only to find themselves thrust into the trough at its back; and so it went as the hours crawled past. The wind whipped up, backing into the north, blowing up a gale, whistling through the narrow passes as a cold rain pelted their faces and soaked to the skin. And when they would pause for a moment's rest, goose-bumps would suddenly spring out over every inch of their flesh as if in silent protest at even this respite. And so, on they hiked, utilizing the sudden tempest as cover to cross the road and then keep its thin, snaking line rising and falling like a hopeless drunk far off to their left. They hiked on this way all through the morning into mid-afternoon, slogging along, screening the rain from their eyes with upraised hands, searching for the first odd movement ahead. And when the road chose to curl in too close for comfort, they gave it a wide berth, circling wide, careful to keep to the shelter of the deep forest ridges, hidden from sight.

By the time the rain slackened, like sopping wet rats they found themselves scaling a particularly difficult hillside. Michelle, who had marched the whole distance without so much as a peep of complaint, turned finally to Cil.

"Is it time for a break?" she inquired, panting for breath.

Cil, detecting the plea in her voice, surveyed with alarm the hollow look of fatigue etched on her face, the careless manner in which she carried her weapon, the droop in shoulders normally firm and erect.

"Can you make it to the top of the ridge?" he asked with concern.

From that weary face—the eyes suddenly blazed.

"I can make it anywhere you can, Major!"

By the time they topped the ridge, as if at the stroke of a wand, the storm proceeded to blow off south, the sun breaking through to beat down in a blaze of heat tempered only by the shade of the overhead foliage and the caress of the breeze. It was like stumbling from an ice-cold shower straight into the oven; and from this height, the forested alpine peaks shot up to the heavens all round, steep and unyielding, as far as the eye could see—the greenest of greens—the forest primeval.

Below, through the tall oak and fir at the height of the ridge, giving way below to a stand of pine and small poplar, they spied the cleft of a gorge and the gray-green course of a stream threading along its crease.

"Let's hold up down there by the stream. What do you say?" And they were halfway down the rugged slope before stumbling upon a trail that led through the woods.

Once again Michelle lifted her voice.

"Would the trail be too much of a risk?" she ventured.

One such plea from Michelle D'Orleans, let alone two, struck Cil as so strange that he surveyed her more closely. Though her face remained set and determined as ever, the spark had departed her eyes, and he could see a slight limp which she struggled to conceal. He scrutinized the path once more; it looked overgrown and untrodden enough, but well did he comprehend the danger; and for a moment he weighed the prospect of land mines or sudden ambush against Michelle's depleted condition. It had been authoritatively estimated that four to six million land mines dotted the landscape of Bosnia-Herzegovina, the majority uncharted.

"Better not—we'll rest here awhile." And when they resumed, increasing their distance from the newfound trail, he redoubled his vigilance. But upon safely reaching the base of the gorge, Cil chuckled at himself, at his own excessive caution.

It must have been a local storm, for here away from the fury of wind and rain, the ground remained bone dry, the sun delicious and bright, slanting in through the trees to dapple the carpet of needles with its full soothing warmth. Farther downstream, Cil spotted huge limestone boulders through the underbrush blocking the rush of the stream, the giant rocks causing the waters to pool now and again, fashioning the place ideal for swimming.

The heat of the sun combined with the sound of the stream and the sweet fragrance of clean mountain air served to dispel the aura of danger which had dogged them so long, supplanting it now with a buoying sense of well-being. In the full flush of sunlight, Cil now following behind, suddenly spied something.

"Damn—look at your legs—why didn't you say something?"

"Ah, *Cherie;* it is nothing," she gasped through her exhaustion. "By tomorrow, you'll see; they will be good as new."

"Hand me the kit in your pack," his eyes focused on the ugly red scratches crisscrossing her legs, aware that infection in the wilds can prove nearly as treacherous as the enemy itself.

"First, *Monsieur,* must I heed the call of nature." Her smile came thin and wan as she vanished behind the cover of the trees.

Exhausted, Cil threw down his pack and leaned his weapon against a tree nearby, noting that poor Michelle must indeed have been in agony since she had not even stopped to remove her pack. He sprawled on all fours to drink from the stream.

As he sipped of the cool mountain waters, a sound caught his ear—the snap of a twig. He turned to greet Michelle.

It was not Michelle. Towering above him loomed a man—a broad-shouldered man with a murderous snarl. Cil could feel the cold pressure of a rifle barrel shoved against his right temple, could feel the fine hairs rise on his nape.

The man stood rigid—barechested—muscles taut—clad only in clinging-wet fatigue pants and a foreign soldier's softcap, the cold steel of the rifle barrel pressed hard against Cil's head.

To snatch a better look at the man, Cil slightly twisted his head—to be instantly rewarded with a kick which snapped his head back, stunning him; his vision clouded. When his senses returned, the gleaming red star on the man's visored cap glinted brightly in the sunlight.

Cil found himself helpless, totally helpless—his weapon out of reach, leaning against the tree trunk, woefully distant.

He failed to catch the tiniest flick of movement from back in the trees—the bare glint of sunlight; but he did catch the sound. A muted *wooaump,* like the sound of a wet dishrag flung hard against a kitchen wall.

With strange fascination, Cil watched the soldier's eyes, watched the way they suddenly sprang wide with shock and amazement, while deep at their core, he could read the terror signaled by the brain. And from the man's suddenly constricted throat, Cil could hear clearly the low strangled cry.

Then the man fell, not quickly collapsing as one might have expected, but slowly, almost mechanically, like the felling of a great tree, the man's huge frame pitching forward, rifle in hand as if the mind had not instructed the hands to release it. A huddle of rocks at the edge of the stream broke the fall, but the face and torso fell flat, splashing in the stream.

Now, with the man's back plainly in view, Cil came up with a start. He could see the black handle where the knife had plunged shaft-deep in the flesh between the man's shoulder-blades. A thin serpent of crimson crept along the hollow of the back to drip and be lost in the flow of the stream.

A single thought raced through Cil's mind. How many others lurked out there in the trees?

15

Michelle D'Orleans, at age twenty-four, had never seen a dead person up close—certainly not a corpse produced by her own hand. Her first reaction? Taut, shivering panic! Long ago as a trainee in Israel she had found herself on patrol during a skirmish when a pair of Arab terrorists had been shot breaching the barren frontier. But there, her compatriots had also fired, which impersonalized the event, and all had occurred at a comfortable distance. Here, it was totally different. Once she had slain the Serb trooper threatening Cil's life, she had taken one look at the dead man's half-naked body, and the very thought that she had extinguished the life of a fellow creature, let alone a human being with a vicious throw of a long knife—her stomach clenched; her blood ran cold, and only a supreme effort of will altered her emotion to anger—then rage.

As she emerged from the bushes, she turned the full force of that anger on Cil. After all, had it not been his own carelessness, his own lapse of judgment, that had prompted, indeed, invited the attack! Had it not been he, who, having applauded her skills and success in the training, had thereafter inexplicably turned against her to fight her every step of the way once her assignment to the mission was announced! And when he had failed in that, had it not been he who had then manufactured an elaborate excuse to bar her from the mission? A suicide mission? Hah, *Cherie*! Was not every such mission a suicide mission? And what of that whole business of *Sonya*?

By the time she reached the body of the dead soldier lying face down in the stream, the paling face obscured by the distortion of the current, she had once again regained her nerve—and wasted no time in demonstrating the fact. Placing her left knee in the small of the corpse's back, and pursing her lips with the effort, she tugged the knife from the bloody hole between the shoulder blades, mindless of the rude sucking sound. As if that were not enough, blithely she rinsed off the knife in the stream—as one might in the process of cleaning a fish. Her task completed, she turned to Cil.

But now she saw that Cil, as usual, was one step ahead, moving swiftly to tame the crisis at hand. In the space of three minutes, working as a team as instilled by the training, swiftly and systematically did they sweep both banks of the stream in a stealthy, moving crouch, weapons on automatic at the ready. Once establishing that the soldier had almost certainly been alone, the fact further confirmed by discovery of his clothing downstream on a flat boulder at the side of a pool ideal for swimming, Cil was short and terse with his instructions—though she could detect just the subtlest hint of appreciation in his tone.

The bare-chested intruder's military tunic and shirt lay neatly stacked atop the huge boulder, his cartridge belt discarded and resting nearby. Placed next to his shirt was an oversized wristwatch with all the gadgets, the sort common to soldiers all over the world. The watch read 4:52 PM.

"The body!" cried Michelle. "We can't just leave it."

"Come—quickly." On his command, taking care not to step out of the stream's bed, they retraced their steps to where the corpse of the intruder lay upstream. Grunting with the effort, Cil hoisted the limp body onto his shoulders.

Then careful to avoid spilling blood on the rocks rising out of the stream, he carried the dead man back down to the flat boulder where the man's clothes still lay folded. When, upon Cil's instruction, she spread her white knitted shawl on the boulder—arranged like a butterfly with its wings spread wide—he carefully positioned the corpse face down on one side of the shawl, with one arm extended across as if caught in the embrace of a woman. Then the soldier's rifle was set at the base of the rock, just out of reach. Next, the neatly stacked clothes and cartridge belt were scattered, along with the man's cap, as if discarded in haste, the crystal of the watch smashed on the rock, and the watch restrapped to the wrist of the corpse. The task completed, Cil turned to Michelle.

"Hand me your pants!" he demanded.

Michelle, nonplused, looked dumbly down at her dress.

"No, no; your panties," he insisted, only to be greeted by a bucolic stare.

He tried a third time.

"From the change of clothes in your pack—hurry!"

And when she had rummaged through her pack and delivered up the delicate item, he first checked the label as he had with the shawl (which displayed no label whatever), to confirm its native manufacture. Then, while she watched, he tore the lace panties roughly with his hands, arranging the torn garment a certain way as if carelessly discarded at the base of the rock at the dead soldier's feet. Finally, with Michelle looking on, an astonished expression drawn on her face, Cil reached under the body, unfastened the man's belt, and hauled his pants down to half-mast at the knees.

"Now, just relax and keep an eye out," he told her. "Up that way, up the path," lifting the stunned Michelle into the air bodily, weapon and all. Then turning so he was facing the stream, his back to the trail, he carried her, walking backwards, until he arrived at the edge of the path where it reached closest to the boulder. There he set her down, and together they produced the distinctive scuff marks of a ferocious struggle. Satisfied at last, he dragged Michelle bodily along the ground and back down to the boulder, careful to step precisely in the very tracks he had made previously.

The job completed, they repaired upstream, again careful to stay in the current, returning the scene of the encounter to its natural state, taking care to wash away all trace of blood from the rocks. Once Cil had reshouldered his pack, they hastened upstream, again keeping to where the current ran swiftest, scouring the banks of the stream with their gaze for the slightest out-of-the-way movement.

After wading upstream against the current for a quarter of an hour, they came upon the steel bridge that carried the main road over the stream. There, one at a time, careful not to touch the bank on either side, each weighted down by their pack, weapon slung over their shoulder, they hoisted themselves up onto the steel latticework of the bridge, then the roadway.

From there, they crossed to the far side of the road. After a bit of hard climbing, they ascended a high knoll to a perch in good cover above and overlooking both the bridge and the path of the stream below.

There they sat, anxious and waiting, alternating their gaze between the bridge, the path of the stream, and the position of the sun.

It was the thought of search dogs that bothered Cil most. With the killing of the soldier, how soon would they come?

16

Cil's watch read 5:40. Already the late afternoon sun cast bleak shadows down the slopes of the blue-gray mountains of Bosnia-Herzegovina. Perched high on an out-cropping of rock overlooking the road, Cil conveyed the impression of a seasoned old eagle perched on a crag pro-tecting his mate. But he knew the impression for the lie that it was. He peered down at the path of the stream below the bridge; that was the direction from which they would come.

The question leapt from Michelle's tongue. "Will they catch us and kill us right here?"

"No," he told her flatly. But now as he watched a solitary car pass below on the roadway, he was thinking of the dogs; he had not told her of the dogs. Truth was, he had struggled to fight the subject of dogs from his own consciousness. Cil was afraid of dogs. Severely bitten as a child, he had never been quite able to rid himself of the fear; too, more than once had he been pursued across hostile territory by packs of vicious, baying dogs. He knew what dogs could do to a person; it wasn't pretty to recall what razor-sharp teeth could do to a human face. That was the reason he had not mentioned the dogs.

And now he cursed himself at how stupid and amateurish

he had been. His own inexcusable carelessness had practically invited the attack back there at the stream. And if it hadn't been for Michelle? Now with the killing, the dogs would come.

His little masquerade may have delayed it, of course, may with luck have momentarily diverted attention away from themselves, but delay was their only hope. Then again, he might instead have buried the body. But digging took time, especially without a shovel or entrenching tool; and a pack of dogs could sniff out a shallow grave in no time. He willed his muscles to relax, stroking the stubble of whiskers on his chin as he pondered, once again lifting his eyes to gauge the angle of the sun.

"How soon will he be missed?" she asked sharply, not fooled by his silence.

"Hard to say." He plucked a spear of grass from among the rocks, and with all the dramatic casualness he could muster, he stuck it between his teeth. After a while, he reached in his pack, fished out two cans of C-Rations, opened them both, handing one to Michelle. "Here, best keep up the strength; they aren't half bad, you know," he lied. He spat out the grass stem and began wolfing down the contents of his tin. Yet, except to check the angle of the sun, his eyes never left the road and the stream below.

"How soon?" she persisted. "Please, *Monsieur*, don't play me for a child."

"Morning, maybe," he hedged. "Eat what you can."

As a soldier himself, Cil knew full well that the Serb trooper would be missed at evening formation. He removed the flask of clear plum brandy from his pack along with a tube of salve from the first-aid kit. He offered her the flask; and when she refused, he took a good swig, felt it burn as it slithered down the lining of his throat, and waited for the fiery liquid to begin to do its work.

"They will soon come with the dogs, won't they?" she demanded anxiously.

"Not till they find him." He avoided the question.

"We must go."

His voice hardened. "Only under cover of darkness."

"But that will be hours."

"Two at the most—now take a sip of this," softening his tone. "Then, take off your shoes, and stretch out those legs."

Beneath it all, Michelle D'Orleans was frightened, terribly frightened, more frightened than she had ever been in her whole life. She had not realized that a mission could be so terribly different from the training; and her emotions, if not her mind, resented the fact, as if someone had played some foul and monstrous trick upon her. And more, she resented Cil—his unalterable bearing and confidence, and too, the way he would outright lie or color the truth in some stupid way to try to put her off. After all, had it not been she who had saved them? And then there was this thing of his drinking. Oh, she counted herself no prude, but she had been brought up under strict Catholic standards. Oh yes, and there were definite rules about that sort of thing. And no matter the crisis, regardless of how frightened she was, there was a time and a place. Yes, she had been taught that—especially about drinking—and this was certainly not the time or the place—but he had forced her.

"I didn't know you were a knife thrower," he said suddenly, smiling.

She spoke through a cloud of resentment. "Major, there is much about me you don't know—so don't bother even trying." She regretted the remark as soon as it slipped from her lips; but he seemed to ignore it.

Once she had removed her tape-reinforced street shoes—albeit reluctantly, for she was fearful of being surprised and caught in this place, he had stretched her legs out over his lap and commenced busily working the salve into her blistered feet. She could tell that the brandy was taking effect, for her mind was all over the lot, but a queer luxurious sensation seemed to drift in, flooding her body. Though still gripped by her fears, inexplicably she found herself feeling oddly expansive and elated. Yes, it had to be the brandy talking.

But there was more. She could see that her plan at last was finally beginning to bear fruit; she was back in her native Europe, doing something, something big, something of which she had always dreamed. She was fighting for a cause, for a people, her own people in a sense, those she had known and loved in her childhood who lived not so far from here, in what had come to be known as The Krajina. And best of all, she was not alone.

Being here on European soil was sort of like coming home, what with her father in the south of France and not so very far away; and then there was cousin Sonya, to the east—in Bucharest. Yes, and now she herself truly an operative on foreign soil.

Cousin Sonya had been an agent once, though the very idea still came as a shock, for she had never quite been able to visualize it, for that was not Sonya. Of course, that had been *before*; but still—Sonya? No, no; that was not the Sonya she knew, not even the Sonya she remembered as a little girl. Heavens no—Sonya? That frightfully elegant lady of charm and wealth, a woman with twenty servants, a woman with a Count and a chateau outside of Bucharest. Why, Sonya was a woman with three hundred shoes!

Despite her fears, Michelle found herself lying there quite calmly, eyes closed. She could feel Cil rubbing the salve over the scratches on her legs, but it didn't seem to hurt. She could feel his hands running over her bare skin, and a slight tingle lifted up her spine. She could feel herself smiling inside, his hands so strong; and she didn't even seem to feel the sting of the salve anymore. For the first time, she turned to him and smiled—a radiant smile straight from the depth of her. "You are a little familiar, are you not, *Cherie*?"

It was later when the sound came—hours later—so much later that the shades of the Bosnian night had already descended in that very strange way never quite familiar to outsiders, as if some giant of the heavens had suddenly slammed down a huge iron gate that shut out the world.

Amidst the black mountains of Bosnia, the weight of the night and the sounds it produces are legendary. The echoing wail of the wind shrieked down the slant of the ridges, the sound wending its way in its journey over the ledges and through the dark forest. There were ever the sounds of the night, and the night thick as pine-pitch: the eerie creaking of a nearby branch, the sounds of scurrying night creatures setting the mind to work, setting the nerves on edge. And all combining to prepare the stage—conjuring images of elves and goblins of the night who somehow inhabit this queer, far-off land.

Local folklore had it that seldom were the indigenous inhabitants so foolish as to venture out into the still forest after dark, to tempt the ghosts of night without good reason—for strange things happen out there in the night.

These two American operatives remained blissfully unaware of the incident, for it had not yet happened; but not long hence, in the throes of this earthly tempest of war—and not far distant, a key foreign diplomat, journeying through the night toward Sarajevo along a mountain road not terribly dissimilar nor distant from this one, had suddenly and violently met his end.

The official version, quite terse, suggested that the wheels of the white painted UNPROFOR armored car in which he was riding had slipped from the road due to torrential rains, plunging the vehicle over the cliff—and that may well have been true. One moment there were the confidence and security of heavy armor and solid ground, the next, the floating sensation of cascading down. But the quiet talk among the villagers would tell a different tale, for such were the ways of the Bosnian night, and the strange way it had of paying homage to distinguished foreign guests.

The sound came as abruptly as had the night. A sudden ear-splitting *crack* as Michelle and Cil lingered atop their dark, silent perch....

Cil felt Michelle jump—her arms spring wide and cling to his neck.

Both froze—stock-still—listening. As Michelle herself had put it: would they catch them right here on the very first day?

17

A few miles north, in the commander's suite at Bosnian Serb headquarters, a golden circle of light fell on the spanking-green velvet billiard table. The time was 8:42 PM. A light rap sounded at the bathroom door.

"Yes, Pavlov. What is it?"

"Comrade General. Do you wish something?" inquired the ever accommodating adjutant with the graying hair and inscrutable Mongolian features, who wore on his uniform the shoulder patch of a Captain of the Russian Army. Waiting, the aide tugged nervously at the corner of his mustache which sat on his upper lip like some dark hideous moth with wings sprung wide as if about to take flight.

"Bring me fresh towels," ordered the general.

Seconds later the door opened and Pavlov entered. The aide deposited a pile of towels on the rack next to the tub where a bearish mass of human blubber thrashed in a mountain of suds.

"Yes, yes, Captain; that will do."

The aide departed the bathroom, leaving the door standing ajar. He moved to a soft chair next to the window from which he could look reassuringly down upon the neat ranks of tanks and artillery pieces stretching to the far wire marking the end of the military compound, the scene faintly illuminated by the perimeter lights. Looking at that mass of armor always gave him comfort and confidence; he could see with assurance that the line was increasing with each passing day, and that made him smile. As the captain sipped his vodka, feeling now more comfortably safe, he threw a remark at the partly opened door.

"My inspection of the guard posts and the towers upon the dam is completed, my General. All is well."

"Don't be too smug, comrade."

"I miss your meaning, Sir."

"What of the mystery man, Private Lajtner? Have you discovered his whereabouts?"

"Ah, not yet, my General. The patrols are still out, but there is no cause for worry—the man is a beggar, a history of reckless, wayward behavior. I expect he lies drunk in the woods, or perhaps in the arms of one village wench or another in exchange for a favor. I am sure there is a simple and forthright explanation."

"Are you?" The general puzzled at how it was that lower grade officers invariably had a quick, simple, final, and absolute answer to all things large and small while a general, with a mountain of experience at his back, could scarcely be certain of next morning's coffee. Nonetheless, he went right on wiping the soapy cloth across his neck while he contemplated the confident, almost jovial tone of his junior.

At last the general rose from the waters and swung his great bulk over the lip of the tub like some great white arctic beast, vast and dripping, shaking clumps of frothy suds among his paw prints before toweling off and donning a lounging wrap. In time, he joined his junior officer in the sitting room, dropping heavily into the cushions of the elegant sofa specially shipped all the way from Moscow, positioning himself opposite his adjutant. He leaned over the coffee table, took a black cigarette from the case lying on the smoked-glass surface, affixed it to a gilded cigarette holder, and paused for the captain to touch it with flame. Russian generals often had plush accommodations, even in the field, but this room was so meticulously appointed as to suggest a fetish for culture and refinement.

"Tell me of Lajtner and of the patrols, Pavlov. What number was dispatched—when and where?" The general fingered his favorite leather riding crop never far from his side. For a moment, he eyed the carved bone figure adorning one end, the exotically chiseled Arab head set on the ebony body of a naked child; the spectacle never ceased to intrigue him.

"As to Private Lajtner," replied the adjutant, "he was last spotted leaving his post at the checkpoint next to the steel bridge at 1500 hours. When he failed to report at evening formation, a report was duly made and patrols dispatched. At this moment, two armed patrols search the roadways, a third is directed to the west side of the lake above the dam where soldiers are known to bathe by the shore."

"Yes, yes; I know all that—but no trace has been found?"

"It is early. The man has a poor record. You know this Serb rabble, my General; the man could be anywhere. I'm sure it is not a matter for concern."

At this, the General lifted one sharp brow. "Yes, yes; and the more certain you are, Captain, the more convinced I become to the contrary. You say the man was relieved of guard duty at 1500 hours. And you have personally interviewed the sentries at his post—the men of his unit?"

"Well, ah, my General; not exactly, you see...."

"What!" The gargantuan figure in the tent of a robe jumped to his feet with surprising agility.

The blow came as the captain, still seated and relaxed, was placing down his glass on the coffee table and formulating a response. It was a sudden snapping blow across the face of the knuckles with the splayed end of the leather riding crop. On the instant, an angry red welt could be seen rising on the soft yellowish flesh; it seemed to freeze all sensation in the hand.

"You say, you have neglected even to speak to his comrades?"

"Yes, my General. I mean no—but we are secure in this base, Sir." The captain, paling even under the platinum-yellow skin, was on his feet in all-out retreat from the easy chair like a mouse in attempt to escape the spring of the trap. "Why, my General, just look at the rows of tanks beyond the window here...."

"Hear me well, Captain," the general cut in. The great face of the general remained strangely impassive, though the eyes seemed to lighten, almost like an albino's, the voice, barely audible, uttered scarcely more than a whisper. "I want that man found—tonight."

"Yes, Sir." The Russian captain, himself nearly fifty, could feel himself aging with each passing second, the skin of his cheeks stiff as old parchment. The pain in his hand was fierce; he thought the knuckle above his index finger broken, but he dared not protest or flee from the room. He stole a glance at the face of his general, at the pink cherubic pigmentation of the skin, at the great enormous head showing not a single wrinkle, the forehead, smooth and broadset, yet the face devoid of important feature save the eyes. And how those eyes dominated the face. Wide-set intelligent eyes now again large and clear, deep baby-blue pools that looked startlingly gentle—a child's eyes. And now the eyes were smiling again.

"Pavlov," declared the general, "you look down at that line of tanks and guns, and you feel safe." The general looked beyond the window at the beam of the spotlights on the great white wall of the dam one mile upriver. "But now," and he looked down to inspect the leather thongs at the end of this riding crop, "you see that impressions, Captain, can be deceiving.

"Now hear me well, Captain—this Private Lajtner—I must know, what is his routine? Who are his friends? Has he ever before been known to violate the bounds of the defense perimeter? Get a list of all habits and vices. I need to hear it straight from his comrades. Meantime—double the patrols. I want the roads scoured for any and all unusual activity. And, oh yes—I want to hear from our friends in the village." The general's voice remained a whisper; he eyed the carved head at the end of the riding crop. "Oh, and Captain—dispatch the special canines."

18

Ten seconds had elapsed since Michelle, seized with panic at the sudden *wham*, had leapt into Cil's arms. Twenty—still no further sound came—thirty—the night held the specter of chill cavernous darkness.

Slowly Michelle released her death grip from around Cil's neck. A full minute passed. No hint of movement—no follow-up sound. Michelle wished beyond hope to take Cil's hand, gently, as though if she squeezed it, her whole world might collapse. Instead, she held her breath for a very long time though the frightening sound went unexplained— one of a thousand mysterious tricks of the Bosnian night?

Stealthily, as if their lives depended on each feather-light step, they made their way down through the stillness, down from their high perch to the side of the road. No foreign sound came as they paused in leafy cover at the side of the road; the smell of fresh asphalt came to them strongly.

There had to be a checkpoint. Somehow Cil knew it in his bones. But where? Perhaps they had passed it in their circuitous trek through the hard country. And by now the absence of the dead Serb soldier had surely been reported— but had he been found? His mind conjured images of gun barrels, shiny with oil, stabbing out of the blackness.

A sudden burst of light made them both start, a swift explosion of light to reflect and bounce off the ridge at their backs. Cil turned to Michelle.

"Wait for the car to pass—then follow behind." They waited for the hum of tires, then the glare of headlights approach and sweep past. They watched the beams of the headlights as they bore tunnels of light through the darkness ahead, for a few seconds clearing a path before the void of ink filled in behind. "Weapon steady," Cil commanded. "Move when I move. Don't make a sound. And listen, try not to fight it. Same as in training, the dark is our friend."

Once the taillights winked out in the distance, caution guiding their feet, they advanced up the road to the limit cleared by the headlights, then hid again, lying in wait—hiding and waiting, hiding and waiting, a maddeningly slow process. Finally Michelle plucked at his sleeve.

"The rendezvous point, how much farther?"

"Not far—hard to say."

"*Monsieur*," she said, voice alive with prideful condescension, "I could crawl faster than this." But he ignored it.

"With luck," he said, "this fresh tar will stamp out our scent."

That ended the discussion, if not the reaction. They went on this way, advancing by fits and starts, moving at the speed of a tortoise. In the space of an hour, they had covered less than a single mile, and Cil could hear the "I told you so" in her every footfall. At this hour, traffic in the mountains was next to nonexistent, the wait between cars interminable. And then finally, as the next car slid past, Michelle's tone filled with excitement.

"Look—look there!—where those headlights started around the bend!" But Cil spied only the pink dots of the taillights slide away and blink out. "There's something up there," she insisted. "Watch the bend."

Weapons leveled, on soundless feet, they crept along the

pavement under cover of darkness, aware that the first glow of headlights from behind could signal disaster. And then, when they had advanced close upon their objective, it seemed the night elves had tricked them again, for a burst of light from the rear sent them sprawling for cover.

Flat down on their stomachs, their necks craned with caution, they waited—watching. Presently the burst of light from behind narrowed to approaching headlights, followed by the distant growl of a heavy engine. In a few minutes, the reflected light of its passing revealed the outline of a dump truck. It lumbered on past, coughing and grinding, belching out a cloud of choking exhaust fumes that clung to the road.

As soon as the ancient truck reached the curve up ahead, abruptly the shadowed figure of a man bolted out into the splash of the headlights. A tall man, the lantern in his hand waving in quick, jerky motions, bathed in the bright pool of light. A shouted command ignited the truck's brake lights, and the heavy truck ground to a halt. At once, a string of curses emanated from the truck cab.

As if on cue, two other uniformed figures swarmed out into the pool of light. At their appearance, as if the perpetrator were suddenly stricken, the string of obscenities from the cab died on the wind, followed by a sound like the crashing of a blunt object against heavy metal. One of the headlights winked out.

In a shallow ditch, Michelle and Cil lay still as death. They could feel the wet grass and smell the exhaust fumes. Over the noise of the truck's engine, the sound of the voices came to the pair only vaguely. At the tinkle of glass striking the pavement, the ancient truck gunned its engine, and spitting and belching, it roared away into the night. A moment passed, the lantern switched off, the darkness was total.

"I count four," reported Michelle in a bare whisper.

"Four, yes. And the uniforms. Did you catch it?"

"Same as the sidewalk policemen in Mostar."

"But listen." Without the noise of the truck's powerful engine, the voices came to them clearly.

"Serb!"

"Shhh. Wolves in sheep's clothing. Masquerading in the garb of the local police—as if the natives couldn't tell."

"Then why...."

"Quiet."

"But how do we get past?" she whispered softly, "around that curve...."

"Not a curve," he corrected. In the reach of the truck lights, Cil had spotted the symmetrical rails. "A bridge. A long steel bridge set off at an angle. Shhh!" Suddenly a burst of light ignited the sky.

"What is it?"

"Get back—a *searchlight!*"

19

At the door of the guard hut, a hastily constructed shack of tin and boards set against the side of the bridge, one Serb private was speaking.

"Will you listen to that ungrateful bastard—cursing us? Us who come to save him. Stupid bastard Muslim."

"Very brave," added the second private, swiveling the searchlight mounted on the edge of the bridge, rotating its beam, aiming it into the gorge below. "Best to abandon the lot of filthy Turks!"

"Hah," uttered the third. "You see how fast the great Mohammed loses his tongue when we all come to greet him."

"Enough!" snarled the corporal, rifle in hand. "You have your orders—a patrol at midnight to search for Private Lajtner!"

"What a break," grumbled the second private, catching a lone deer in the searchlight beam below the bridge, a speckled fawn traversing the base of the canyon below. "Another night without sleep," he grumbled. "And all for the likes of Lajtner, the lazy oaf, who no doubt slumbers somewhere under a tree."

"Look alive!" commanded the corporal, swinging out the

butt of his rifle in a menacing gesture for no apparent reason, so that it grazed the shin of the second private manning the searchlight. But the private, insensitive to minor physical punishment, paid it no heed, his full attention suddenly focused on the fawn whose eyes shone like large yellow buttons in the beam of the spotlight, the fawn charging madly into boulders and trees to escape the dazzling light.

"Hey, look," cried the third private, raising and cocking his weapon as the others crowded around, and the crash of a discarded beer bottle sounded off a rock far below. At first, the men seemed merely amused until the first surge of blood-lust began to take hold. "Hah, look at her spring, like a cat with a kerosened tail."

"Get the little fundamentalist bastard," shouted the first.

"Watch this!"

The first three shots flew wide, merely raising a deafening clamor, echoing off the canyon below, causing the fawn to spring ever more frantically. The fourth shot winged the young deer so that a dark stream of blood spurted from a wound in the neck, spattering the legs; it thrashed only weakly in a grotesque, circular pattern.

"Watch the car," growled the corporal, his eyes squinting down the road through his spectacles at a reflection of approaching headlights caressing the treetops.

"We stop this one?" inquired the first private as the oncoming headlights popped into view.

"Not if it is but a poor farmer. Only if it is suspicious!" commanded the corporal.

"But Comrade Corporal—unless we stop every one, who can tell in the dark which is suspicious?"

"Do I make the orders?" snarled the corporal. The whack of the gunstock struck off the young recruit's skull, causing a small echo to ricochet off the steep canyon walls.

20

The rendezvous point, a remote Swiss chalet on the far side of the village, crouched like a hound dog on a rise above the road, the house shrouded in darkness but for a dim orange bulb set at the peak of the roof. Not much of a house really—a crudely constructed shack flanked by a stable.

The two strangers circled around to the back of the house and rapped lightly at the door, twice—then once—then twice again. Expectantly they waited. Anxious murmurs erupted from within, followed by a flurry of scuffling feet. The curtain in the second story window ruffled aside, a breathless motion; then an interior light snapped on. It was 12:05 AM.

Slowly the door inched ajar. Then abruptly a short stocky man with the shoulders of a bull reached out one meaty arm, seized Cil by the shirt front, and hauled him inside. Then the man, noting Michelle in the doorway, nodded graciously, and helped her inside, noiselessly swinging the door shut behind them and bolting it securely.

A frail-looking woman of about seventy, with unkempt hair and the twitching cheeks of a field mouse, scampered frantically down the stairs from the second floor, one hand clutching together her housecoat.

The Divan—the windowless all-purpose first floor room of old Turkish construction, used in harsh weather for cooking, eating, sitting and sleeping—looked clean and neat and compactly furnished. The smell of wood smoke issued from a cast-iron cooking stove set next to the back door, an ancient coffee pot steaming eerily on its lid. A small round table with crudely crafted chairs occupied the center of the room above a bare wooden floor that spoke of a life of endless toil and poverty. Yet, incongruously, covering the table lay a delicately embroidered cloth with matching napkins rolled in finely-carved wooden rings, all neatly arranged to mark each place. Tacked to the right-hand wall above the table was a poster-painting of a dying Christ, and on shelves below was set a miniature altar surrounded by carved figurines carefully arranged as might be found in any strictly religious Catholic home.

Rifles and shotguns and the equipment of a hunter cluttered the corners of the room; and tacked to the left-hand wall below the stairway was a bear skin so black and enormous it somehow seemed real and alive.

"Zeljko is the name," growled the old man fiercely. "You are late—woman!" And in addressing his wife, he neither turned nor looked at her. "Whiskey! Why you are late?" the challenge exploding in his native Serbo-Croatian tongue.

Cil turned to face the man squarely, but responded in English. "Trouble—trouble on the way."

"What trouble?" the old man's manner remaining at once testy and guarded—though the language was *English*. The old woman, her movements quick and jerky, moved to a shelf in the corner, returning with three chipped coffee mugs which she set on the center table. With a nod, Zeljko motioned the newcomers to be seated at the table, turning his own chair around to sit in it backwards, his thick-muscled arms resting on the curving back of the chair, his heavy square whiskered jaw jutting accusingly.

"Tell me—what trouble?" he demanded in the manner of a prosecutor.

"We killed a man."

"What—kill, you say?"

"That's right. A Serb soldier."

Michelle glimpsed terror on the old woman's face as she caught her husband's eye, but he reacted calmly.

"How you know he a Serb?"

"The uniform."

The old man's voice lashed out. "All soldiers have the uniform. One look like all other."

"No." Cil's tone remained cool and controlled. "Papers. In his wallet, the man had papers."

For a moment the old man sat back in his chair, ignoring the world, picking at his teeth. "The killing—where?"

"By the stream, south of the road block."

"They spot you—they follow?" he asked quickly, glaring at Cil.

"No. Unless they have dogs."

"Dogs?" Michelle observed the way the old man tensed in his chair. "Much soldiers—much equipment—and dogs! Our men, they watch enemy compound all hours the day. What time the killing?"

"Two—three hours before dark—4:30 your time."

The old lady stood over the table struggling to steady the upturned bottle of whiskey with both hands; yet, when she attempted to pour, her hands shook uncontrollably. The old man, however, though his faced flushed with rage, retained his composure. He tossed down a stiff drink as the woman, catching her husband's eye, gestured slyly and made for the stairway.

The old man excused himself to follow, and somewhat later from above came noise of a muffled conversation, then the gruff sound of a male voice. "Woman—some day, your nerves, they be the death of us all. Keep watch on the road; soon come the patrol."

In a minute, old Zeljko reappeared with a map.

"Show me close where you kill the Serb." But now patient deliberation had come to his voice.

Cil studied the map for but a few seconds though it was of stringy brown paper and a larger scale than his own.

"There." He planted a finger where the stream bed ran east of the road.

"And you bury him there, yes?"

"Bury, no." And when Cil had completed his explanation, the old man sat back, frowning, thoughtfully rubbing his gray stubble of beard; but after a moment the frown was replaced by a slight sparkle in the eye.

"And the car? Show me clear where you give up the car?"

When Cil had carefully described the dump and his procedure of disposal, Zeljko leaned so far back in his chair that his head brushed against the poster of the Savior. For the briefest instant, his countenance exhibited a line of strong, square, white teeth, a noticeable space invading the upper two at the front—which in no way detracted from the warmth of his smile.

"Still, there must be precautions," he said at length. "Woman—more whiskey."

He lapsed into silence, waiting for his whiskey, while his wife, her face a knot of suspicion and fear, ran downstairs to splash each mug with whiskey. After which she remained only long enough to, with quick, precise movements of her hands, reposition the napkin holders in front of each place with determined exactness.

For a moment Cil carefully studied the old man, the worn overalls, the denim shirt mended almost beyond repair, and on his feet, workboots muddied and ancient. So far as Cil could see, a bright crimson scarf thrown round his neck appeared to be the man's single concession to vanity.

Once the old mountain man had tossed down his whiskey, Cil spoke with insistence.

"What about the dogs?"

"Later, later; we are to see. Now show me." The old man tapped an impatient forefinger against the map. "Show me here every inch of the way from the killing to my door."

And while Cil traced the route, the old man scrutinized each move of his finger on the map. Then, for the first time, the old man turned to Michelle, though his words were for Cil.

"And this—this is your woman?"

Michelle came to her feet with such alacrity, her chin upturned in the process. "I am the woman of no man," she challenged. "And about the killing. It was I that...."

"It was she who spotted the guard hut," Cil put in quickly. "And thank God for that!"

Old Zeljko had not spied them while she remained seated at the table, but now with her standing, he observed Michelle's light street shoes and the patchwork of scratches and welts that quilted her legs below the hem of her dress. A curt command brought his wife scampering back downstairs to fetch and return a few minutes later with a set of men's workclothes and a pair of sturdy woman's hiking boots, a small item tucked in the top of one boot. Then, as shyly as a country bumpkin, the old man plucked out the tube of disinfectant and slid it across the table to Miss D'Orleans.

"Is all there is here in the mountains," was all he would say, and she took the time to pass her thanks to him through the warmth of her smile. "Rub it on good," he admonished. "Then we go."

At this last, Cil addressed him curtly, nodding at the map.

"Here, on the map—show me the way to the ruins."

The old man's reaction came swift and direct, his finger drawing a straight firm line from their present location. Cil came up with a start as the old man's finger traced across a snaking blue line on the way to its destination.

"But that river? Why, even in daylight...."

"Tonight!" snapped old Zeljko. He was looking at Michelle. "With the killing—we go tonight!"

"With the rain, the river is up!" Cil burst out, and he, too, looked at Michelle. "A night crossing—that is impossible!"

For once, a chuckle of amusement erupted from way deep in the old man's chest.

"Here in the mountains, Americano," all the while coolly eyeing Cil, "the impossible is the way of our life."

Without more, Zeljko jumped to his feet. "Woman!" He shouted up the stairway. "When the patrol, it is past, saddle the horses. We go." He plucked a jacket from a peg on the wall, snapped up his rifle from where it leaned in the corner, sniffed the coffee pot on the stovetop, then stole off into the night.

21

The three riders, in pale moonlight, shot away from the house, cascading down, galloping through the trees in a lather. It was only when they reached cover at the hem of the forest that the little troupe held up, Zeljko cocking one ear to the wind.

"Listen—listen fast," his tone triumphant. "Tar oil— already they begin the spray of the road. Then let those bloodhounds fill their fat noses. Hah!—they not smell a good beef in a week."

For the first of August, it seemed astonishingly cold here in the mountains, and Cil could hear the low-throated rumble of a distant engine; it sounded like the same ancient dump truck encountered at the roadblock on the way in. He glanced at the luminous dial of his watch, thinking of the patrols, of the Serb trooper lying dead back there on the bank of the stream. It was 12:47 AM.

When they had progressed but a few miles down a trail through the woods, the old man in the lead abruptly lifted his arm, like a cavalry captain reining in his horse. The riders dismounted. And now in the stillness, their ears caught a new sound. Without explanation, Zeljko advanced on foot, leading his mount in the silvery half light of the moon.

When he reached a certain spot, he halted, inclining his head—listening.

Michelle emitted a gasp and drew back. In speckled moonlight through the branches, the giant trees seemed to march along the forest floor in normal fashion until they reached a certain point. And then there was nothing—an open abyss. It appeared they had come to the end of the earth, a void so deep and so vast as to echo only of time and time past; only the muted roar of the river below could be heard in the night.

"Bad, yes," allowed old Zeljko matter-of-factly. "But with friends on our heels—is no other way."

Michelle and Cil, shocked into silence, unwilling to admit, much less share their own fears, paid one another not the slightest attention.

Without ceremony, the old man led off. Rather, his great muscled plow horse led off over the edge while the old man, on foot behind, inched forward slowly, clutching the thick, swishing tail of his horse for support. Michelle and Cil watched in solemn disbelief as the old man, in what could only be viewed as a monstrous act of faith or contrition, willed himself over the edge and down into the abyss. To the observers, it seemed a right of passage reserved for the condemned. First, the huge plow horse, then the old man—both swallowed up by the night.

Only when both had vanished from sight did their disappearance evoke the most god-awful clamor. Thrashing and crashing noises seemed to rise up from the very bowels of the earth, only to die away as quickly as they had begun, the sounds replaced by the same ominous thunder of swift, rushing waters from somewhere below.

Placing aside their separate fears as best they could conceal them, the two trained operatives followed in turn under full pack, assault weapons slung over their shoulders, each in turn and by example grasping the tail of their horse. And then, swiftly as the earth dropped away, pure desperation flung out desperate hands to grasp at rocks and roots and low-lying scrub brushing past. Led by their mounts, robbed of breath, each descended behind bright, sparking hooves striking stones in the darkness, one moment the horses pawing gingerly down the steep graveled embankment, the next, the great beasts stumbling blindly, hooves clacking and skidding, kicking up miniature rock slides.

And then, at last, they were down. Shaking off dirt and debris as they shook off their fears, buoyed by the security of *terra firma* once again firmly planted underfoot, with the combs of their hands they brushed twigs and leaves from the strands of their hair, struggling to conceal a frantic gasping for breath.

Here on the riverbank, talking was out of the question; the noise of the black, rushing waters required one to shout to be heard. Close by the shore, fingers of moonlight gilded the ripples and cast them in silver; but farther out where the water ran deep, the current swept along, dark and swift.

Zeljko, leading his mount, wound his way among the huge boulders lining the riverbank, traversing mounds of smooth pebbles that slid underfoot like pebbles of ice, until he reached the spot that he wanted. In a calm, almost business-like manner, he unhitched a coil of rope notched over the pommel of his saddle, which the others had earlier failed to observe.

"We cross here!" he bellowed over the noise of the current, and Michelle stepped up and shouted in his ear. "How deep?"

"All the horses can handle," the old man now fully absorbed, toiling with the coil of rope as he turned to Cil.

"Watch!" he shouted. "First I go with the rope. You hold rope in both hand." He was shouting, but his voice could barely be heard. "When the rope no more move in your hand—follow. Send first the girl." He waited for each's nod of understanding. "If the horse lose his feet in the current, ay, let him go!" And now he was much amused, grinning like a child, showing his big, square, white teeth as he nodded his head. "Then is my job to reel you in." He crouched low where he stood, demonstrating with the rope, hand over hand, and again waited for the uncertain nods.

Old Zeljko, winding one end of the python of rope around a tree trunk jutting from the riverbank, knotted it double. Then, mounting up with the coil of rope over his shoulder, cautiously he coaxed his big plodding plow horse out into the current, paying out rope as he went. Then the rump of his horse was down in the current, all but submerged; and all that could be seen of the old man in the pale light was the outline of his back, stretching out the distance. Cil held the rope, feeding it out through his fingers, a dark living thing, slithering, feeling the prickly strands of hemp attacking his palms, feeling the slow steady motion of the rope as it gathered dimension and weight, gauging its tension. Finally it stilled in his hands.

Then the rope pulled taut and remained so, and he could tell that the old man had secured the rope to a stout object on the far bank of the river. He turned to Michelle.

She was standing very close; he could smell the perspiration and the musky woman scent of her. He thought he caught a smile on her lips as she nodded and adjusted her pack. And then she mounted up, and he was thinking of the smile, but she was all sternness as she seized the taut rope from him and slipped it under her arm to slide through as she advanced on the river.

On the far bank, the old man was worried, his thoughts clouded, guilt-ridden. "I do not know what my old friend and colonel would do with his niece in these conditions." Standing there alone, he was speaking into the roar of the river. "Surely he does not let her stay the night in my humble house—not with the danger—ay. He, too, know what happen to a woman if they find her." Unconsciously he crossed himself. "No, no; you are right to come—but dear God, what if I lose her now here in the current? What could

I tell him? What would I think if it were my child, my Nedo?"

Then he checked himself. "Zeljko, you bumpkin, you act the fool. What if? What if? Hah, he would do as you do—exactly. But no, he does not stand here by the river to whimper like a whipped pup." Still, old Zeljko could not clear his conscience. "But only do I wish it not the little niece of my colonel."

Michelle D'Orleans leaned forward in the saddle. With one sharp thrust of her heels to the flanks of her mount, she started across, holding the reins in her hands, her back sternly erect, the safety rope moving steadily through the crook of her elbow.

Cil could not help but study her progress with rising alarm. The roar of the current thundered in his ears. He could see the great inky mass surging on past. He wanted to speak, to shout to her; he wanted to shout out some warning to aid and assure her safe passage. But already she was away, moving across.

He watched her ride forward into the current—lower, ever lower, above the bulk of her mount. And then he saw. When the withers of her horse reached the level of the current, instead of grasping the rope more tightly, to his shock and amazement, he watched her *cast it aside* with an arrogant gesture.

Cil, with uncomprehending eyes, stared at her moving away. Vainly he clutched the taut rope at water's edge, clutching it sympathetically in both hands—as if that might save her. He watched her slim back recede into the night, and somehow the sight of her moving away drew her closer to him. He watched the silvery beam of moonlight play on her back, then shrink with the distance to a vague shimmering glow. He could feel the pound of his heart in his chest, and it surprised him. Now the horse was far down in the current, and the outline of her back scarcely more than a mark on the surface. She was nearly across. Though he never prayed, he prayed now, fervently. The seconds seemed months.

And then he felt it—the slight snap of the rope in his hands. The signal—she was over!

When Special Forces Operative Michelle D'Orleans safely reached the far bank and dismounted, the old man beckoned her to the lee of a huge boulder where the roar of the current was less.

"I sorry about the crossing this night," he said, "but, well, you see, there is no choice." He was shouting to be heard; he was shouting in the way some men might if trying to appease their conscience. "Before, I think to cross in the morning light, but now, you see...."

"It is all right," she cut in. Michelle, seeing his pain, placed a silent kiss on the old weathered cheek.

"You ride very good," he shouted, and with his heavy hand, patted her shoulder, roughly, like the paw of some great friendly beast.

Cil, alone on the opposite bank, steadied himself and untied the rope from the tree. Securing it round his waist and knotting it carefully, he leaned forward and spurred his mount down into the stream. The water was ice. The thunder of the current deafened his ears. As his mount sank ever deeper in the current, he could still smell the sweat of the horse, feel the goose bumps standing out on his legs—and he could sense the rise of his fear. The black roaring force of the current tore at his thighs.

Now his mount was low in the current, oh, so low—and deep. With the saddle all but submerged, Cil suddenly felt a slight floating sensation. Fear changed to panic, the panic hooking his boots ever more securely in the stirrups, forcing his legs to squeeze the flanks of the great animal so tightly that his thigh muscles ached.

When it came, it came quickly—at first, a quiet second of weightlessness—a stab of foreknowledge. Why, he seemed to be drifting—drifting free—sliding away. He was down in the black water—holding his breath—hands grasping the rope. The horse! Where is the damned horse?

The force of the current was driving him down. Where his hands clung to the rope, the tug of the current yanked both arms straight up over his head, as those of the condemned on the gallows clasping the rope as they kicked open the trap. He hung on the rope, the entire weight of his body dragged by the pull of the current.

After a while, his mind seemed to change, even welcomed the sensation of weightlessness, enjoying the sensation of the hemp biting into his hands where he held it. He could feel the rushing water caressing his cheeks, pleasantly. He inhaled his first mouthful of water, yet still he hung on, the current sucking him down. He could see himself as a small boy crying into his mother's full gathered skirts, she patting his head with a comforting hand. He could smell the aroma of the colonel's pipe, see that clever smile slightly slanted, like Sonya's smile.

What he could not see was the great muscular frame of old Zeljko, hunkered down on the far bank, leg and back muscles taut, straining, the tug of the rope so great on his arms as he hauled away as to cause the heels of his boots to begin to slide in the pebbles of the riverbank, his hands burning under the terrible weight of the rope.

Cil could not see his own body swaying with the current at the end of the rope. Nor could he see the expression on the face of Michelle.

22

With a sense of rapt anticipation, the riders broke over a rise below the peak of the mountain. Suddenly above them towered a medieval ruin, its silhouette at once ghostly, mysterious, its ramparts somehow suspended in the abundant moonlight, its outline stark in silvered relief against the night sky. To Michelle D'Orleans, as she sat astride her mount peering skyward, it was dreamlike—a great fairyland castle shimmering in the moonlight, peering out above the mists that clung to the treetops. Above the parapets grew needle-like spires and turrets that spiraled up into the sky. The castle commanded a view of the landscape for miles.

As they moved on up the trail, Michelle's mind was on Cil. She could still see it clearly in her mind, how at first she had been so sure she had lost him to the river; and once again she berated herself. Charged with full knowledge that Cil was no horseman, never should she have permitted him to attempt the crossing alone. Vividly did she recall how she and the old man had dragged him from the dark waters, evacuated the water from his lungs, restarted his breathing, then labored to restore circulation and warmth by rubbing his arms and legs. And it was still with an aching inner pain that she recalled his first words as he came back to this world. He had cried out for help. He had cried out for his precious *Sonya.*

Zeljko was riding behind the mount of his charge, the niece of his colonel. He was recalling how, back at the riverbank, they had positioned the wobbly American on the broad back of the workhorse, propped up and bound with rope to his, Zeljko's, own back. And now Zeljko could feel the pressure of the American's arms around his waist, and he could tell that the Yankee major was finally coming back to himself. But still he puzzled at how the High Command could have thrust upon him this Yankee officer—a man who could not even sit a horse! What good could such a man be on a mission in these mountains? Yet, even his, Zeljko's own brother in America, Marko, servant of the colonel, had known this Yankee in the past and vouched for him stoutly. And not only Marko, but Zeljko's old friend and commander, the colonel. After all, had it not been Colonel Anastasi who had named the man personally?

For a moment the old man looked off in the distance, shaking his head. No, he himself would reserve judgment. For what could you do with a man foolish enough to reveal himself to a Serb trooper in the very first hours—then wait on a woman to come to his rescue? A woman! Oh, it had not been stated in so many words, but it took no brains to see it was the woman who had saved him.

And then, what of this queer business to stage a false rape? Yes, he had to admit, a clever piece of business. And it might even throw the enemy off the track; but where would it lead? No, he didn't like it. Just like those movies of the old American west on late night TV from Belgrade. Hah—cowboys and Indians—just like a damned foreigner.

And what of his poor Theresa left back at the house— what of her safety? But at the thought, he pulled himself up short. No, he was a soldier again; a soldier could not permit himself the luxury to think of such things.

And the girl? Yet, he had watched her skill as she worked over the half-drowned Yankee major. But Lord—a woman against the Serbs?

No, no; she was a child, and a reckless child at that. For, hadn't he watched the insolent way in mid-river she had thrown off the very safety rope against his instructions? Bah! A mere headstrong child—anything but not a well-trained, disciplined soldier. And for what? All to impress the Yankee? The old man gave his shaggy head another shake of bewilderment. Still, what other reason could there be? For hadn't he himself, Zeljko, seen the way she had worked over the major to bring him around? Hell, even an old man could spot that kind of feeling in a woman when he saw it. But then, afterward—and still he puzzled at the change in her behavior. For, as soon as the Yankee had finally come to, instantly was she the very picture of a prim, clucking barnyard hen pecking away the attentions of the rooster!

No, no; the set-up was a disaster. With his own son, Nedo, exposed on the far shore of the lake with that Englishman, there could be no room for mistake.

Cil, riding piggy-back on the old man's horse, could feel himself finally coming around. He could feel the exhaustion deep in his bones and knew it must be even worse for Michelle. Yet, there she was, riding ahead, back ramrod-straight, the very picture of the damned colonel.

And he could only guess what they must be thinking of him, with first the killing on the way in, and now nearly lost in the river? And then there was this old mountain man. After all, what use could a sharp-tongued, cantankerous, old man be? What could he possibly know of discipline, tactics, and stealth? Cil's mind darted ahead.

It was the official thumbs-down on radio communication that troubled him most. Obviously Washington was sufficiently dubious about the success of the mission to insist on absolute deniability above all else. And now that he had made such a fool of himself in this very first stage, he could see dark clouds ahead. To display the slightest physical or command weakness before a man of the mountains like Zeljko, well, that could only serve to compound the problems that lay ahead.

Cil was thinking of the tactical situation; the castle was far from the ideal site from which to stage an operation. While a convenient location, there were serious drawbacks; chief among them was the existence of only the single escape route. As distinct from the mode of fourteenth century warfare when a fortress was as impregnable to most as heaven's gates, in modern warfare the possibility of his small force being surrounded in a virtual trap with all avenues of escape cut off amounted to a daunting prospect indeed, the more so when considered against the prospect of incessant bombing, or mortar and artillery attack. Still and all, if his small band were to be limited to primitive means of communication, it was best, at the least, to command the heights.

At the edge of the trees, with the castle looming above them, the old man pulled up and dismounted. Raising his head to the ramparts, thrice did he give the shrill squawk of a wild bird, then stand back, awaiting the return call.

But no signal came. The others sensed his alarm. The only sounds were the restless snort and pawing of hooves on soft ground, and the eerie murmur of the wind in the trees—a plaintive, mournful sound.

23

The castle gate stood naked and unguarded. One good shove swung it wide, and Michelle could sense the old man's stunned chagrin as the little party passed without challenge.

Once within the courtyard, she could see that the castle was indeed a ruin as the three in the cool night air picked their way around piles of corroded stone and rubble from the crumbling outer walls. In places it was impossible to tell at what level the courtyard had originally stood. And now, wary, with clear trepidation, they inched open the heavy entrance door, peering inside.

The Great Hall stood enormous and airy, all but vacant of furnishings, and Cil noted its crude construction of rough-hewn stone—the floor, the walls, the towering ceiling. In deep shadow and dominating the room hung an ancient chandelier, the great pointed structure hammered out of wrought iron and poised on a length of chain, like the Sword of Damocles, above a center table.

On the long-planked table huddled two figures before a lone candle playing a game of cards. The light of the candle cast bloated shadows of the cardplayers on the great wall at the back of the room.

A tall, proud-looking woman, perhaps in her mid-thirties, stood remote from the players on the left of the room, laboring before an open hearth. She bent to stir a pot above the flame.

At the first bark of the old man's voice, the cardplayers started like thieves in the night.

"You there—One Eye!" And even in the firelight, Michelle could see the way Zeljko's face flushed crimson. His great shaggy head thrust forward from his shoulders like a man girding for battle.

Both of the strange men were short and swarthy, the elder sporting a black patch over one eye, and it was toward him that Zeljko directed the force of his wrath. "Once more fail my orders, and I kill you where you stand! Now go—take the watch!"

The one-eyed gypsy leapt away like a fly from a wall, snatching up his carbine. He flitted up a set of steep inner stone steps that the others had failed to earlier observe, and which led to an archway in the wall high above them, leading out onto the ramparts.

"Worthless trash!" spat the old man, still raging. And as swiftly as the one-eyed gypsy vanished from sight, the old man himself quit the room. The others had seen the hurt and shame etched on the old man's face that such an important order had gone unobeyed. But in a moment Zeljko reappeared, loaded down with a bulging wineskin.

He nodded to the tall, gently-smiling woman at the hearth before turning on the remaining cardplayer.

"Go, you rabid Chipmunk! Go this minute and tend to the horses."

But at the mention of his name, the second gypsy, Chipmunk, a bare wisp of a man, beamed at the others with a carefree air. He was dressed in loose-fitting clown clothes the colors of the rainbow, bright with long flowing sleeves, his baggy pants secured at the waist with a crimson sash. The little man, completely unhurried, bowed from the waist at the strangers in a solemn, theatrical gesture, seemingly unaffected by the old man's abuse. Adjusting the checkered kerchief covering his head and trailing off down the neck, he took leave of the room with a flourish of color and movement, with each tossing goose step, kicking up his loose-fitting velvet pantaloons as he carelessly made for the door.

Holding a candle before him, Old Zeljko guided Cil and Michelle to a room at the back where he excused himself to check on the lookout. A cache of ammunition and weapons, odd blankets for bedding, and other supplies were scattered about the room, and Cil took a quick inventory once he had slid off his pack. Then guided by the wavering candle, the newcomers swiftly reconnoitered the lower back rooms of the castle.

When they reentered the Great Hall, the tall, proud-looking woman was still tending the open hearth, and now at closer quarters, Michelle could see the delicate hands, the kind open face, and, too, that the woman was clad in a dress far too finely cut for her surroundings. Fingers of steam licked above the lip of the cast iron pot on the flames, a spicy aroma scenting the air with a cheerful note of welcome. The woman, noting the haggard appearance of the travelers, came graciously forward and offered a curtsy; a quiet open smile played on her lips. And now alone with the new arrivals, she pressed their hands in turn, addressing the pair in flawless English.

"I am Bogana of the village below, but please call me Bogey, everyone does." She appeared most alert and composed, a note of refinement in her voice and mien, her dress wholly incongruous to her surroundings, her teeth, small and white and exquisitely formed.

"Zeljko has been so worried for your safety," she said. "Please take my word, you have long been expected, and you are welcome—come." Her tone was at once sincere and sweetly maternal. "Sit with me; try some of my hot squirrel stew. I think you may find it warm and tasty. Yes, yes; in no time, you will feel yourselves again."

Cil, still a bit unsteady on his feet, sat thankfully down at the table while the woman, Bogey, served steaming bowls of the delicious stew. Shedding all inhibition, Cil and Michelle ate ravenously, shoveling the food into their empty stomachs without formality.

Now openly concerned with Cil's condition, the more so for the presence of another attractive woman, Michelle made a show of fussing about, tending him zealously, then picked large tin mugs from pegs on the wall, and served the sweet red nectar from the wineskin the old man had provided. Cil finished one cup only to have Bogey, with ever the considerate eye, refill it under the ever watchful glances of Michelle. When at last they had finished the meal, Michelle insisted that Cil change out of his wet clothes, then sit before the open hearth while the two women busied about cleaning up. Yet, once Cil found himself exposed to the warmth of the fire, he suddenly felt the depth of his exhaustion. But Michelle in her youth appeared quite immune to fatigue as she went about her chores, displaying open deference to this woman Bogana who called herself Bogey, even more to Cil whom she clearly considered her charge.

When the old man returned, Cil, feeling somewhat renewed, first drew Zeljko aside for a few moments, then seated he and the two women opposite himself at the table. Once cigarettes were offered around, and everyone lighting up and sipping the cool, local wine, Cil spoke firmly and plainly, first addressing the old man.

"Baxter, the Englishman? He has already arrived?"

The old man looked up and nodded. "Three days past. He take up position on the hill opposite—with my boy, Nedo, and his band."

"And besides the two gypsies, how many sentries have you posted?"

"Only the childish gypsies and myself, but the twins, they

are expected tomorrow."

Michelle's eyes met Cil's only briefly, but Cil looked to both women.

"All right. I have spoken already with Zeljko, and we are agreed. From here on, Michelle, you take charge of communications and all operations here at the castle and the surrounding grounds and approaches: lookouts, provisions, and supplies as well as care of the men as they arrive. It seems that Bogey here," and he proffered her a knowing glance, "can show you the ropes."

And now he addressed them all, and there was newfound authority in his voice.

"From this minute forward, the operation begins. It will be over in a matter of days. That's right—days. And it must be clearly understood, Zeljko and I will be fully occupied with operations. If problems arise, somehow you women must deal with them yourselves.

"And one thing more—there have been mistakes. There will be no more mistakes." And now he grinned. "Especially my own." And there was cheer enough in that bashful grin to embrace the whole party.

At length, Cil eyed each one of them in turn. "Be sure to remember—security comes first. All weapons, supplies, and ammunition must be removed to the tunnel at dawn. No sign of life may be left to a curious eye, do you follow? Inside the castle or out. From here on, I'm sorry to say," and he turned to Bogey and nodded, "there can be no fires, cooking or otherwise, within the castle ruins. Few things carry more distance than the sight or smell of a campfire. Now, where are the horses hidden?"

"Down from the castle, under cover of trees," replied Zeljko.

"Good. Then let's get a native gypsy lean-to set up by the horses, a simple structure of raw canvas, you know, with gypsy clothes hung about, drying in the trees. Yes, and a cooking pit. That ought to explain the odd human presence in case of an enemy patrol straying afield—and, too, the horses so close to the castle and the number of telltale hoofprints." Cil looked inquiringly at Zeljko. "Horse stealing, I take it, is not yet a lost art to gypsies in the region?" to which the old man nodded sagely.

Once old Zeljko had received his orders and seen Major Cil and Miss D'Orleans to their quarters, not trusting the frivolous gypsies, he mounted the steps to the high parapet, and there dispatched the gypsy, One-Eye, to the lookout post guarding the mountain's northern approaches while he positioned himself in the ramparts where he could scrutinize the alertness of both gypsies at their posts, and if need be, signal them with an assortment of bird calls. It was 3:24 AM.

The night, hushed and placid under a benevolent moon, gave old Zeljko in the ramparts a sense of peace and wellbeing as he looked off down the mountain at the shimmering waters of the lake at its base, and the dam to the left. From the far shore of the lake rose the dark silhouette of a hill with a rounded top bare of trees, like some broad-shouldered giant with a light-colored cap rising up from the shimmering waters. He stood thinking of his only son. At this hour his Nedo, too, would be standing watch on the crest of that hill.

And what about the safety of his beloved Theresa, his woman, left back there alone at the house? He crossed himself hastily and looked to the sky. But surely it was true; he himself had been given no choice; he had had to leave her; why, an empty house at the edge of the village with patrols out?

No, he did not know about this Yankee major. For his own money, he would take a plain mountain man any day, a man like the giant Moslem known as The Professor, who knew these mountains as he himself knew them.

And the girl? He wondered what the niece of his old colonel really thought of his own woman, Theresa. And as the mind of an old man is wont to do, his mind floated back over the years to another day and time. He could see it right there in his mind good and clear.

He recalled the very day of his wedding fifty years past. He and his Theresa, yes; they had both been young and eager in those days. It had been just after Marshall Tito had formally taken over the government in Belgrade, and he, Zeljko, been released from his first hitch of military service, so there wasn't much money. For sure it had not been much of a church, just the old village chapel. And the whole village there, all his comrades and good drink and having a time. Yes, that and the brown-hooded old priest. Oh, how the liquor had flowed on that day. And those damned ole two note bells. That was the way he always referred to those ancient chapel bells—three bells there were, but only the two ever working.

Now his great chest expanded. Yes, that was his woman, with a damned good eye with a needle, if he did say so himself, and a fine worker, too. So what if she might be a little nervous in these last troubled years? Why, hadn't she borne him a good strong son?

His features saddened. In the crossing this night, he had lost a fine horse to the river. Not just any old horse, but his long-time companion, *El Perezoso* (The Lazy One). It had been a sickly *El Perezoso* that he had purchased as a young colt from the kindly old Jew whose people had, centuries earlier, fled here from Spain, so he had kept the name. Yes, and had it not been he himself who had tended and nursed, who had fed and trained that ornery bastard colt through every affliction known to man? *El Perezoso*, who year by year had since toiled at his side in the quiet poverty of the fields. Yes, it was true; he had become used to that stubborn, lazy, good-for-nothing. And now comes this smart young Yankee—who can't even sit a horse.

He was thinking again of the American. Still and all, a man had to be given his due. There he was one minute, half dead by the river, and then, not two hours past it, taking charge and barking out orders like a damned general. What had surprised him most was the fact that the man was not handing out blame about he himself, Zeljko, and the gypsies' falling down on the job, but spotting with a quick eye what must be done and spitting out orders like nothing had happened. Well, it was true; if he had his own way, he would have gone for a mountain man. But if this is what his brother, Marko, could support, and what his old colonel commanded—well, his colonel was his leader, and he would do his duty.

But it was a hard pill for a man to swallow just the same—and how all those things could happen to one man in a single day?

At this moment, old Zeljko was looking across the lake at the hill opposite where preparations would already be underway. He felt a chill wind at his back as he reflected upon the American major and the mission ahead. What was it his woman always said? "On some poor creatures of this earth, bad luck grows like a wart on the nose."

24

August 2, 1995—5:47 AM....Day 2. On the second floor of the headquarters building in the Serb compound, General Nikolai Kerenofski, line general of the Russian Army—Balkan Sector, hovered above the situation map. The map was draped over the billiard table, and the general stared into the yellow circle of light beaming down upon it. In full battle dress and at his full gathered height, he cut a commanding, if somewhat bulbous, figure. Of such stature was he, in fact, that his head nudged the shade of the overhanging lamp, and the movement of the green glass shade sent sinister shadows gliding across the face of the map and the dark gradation lines of the mountainous terrain. At the general's right hand stood his mustached adjutant, Captain Pavlov, looking especially pleased with himself as the general spoke again.

"And you say, Pavlov, that the corpse of Private Lajtner was found right here, by the stream?" The end of the general's riding crop slapped lightly at a thin blue line on the map, at a point not far from the main road south of the village.

"Yes, my General," said the captain importantly. "Once discovered, I personally observed the dead Serb lying face-down on a boulder with a stab wound in the back."

"Yet, the man outside the defense perimeter—alone—with no sign of a struggle?"

"Alone, Sir, yes. With no sign of a struggle at the immediate site, though on the path nearby the dirt showed scuff marks of a struggle, signs of a man's footprints brushed over—as though someone had been dragged or forced down to the boulder."

The general's brow furrowed at this last. "And you say the corpse was dressed in fatigue pants and boots only, the rest of his clothes scattered about? Tell me of the clothes."

"Yes, Sir; pants and boots only—and the pants—ah—pulled down to the knees." The captain, in his embarrassment at relating the lurid details of the matter, failed to observe the expression on the general's face. "The man's rifle was leaned against the boulder just out of reach, and his shirt, tunic and cap were scattered about. His cartridge belt, too, Sir—as if the man had, ah—disrobed in a hurry."

"And what makes you think there was a woman involved?"

Captain Pavlov glanced at his superior quickly. "A woman's white shawl was found stretched out across the rock, part of it under the body, and that part soaked with blood. A pair of woman's lace panties lay on the ground, ah, ah, at the feet of the dead man, the garment badly torn as if ripped apart by powerful hands." The captain stooped and picked something from a box on the floor, holding the delicate article up for the general to see. "Here, Sir; well, ah, you can see how they were torn."

With none of his inferior's hesitation, the general took the garment in his hands, examining it for a label.

"Made in Belgrade," the general noted. "Or, at least—so says the label."

"You will recall, Sir," Pavlov continued, "I told you last evening after reviewing the man's personnel file, Private Lajtner had a bad record, a history of this sort of thing." A smile of disdain appeared on the captain's lips below the broad mustache. "You see, Sir; the man is a Serb."

For a moment, the general's large baby-blue eyes squinted in thought. Somehow, it is all too pat, he was thinking, but he said, "Show me the shawl."

Once again Captain Pavlov stooped to the box of clothes; he pulled out the white, crudely knit shawl, stiffened in part with dried blood. He passed it into the general's hands which still held the lace panties.

"I see no label on this."

"No, my General. It is the homespun shawl common to the women of the village. There would be no label."

The general gave his aide a sharp look of challenge. "And this is precisely the type shawl made by the women of the village—you are sure of that?"

"I would stake my life on it." Pavlov's normally noncommittal eyes now sparkled with assurance; his voice held even a hint of a swagger.

"You may have to, Captain." said the general mildly, fingering the broad patch of dried blood on the shawl where it had lain under the corpse; then he handed back the shawl. "Yes, Captain, you just may have to—and perhaps the rest of our lives as well."

"Yes, Sir." At this turn, the adjutant's look of self importance vanished; his eyes once again assumed that glassy, vacant look fashioned long ago when confronted with superior authority.

"How many patrols are still out? What are their orders?" The general's plump fingers still held the delicate undergarment.

"Doubled patrols as you ordered, Sir. Two still search the banks of the stream and the footpath with dogs. One scours the shore of the lake and the river beyond. The remaining three search the village house by house."

"Intensify the search of the village and tighten the defense perimeter. And, Captain, you take personal charge—is that clear?"

"Yes, Sir. But speaking of the defense perimeter, there is that thing I mentioned before. You remember, the old goat herder. Still he insists on watering his goats in the lake."

"Can he not see the sentry posts marking the line of the defense perimeter?"

"To be sure, my General. But before our troops came, this basin was part of his land. And he claims that his goats must have water."

The general paused not a moment in thought, still holding the intimate garment in his delicate hands. "Can the sentries not act?" he growled.

"Sir, the man says simply, 'What are you going to do, shoot me?'"

"Well?"

"Well what, Sir?"

"Then shoot him—our troops could do with fresh meat."

The general's command left the adjutant blinking.

"Oh, and Pavlov, there is one other project. If the villagers have set about to slaughter my troops, perhaps it is time to teach them a lesson. Listen...."

25

Cil stood high in the ramparts, basking in the rays of morning sun. He stood above the mountain, above the courtyard—above everything. Only the distant peaks ranged higher, dark and majestic, faintly capped with snow. In the tension of yesterday's climb through the mountains, Cil had been blind to the beauty of the landscape, but now it rolled away before him in all its Alpine splendor. These great castle ruins perched above the emerald waters of the lake, the lake surface shimmering in the morning sun—the broad circle of mountains whose abrupt leap to the sky momentarily robbed the lungs of breath and produced a slight touch of vertigo—and from below the wafting scent of evergreen blended with a trace of wood smoke blown on the wind. Seemingly remote from the ravages of war, the majesty of the land seemed to embrace him. He felt refreshed and vital, fully recovered from his bout with the river.

But now Cil's stomach tightened, and the deeper he thought, the more intense his emotion. In a gesture of disgust, he dislodged a stone from the ancient wall to, seconds later, thump the ground below with an audible thud.

Orders had explicitly called for the old man to be prepared with workers in numbers sufficient to get the job done. Yet, upon his arrival, what had he found? A pair of giddy, card-playing gypsies, and prospect of another two men due to straggle in. Amateurs—without a crew of disciplined workers, the mission was little more than a joke.

Overhead swooped a hawk, gliding on a current of air, searching out an unsuspecting squirrel or hare—predator and prey, the classic equation, Cil mused. Which are we? Or could we be both?

He looked down the forested slope of the mountain. Directly below lay the foot of the lake with the dam to his left. Across the lake and rising steeply from the opposite shore ascended a steep wooded hill with a bald spot on top. Cil's earlier study of the map told him this was Bald Hill where the Englishman Baxter camped with Zeljko's son, Nedo, and his small band of irregulars.

Cil lifted the field glasses from his chest and swung them left, beyond the emerald sweep of the lake, past the great white wall of the dam, south, to where the thread of the river below the dam tumbled, foaming and white, through a narrow gorge chiseled through the mountains. He looked farther down to the point where the gorge widened out into a basin. Yes, that's where the Serb compound would be. And on either side, the basin closed in, wedged in by steep sloping ridges as if caught within the arms of two giant pincers. With a steady eye, Cil studied the way those pincers held the river basin in its grip. A voice from below broke his concentration.

The voice rose up from the base of the wall with the rasping quality of a spade thrust into gravel, though the sound was not unpleasant.

"Major. The day, she's already half spent. Come!" shouted old Zeljko from below.

As Cil made his way down the stone steps, he met the one-eyed gypsy of the night before, the man climbing toward him with rifle in hand and wearing a black eye-patch. In response to Cil's question as to who had dispatched him, the gypsy's only reply was a broad lascivious grin as his hands drew in the air the silhouette of a well-endowed woman, the grin on his lips both wide and obscene. But Cil's interest was focused elsewhere.

"Tell me," spoke Cil upon reaching Zeljko below. "How did you sleep?"

"Good. Always good in the mountains—same as my son." Then Zeljko was off, striding down the mountain, arms swinging loosely at his side, his rifle held lightly as a toy in his hand. Struggling to keep up, Cil could see how thick-necked and heavy-shouldered the man was, and how he carried himself in the woods like a man half his age; he judged the man's age at not under seventy.

The pair headed into the evergreen forest below the castle, on the opposite side of the ruins from which they had approached it the night before. They moved past the horses concealed in a thicket of trees, picketed in a tight circle; the walking was easy.

"In case of attack," said Cil, "should the horses be left unattended?"

"Is the duty of the one on his way from the village."

"It's not easy to do from the village," Cil reproached him gently.

The old man halted in his tracks. "I go for the second gypsy."

"On the way back, " said Cil with an easy smile, noting the look of simple gratitude on the old man's face. "Right now he helps the women move the supplies to the escape tunnel."

They had been moving briskly over the forest floor for a quarter of an hour when Zeljko held up in a shelter of trees.

"We are close. Stay low," he warned, crouching low; and they crawled the last yards on hands and knees, out onto an outcropping of rock.

Below, the evergreen slope fell away so sharply that for

an instant one was taken aback, the pitch of the cliff so steep that the whole panorama seemed to spill out before them. The near side of the dam was almost directly below, and a quarter of the way out from either end of the dam, makeshift guard towers squatted like huge insects on stilts on the crest of the dam, the near tower so close that one could almost reach down and touch it. Raising his field glasses, Cil could see the dark knots in the boards of the access ladder, and upon the railed platform, a fifty caliber machine gun mounted between two troopers standing erect and alert in green camouflaged combat fatigues. On their heads, visored caps pointed out at the clear, open waters of the lake, the mineral-rich waters only slightly opalescent, much as the lakes of Switzerland. The surrounding beauty drew sharp contrast to the murderous snout of that mounted machine gun.

Where Cil and old Zeljko lay stretched flat on the hard limestone ledge, hungry black ants penetrated Cil's clothing and bit him at will, though Zeljko seemed to pay them no heed as he busied himself, pointing out landmarks and other points of reference. Below the dam on the far side of the gorge, Cil could see a jeep, a mere toy in the distance, moving away south down the road that hugged the far bank of the river, the car moving fast, throwing up a rooster-tail of dust.

"That jeep," said Cil. "Where does it go?"

"Just there, down River Road, to the Serb compound one mile down." The old man lifted a brawny arm, aiming it downriver where the broad basin below the gorge opened up below the dam.

The enemy compound was screened from view by the trees, but a light powder of dust could be seen rising above the treetops and drifting on the breeze over the road and the river. Closer in, Cil could see where the road forked left, passing over a steel-framed bridge below the dam where it crossed the rushing waters of the river. But now Cil was looking directly across the foot of the lake, along the white crest of the dam to where River Road coming up the river from the enemy compound hooked away from the far side of the dam and vanished from sight between the far ridges.

"That road on the far side, where it hooks away from the dam through those hills?" Cil asked. "Where does it go?"

"Look close," the old man said, extending his chin. "She ducks through that pass to a guard post south of Bald Hill, then back to the main road. You know that bridge you cross last night in the dark?" The old man was now sitting comfortably, scratching his back against a cushion of rock, a chew of tobacco ballooning his cheek as Cil fixed his gaze on the bridge across the river below the dam.

"And that road down there where it crosses the river, where does it lead?"

"Curve back of the mountain here," and Zeljko patted the ground where he sat. "Back of Castle Mountain here—to another post of the guards."

And now Cil put the real question.

"Tell me," he said. "To cover that bridge, how much would the river have to rise?"

The old man's cheek moved in and out as he pondered, chewing his tobacco. At last, he shrugged, as if it were a stupid question.

"Hah," he mumbled, "Maybe five, six feet—but never happen; the dam, it hold back the water real good."

"And the same rise to reach the level of the basin where it widens out there—downriver below the gorge?"

The old man nodded; another stupid question.

"The back of the dam," Cil prodded. "Think of it at night. Where are the lights?"

Old Zeljko fell silent for a time; he let go a prodigious spray of tobacco juice which picked off a grasshopper in mid-flight at three paces and propelled it over the cliff.

"No problem from there," he replied with impatience, nodding at the guard towers perched on the white crest of the dam. "The searchlights, same as the machine guns, they all aim at the lake—mounted way forward. Don't ask me why."

"What others?"

"Generator room, windows back of the dam." He held up three meaty fingers to signify the number of windows. "But high up." He scratched himself and spat at another insect but missed. "Maybe ten meter up, over the dirt dam, so that give no problem."

"And the power station?"

"No, no. No light at night there." Suddenly the sound of aircraft engines could be heard revving up far downriver.

"No others?"

"No more, those only." There was a half-hearted stray spurt of tobacco juice as if the man was tired of the questions.

"No spotlights at the back of the dam?" But from night aerial photos, Cil knew better, and he leveled his gaze at Zeljko.

The old man had been wiggling once again against the rock at his back to crush a bothersome ant, and now he looked up, a little chagrined. "Yes, yes; two at the base, but fixed; shine only way high, up the white wall."

"But no beam down low at the back? No light on the earthen dam at the base?"

"No, no. Only high up, like I say, high up the white wall."

"What about car lights, from the far side, moving up the river?"

"That is so." He shrugged, looking annoyed.

"No others?"

For a moment, Zeljko held his tongue, then: "From the take-off planes!" His big toothy grin flashed, and they both laughed.

"One thing more. Tell me what you know of the spillway of the old earthen dam, from years back when they filled it in and built the big dam over the top."

"Hah!" The old man let out a hearty guffaw. "That is the

very big secret! But us who hunt the mountains, we watch it all real good." He was beaming proudly, exposing the space between his strong, square, white teeth.

Just then a cargo plane lifted off from a slit in the trees downriver. It rose steeply on the blast of the wind. The old man reached out one meaty hand and tugged Cil roughly back within the cover of trees.

"Like I say, we see the government fill over that baby dam—and the old chute of the water, she stay plugged to this day."

"With what, do you know?"

"Hah!" At this, Zeljko threw his arms into the air with wild animation. "A sloppy job! Dirt and rock, that is all—not with the concrete—that I know." His shaggy head shook vigorously. "No, no; no concrete; concrete might cost the thieving government bastards good money. Today, like a rusty bucket, she leak. Take my word."

Cil's voice became more crisp. "How do you know it leaks?"

"Hah! Whole town know she leak! One day I get the word." And now a note of reverence crept into his voice. "Even it reach the ear of the big cheese, the big marshall in Belgrade—old Tito himself!" Zeljko raised one meaty hand before his chest, then he flapped the hand with a rapid play of the wrist in the peculiar gesture used by the indigenous peoples to signify disaster. Again he displayed his broad toothy grin.

But if Zeljko thought it a joke, Cil was dead serious.

"The old spillway in the earthen dam, you say it was plugged with dirt and rock only?"

Zeljko nodded solemnly.

"And the rocks, were they filled in by men or by big earth machines?"

"Mans only. Many mans."

"What about noise?" Cil pressed. "The generators built into the high wall of the dam, they make much noise?"

"Much noise, no—much, *much* noise!"

"And they run all the time?"

"Like the river."

Suddenly Cil's questions took a personal turn.

"Your wife—last night I could see how upset she was." Cil surveyed Zeljko closely. "Is she safe in the village alone?"

The old man began his answer, then checked himself; he was thinking of her there all alone, of sniffing dogs and Serb patrols, but he stifled the thought; instead he gave out a chuckle. "Ah—she the nervous one, yes—but always dependable. You have no worry with her."

Cil sensed the overplay but chose not to pry. Instead, he sharpened his scrutiny of the old man, studying his features minutely.

"Look, Zeljko—I need your help. We're on a close timetable. I need shifts around the clock. How many men can you find me?"

"Many mans in the mountains," he replied slowly, pondering the weight of the request. "But not all strong. Not all to be trusted. How many you want?"

"We'll need four lookouts. Two at the castle, two guarding the mountain approaches, one with the horses at all times in case of attack. We'll need five in each crew. That's twelve more, not counting the two you're expecting today. Can you do it?"

Zeljko shrugged. "I do what I can."

"How soon?"

"Some tomorrow. Maybe some the day after."

"No maybe. And they must be told nothing."

"I hear you clear," acknowledged the old man gravely. "But you say, mans to be trusted."

"That's right."

It was then that they came—they came without warning or sound—out of nowhere. The passing of the pair of F-18 NATO fighter aircraft was instantaneous, followed first by a sound like a rogue wind through the tall branches—then an ear-splitting *whooooosh*. The crash of sound was so loud and unexpected that it caused Zeljko to jump clear off the ground. When he recovered, he crossed himself, swiftly.

It was only beyond their passing and Zeljko's fighting for control of himself that the two men moved away, back up through the trees toward the castle ruins.

26

As Cil and Zeljko hiked back up the mountain, Cil found himself reflecting upon his observations of the old man. After the debacle of the previous night, he had been interested in an overview of the dam and environs, yes, but more importantly, a chance to observe the old man and feel him out; and in that, he had been frankly startled at his discovery.

He could see now that old Zeljko was far more than some crude and simple mountain man. True, he was clearly a throwback to former times, even in this ancient land, but beyond the harsh exterior lived a stubborn man, fiercely loyal, yet highly sensitive to the logic of the wilds and the rhythms and symmetry of this, his world of the mountains. Cil had studied the man's reactions as Zeljko labored to answer his questions. He had watched the man struggle to bridge the gulf between his own private world of signs and habit and instinct, and the foreigner's unknown world of technical facts and timetables and mechanized monsters howling past at the speed of sound.

And, too, Cil had observed the man's simple patience, the practiced way he had paused by a tree trunk to coax a fat squirrel down from its perch with a clicking sound of his tongue. Cil had watched until the little creature, at first apprehensive, gradually laid aside its defenses and climbed into the old man's big callused hand to be petted and comforted and finally released. Cil had watched the way the old man listened without listening to the sound of the wind and noted the man's talent of observation, of Cil himself, of the first hint of danger. And Cil judged that there was more in what the old man saw and sensed than what he disclosed in so many words.

This was not a man to take orders and march to the beat of a drum, but Cil had a hunch that when the time came, this man would do his duty on his own terms. Yes, Cil could see why the man had been Colonel Anastasi's choice, for, when the hard times came, Zeljko would not be a man to shrink from a fight. No, he could go easy with this man; in him he could see a valuable ally, and if he could not be made to bend to a mold and carry out orders in the normal course, so be it. Given leeway, the man would show himself—and Cil could learn from a man like this.

Upon reaching the horses concealed beneath the hem of the forest below the castle, Cil adjusted the pickets while the old man scaled the high knoll to summon One-Eye, the gypsy, to attend them. When he returned with the gypsy, Cil addressed Zeljko with wry challenge.

"What do you say we check out the tunnel?" He was anxious to assess the true value of the escape tunnel in case of attack.

Zeljko beckoned the gypsy with a flick of the hand, and Cil fell in step with the old man as they headed for a hollow where flat layers of slate seemed naturally arranged, screened as they were by thick brush and undergrowth.

"I wonder," the old man snapped at the gypsy scornfully, "if for only one second you can hold in your head where in the tunnel you leave the lamp?" Cil could see that Zeljko had yet to recover from the gypsy's open disobedience of his orders the previous night.

"I know clearly," the gypsy told him with sarcasm, relieved, nonetheless, to escape the squadrons of swarming mosquitoes around the horses.

"Then follow us close to the entrance—and try not to lose your way back."

Upon reaching the lower tunnel entrance, the gypsy lounged against a tree trunk while Cil, in league with the old man, slid aside the covering stones.

With the cave mouth exposed, Cil noted the inner walls neatly stacked with the supplies and equipment he had ordered moved down from the castle. And Cil could see the look of stunned surprise on the old man's face that Cil's order of the previous night had been obeyed with such care and alacrity.

Once the lantern was located and the escape tunnel entrance closed at their backs by the gypsy, the atmosphere within the tunnel altered abruptly. The air within the closed cavern turned clammy and cold, stale and musty, almost as if they were sealed in a tomb. And here the blackness was penetrated only by the thin spear of light from Zeljko's lantern, the beam leaping and bouncing off the walls with swift, jagged movements. Cil, having suffered from mild claustrophobia since a child, panted for breath as if suddenly thrust within some dark and alien world.

To navigate within the bowels of the cavern meant to stoop low and forge ahead slowly while splotches of light from the beam of the lantern poked and stabbed at the narrowing passage ahead. Cil in the lead, with Zeljko stooping behind with the lantern, inched past cobwebs hanging from ceiling and walls, moist, hoary fingers poking out at his face.

Cil could hear the slurp, could feel the sudden slip and slide of mud underfoot, the floor littered and crawling with small mushy things, and always the fetid smell of creatures long dead. Points of dancing light displayed narrowing walls of crudely cut stone, green with age and coated with slime. Cil, holding his breath at each forward step, now and again felt a spatter of wetness on the back of his neck. Starting at the touch, each time he would fervently hope it was no more than the innocent dripping of ground water.

Up ahead in the darkness, his ears picked up a curious sound, an odd fluttering noise.

"Now we climb," the old man's voice echoing hollowly in the blackness. "Watch your hair for the bats." And at the warning, Cil found himself instinctively ducking his head against the very prospect, and it required a conscious effort to take the next forward step.

The tunnel had been rising slowly by fits and starts, but now it climbed in earnest, and in the uncertain light, Cil, brushing wet sticky cobwebs from cheeks and hair, caught a wisp of furry motion close over his head. On closer inspection, he spied rows of paired wings hung from the ceiling, shuddering rodent-like creatures, furry and dark, suspended by wet-looking feet so close over his head. Easing silently past, he saw that if he moved cautiously, the bats barely stirred, but the slightest noise or wayward movement triggered an explosion of sound—a hundred dark wings thrashing just there above the hair of his head.

And then at last, there it was—a distant point of light. The relief was a palpable thing—and then they were out.

The old man, the very picture of nonchalance, stood by on the dry stones of the courtyard, blowing away cobwebs from the sights of his rifle, observing Cil as he clawed with his hands at the strands of his hair, feverishly, raking at the nasty webs that knotted and snarled there. When a pair of black spiders dropped from his hair, with the heel of his boot Cil stamped them flat with a vengeance. Amidst his labors, Cil chanced to glance up at old Zeljko—whose face was beaming.

"An experience, no?" the old man chuckled.

Cil's immediate reaction was one of stunned chagrin, but then abruptly he clapped the old man on the back and roared with mirth at the discomfiture he had brought upon himself. Arm in arm, the pair marched over the courtyard toward the door of the castle. Cil was beginning to feel a keen affection for this rough-hewn old man, and after the episode in the tunnel, he could feel the first spark of true feeling growing between them.

As Cil entered the Great Hall of the castle, Zeljko hung back, surveying the hem of the forest below the clearing with a wary, searching gaze. Zeljko's thoughts were in turmoil. He had barely slept the previous night for fear of the patrols—and today the threat would be worse. If the corpse of the Serb trooper had not been discovered during the night, surely it had by this hour, and by now the hills would be crawling with mad-dog patrols. It was the welfare of the "Little Giants" which occupied his mind. The Serb defenses were difficult enough to penetrate under cover of darkness—but to attempt a river crossing in the light of day?

Upon entering the vast stone space of the Great Hall, Cil was startled to discover the tall Muslim woman, Bogey, alone in the castle. He was further surprised at what she was wearing. He found her clad in a skimpy silk summer dress which showed off to advantage her womanly features, the dress cut low in front, the hem concluding in the smooth roundness of the thighs. Cil was somewhat shocked at the God-given endowments he had failed to notice in the confusion of the previous night.

"Where's Michelle?" he asked, a bit self-conscious.

"At the north lookout post." The woman was scooping up the last dead embers from the hearth, yet surreptitiously nibbling with her eyes at his graceful, lanky countenance. "She guards the mountain approaches on the river side."

Cil, starting for the door, turned back to Bogey. In the play of her movement, he could see the full thrust of her womanly curves directed his way, disquieting, subtle, mysterious.

"All is moved into the tunnel?" he asked with added sternness.

"Just as you ordered," she told him, still with a slight sway of the hips as she went on appraising him, smiling fetchingly if shyly, yet with an intensity as penetrating as it was revealing. "But wait." And for a moment she moved close enough to convey the scent of her perfume. "Must you hurry?" She gave a playful, fetching smile, her hand lifting to make a fuss of picking the remaining cobwebs from the strands of his hair, the movements of her fingers both gentle and expert.

Cil had not thought much about it before, but now he wondered just what the story was with this woman, Bogey. Was it fact or only a trick of his imagination that during the night in the communal sleeping quarters, she had sidled in her sleeping blanket up close to where he lay? No—it couldn't be.

As soon as Cil was out the door, old Zeljko, who had been waiting impatiently for him to leave, entered the Great Hall, and no longer able to contain himself, fired the question at Bogey.

"The brothers? No sign of the brothers?"

"No sign. But it is early—not even mid-day." Her voice came gentle and reassuring, but the old man paused only long enough to grunt his acknowledgment before scrambling up the hard stone steps two at a time, rifle in hand, ascending to the height of the parapet where the gypsy, Chipmunk, was standing watch.

The gypsy seemed to be engaged in some sort of odd game. First he would hold his right hand over his right eye, then lowering the hand to his side, lift the left hand in turn and with it cover the left eye, then repeat the whole process with the utmost solemnity.

"Any sign of the brothers?" Zeljko demanded, his voice urgent.

"No, Old Man," came the careless reply of the gypsy,

once again covering one eye with his hand. "Nothing y-yet." It was not the strange conduct, but the answer which infuriated Zeljko.

"What the hell do you play at?"

"With One-Eye, I have a w-wager. That with two eyes I can see t-twice as clear and far as he with but one; it is my th-third test of the theory."

"Away with your nonsense," growled Zeljko. "No sign of patrols?"

"None, Old One; n-no sign."

"And your cousin, One-Eye? Does he, too, battle with nonsense? Do you keep watch on him like I tell you?" The old man was looking off, scowling down from the ramparts at the base of the knoll where the outline of the second gypsy could faintly be seen within the cover of the trees, tending the horses.

"Oh, he is in b-b-battle all right, but not with the little green men of the mountains, no." And now Chipmunk snickered, exhibiting fine white teeth in a smile that instantly lit up his face. "Right now he makes w-war on the mosquitoes. See there; he swats like a man p-possessed!"

The old man was scouring the base of the clearing with his field glasses, searching for the first, false movement. "What else—what else? You see anything out of the way?"

"Nothing, Leader."

"With discovery of the dead soldier, enemy patrols swarm through these hills more thick than the flies that sit on your tongue."

The gypsy shrank back at the words, his eyes oval moons. "Th-then what of the Little Giants who c-c-come with supplies? Do they not al-already ride in great danger?"

"Bah! The Ox, who last night take charge of the spray of the road, he knows of the killing. And the Professor, don't worry for him. He know the way." The overplay of the old man's words spoke more to convince himself than assure his companion, but the panicky gypsy was persistent.

"But loaded down with the c-c-compressor—and the long tube for br-breathing, Leader? They can move only slowly."

Zeljko, unwilling to share his feelings, much less his fears with this gypsy, glanced up at the position of the sun.

"And you know," the gypsy put in, "how s-s-swift and cold runs the river at the c-crossing!"

"No, no—they cross many times," the old man rebutted, a trifle agitated, shielding his eyes and watching a staff car pull up on the far side of the dam.

"Yet, never loaded down with a h-heavy compressor," insisted Chipmunk helpfully. "And what of a patrol hidden in the g-g-gr-great boulders lining the b-bank of the river? In all cases, killing of the hated Serb is a b-b-bad omen."

The gypsy seemed to be reading his mind, and given the state of the old man's emotions, this last remark laid his nerves bare.

"You damned gypsies—frightened rabbits every one! Life to you is the stupid game of blind man's bluff—life in the tea leaves! To you people, nothing has weight, for nothing has meaning."

Little Chipmunk recoiled at the old man's barrage. "Wh-What you say with much harshness, m-my Leader, is true. But I-I have feelings, too. I, too, have f-fear, not only for myself, but much also for the L-L-Little Giants."

At this, the old man fell silent. When at last he spoke, his voice was so low he seemed to be addressing himself.

"With the grace of God, they pass with safety," the old man said and crossed himself.

"And the Yankee m-major, what of him? Is he to be tr-trusted, Leader?"

The old man did not hesitate. "The Yankee, he is a rock. I say you take his orders." Zeljko lifted his field glasses to follow the path of the staff car as it moved down River Road, throwing up a cloud of dust as it moved toward the Serb compound.

Suddenly the field glasses fixed on a distant speck on the opposite side of the river below the dam, far down near the enemy compound. Adjusting the lenses, Zeljko could make out what looked like a small human figure sitting on the bank of the river. What is this? And then Zeljko nodded to himself—he had been told of this man.

"On your journey in with the two f-foreigners, there was trouble on the way?" prodded Chipmunk.

"No trouble," lied old Zeljko, lowering the field glasses and thinking to himself how close it had been at the crossing. "Why?"

"The girl is s-slender, with the tender skin of a child, not the r-r-roughness of the mountains," said the gypsy, looking closely for the old man's reaction.

"Hah, Gypsy, your brain is sawdust. That girl there is a fighter," declared Zeljko in a tone both mixed with protectiveness and pride as he thought of his leader, the colonel. "I wish only for ten more the same—then can you play your silly gypsy games and sleep in the sun."

"Then I breath e-easy," nodded Chipmunk, displaying an acknowledging smile.

But the old man's thoughts were far away, and once more he checked the position of the sun. No longer can I wait, he thought to himself with agitation; but when he spoke, his words were slow and measured. "I ride east in the hills for more men. You take the order from the Yankee—understand?"

"Clear, Old One. Do not w-worry your head."

"Is my business to worry!—yours, to follow my order."

Zeljko hurried down the hard stone steps, rifle in hand. If he were to round up as many men as the Yankee major ordered, he could wait here no longer.

27

North of the castle ruins, above the head of the lake, a pair of giant riders pressed their horses for speed. They moved at a hammering pace toward the cliff overlooking the bank of the river where the party had crossed the night before, a spotted-gray pack horse trailing behind, sagging under its burden of equipment. Upon nearing the precipice, both men dismounted, then advanced on foot, warily, leading mounts glistening with sweat under the dazzling noonday sun.

So solemn was their appearance, so grave their mien, that the pair of riders might well have been clergymen on a mission of the Lord in another place and time, or a pair of morticians of impressive rectitude going about their somber task. The pair, though men heavy through the shoulder with big barrel chests, seemed almost raw-boned because of their unusual height and stiffness of carriage. One, Ari Akheem, the taller of the two and bald as a granite ledge, wore a spade-shaped beard, had a hawk-like appearance, and the serene countenance of a doctor or professor. He carried about him such a keen, yet gentle look, that when he spoke, others listened. The other, Agar, his twin—though clearly not an identical twin—had as a child been dubbed "The

Ox"—and not without reason. Both men wore on their heads the tall fez of the Muslim, which increased their height and gave the impression of their being veritable giants.

Upon reaching the edge of the precipice, suddenly the taller man shoved his twin back.

"Get down!"

Both crouched and froze. Slowly, with the quiet of the angels, they backed their horses away from the edge and secured them in the safety of the undergrowth. Then, sprawled on all fours, peeking over the lip of the canyon wall, the two men eyed the progress of the enemy patrol below, slogging its way along the near bank of the river.

"May the robes of Allah be soiled!" cursed the Ox.

"Calm yourself," soothed his bearded twin, Ari Akheem, known in the village as the Professor. "We could not be more fortunate." He spoke softly with patience and calm encouragement. "Two minutes more and our carcasses would be drying in the sun, picked off that cliff-face like two fat milk cows. Or think if they caught us in the river. No, no, little brother, today is our lucky day."

With a shrewd and quiet eye, the Professor watched the movements of the string of men below in the scorching heat of the noon-day sun. With care did he study the droop of the shoulders and the wearily nodding heads as each patrol member trudged along, boots clumsily slipping and sliding at each footfall over the shifting pebbles of the riverbank, the patrol picking its way among the maze of great boulders lining the bank where clouds of mosquitoes swarmed over the rocks. "Watch them go—and remember. With each forward step, a dozen new mosquitoes kiss their soft skin with pride and affection. Another hundred meters, Little Brother, and our heathen friends will give up the game, cursing in terms even more harsh than your own."

Calmly the Professor tugged a small bottle from a line attached to his belt; he unscrewed the top and passed it over.

"Yes, Brother, count the blessing that Allah bestows, and drink of the blessed waters."

The Ox, however, remained unconvinced, grumbling under his breath. He took a healthy swig of the cool spring water and passed back the bottle. Lying there in the grass, he stared down over the edge at the slow-moving file of uniformed men. He was counting the number of rifles.

"I tell you, the sun will be down before they move out!" blustered the Ox.

"Patience, man, patience. First, permit our little stinging allies a little more fun."

"But that will be hours! And supposing they scale the canyon wall?"

"Calm yourself. To the north, the walls of the canyon are steeper yet. And notice, the prowlers are led not by a lieutenant, but by a mere corporal; corporals do not think of such things. Ten minutes more and our little friends will lose all taste for adventure. Here, another sweet sip of ice water while I keep watch."

"Very well, Brother. It may be that at birth you were passed the fat brain. But do not forget, it is I, Agar the Ox, who could tear those savages to shreds—as I can whip your ass any day of the week!"

As the Ox lay in his bed of soft summer grasses, the Professor crept north along the rim of the canyon wall, keeping the patrol in view, carefully eyeing its slogging progress until the insects and the blistering sun combined at last to break its will. He watched the soldiers as finally they turned in their tracks, retracing their steps until, a quarter of an hour later, they disappeared around the bend in the river far to the south from whence they had come.

Suddenly, above the muted roar of the river below, the cry of a wild bird sounded—then again the peculiar squawking noise. Ari, the Professor, lifted his gaze to sweep along the wooded bluff above the opposite bank of the river. And then he spied the familiar figure, arms waving above

28

It was early afternoon when, for the second time this day, Cil found himself high upon the castle ramparts surveying the landscape below. For better than an hour he had been gauging a haze of oily black smoke funneling up from the base of the mountain. The evil tail of smoke, blowing on the wind, seemed to be coming from the north in the direction of the village. The sight of it troubled him. He sorely wished he could consult the old man, but already Zeljko had set out through the hills to round up more men. So concerned had Cil been, in fact, that he had summoned Bogey from below; but unable to offer explanation, she had returned to her duties.

Searching for explanation and wondering if it had to do with the Serb forces, Cil raised his field glasses and trained them on the road on the far side of the dam, but he could discern no unusual activity. Far down River Road near the Serb compound, Cil spotted a black dot on the opposite bank of the river. "Hmmm. Now, who could be lounging so comfortably—and so close to the enemy compound?"

Just then Michelle appeared, and he drew her attention to the smoke, but something more immediate caught her eye.

"Oh look, the riders! They've finally come." And Cil

peered down to discover two horsemen galloping in, leading a gray packhorse. "The old man was so worried," she cried. "You go; I'll keep watch—and, oh yes," lifting one wary brow, "take care that your eye does not stray from your business." He turned to catch her expression, but already she was raising her field glasses, so he descended the stone steps to find Bogey in the Great Hall excitedly greeting the new arrivals, then bustling about to rustle up refreshments.

Cil was not sure what to expect when first he set eyes on the giant twins, but whatever his expectations, one glimpse at the new arrivals swiftly put them to rest. The two men were enormous, tall, very tall, and thick through shoulders and chests. And they seemed to move with an odd, almost stately air in their strange, stiff-braided jackets and dark trousers that reached to the ground. If Cil had expected hard-faced ruffians with dark swarthy faces and eyes and hair to match, then he was mistaken, for the faces, though forceful, well-chiseled, and tanned by the sun, were open and expressive with eyes that sparkled in their blueness. They might have been Viking conquerors, but for the fezzes adorning their heads. The taller and more stately of the two, introduced by Bogey as the "Professor," carried an almost ponderous dignity both in movement and speech, yet there was an unmistakable masculinity about him, somehow enhanced by an easy manner and quiet mien. And when the man set aside his tall fez before seating himself at the table, Cil was startled to see that the man was totally bald with a starkly white dome of a head above the hawkish face and well-trimmed yellow beard. As they seated themselves at the table, and water in preference to wine was passed, Cil was further reminded that the old man, Zeljko, had referred to the twins as Muslims. Cil addressed the Professor directly.

"Up top, I spotted smoke. Could it be from the village?"

"It is hell!—it is a nightmare!" burst the shaggy headed

Agar Akheem, introduced simply as the Ox, but he fell silent as his twin, the Professor, lifted his hand in a calming gesture to restrain him. The bearded Professor turned to Cil.

"What your eyes see is no lie." The Professor spoke slowly and deliberately in somber tones. "In the village, there is much suffering—even death."

At confirmation of the other's words, Bogey started in shock, nearly upsetting the serving plate.

"Trouble?" pressed Cil.

"Trouble? Rape and pillage and murder!" raged the Ox, balling his fists and red-faced with passion.

"Yes," the Professor agreed quietly. "The advancing blight on the land once again arrives at our village."

"Worse!—worse than ever I've seen...." cried the Ox, choked with emotion and flailing his arms before his voice trailed off and his gaze sank to the plate laid before him as if further explanation was beyond words.

In a subtle upward motion of the head, Cil gestured to Bogey who set off to relieve Michelle at her lookout post on the high wall. So stunned was the Ox, in fact, that as Bogey moved off, Cil failed to lift his gaze in customary fashion in pursuit of the sway of her hips and the toss of the firm, rounded buttocks mounting the stone steps.

Now that Cil's focus was drawn to Bogana, he was surprised to see that since their earlier encounter, she had changed out of her skimpy silk dress—and into this plain black and white heavy curtain of a garment that reached to her shoetops, typical of Muslim village women to conceal suggestion of their womanly features. Over her shoulders draped a white, coarse-knit shawl, which, as she departed, she slipped up over her head and wore as a hood as if to mask her face.

When she was gone, the Professor continued.

"The mosque. Its ancient minaret has fallen. After five hundred years, the heathens have seen fit to dynamite the sacred symbol of Islam and level it to the ground."

"A pack of mad dogs, I tell you!" raged the Ox.

"It began last evening just before twilight," the solemn-faced Professor began again slowly. "Patrols in the village are not something new; they had come in weeks past. The silence of the evening broken by loud pounding on doors, then gruff questions. But early this morning, all of that changed."

The Ox stiffened at the thought. "Savages. They broke down doors. In uniformed gangs they came! The raping, murdering bastards!"

"What my brother says is true," affirmed the man with shrewd eyes and flowing golden beard. "But it started slowly. At first a quiet rap on the door of the local stool pigeon. That followed by the usual clatter of gates and shutters by the roused villagers all up and down the street, the sound of it, agitated, rhythmic. Then a random stone cast in protest from behind a courtyard gate, followed by more, then vulgar hand gestures by one defiant child, then another. That was the spark; the soldiers became aroused.

"Villagers in nightdress routed from their homes. Serb troops and uniformed toughs. Every minute the frenzy gathering momentum, with the slightest act of resistance answered by men hauled out and beaten—then shot—women dragged off and systematically raped."

Cil's face was pale as he spoke.

"What provoked it?" He faced the bald, bearded man squarely, and the Professor returned the gravity of his stare.

"Who knows?" the Professor shrugged. "Whatever provokes such a thing?"

Cil and Michelle, seated opposite one another, exchanged troubled glances as the Professor went on.

"It is a sickness fallen over the land," he said gravely. "Are the words not familiar to you? As in the days of your own President Nixon's Watergate, when, who was it, a young White House aide who declared that a cancer had fallen over the Presidency?"

For a second, the Professor allowed himself a faint smile.

"Oh, do not look stunned," he added good-naturedly. "Despite your western press, we are not all in this land ignorant bumpkins—an ancient savage race and throwback to medieval times." He was quite amused, but his face again sobered as he reflected on events.

"A wall of hatred has divided our peoples for centuries. But now the Serbs have refined it and set it in motion. A cancer, yes— 'Ethnic Cleansing,' I believe is the term coined by the western press in its lily-white pages."

He paused, his face transparent. "To you, perhaps, it is only a phrase. But to us here of this land, it is a new wave of people plowed under, plowed under by the same black hand—in truth, a cancer, a malignancy of mind and spirit, requiring in each village only the right spark to ignite it."

The Ox stepped in. "I tell you, those who resisted were hauled out and shot!" The Ox had no stomach for history or logic. "As a lesson, young girls down to the age of ten— their clothes stripped off—just thrown down and raped." His eyes were huge saucers. "And all the shooting—shops looted—houses burned!"

"It is true," acknowledged the Professor wearily. "The village schoolmaster was singled out for special treatment." He paused, sucking in breath to gather himself. "There in his red and white striped shorts, shoved off through the crowd in the morning sun—an ax produced—a stout wooden stake cut and prepared, the stake sharpened on each end—a hole dug."

The Professor was blinking his eyes, remembering. "I shall never forget it, that woman there on her knees in the grass, the man's wife, twisting that little green handkerchief held in her hands, her eyes rounded and staring, the family's small children also watching.

"They laid the man flat down in the dust of the street. How strange it was," still blinking his eyes. "To hear the odd choking sounds that jumped from his throat. Then they splayed out his legs like a pig to the slaughter, and with one mighty blow of the ax, his buttocks split, the stake driven straight up his rectum. Then the stake that impaled him was raised up as if to place the man in a standing position, the lower end of the stake set in the hole that had been prepared in the ground. I could see the high, ax-sharpened point of the stake protruding right out through the white stomach. Only later did he succumb."

It was then that Cil's stomach knotted, and Michelle D'Orleans darted for the door.

"Monstrous," exclaimed Cil.

"Yes, but Sarajevo—in Sarajevo it is worse. Yet, why do I go on? The whole world knows of Sarajevo; it is the start of the fourth year for them. All that puzzles me is—why the world sleeps? *Why?*"

This odd bearded giant with the hawk-like face and white, cannon-ball head dropped his gaze to the surface of the table. Despite the grizzly tales, he began eating normally, downing cold, well-browned tarts stuffed with spinach which Bogey had long since laid before him; he ate gravely and quite formally. It was then that Michelle, head bowed, her body supported on wobbly legs, reentered the room. Cil could see that her face was chalk-white, pasty-looking. She sat down quite without expression, and Cil fought the impulse to go to her.

"But what drives people to such savagery?" Cil asked instead.

"An ancient curse," responded the Professor between mouthfuls as his brother barely picked at his food. "Have you never seen the handsome young man, the ringleader of the village in his fine sporting jacket of three years past which should be hung in school? And he and his friends sitting there where daily they gather on the stone wall by the village square? It is a sight as old as the world, except in our land it is different. The handsome ringleader is barely past adolescence with a sneering expression and razor-sharp wit.

"The boy's father works in the local mill, so the boy has no real education, yet he has grown used to the others on the stone wall looking up to him. And when one of his fellows, better taught or better read, speaks of wonderful things foreign to the handsome young ringleader's knowledge and experience, affront is taken to his position as leader, and he slaps the boy down. Oh, I don't mean with fists—a minor humiliation will do, enough to cut the boy down in the eyes of his friends.

"But as more books find their way into the village, as the information of the world filters in, the threat to the ringleader increases." The Professor permitted himself a slow, sardonic grin. "In other lands, boys with ideas leave the village to go on, but here, alas, it is different. Here, the young bully with no learning and no chance, he looks to the town graveyard and unburies old hatreds. It is these that he, as his father before him, dusts off and employs—to keep his fellows down."

"And they call *us* Turks!" interjected the Ox.

"There, you see?" responded the Professor, stroking the golden strands of his beard. "We have no Turks in this land. The Turks conquered the Serbs in the year 1387 on the Field of the Blackbirds in the province of Kosovo, which the Serbs now call their own, though it is 90% Albanian. The Turks were defeated and thrown from our land in the year 1878. Yet, as my brother says, we Muslims today are still referred to as *Turks*.

"Yes, yes," he went on. "Old hatreds die hard. The province of Kosovo, historically a region of Albania, was taken by Tito and made part of Serbia to appease the Serbs; but because the region remains peopled by Albanians, this province of Kosovo, where the great battle of conquest was staged six centuries ago, remains a constant irritant to the Serbs and a source of eternal jealousy and hatred. It is these old hatreds that are employed by the boy on the wall to keep his fellows in line. And it is these hatreds that pit boy against boy, man against man, family against family—and that finally turns Slavic brothers of the same root, name, and language into savages."

He sighed, as if with resignation. "But it is not simply these ancient hatreds which threaten us now, but those fatheaded Serbian nationalists masterminded from Belgrade in their quest of political goals—say, a Greater Serbia, for instance. Strange, is it not, right here in our native Bosnia-Herzegovina, a Republic of Serbs, Muslims, Jews and Gypsies—where one third of the population today intermarries?"

He turned to the Ox. "My Brother, finish your tart. We must see to the horses. Then when the old man returns, we take another step in our journey." He looked into the faces of the others. "If I may be trite, *today is our day for turning in plowshares*."

29

"*What*—blood in the streets, you say? *Who* let it happen?"

"My General, a thorough search of the village—as you ordered. The Serbs—well, somehow word got out, and the Chetnik irregulars in from the hills got out of hand."

"Out of hand?" snorted the general, adjusting the silk belt of his robe. "Six dead in the streets—rape, pillage, and murder—the mosque burned to the ground. That is not 'out of hand,' Captain—that is a *massacre*!" The general's face flushed sunset-pink. He gripped the handle of his riding crop with a firm meaty hand.

"I cautioned the patrol leaders personally, my General," muttered the mustached captain, retreating a step, his eye never straying from the weapon held in the general's hand.

"Cautioned? I placed you in command. Do you not perceive what this portends? Dammit, man! And what of the identity of this young village maiden we seek and the assassin of Private Lajtner?"

"Captain Pavlov swallowed hard, his timorous gaze never leaving the riding crop. "Even under pressure, my General, the men of the village swear they do not know."

At this, the general's demeanor underwent an abrupt if fitful change; he fell silent, his massive bulk dropped pen-

243

sively down onto the broad sofa. He laid aside the riding crop, and struggling to control his emotions, poured himself a glass of vodka from the decanter on the ornate coffee table. Then, assessing the nerves of his adjutant, he poured the man a glass as well.

"You'd better be seated, Pavlov—before you fall. Here—an ounce of piss for your liver." The fury of the commander had passed. The ability to control his temper was a talent of necessity which General Nicholai Kerenofsky had cultivated assiduously over the years since his early years as a young officer in the Caucasus. Anger would solve nothing this day; information was the armor he sought. "We both know this thing of ethnic cleansing. Is that what took place in the village today?"

"Not by my men, General." The aide took a healthy swallow of the smooth clear liquid; a bit of courage flowed back into his veins. "I myself remain a comrade and officer of the Russian Army. No, no; it is the human garbage I lead; it is the Serb rabble that got out of hand. As the general well knows, it is these savages who for more than three years have ravaged this land."

"But not here, Pavlov—not here."

"No, Sir, not here, but look at Zepa and Srebrenica and the other eastern enclaves. Even back home, the Moscow newsboys cry out the story."

"Were there rapes?"

"Ah—I think a few...."

"Of children as well?"

"A few, Sir—perhaps."

"You say the villagers deny knowledge of the Lajtner killing as well as the identity of the girl and the assassin? Even under torture and threat of death?"

"I know of no public torture," the captain protested, though there appeared a noticeable waggle to his mustache. "But no, they say they know nothing."

The general calmed. "Hmm—even after killings in the

street?" He muttered to himself, stroking one jowl pensively. "Now, that is strange."

The commander was silent for a time. At length, he spoke softly. "Pavlov, I wish every inch of these mountains searched. Every inch, is that clear?" his voice so low it could scarcely be heard. "If the attack on Lajtner did not come from the village, then others are out there."

"As you say, Sir. But with our compound secure, and the men of the village who fight with only pitchforks and rakes...."

A slight shiver of foreboding passed over the general, and one glance at his expression cut the adjutant off in mid-sentence.

"Do not play the fool, Pavlov. We sit here surrounded by a simple people, it is true, but a people proud, nonetheless. A people of courage and passion who have fought one another for a thousand years, a people capable of the kind of courage and cruelty which springs only from a deep wellspring of abuse and repression. And that, Pavlov, is the most savage force on this planet." He raised his head to the window facing north. He peered long and hard at the great concrete dam, standing stark and white, almost majestic in the noon-day sun. "Perhaps even more powerful than the watery serpent that lurks behind that thin skin of concrete.

"The unpleasantness in the village was but a symptom of a sickness which runs deeper," he went on. "A sickness like the rotting of the soul. A sickness that comes when the hates and frustrations of centuries arise from within and cry out for release. It matters not whether it erupts this day from Serb or Muslim, from Croat or Jew or Gypsy. Once unleashed, this force, mindless as a torrent, crashes out to spread and flood and multiply. It follows the folds of the land as a scourge, devouring all in its path—a force as useless as is that ancient castle up there on the mountain—and only does it recede when the cycle of hatred and destruction has gone full circle and its appetite is at last appeased."

The general shook his head as if rousing himself from a dream.

"Yes, Pavlov, that is what we face. So do not speak to me of pitchforks and rakes. Once we of Mother Russia were such a people—but that was long ago."

"You speak with great eloquence, my General, but one must not take lightly the awesome weapons of modern war which lie at our fingertips—state-of-the-art tanks, computerized missiles capable of dropping a shell on the back of a fleeing rabbit at a distance of forty miles."

The chubby commander sprang to his feet. "You talk of tin; I speak of power!" He swung the glass in his hand in a great curving arc, in such agitation that the medals pinned to the breast of his robe shook themselves with a fury. "Pavlov, hear me. It is what flows in a man's veins that determines the outcome of battle, not the number of computer chips pressed into a weapon. And if I am in error, then explain to me the lessons of history, Captain. What happened to our old adversary, the Americans, in Vietnam? To our own armies mired in the nationalism of Afghanistan— now Chechnya?"

The general, ensconced in the tent of a robe, resumed his seat, his tone once again distinctly professorial.

"Take the Americans, Pavlov. In the war with Iraq, the Americans had a President who sought to repair an image of weakness. To prove himself as a man, he bombed 130,000 poor souls into submission within their own self-dug graves below the sands of the desert. And now this new American President begins the cycle again in order to assure his own re-election. Is this his new Vietnam?

"As before in Vietnam," he continued, "they are starting small—cautiously. Already they have placed planes in Italy and Greece, five hundred troops in Macedonia to watch the southern flank, others in intelligence operations in Albania. Already their NATO planes make a phony show of No Fly Zones although we fly new troops in every day of the week.

Masquerading as peacekeepers, the West slowly, systematically, infiltrates their crack combat units, hiding under the blue helmets of the UN, all the while carefully positioning their troops along the Croat-Bosnian frontier as 'Advisors' to coach the Croats in the latest combat tactics."

"But, my General, five hundred troops here, and a few Peacekeepers there—that is nothing."

"Ah, my good Captain, that is nothing today; but hold on; do not forget the 25,000 US troops promised to NATO to assist in a withdrawal of the Peacekeepers—or to police a solution. And if, Pavlov, if an incident should arise? Well, there you are, the Americans will have the excuse their Congress demands to permit them to pounce. In the meantime, they sit back, fail to enforce the West's UN embargo against shipment of arms to the belligerent factions and turn a blind eye on the troops and weapons which pour through the sieve from Iran and North Africa in support of the Bosnian Muslims—and all with impunity under the banner of Islam." The general shrugged. "Ah, Pavlov, I do so wish that our young American President who soon faces new elections had not taken it upon himself to so obviously hide in his youth from the draft. Then, perhaps, we at this instant would be at home, snug in our own warm beds."

"Still, we are safe here—and undetected," responded Pavlov airily, feeling his vodka at this hour of the day, not observing the way the general fingered his riding crop. "It was a true act of genius to secrete all these heavy weapons here in the mountains."

"Safe!" The splayed end of the leather riding crop snapped against the glass tabletop, upsetting the gilded cigarette lighter, but this time sparing Pavlov's hand by a matter of inches though he jumped as if stung by a direct hit.

"You think we are safe," whispered the general. "But we are not safe; and we are not undetected. Captain, I have warned you before of this false notion of yours. Only a fool could imagine this movement of heavy arms and troops to a remote outpost could go undetected by the Bosnian Army, or by the Croats who surround us. As surely as we sit in this room, Pavlov, our presence is known—if not by the combatant factions, then by the Americans with their air patrols and electronic AWACS flights, their spy satellites and U-2 planes—or by their NATO and UN surrogates.

"In fact, my good Captain, I lay you odds that at this very moment preparations are underway to destroy us. If not today, then tomorrow and tomorrow—but surely one day soon.

"Has your electronic monitoring of their radio communications turned up anything yet?"

"Nothing yet," acknowledged the captain.

The general exhaled a sigh of exasperation. "The fools who sent us to this damn awful place ought to be shot! My tongue lacks adjectives to do them justice."

At the blasphemy, Captain Pavlov's bush of a mustache stood almost on end; he drew back even more suddenly than at the snap of the riding crop.

"Most Revered Comrade General—one must be careful of how one speaks—lest the walls interpret and write it as treason!"

The tent of a robe sat quiet and composed, and then it heaved majestically back in the cushions to give its master pause to ponder the thought; the general smiled.

"Don't fret, old comrade. These days, even the Kremlin permits a flabby-fisted old general the luxury of a word of treason now and again. In a fallen empire, it is one of the last privileges of rank. And now, where are the little ones?"

30

The cloak of darkness had already slipped over the shoulders of the mountains by the time Zeljko made his way back to camp. And now in company with Michelle and Cil, he mounted the hard stone steps of the turret above the high wall. At this elevation the air held more nearly the nip of a late autumn frost than what one might have expected in the first days of August. The moon on the rise shot a silver lance down the lake as Cil rushed with preparations.

Unslinging both M-16 military assault rifle and pack, Cil rummaged about in the pack until his hand fell upon the fat barrel of the signaling rifle. Assembling the components in the dark by feel, he then produced penlight, pad and pencil, passing these items to Michelle. All the while, the old man fixed his attention on the dome of Bald Hill, its treeless pate towering above the far shore.

"OK, ready?" prompted Cil, turning to Michelle who sat at his feet, pencil in hand. "When the first flash comes, take down each letter just as I say," he coached, as she switched on the penlight. "And be sure—shade out every fragment of light."

It was nine on the dot, the prearranged time for the signaling, but no flash of light came from Bald Hill. Five minutes passed—ten—still nothing.

"Why not signal them first?" prodded Michelle.

"Too risky; they're at the lower level. To beam our signal down at them means it could be picked up by anyone in proximity to that hilltop. Be patient; it'll come."

The old man tensed with the passage of time; he shifted where he sat, nervously rubbing his back against the inner stones at the top of the turret, all the while his gaze remaining fixed on the dome of Bald Hill. And then, finally, he could contain himself no longer.

"Is not the habit of my Nedo to be late."

"Take it easy; it'll come," Cil assured, though his words only served to heighten Zeljko's anguish. The luminous hand of Cil's watch slid down to 9:17.

The old man sensed the rise of the moon at his back as the wind rippled the surface of the lake below, painting it with tiny crescents of silver. His impatience transformed to worry, then to anger. Damn it, Nedo, where does your wondering mind carry you this time? Why is it you fail in your duty this night? Why, boy, why? He was reminded of the obstinate nature of the boy, of how he himself, Zeljko, had taken great pains to get the boy a start in the local pulp mill, hoping with hard work, a quick wit, and the dexterity with the hands that came from his wife's side, he would make a good foreman one day. But it was not to be; the boy didn't want it; he yearned for the quiet of the hills just like Zeljko himself, for distance from the crowd, for the magic of nature, for the game and thrill of the hunt; and soon he was let go at the mill. Nonetheless, old Zeljko thought proudly, the boy has a head for the mountains, and when the scent of war had come to these hills, who was it who lost no time in recruiting his friends? And from these hills, is it not his own small band which hammers the Godless Serbs? With each passing week, he finds new recruits from the mountains.

The old man's anger softened. He fixed on those far off days when Nedo was a boy. He recalled how the little tike would follow him through the hills to hunt bear and wild boar. He recalled how together they had tracked a black bear for days through the snows of these very ridges, and the nights freezing, and how it had been the spirit of the boy, the eagerness of youth which had shoved the father on to the higher peaks, until finally, in the chill mountain air on the fifth day, a clear shot rang out. He recalled how he had cleaned the mighty bear right there in the snow to lessen the weight, then struggled, dragging the carcass mile after weary mile down the ledges, through banks of blowing snow and sloping timber, until the muscles in his thighs cried out for relief. But the boy would not give up, and he remembered the pride and excitement in the little boy's face when at last they had staggered into the village, the great carcass in tow. And now, standing here, he recalled how the light in the boy's eyes had never to this day been extinguished.

Something jerked the old man out of his reverie, and he muttered under his breath. Oh God, let him be safe. Though there had been no sound of guns, the old man knew firsthand of the patrols; he crossed himself properly and said a Hail Mary.

"What time is it now?" asked Michelle.

"Nine twenty six" Cil could feel the tension building in the muscles of his throat. Their eyes met, but no words passed their lips.

Michelle rolled the cigar-like shaft of the penlight between long slender fingers exquisitely formed. Surreptitiously she raised the hoods of her lids and studied the rough, determined features of Cil in the moonlight, the smooth-muscled planes of his stomach and chest outlined under his khaki shirt. She could see his face framed as it was by a mane of tawny-brown hair which tumbled thickly, ruffled and unkept, to a rough-sheared line at the base of the neck, the stray ends of his hair glimmering now strangely in the moonlight. She could see the firm set of the chin under a short stubble of beard as his arms braced resolutely against the stones of the turret. The lines of the face were heavy and strong, shadowed in the odd light, the effect heightened by high cheekbones broad-set, the straight, well-chiseled nose with proud flaring nostrils, the determined line of the full, mobile mouth. Yes, she agreed inwardly, he might have been considered handsome were it not for the length of chin and severe line of the jaw which left no doubt of an unswerving purpose and will.

Suddenly she was seized with a bout of conscience. She was pondering what the bearded Muslim called the Professor had told them earlier at the table in the Great Hall. Could it be that her killing of the Serb Soldier had led to murder and rape in the village? No, no; no such claim had been made. But still the plague of conscience would not free her, and her thoughts turned to those things she had done at the start of the mission.

"I'm a reckless, selfish child!" she silently reproached herself. "That should be your name—just as father reminded you as a child a hundred times a day." She knew that but for her, Cil never would have come on this mission, but instead be safe and settled by now in the hills of his precious New England—once again a civilian. "What is it about me that jumps first and...." A soft sigh overtook her, "if ever you think at all. Yes, this time you have gone too far; you have risked the life of the one...."

And now her thoughts ran back. In every way known to feminine charms—well, almost every way—she had forced him, lured him, dared him, insulted his manhood, trod on his vanity, insulted every shred of his being. And yet, against that man's plain stubbornness, all her wiles combined had failed to turn his head—until, that is, she had stumbled upon his one area of weakness through her Uncle Mavro. Still she did not understand the details of that long-ago mission that had robbed him of pride and destroyed his reputation and confidence. But still, finally, she had found that weakness and played on it with the claws of a cat. Yet, still and all, even in her vanity of vanities, she consoled herself with a thought, and it eased the throb of her conscience. For anyone who knew Cil knew also that he was not a man to be tampered with, to be truly dissuaded from the course his compass had set.

For a moment, she took comfort in the notion, and some of her guilt slipped away. But deep down she knew just how shamelessly she had stretched and torn at the truth, rewoven the moral fabric, until at last, his conscience would not permit him to refuse her.

She shook her head to clear it. She had felt a premonition, and it frightened her. She knew that it was she herself who had placed him in this danger. And she was frightened by this other thing, too. But that was her secret, and she would hold it within her breast. No, she would be strong; she would never ever even let him guess.

And now she looked off over the cool waters below them, ruffled and shimmering in the wind. She looked up the steep slope beyond, up, up—to the spot where the gray clearing on top ran hard against the blackness of the surrounding trees. She shivered. She kept her gaze glued to the spot as the minutes crept past.

"There!" she cried out. "See there!" There was no mistaking it, a fine point of light barely visible to the naked eye, beginning to blink from the hilltop.

"Zeljko." Cil spoke calmly. "Move down to the parapet and see if you can pick up the beam of their signal at that height. If you can, move farther down, down until you no longer can see the slightest trace of the light." He pointed at the courtyard below. "If you see it from down there, wave your arms. We don't want our friend Baxter spraying that signal all over the whole damn side of the mountain."

As the flashes of dots and dashes in International Morse Code streamed in cadence at the center of Cil's mind, Zeljko moved on down the steps, and Cil dictated each letter to Michelle, seated at his feet.

"L E P P R word M E T E R I N E word A B L word— and so on for twelve solid minutes.

The old man rejoined them, reporting a dim signal from the height of the parapet, but nothing from the level of the courtyard. Then came the sign-off, and Cil squared the fat barrel of the signaling gun and squeezed off one rapid parting flicker.

When Cil hauled Michelle to her feet, he noticed her rubbing and rubbing her hand.

"What's wrong?"

"When you asked me up here, I didn't know——to write a book." In the moonlight, he spotted tiny crinkles at the corners of her mouth. Without hesitation, he stepped up and tasted its warmth as they all started down the steps, the old man in the lead. When they had descended to the level of the parapet, Cil whispered in Michelle's ear, and she moved on ahead.

"Zeljko. Your son, you have trained him well." And even in the moonlight, Cil could see the warm turn of the old man's lips. "Now let's get the message to Mostar. Which of the men will you send?"

"No, no; I myself go."

"Oh no, you're far too valuable to me to run that risk. Besides, tonight we begin at the dam."

"No." Zeljko spoke with finality. "I go. Now with the killing, they look with the sharp eye. Mine are papers that work. If we start the dam now, still is there time."

Cil could see from the old man's tone that he would not be dissuaded, so he changed the subject.

"You say you could dig up only seven men in the mountains?"

"But seven. The rest—too small, too lazy, or not with dependable tongues. I know are less than you order, but all are men of heart."

"And horses? What about the horses?"

"As many, maybe more. All arrive under cover of night, with equipment you say—and the tin wagon for the dirt."

"Yes, the dirt," Cil was reminded. "Have you figured an answer to that one?"

The old man paused for only a second.

"In my country of the blue mountains," he said slowly, "with patience and prayer, life speaks to all things."

31

The spirit of excitement and anticipation that swept through the little party as it made its final preparations charged the atmosphere like an electrical current. At precisely 10:25 PM, the small troupe set off down the mountain for the dam. The giant Sons of Islam had covered the faces of the tools and compressor with burlap to prevent loud banging on the rocks during the descent, and now, hoisting their packs, guns slung on their shoulders, the group moved down the knoll before the castle, stooping under the weight of the tools and equipment they carried. The Professor carried the fuel and a coil of thick plastic pipe while his twin lumbered under the weight of the compressor. Zeljko, like an over-anxious scoutmaster, led the way, setting the pace and ever watchful, prodding the others along. Michelle and Bogey followed with the shovels while Cil brought up the rear, laden with picks and axes and a host of carefully wrapped lanterns and other supplies.

At the base of the knoll, the others rested while the old man led Bogey to the horses and the waiting one-eyed gypsy who lounged atop a boulder, polishing off a bar of candy earlier pilfered from the stores, hurriedly licking the last remnants of chocolate from his pencil-thin fingers.

"On your feet, Captain Kidd!" growled the old man with impatience. "The woman looks after the horses. And, Gypsy, I hope what you steal gives you much strength—check your rifle; we are off to the dam."

When the gypsy was out of earshot, the old man turned to Bogana; he spoke in that rough-mannered way of his.

"Here, you be safe. If someone come on you, move away from the horses into those trees; always can I find new horses. But in all cases, take no risk. And do not worry your head, the tender foreigners with me, they come to no harm."

For a brief moment, she leaned forward to stroke his cheek, almost as if he were her father, before he moved away through the trees after the others.

The old man hurried the small band down a sloping forest trail, moving south, to the left of the morning route used to inspect the terrain. Cil chafed under the weight of his pack; he could feel the straps dig painfully into his shoulders, and where the pack braces rested against his back, his shirt was already wet and clinging. From Agar the Ox in front, the odor of stale sweat came to Cil strongly. With each forward step, the big man emitted a heaving grunt of effort. When the trail ended abruptly at a limestone ledge overrun by a gushing stream, Cil placed down the shovels taken from Bogey. Dropping to his knees to peer over the edge, he could hear the waterfall splashing on the rocks below.

"Is possible if you take it slow," assured the old man. "I go first. Lower the equipment to me." He took a coil of rope slung over his shoulder and handed it to the Professor, then snaked his rugged frame over the edge with startling speed and agility. Cil could see that the old man had traveled this course many times before and knew it by heart as he vanished from sight down the sheer limestone face.

When the equipment had been lowered by rope, and all stood safely below at the foot of the ledge, showered by the spray of the waterfall, once again they loaded up. Stumbling under the weight, sliding on the stones of the streambed slippery and slimy with moss, they continued on down, the shallow current tugging at their pant cuffs, brushing their ankles pleasantly. The stream snaked and boiled down a series of crests, falling off through the trees for nearly two miles to a point where the slope leveled out and the stream, choked by the undergrowth, made a sharp bend and dove underground through the limestone bed. Zeljko in the lead raised a finger to his lips.

"Close now—take care!" he cautioned in a gravelly rasp, swiveling his head about, watching through the trees with ever a wary eye. "Away from the noise of the stream, step with the feet of a cat. When you come on the clearing, stay close. Cross on my signal."

In a moment they were through a growth of prickly high bushes. Cil tripped and nearly lost his footing, stumbling over the ties of an abandoned railway bed. Ahead, filtered through a stand of new-growth pine, he could see a glow of bright light like a road traveler first glimpsing the distant lights of an athletic field. He forged ahead, inching toward the light, needles of pine swishing playfully against his stubble of beard. And then as he stuck his head through the boughs at the edge of the clearing, he froze and shrank back. Fear, like a cold wind, gripped him at the sight.

Before him lay a clearing. The clearing bathed in a pool of white light, gauzy white light rising out of the mists from the river beyond, like a scene from one of those old English movies filmed in the moors. Above him in the eerie light loomed a structure of epic proportions. When he had first seen the silhouette of the high-perched castle cast against the night sky, he had thought it the most awe-inspiring spectacle he had ever beheld. But now he could see he was wrong.

Thrusting into the sky as high as the eye could see stood the great wall of the dam, stark in its majesty, ghostly steep in its whiteness. Spotlights widespread and positioned at its base threw twin circles of light high on the naked wall. Where the twin beams struck high up on the wall, they created what appeared to be sickly white eyes staring down in the night, seeming to bring the wall to life—a great otherworldly creature rising out of the mists, at once malevolent and ghostly and looming above him. The glare of those eyes—huge, penetrating—fascinated Cil, and for a moment held him spellbound. And when he turned to Michelle, he could see that those eyes had had the same effect upon her, for she seemed to stagger and cling to a sapling as if for support.

Cil lost all sense of the others around him. He stood gazing dumbly up at the great edifice, drawn by those huge hideous eyes and the high dam that dwarfed him. He stood there, shaken, contemplating the strength of this ragged crew when weighed against the force and power of the mountain of water held back by the dam. The thought was overwhelming. It took an effort of will to steady his nerves as the others crept up from behind. Towering above at his right hand, the slope of the mountain crashed down against the wall of the dam, a rude and hellish sight as if two leviathans of another world were locked in a death grip—as, indeed, perhaps they were.

For a second he peered down at the puny picks and shovels he carried in his arms, then stared up again at the great wall of the dam. His fear turned to anguish. The thought of Colonel Mavro Anastasi flashed through his mind, and he could envision the man's countenance as clearly at this moment as he could see the wall of the dam. The big man back home and safe, seated piously before a crackling fire in the quiet of his study, the big hands stoking his pipe peacefully, then smoothing the arrogant spread of his mustaches.

The stark realization of the trap they were in struck Cil like a physical blow. He dropped the load in his arms onto the soft earth at his feet, his eyes still fixed on the dam. In fear and confusion, he first looked to Michelle to assure she was safe, then, for a moment his hand reached back involuntarily to touch the blade of the broken sword couched in his pack, to feel the security of it.

With that touch, his anguish turned to rage. The whole lunacy of the mission welled up in his mind. To entertain for one minute the delusion that a threadbare troupe, disparate and untrained, could bring a monster of this dimension to its knees was no more than cruel, comic folly. But he found his nerve and looked about him.

To Cil's immediate left loomed the low wall enclosing the power station, the wall topped with strands of razor wire gleaming odd menace in the silvery moonlight. Dead ahead, across the clearing and beyond the reach of the spotlights, stood a row of weeping willows, dark in the shadows and dwarfed by the dam, presenting in the uncertain light the specter of a row of mourners lined with heads bowed on the bank of the river.

Then Cil spied something that had escaped his notice. The light from the pair of ground spotlights, set a good distance apart, threw beams of such brilliance on the upper reaches of the dam that the dam wall at the base was cast in deep shadow. So dark was the base that Cil could scarcely make out the outline of the gently rounded mound of earth and ledge upon which the concrete dam was constructed.

With Michelle at Cil's side, the remainder of the puny band lined up at the edge of the clearing and set themselves. Then Zeljko pumped his arm straight over his head as if leading a charge.

The party exploded off the line. Crouching low, grunting under the collected burden of tools and equipment, they bolted into the flood of reflected light, stampeding out over the narrow clearing.

Once safe within the concealing shadow of the mound, all flopped down on the slope of the earthen dam, panting and gasping for breath. And from this vantage, Cil could see that the mound of the old earthen dam was overgrown with new-growth maple and poplar, the tallest of the young trees leaping ten meters or more up the wall of the high concrete dam above with the uppermost leaves shimmering like Christmas tinsel in the reflected glow of the spotlights playing high on the chalky wall overhead. As he and Michelle scaled the mound, he found the top of the mound oddly roofed by a lip of concrete jutting out six feet or more from the base of the great concrete dam to form a narrow shelf, high as a man's head. Here where they crouched, an odd sound came to them, a steady whirring noise.

"This way." The old man led the party along the crest of the mound. As they moved along beneath the great wall of the dam, a bar of golden light peeked out of the wall from three tiny squares in the generator room at the height of the tallest trees. The whirring noise was more distinct here; and as they moved close in under the bar of light, the steady whir of the heavy generators altered to a roar, filling the senses and drowning all sound of the big dam's spillway beyond and the river it spawned.

Here on the crest of the earthen dam, Cil conquered his fear and resentment, and, too, the rage that for a moment had threatened to consume him. He watched the old man position Michelle, then the Gypsy in the deeper shadows under the lip of the dam at points with a commanding view of the line of approach. Then Cil counted out the spare clips of ammunition, stacked them within easy reach, and received a nod of understood assurance from Michelle in her perch. Swiftly Zejko led Cil and the giant Muslim twins along the wall of the dam to a spot where he halted and wriggled out of his pack.

"Here!" Zeljko shouted over the roar of the generators. He picked up a spade and banged its tip down against what seemed a three-foot square cover of rotted boards lying flush with the ground. With three crashing thrusts of his spade, the rotted boards parted, collapsing, and dropped away to disappear into the black mouth of the hole.

Cil got down on his knees, gripping the sides of the square hole, the concrete sides coarse sandpaper on his hands. Slowly he lowered his head into the darkness until, even over the roar of the generators above, he could hear the faint gurgle of water below.

"Don't fall in," warned the old man in jest. "Or you find yourself in Mostar!" They stood there in the dark shadows, Cil, suddenly giddy with joy, clapping the old man on the back, for old Zeljko had indeed solved the primary riddle—the problem of disposing of the dirt. A catch basin of this size and dimension feeding directly into the river was truly a Godsend.

With Michelle and the gypsy standing watch, the rest in turns set about turning their spades into the loose dirt at the side of the catch basin. When a cavity of adequate size had been opened in the blackness under the protruding lip of the dam, the crew began burrowing on the horizontal, using the mountain of concrete above as a ceiling, and the noise of the generators as cover—and good cover it was.

After discovery of the catch basin, Cil's shovel moved eagerly, fairly singing through the packed earth. Once they had progressed well under the concrete wall of the dam, the shaft was steadily widened and deepened so that two men, though stooping and cramped, could dig shoulder to shoulder while the others shoveled the loose dirt back into the catch basin.

Finally, when they were well along and making steady progress, Cil put down his shovel and gestured to the old man. Within the tiny shaft, the roar of the generators seemed muffled, the hearing better.

"You go ahead," Cil told him. "We'll keep on." It was 1:25 AM.

"You know to get back?"

"No problem."

"Be out before first light!" Zeljko warned. "And take care with the girl."

Cil patted his back in the darkness.

"I show the bearded giant the trick to cover the entrance," explained the old man, turning to make his stooping way back through the opening to the spot where the giant Muslim brothers were shoveling the dirt into the catch basin.

The iron man, Agar the Ox, joined Cil in the digging up front while the old man drew two woolen blankets from his pack and shouted instructions into the Professor's ear. When the old man was content with the tall Moslem's understanding, he nodded at Cil, then slipped away into the darkness.

With the old man gone, the three remaining took turns with two at the digging, the third at the catch basin. Farther in, the bearded Professor and Cil began to deepen the shaft, increasing the headroom to a full five feet before gradually fanning out, expanding the width to six. In deepening the shaft, Cil's spade clanked heavily on something metallic, striking and bouncing wildly to the side. A few minutes of hard digging revealed a python of cast iron twelve inches thick, which the men traced back to the catch basin. They kept on with the shaft, following the path of the cast-iron pipe.

Now with the precise direction of their task confirmed, Cil wished the old man were there to share their excitement as the giant twins and Cil burrowed on with a zest that defied the pain in their arms and the soft watery blisters rising on the flesh of their hands.

While they moved steadily forward, the Professor took advantage of each lull in his toil, rigging with the use of the heavy blankets two light baffles from floor to ceiling, framed with wood fashioned from green saplings. It seemed the roughest makeshift affair, but allowed the advantage of light from a lamp wedged flush against the dirt of the wall. They went on digging with no sense of time as the hours rolled past, the men coughing in the dust, following the path dictated by the line of pipe. Finally, the Professor slapped Cil on the back.

"Soon will be first light. We must go."

Cil and the furiously panting brother, the Ox, threw down their spades, stowed the gear in the tunnel, then went outside and sat spent and exhausted, spitting the dust and grime of suspended dust particles from their mouths. Both men sat bent almost double in the wedge where the earthen mound met the concrete lip overhead while the Professor rigged a makeshift cover for the entrance, pressing scrub pines and poplar saplings into the soft earth as a veil.

Here in the deep shadow beneath the beams cast by the spotlights, all was inky black, and the little party was forced to leave with no assurance of the effort to conceal the entrance. As they collected Michelle and the gypsy, then crept away, they took comfort in the fact that the shaft mouth lay wedged under the shielding lip of concrete.

When the party had retraced its steps across the clearing and railway, then up the score of terraces of the soft, chuckling stream, mounting the sheer, rocky ledge below the waterfall, Cil was concerned to find Michelle continually lagging behind. He took her by the hand. Together they branched away from the others to relieve Bogey where she tended the horses, and once alone, found a nest of evergreen needles next to the fidgeting horses. As they seated themselves in the milky pre-dawn light, Cil drew a flask from his pack and passed it to Michelle.

"This native plum brandy isn't so bad," he encouraged. "Try some."

Surveying him at close quarters in the pre-dawn light, she brushed aside the aluminum flask.

"*Mon Dieu*," she exclaimed. "Why, this night the Serb

265

patrols might as well stay home. They couldn't find you at night on a bet. Look at yourself, you're a black man." And in reaction, Cil hurriedly wiped his face with the lining of his P-jacket, put the comb of his fingers through his hair, then determinedly spanked the dirt from his clothes. "The digging," she pressed. "Tell me, how did it go—really?"

For a moment, Cil remained silent. "A beginning, and so far, a breeze. Later comes the hard part." Then he could contain himself no longer. He fairly tripped over his words in haste and excitement to explain, finally remarking, "And the old man was right about the cast-iron drain pipe. It's a compass straight to the leaks at the front of the dam. And the Muslim twins—tough, very tough and steady. The two of them—why, they dig like moles in heat!"

But now her face clouded. "As I sat there on watch all through the night, that giant wall over my head, I was thinking...."

"Yes?"

"You know, you cannot simply unleash that great flood of water without first warning the people downriver. Out of simple humanity—you, you must give them warning."

At that, Cil came erect where he sat.

"You know the orders," he reminded her harshly. "At all costs, we maintain radio silence till the operation is completed. Besides, any warning, any warning at all would only be intercepted and increase the danger to the crew in the shaft. No—it's out of the question. And anyway, you know the engineering estimates. The great dam overhead is to remain intact with its stout footings and the ledge most of the way across underneath. No, no; the flooding is supposed to be gradual."

"But can you be sure?"

"Don't worry about it," his tone dismissive; but she could tell from his voice that he, too, had been wrestling with the same question.

"And Zeljko," she added, for the moment not wishing to

press the subject. "He's not a young man, *Cherie*. Where is he off to?"

"To meet his contact. Insists on going himself. He's convinced his papers are the best of the lot."

Michelle seized his arm. "Through enemy lines?"

"He must."

Michelle was left frowning; then later she sighed and a faint smile came to her lips. "You know, Zeljko said the loveliest thing when he left me at my post by the dam." When Cil perked up, she read his interest and squeezed his hand, but smiling, she turned his question aside. "Oh, it was nothing really; he said not to worry, that's all."

"Worry?"

"That he would not let you be killed."

Suddenly Cil sensed how upset she was. He took her in his arms and held her close, trying to sooth her, running his fingers through her soft, springy curls. When finally she calmed, he gripped her arms roughly, dramatically.

"Dammit, woman—you're supposed to be a soldier!"

Stunned, she turned to confront him. Then observing the mischievous glint in his eye, she tossed her head quickly and shook it in disgust.

"Oh, you damned fool!" she scolded. *"Sacre Bleu*—I should have known you had no heart."

She was silent for a time, after which she turned to face him squarely.

"You know, *Monsieur*—I don't know why I worry for you. After all, I hardly know you." There was clear implication in that lilting voice which Cil had not detected since that day long ago at the colonel's New York villa.

They sat in silence, listening to the first chirping of the birds in the trees, breathing in the fresh scent of evergreen blended with that of moist earth, peering east through the trees for the first break of dawn. He could smell the sweetness and feel the warmth of her. He took her in his arms, drawing her to him. Little by little, the moist tenderness of those wanting lips stirred fires long dead within him.

Later, Cil reached up and stroked the softness of her cheek. He felt a wetness, and it startled him.

"What is it?" he asked.

"I'm sorry, most likely nothing," she replied cautiously; but then the words gushed out like water from a tap. "It's, ah, it's just that more and more the headaches—they're coming back. Twice today I felt my head spin and started to fall. Bogey helped me." Then abruptly she caught herself. Her hand sprang to her lips as if to block the words. And then he felt the tremble of her shoulders. "Oh, *Cherie*—I'm so sorry! I, I did not mean to be so weak; I did not mean to tell you. I told myself I wouldn't—no matter what. You must forgive me; I won't do it again." She clung to him with the clinging arms of a child as if for dear life, and the tears flowed down her cheeks as her head nestled beneath his chin. Her breath came in tight gasping sobs.

The words stabbed out at him. The start of a morning breeze tossed wisps of her hair across his face, and the tresses licked at his ears and his neck. For a while he was breathless; but when he spoke, the words were gentle and low.

"When did they begin?" he asked.

"On the way in as you thought." Her voice was high-pitched as if she were panic stricken. "Somehow I was so sure they would—that they would go away as the doctor said, but then—but now—they only get worse." She hesitated. "Finally since I've found you—oh, I just couldn't bear to lose you now." The sobs were deeper now, racking her whole body. "Hold me, *Cherie*, tighter—even tighter if you can."

Finally, when she was better, she paused to ease her breathing; then, "You remember when I killed the Serb trooper cool as you please?" and he nodded. "Well," and now the words gushed out. "This time, while I waited out there on the mound—oh, how frightened I was for you. I was so sure something would happen, that you would be caught—or a cave-in. That, that I would not see you again to tell you of my...." She paused. "And of my guilt, my guilt for bringing you here against your will and your judgment. You must know how sorry I am for getting you into this situation. And now above all, I fear something will take you from me." She thought of the blackouts. "Or me from you."

Cil's voice, when it came, was once more steady and low. "Please, you mustn't talk nonsense...."

"But you don't understand!" she cut in, her words a plea.

"As for your head," he told her gently. "I, too, spoke with Doctor Rutledge. He said there would be headaches, and they would likely go away, then return," he lied. "And eventually, after months, they would go away completely. It's not been a month; you must give it a chance." And he lifted her chin and kissed softly the moist petals of her lips, then her eyes, the gentle slope of her upturned nose; she seemed to loosen, to begin to relax.

In a few minutes he could feel her breathing against his neck become regular, then deepen. He tried to regulate his own, to loosen the fear that suddenly gripped him.

He thought back to his last conversation with the doctor while Michelle and the colonel were busying themselves packing her things that last day at the hospital. He strained to recall the exact words. "There will be headaches for a while," he had said, "but slowly they will diminish, eventually go away entirely." Then he had warned of a tumor. "Rare, very rare," were the words. He had warned to watch closely for recurrent headaches once they had vanished completely. "Above all, watch for sign of blackouts or dizzy spells. At the first sign, get her to me—quickly." Those had been close to the exact words.

Dear God, he thought. And I let her come! And as they lay together wrapped in their own private world, he sensed himself inexorably bound to her. For a moment, he felt helpless and weak; he could feel tiny goose bumps come up

269

on his flesh and a lump in his throat, but he set his jaw and the steel of his will against it. "No good to worry," he told himself. "In two days, three at the most...."

32

By the time Cil returned from watch, the early sky, though light, hung low and leaden, a chill wind whipping the branches overhead. He pulled his P-jacket closer about him, then made for the knoll and the castle beyond. In the Great Hall, he came upon Bogey folding the bedrolls. Inexplicably, he found her clad in a flowing silk oriental dressing gown that was nothing if not skimpy and revealing, yet she wore it as if accustomed to these mountains and immune from the cold; she greeted him cheerfully.

"Join me," she said and bowed only enough to open the front of her gown and expose a generous cleavage, round and smooth to the eye as satin. She motioned him to be seated at the long table, then poured him a mug of coffee from a thermos. "We are deserted."

"The old man," he asked urgently. "Any word? And where are the rest?"

"The grinning gypsy, Chipmunk, he takes the post up top while the old man sleeps in a room at the back; he returned at first light."

"Then he got through."

"Barely. Thanks to the uproar and confusion in the village."

"Thank God—what of the others?"

"Ari and the Ox returned to the dam before dawn. I only know because they woke me to pack provisions—bread and cheese and goat's milk to sustain them."

"What?" Cil's immediate reaction was surprise, then anger. He had issued no orders for return to the shaft, and he cursed himself for deserting his charges and leaving the giant Muslims to their own devices. "Went back, you say— without so much as a lookout?"

"Oh!" She drew back at the rush of color to his cheeks, her tone apologetic. "I have spoken out of turn."

"No, no. They did the right thing." There was a lull in conversation clumsily filled by Cil's fumbling in his breast pocket as ten thoughts at once raced through his mind. He held a cigarette out to Bogey who brushed his hand for only a second too long as she accepted it, a lingering, intimate gesture. Taking the excuse to stand close above him while he offered a light, she made a show of tidying his hair, combing it out with her fingers. She seemed to have a fetish for his hair; she stroked it fondly, and he caught the scent of perfume and could feel the pressure of her delicate touch; she knew just how to use those fingers.

"About Michelle," Bogey ventured. "At risk of again speaking out of turn, I must tell you of her condition." She was still stroking his hair with her fingers; it was almost a caress.

"Yes, yes—the headaches and occasional dizzy spells, you mean." He got to his feet; he moved away to a respectable distance. "She told me of the two yesterday."

"Headaches—dizzy spells?" her face suddenly a storm of disbelief. "I'm talking blackouts—each longer than the last. Yesterday I counted five! Yes, and trouble to awaken her— even with smelling salts."

Cil could feel the color drain from his face. He held his tongue.

"You understand the danger, yes?" and though he didn't

answer immediately, she could read the answer in the set of his features.

"If there is a way," she said softly, "we should try to get her out now."

"Yes, yes. And Bogana—I want to know at once of any new spells. It's not that she, ah, doesn't tell me, but—well, perhaps some detail is lacking."

"I understand," she said, and he could tell from her tone that she did; and he got the distinct feeling that this woman before him, shrewd and sensitive, refined in her way and delicate, was anything but a peasant of the mountains. To alter the train, he put the question.

"Miss Bogana, you are not really a woman of the mountains?"

"What makes you say that?" She was suddenly smiling; an inscrutable expression flitted across her features while playful sparks flashed in her eyes.

"Your speech and manners—the subtle awareness back of that mask of yours."

"You are too kind," she said simply. But there remained something in the inflection of voice and the change of the smile, at once inviting, yet evasive, and as she turned from him in a lithe, graceful movement, the lines of her womanhood appeared all the more openly revealed to the eye.

"No, tell me; I must know—who are you really?"

She gazed at him now with a winsome air, but a promise of something she seemed intent to conceal hid in the shadows behind the long lashes. "Perhaps the day will come," she said softly and curtsied, then drew back suddenly with an unapproachable air. "In the meantime, we must look after *your love.*"

For an instant, Cil was stunned by her brashness, and, too, by a detected quality of voice both conspiratorial and faintly obscene; despite himself, he blushed. Then he brushed off the veiled suggestion, and his manner again became formal.

"If you could help look after her," he said. "For the next few days...."

"No need to ask," she said quickly, interrupting. "In all events, I would consider it my duty." He nodded and their eyes met. "And, oh," she said, "please, there is one more thing."

"Yes?"

"Major Cil, despite what you may think, we are not all of this land but beggars and thieves—and if I seem no more to you, then, so be it. For, perhaps now it is true—and I make no excuse for it."

She looked away before going on. "You see, this war does strange things—makes us all even strangers to ourselves. And would it surprise you to know that, less than four years past, culture and education flourished in our cities now reduced to waste and rubble—as we, too, now reduce ourselves to begging for favors."

For an instant, Bogana seemed to hesitate, then her expression changed, hardened.

"I will not, just now, bore you with the threads of my past," she told him, "but I ask one thing: if, in this military operation of yours, you intend to blow the great dam, for my people, you must do one kindness."

"Yes?"

And now her words began to flow out. "You cannot—under God's law—cast down the waters! No, no—not without warning. Not without warning release the fury of that flood upon our villages downriver—upon Mostar and Metkovic."

At this request, abruptly she turned and gave him her back.

"I do not ask for your reason, Sir," inclining her head, her voice nearly choking, "I ask for your soul and your heart."

Cil, who had begun to relax, now stiffened. It was the second time in so many hours that he had been reminded, and now as he moved toward the stone steps that led up to the ramparts, he veiled his reaction behind a cloak of authority.

"When the old man awakens, send him to me on the wall. And, ah, Bogey," in a quiet voice, "thank you."

When Cil arrived at the height of the parapet, he found, to his amazement, the diminutive figure of the gypsy, Chipmunk, clad in a many-colored jacket of splashy reds, yellows, and purple. The man was huddled behind the protective shark's teeth of stone, out of the blast of the wind.

"Damn, man—if you must wear that coat in broad daylight, at least turn it inside out."

"V-Very good," muttered a compliant Chipmunk, reversing his jacket. "Though there is a s-slight chill." Teeth chattering, he flashed a game smile, wiping from his chin a telltale stain of purple wine.

"Any sign of patrols?" And when the little man shook his head, Cil contemplated him thoughtfully for a moment. "Chipmunk, I wonder if you'd do me a favor; would you go down and watch the horses for me?"

"My pleasure, Sir May-jor," he declared with a crisp salute. "Trouble your m-mind no more, for it is done," and smiling graciously, he reached for his carbine.

"The woman with the fair hair sleeps by the horses in the lean-to in the lee of the wind. Stay clear, but keep an eye on her for me, would you?" and Cil winked.

"Have no worry, Ch-Chipmunk is here." And again the grin that sparkled, again the crisp salute.

"Let her sleep; she is not well."

"I understand not merely your words, but the meaning that lies at their back—fear not."

For an instant, Cil placed his hand on the little man's shoulder.

"Look," he said. "Stay close to her. If you notice anything, you know, out of the way, let me know—*pronto*."

The bronze-faced Chipmunk gave still another salute before skittering off down the steps; and Cil, once alone on the parapet, struggled to turn his mind from Michelle. With the wind whipping past his ears and ruffling his jacket, he contemplated his upcoming mission this night. And as he looked out on the white ruffled waters of the lake below, a sudden shudder of foreboding moved up his spine.

To the south and far downriver below the dam, he watched a cargo plane line up for final approach to the airstrip at the Serb compound. He followed its course until the desperate roar of its engines could be heard as, its wings barely clearing the trees, the plane lifted off to circle for another pass.

"So—this wind is as much your enemy." He waited for the plane to clear before again rising above the stone teeth of the wall and lifting his field glasses to scan the fringe of the forest below for the first sign of false movement. Then he looked far down the mountain, beyond the lake and the dam.

Far downriver from the dam, a speck caught his eye, a solitary speck on the opposite bank where the gorge widened out. He strained through the glasses; he could barely make it out.

It was at that moment that Zeljko appeared, moving up the steps, gingerly, laboring with each step and favoring his right leg, climbing with a decided limp.When he reached the height of the wall, he held up, panting. Cil could see huge beads of sweat standing out on the old man's forehead despite the chill wind.

"What is it?" demanded Cil with alarm. "What happened last night?"

"Close. Very close!" Zeljko, still panting, lifted one arm before his chest, flapping the hand loosely from the wrist in that peculiar way of the indigenous peoples.

"Let me see." Cil stooped, attempting to raise the other's loose-fitting pant leg until a knot of tangled muscle, yellow and raw, showed itself below the knee, bulging out in tightly bound ridges.

"Sit down," ordered Cil. "It's a wonder you can walk at all. How did it happen?"

"The far side of the river—top of the bluff. I run flat on a night patrol. At first, for sure they hear the horse, the way she snort at the end of her climb. But no; they keep up their jabber, and I lead the horse out." He looked a little sheepish. "I trip on the rock in the big hurry. But what of the niece of the colonel? Bogana, she talk of trouble."

For a second, Cil stood silent. "At first I thought it was nothing, but now...." When Cil had finished his explanation, the old man stood motionless. When he spoke, though his features betrayed no emotion, his voice seemed troubled and grave.

"No power can get her out now—look at my leg." He shook his head firmly and crossed himself. "It will be an act of God if the seven with shovels get through—and they come from the east. Is there for her no medicine?"

"Not for this, no." But the old man's message was clear, and Cil abruptly changed course. "The Professor tells of the massacre in the village. What of your wife?"

"Safe—she go with the cousins. Yesterday, the giant twins, they lead her out—to a camp back in the woods. There they not find her."

"Your man in Mostar? The contact was made?"

"This one time, yes," replied Zeljko. "But now all is sealed in—the whole of us—tight as fish in a barrel. What of the digging?"

"So far—good. We ran onto the drainage pipe, traced it back to the catch basin, then followed it forward."

The old man read the consternation on Cil's features.

"I see in your face there is more," Zeljko said.

"Only that the Professor and his twin returned to the dam before daylight without orders—not that there wasn't good reason. There was the question of concealing the entrance as we left the shaft before first light."

Zeljko tensed. "The return, it is against orders?"

"No. I gave no special order either way."

At that, the old man eased; he was silent for a time. "I stake my life on the wits of that Professor; both twins I know since the day of their birth."

Cil, lifting the field glasses from his chest, training them south, down below the dam and the gorge, adjusting the lenses until the speck on the bank downriver came into focus. "Down there on the far bank of the river—way down," he said. "Looks like a person."

"Each day, there does he fish," replied the old man. "Why the Serb put up with such a fool, that is the mystery."

Cil lowered his binoculars. Already his thoughts had switched to the second most important subject on his mind as he sought out the old man's eye.

"I must go to Baxter tonight," Cil declared, and the gravity of his words was not lost on the old man. Old Zeljko did not reply immediately; instead, he looked off at the surface of the lake roused by the wind. When at last he spoke, his voice betrayed both impatience and stubborn indignation.

"Hah—this night?"

"As soon as we get the signal."

"Is no other way? Before, I see the radio pack in your bag." The old man again stared down at the frothing white-caps ruffling the surface of the lake as an icy blast of wind tore at his coat and tussled his dark, shaggy mane. The question hung in the air. Cil could see the muscles working at the hinge of the old man's jaw. He squared off to face him.

"No. Radio transmission is out. The Serbs must surely have electronic detectors to pick up a signal." He gestured with his head toward the top of Bald Hill. "Suicide for them."

"And to cross that lake on this night?" mouthed the old man, stroking his chin.

"There's no other way—here, have a smoke."

Cil offered a cigarette to the old man, but the old man threw the cigarette down with a gesture of disgust. His tone turned harsh and unyielding. "I go keep watch down there," he declared haughtily, his manner aloof, striding off down the catwalk with a bold limping stride.

Cil watched the old man pick his way through the breaks and faults along the top of the parapet. He noticed, as the old man crunched along, that every few paces small chunks of stone would crunch and scatter from beneath his boots.

The man had progressed perhaps a hundred feet along the catwalk when Cil came up with a start and cried out.

"Rock slide!" Suddenly Cil was watching with horror as a whole portion of the top of the wall and the catwalk gave way. He saw dust fly and the old man go down, his hard-muscled frame falling hard in the debris. He watched the man's body being propelled over the edge on a carpet of loosely rolling stones.

Zeljko had vanished. All that remained to be seen were his hands which appeared to take on a life of their own, frantic fingers could be seen clawing at the edge of the wall for purchase.

Cil raced for the break in the wall. He was already in full stride when he heard the crash of debris strike the floor of the courtyard below. Bogey's scream came as she bolted out the door at the base of the wall.

"Hang on! Hang on!" shouted Cil quite stupidly.

Now Cil was close. Zeljko's face shone as ripe as a beet, as oddly distorted as a reflected image in a carnival crazy mirror: the eyes bulging out and veiny—the tips of the fingers so many pieces of chalk, now stark white and bloodless, matching the pallor of Bogey's face as she frantically watched from below.

Upon approaching the spot where the old man hung dangling over the edge, Cil leapt into the air. In the process of his leap, he tossed up one leg and twisted his body so that when he landed, facing out over the edge of the wall, his boots straddled Zeljko's head and shoulders. In one continuous motion, Cil hunkered down in a low crouch so that his boots braced against the outermost stones of the wall while his fingers looped through and hooked under the fallen man's belt at the back. Cil lowered his head until his chin lay buried in the small of the man's back. Zeljko's shirt was wet and reeking of the sour sweat of panic. Then, both men's muscles bulging as one, slowly, inch by inch, the combined effort hoisted the burly frame upward.

When finally the toes of the old man's boots found purchase on the lip of the wall, his legs churned through the rubble like runaway pistons, his body scooting for safety—to finally collapse on a pile of debris.

There sprawled the two men, gasping for air. Bogana, rushing up the steps from below two at a time, sprawled as if in a swoon, piling on the backs of the men. Her arms embraced and enfolded them. She held them in a death grip as fat tears trailed down her cheeks. All three beamed at one another as might inmates on week-end furlough from the local asylum.

33

The four newcomers, heavily armed and anxious men, stood about the cavernous Great Hall of the castle, slapping and brushing the dust of the trail from their clothes. They were not laughing, not joking with relief at a safe arrival as one might have expected but instead shifted uncertainly on their feet, stunned, weary with fear and exhaustion, white-faced and watchful. One, the leader, stood toying nervously with his pistol, observing the sensuous Muslim woman, Bogey, in her revealing dressing gown as she tended the fourth man bleeding from an arm wound.

The moment Zeljko entered the room, Bogey flashed him a warning glance. Remaining only long enough to extract the information he needed, he left the room to intercept Cil, then led Cil to a drafty chamber at the back. Even before old Zeljko spoke, Cil read the alarm on his face.

"Trouble," warned Zeljko. "Before dawn, seven begin through the hills. But four remain. One with a flesh wound. The others lost to patrols on the way." He waited for Cil to absorb the weight of the news. "They are unnerved. Best you carry this." He shoved a revolver into Cil's hands, along with a belt studded with cartridges.

"You say, lost three men on the way in? Where?" Cil fingered the revolver and checked it for balance.

"In the hills to the east." Looking at Cil holding the pistol, Zeljko tensed. "You know to use if you have to?" he asked, recalling it was not he, but the girl who had brought down the Serb trooper on the way in.

"I can manage."

"Is a good thing." That was all the grim-faced old man would say.

He watched in silence as Cil loaded the weapon and slid it under the belt at his waist. Zeljko was arming himself when Cil addressed him.

"You are certain they were not followed?"

The man faltered. "I—I cannot be sure.""

"What?" Cil fired the question. He stared at Zeljko for only an instant. Then abruptly he wheeled and hurried for the door.

In the Great Hall, the peasant leader had positioned himself on the far side of the heavily planked table, flanked by his men. He was standing, back to the wall, his gaze wary, his attention trained on the main entrance door. As Cil strode in with Zeljko at his heels, the peasant leader shifted his gaze and eyed him as if something long dead had suddenly entered the room.

A glance confirmed to Cil what the old man had told him. Except for the leader, these were not men, but mere boys, and from the wide-eyed expressions of wonder and shock, the crude, muddy boots, patched shirts, and dark baggy pants with safety pins closing the fly where once a zipper had been, he judged them indeed spur-of-the-moment recruits impressed from one upland farm or another. Though robust strapping lads, none could have passed for a boy beyond twenty.

In contrast, the leader, a short, swarthy, sharp-eyed man of forty, wore the ravages of life on his features, perhaps a reflection of the arduous life of a barman or horse trader. His features were handsome enough in a crude and primitive way, with a pony-tail that trailed down his back. Yet, at this moment, the eyes, quick and alert, smoldered with suspicion under the dark curving bush of his brows. The face carried the brash and smirking quality of a man long accustomed to pushing people around. Cil halted before him, confronting him squarely.

"I ask you directly—were you followed?"

The peasant leader, ignoring the question, turned to his men; his face wore a mask of disdain.

"So!" he leered. "What have we here—the great Yankee hero?" He allowed his gaze to rest upon Cil's hardened features for only a contemptuous second before fixing on the old man. "I, Slobodan, the mountain commander, come here to serve no foreigner."

"You fool," snapped Zeljko, taking a step forward to glare at the peasant leader who stood before his men with arms folded arrogantly over his chest and the crossed bandoleers studded with grenades that ran up over his shoulders. "Answer the question."

"Why must you ask, old man?" smiled the peasant leader, measuring his words. "Slobodan, the mountain commander, is no fool. Is it only the true native Yankees with feathers in their hair who know to always double back to cover their tracks—as I did? Tell me," he said. "How is it the old hunter grovels for the favor of a foreigner? Already this hero cost me three men."

"The Serb, Little Commander, cost you your men."

"Ha, that is but half truth." The smile died and the mouth twisted down. "It was the provocation that killed them!"

"Provocation?" Zeljko suddenly looked unsettled.

The little commander nodded toward Cil. "By his own hand, he cost me my men. Ask him; it was his provocation that drew the patrols."

Cil stepped forward to face the man down. He could feel the eyes of the room focused upon him. Hands on hips, his military boots planted firmly apart, Cil looked down on the diminutive figure of the stranger from his full gathered height.

"For what purpose do you come here?" he demanded. "To whine or to fight?"

"First you tell." Slobo begged the question. "Where is it you directed your little provocation, eh, Hero?"

The old man tensed, aware at once of the man's direction; but Slobo's words stole the thought from his mind.

"It was your false rape that pointed the finger. That's right. Pointed the finger straight at the village! When you killed the Serb trooper, you planted the body to show he had been with a girl. Am I right? Like someone stabbed him over the girl?" The little commander was enjoying the game. "But everyone knows the only girls in these parts are girls of the village—and so, the assassin as well." The little commander turned to the old man and squinted his eyes. "And now is this thing of the bus."

"What bus?" The blast of Zeljko's voice explored every crevice of the Great Hall.

"The bus of the village school. The big yellow school bus missing since yesterday with twelve small ones on board."

"Oh, no!" wailed Bogana. To this point she had been quietly ministering to the wounded young man, expertly cleansing and dressing the arm wound, but now fear clapped her hand to her mouth. "Oh, merciful God. Not the children!"

The little commander behind the planked table took this opportunity to seat himself. In turn, he motioned his men to follow suit, flanking him. He stared up at Cil's standing across the table facing him. With casual ease, Slobo drew his pistol, opened the frame, spun the cylinder playfully, and set the gun on the table before him while he toyed with one round which he bounced in his hand.

"How you know this?" snapped Zeljko.

"Me? Ha, the whole world knows; I do not lie. From the high mountain passes to the steel bridge at Metkovic—

everyone knows."

Instinct told the old man it was true, but he could not grasp it. "But...."

"No but's!" Slobo cut him off sharply, enjoying the game. "Think of it; the bus of the village school escapes from this earth without trace. Now I ask you, how can that be, when, as we both know in these parts, an old woman's broom cannot disappear from her back step without half the village to know of the disaster? No, there can be no mistake. The children are stolen!"

It was at this point that Michelle rushed into the room. Then, sensing the tension, she froze in her tracks as the peasant commander surveyed her appraisingly.

"So that is The Yankee's whore," Slobo observed, surveying her feminine charms, employing the confusion of her sudden appearance to conceal his actions as his fingers deftly shoved the live round he held into the cylinder. He clicked shut the frame, spun the cylinder, and aimed the weapon straight at Lane Cil.

Cil, all the while observing the man's actions, had also used the time to advantage. He had studied the revolver earlier as it lay on the table and noticed a paint mark on its revolving cylinder. He had noticed, too, when the frame was open, that the the cylinder had been empty. But after once injecting the round, from the position of the paint mark, Cil had noted that the leader in his haste had spun the cylinder containing the round past the firing position. Cil stood three paces from the table.

"All right," thundered Cil. That's enough!" He strode forward unhurriedly up to the table. As if time was somehow suspended, he watched the pistol in Slobo's hand. He noticed a tremor in the hand holding the weapon, a nervous wag of the trigger finger at the moment of decision. He heard the slight shuffle of the man's boots against the silence of the room. He smelled the odor of rubbing alcohol blended with stale tobacco smoke and unwashed bodies; it came to him strongly.

In a single fluid motion, Cil lifted his arm and swung it as a club, not in a clumsy swipe, but in that lithe motion of a tennis player making a straight-elbowed back hand swing of the racquet, so that the back of Cil's hand swatted the raised and pointed pistol from the outstretched arm to flip through the air, careen off the hard stone floor of the Great Hall, then clatter and spin to a standstill at the base of the wall.

Zeljko had already drawn his weapon. He moved swiftly to disarm the others, but Cil waved him off.

"Save it," he ordered. "Expect no trouble from those men." Cil, still eyeing the mountain commander, turned to Zeljko. "Make sure all of them, including our friend here, are generously provisioned. Then see them to the dam. With only four men, not seven, we cannot wait for nightfall." Cil threw a glance at the little commander climbing unsteadily to his feet. "And if there is trouble with this one—well—that's up to you."

As soon as Zeljko had led the men from the room, Cil turned his attention to a more ominous question. If a school bus loaded with children had vanished, there was only one place it could be.

34

The moment Zeljko and the ragged band of recruits moved out of earshot, Cil eyed the two women with such force and conviction that they immediately dropped what they were doing.

"Since the three were gunned down," he told them, "the Serbs can have no doubt of our presence. They'll come looking for the others, following the trail of their horses. Throw everything remaining into the escape tunnel—everything! Discarded equipment—ammo—any weapons the newcomers left behind. Erase the last trace of our presence."

The two women set to work with the urgency of firefighters trapped in a forest with their backs to the flames. In no time, Bogey was wiping the last of the blood drops from where the wounded recruit had bled on the floor while Michelle sprinkled handful after handful of the powdery dust of the courtyard over everything—the floors, the steps, the table, and the benches. With the huge oaken doors swung wide, the wind slid its swift fingers within the great castle chambers, driving out the last odors of human presence, blowing the fine dust to spread and drift to every nook and cranny of the Great Hall.

Cil moved up the steps to the height of the wall to find One-Eye. He felt the first spatter of rain on his face as clouds rolled in so low overhead that tendrils of mist shrouded the turrets above him. Once having dispatched the gypsy to stand watch at the mountain's northern approaches, Cil raised his field glasses, shielding the lenses from the rain with his hands. Slowly, methodically, he scoured the hem of the clearing below the castle knoll. Below the canopy of tall pine, he could see Chipmunk, carbine in hand and kerchief bound to his head, tending the horses where they were sheltered. Swinging the glasses slowly, again he scanned along the line of the forest.

For an instant, he thought he spied movement. Arm muscles taut, he fixed the spot with his gaze as the rain pelted down.

"Jumpy, that's all," he told himself aloud, stamping his feet to fend off the cold. Leaning out between the heavy stone shark's teeth and peering down at the courtyard below, he could see Michelle hauling the last of the bundles toward the upper mouth of the escape tunnel where Bogey, standing waist-deep in the shaft, arranged things below with quick hands. Cil nodded at their quiet efficiency, at how smoothly they worked as a team with petty differences for the moment set aside.

Unshouldering his M-16 assault rifle, Cil tucked the snout of the weapon under his jacket in out of the rain. Again he lifted the glasses and fixed his gaze on the spot below the slope of the knoll at the dark edge of the forest.

Suddenly Cil dropped to his knees. Three uniformed figures in full battle dress and the unforgettable cap of the dead Serb trooper pushed out of the foliage and stepped into the clearing. They moved out away from the trees at a stealthy pace, slowly at first, advancing up the bare knoll toward the courtyard where Michelle and Bogey were still dispatching the last of the new men's spare equipment. In a moment, two more figures emerged from the trees, for the moment similarly screened from the women by the corner stones of the courtyard.

Cil dared not risk calling out from the height of the wall. Instead, from where he knelt, jammed low behind one of the stone shark's-teeth, he motioned furiously at the women below. Consumed by their duties, they paid him no heed. A hundred thoughts flashed through his mind as the enemy troopers advanced; they seemed to come on at surprising speed.

The patrol was close now, very close, the lead trooper a scant twenty paces from the wall, moving cautiously, each advancing soldier swinging his weapon from side to side in a practiced, professional way, searching. The women went on with their work.

Quiet desperation seized Cil. Helpless, he watched the women toiling below. He watched the search party narrow the distance. His lips parted and a panicky rasp escaped from his throat. "Hell with the noise; got to do something!" He seized a shard of crumbled stone from the debris at his feet and let fly the small stone. The stone took forever to reach the floor of the courtyard. "Damned fool stone."

Cil did not hear the stone strike the floor of the courtyard below, but he observed the women's startled expressions as their heads lifted skyward. He thrust out a fist with one raised finger jabbing at the air, motioning furiously toward the corner of the courtyard. After a moment of understanding, Michelle lunged for the last soaking bundle.

Now the point man was so close Cil could make out his features. Under the soaking visored cap, Cil could see plainly the thrust of the hard lantern jaw, the polished sheen of the rain on his cheeks; fat droplets of rain gleamed off the barrel of his automatic weapon.

Cil wiped the rain from his face, but he could feel it replaced by beading sweat despite the pelting rain and the bite of the wind. Below, Bogey ducked from view as Michelle, her white arms stretching out from the mouth of the tunnel, strained to slide the circular cover down over her head.

Another moment and the entrance was sealed, both women tucked safely away in the bowels of the tunnel as the point man stepped lightly up onto the stones of the courtyard, half-crouching, AK-47 assault rifle held at waist-level, the man's attention momentarily diverted by a sound. Cil watched and listened. Even with the wind and the rain, the sound of the swinging doors of the Great Hall carried to him distinctly. The rusted metal hinges creaked on the wind.

Soaked through to the skin, kneeling in a puddle along the high catwalk with one eye cocked over the side, Cil pressed forward for a better look. He could see the point man moving cautiously along the base of the wall, one rain-slick boot treading scant inches from the circular shaft cover. That of his following companion planted itself squarely upon it, but Cil saw no sign in the man's actions that he read something amiss. Then the third man moved across. Soon, all three vanished within the high swinging doors of the Great Hall while their two companions in the rear lingered behind, scouting the grounds.

Cil was certain it would take the three in the castle but a moment to figure out where the stone stairway in the Great Hall led. He was determined not to provide a personal welcome upon their arrival. Gathering himself for the attempt, mindful of the two troopers still in the courtyard, quietly as haste would permit he scampered along the catwalk, racing for the spot where the old man had fallen such a short time ago. As he neared the point of the rock slide, his eye measured the distance to the mist-shrouded turret beyond; it seemed like a mile.

Already too much time had elapsed since the three had entered the Great Hall. As he ran, an image took shape in his mind of the first trooper blossoming in the doorway at his back.

Robbed of choice, weapon slung, Cil took three running

strides and flung himself into the air, hurdling the rock slide with inches to spare. Without glancing back, he dashed down the catwalk with all the deftness of a charging bull elephant. He could hear the debris crunching underfoot to spill over the side. He could visualize the stones crashing in the courtyard below. Still he kept on. At last he reached the end of the parapet and plunged headlong through the doorway into the south turret. His boots only a blur, he sprang up the spiral steps to the square window near the top of the silo. Gasping and spent, he peered back along the catwalk wreathed in the swirl of the mists.

He had made it. A brief sense of relief swept over him. Brushing the rain from his eyes, he spoke to himself sternly to steady his nerves. He waited. He went on peering out the window through the wind-driven rain and slow rolling mists like the swells of the sea.

The first soldier pressed out of the far doorway onto the catwalk, followed by the second, then the third. All three advanced down the wall in his direction, moving as before in a crouching shuffle, slowly, cautiously, weapons held at the ready.

Holed up here as he was, Cil felt a surge of adrenaline pump through his veins. He stared at the lead trooper, squinted his eyes, and dared him to come.

By the way the man gave orders, Cil could see that the second trooper in line had to be the corporal. When all three reached the break in the wall where the old man had fallen, the corporal leaned down to pick up an object. Slowly and inquisitively the man turned the object over in his hands, examining it carefully. He rose and showed it to the others.

Cil could see they were talking it over. From where he crouched, blinking through the mist, it looked like a cup— or a mug. Cil was unconcerned with the object. He cared only whether he had been seen or heard in the wild sprint down the catwalk. Judging by the casual demeanor of the three as they huddled about the cup, Cil guessed not. He lowered the stubby snout of his automatic rifle. He cocked the weapon and heard the hollow metallic clank as he stared through the drifting tendrils of mist.

For what seemed an eternity, the three soldiers huddled on the far side of the rock slide. Then the corporal gave a command. One private, a tall gangling fellow who walked like a duck, made as if to hurdle the gap in the wall. At the very last second, he pulled up short, backing off timidly.

A second command parted the air. For a moment, the spindly private paused as if to argue the point. Then slowly, ever so hesitantly, he stepped back a few paces to get a run on the yawning abyss. Then he was off. Three jerky quick-steps and a desperate leap! His boots landed duckfooted, barely catching the edge. For a moment, he hung there, wavering, flailing one arm in the air like a bird madly flapping one wing, his weapon held in the other until it fell from his grasp. Then he squatted low, pawing the stones at his feet in frantic effort for balance. A few seconds later, Cil heard the muted clatter of the rifle as it shattered on the floor of the courtyard below. Watching the soldier teetering there on the edge, for a split second Cil even felt a twinge of pity—until he spied the third man toss the private his own assault rifle. Cil would know that weapon anywhere.

The corporal, poised safely on the far side of the gap, barked a further command. The gangly private started forward, advancing toward Cil with the same duckfooted gait. Slowly Cil eased farther back into the shadows of the turret. Raising the snub nose of his weapon once more, he cocked his head to line up on the sight. He watched the advancing trooper abruptly brush off his cap; it flopped down into a puddle on the catwalk. Cil fingered the selector switch on his weapon. The trooper ranged closer. Cil could see the lines of the raindrops streaming down the man's tunic, the frightened eyes, the rain-matted hair, the way the mouth hung half-open and slack with fear.

Now the soldier was lost from sight as he entered the

door of the turret below. Seconds passed. Cil heard the tell-tale crunch of bootsteps on the rubble that coated the steps of the silo. He could hear the man as he began his ascent.

In the silence and shadows, Cil waited. The hollow clump of footsteps broke off. Cil's ears strained for the faintest sound.

For what seemed a century, no further sound came, only the patter of the light splashing rain. Nothing. Then the faintest rustle, like cloth rubbing against cloth; then again nothing, only the intermittent noise of the wind whistling past the outer stones of the turrent and the patter of rain. Cil waited; he waited impatiently; he waited with the ugly snout of his weapon aimed down the stairwell.

The M-16 assault rifle has a muzzle velocity of 3,000 feet per second. On automatic, this weapon has cyclic rate of fire of 1250 rounds per minute. It fires a 55 grain copper-jacketed round with a steel core that spins out of the barrel at the rate of one revolution every ten inches.

Cil, with his long combat experience, knew only too well the characteristics of the Russian made AK-47 assault rifle in the hands of his opposite number—and of the heinous rounds that it fired. He knew that each sleek, slim round that the rifle carried had been primarily designed not to kill, but to gut and to maim, for in battlefield conditions it takes only two soldiers to remove a dead soldier from the field of battle, but five or more to remove a thrashing, wounded man— not to mention the psychological effect upon the opposition.

Cil could feel his throat going dry; he held his nerve. He clicked his rifle's selector switch one position, to semi-automatic fire and aimed the snout of his weapon for a stone in the wall, darker than the rest, where the rain-slick tunic rounding the inner wall would first come into view.

He waited, smelling the familiar oily smell of his weapon, not daring to breath, working to fix in his mind whether a head shot or a chest shot was the better bet. He decided the chest—the safe shot.

When no sound came, it played on his nerves. Though he had wiped off the rain, he could feel dampness coming again in the creases of his forehead—ever more wetly under his arms.

Then he smelled it—the best known smell to civilized man. Cil's eyes blinked in surprise as he thought to himself, "Why the fool! He's standing there smoking! Just me up here—and him down there—and all the while the fool just taking his time away for the watchful eye of his corporal—smoking."

In a minute or two, Cil heard the impatient shout of the corporal. After an appropriate interval, the calm and measured response sounded from below.

Cil knew it was over and he sucked in his breath. He waited for the moistness to again come to his throat. Though he seldom prayed, he said a prayer now—of thanks, and once again his body began to feel the bite of the wind as the sound of stomping boots came to him clearly. They were moving away.

35

The rain drove down in sheets as only rain can in this ancient Slavic land. Old Zeljko was doing some driving of his own. He was escorting the band of new arrivals down the knoll, away from the castle. As the men looked back, the image of the castle ramparts thrusting into the blanket of rain-swollen cloud conferred upon the great edifice not only an air of medieval majesty, but etched as it was against a gray and brooding sky, almost an aura of the divine.

With the rain beating at their backs, the little band entered the forest below, bound for the ledges and the back of the dam, the sly-eyed little commander, Slobo, in the lead, followed by Zeljko with a gun at Slobo's back, then the three farm boys. All but Zeljko had been shorn of their weapons. Instead, they carried picks and shovels, axes and saws, and two of the strapping farm lads in the rear lugged a four-wheeled cart. The old man trudged along, limping painfully. As he cautiously scanned the woods ahead, he addressed the surly peasant commander.

"Tell me the truth," he demanded, prodding Slobo in the rump with the muzzle of his ancient hunting rifle. "How is it a man of your experience lose three on the way in?"

"I tell nothing to turncoats!" snapped Slobo defiantly.

"Do not forget who holds the gun."

"Today the gun is your balls, old man. Tomorrow will be different." The little commander twisted his head just enough to reveal the contempt registered on his features.

"I say—speak!" Zeljko again jammed forward the muzzle of the gun at that spot of the other's anatomy where he had long suspected the man's brains could be found. After the briefest pause, the little commander began his story.

"It was in the poor light of dawn, maybe four, five kilometers south." Slobo's voice took on a high-pitched theatrical tone. "Seven strong we ride through the night. Then we dismount, walking the horses up a wooded steepness, keeping always alert, always silent."

Only a deaf man could have failed to overhear the disbelieving sigh at his back, yet Slobo continued undaunted.

"As I say, it was the early light before dawn, mist in the trees. And then, ah—well, they must have had warning.

"Fifty of the bastards if there was one," he went on, "all dug in deep cover at the top of the ridge. They come at us like wolves. I don't lie, a pack of wolves with razor-sharp teeth!" Again the yawning sigh from behind. "They hold their fire until we reach the top, see. And then the bastards open up. In the crossfire, we are cut down like ripe barley before the scythe. One minute, dew on the grass and light the color of goat's milk; the next—the fire of hell on earth! I do not lie; we didn't stand a chance." He was mopping his brow breathlessly, theatrically. "Only by a miracle of God do any survive. Without fog like hell, all still would lie on that hill!"

Tension gripped Zeljko's voice. "What of papers? Do any carry papers or maps? You know—before I just now pass out the new ones—any of the dead?"

"Papers, no. Ha, you forget your own orders, old man. You think I am stupid? 'No light and no papers', you say!" Then he turned and smiled, and his face was almost handsome. "Papers? Hah, I doubt any carry so much as one spare change of underwear!"

"And you hear no word of warning? No—'halt and identify'?"

"None!"

"You sure? Before they open fire?"

"Positive."

"Hmm. Then the orders—they are changed."

"That is most comforting to hear, Old Grandmother."

They went on for a time without speaking; the cawing of a crow in the high branches reported their passing. After a time, the old man spoke again.

"You act the fool in front of the Yankee. Why?"

"His days, they are numbered. No Yankee bastard makes an ass of Commander Slobo before his men!"

"You give him small choice."

"Listen, at this very second do I feel my hands on his lily white throat!" He mouthed the words with truly dramatic flare. "For mercy he kneels and begs before the mountain commander!"

"Over my corpse."

"That I can arrange."

Again a damp blanket of silence descended over the pair as they trudged along the rain-matted forest floor, their clothes soaked through by the rain which beat and lashed at their backs. The old man pricked up his ears, listening for the first discordant note from the forest, but all he could hear were the whistle of the wind and the steady patter of rain in the boughs overhead. To divert his attention from the pain in his leg, Zeljko focused his full concentration on the sounds of the forest ahead. It was Slobo who broke the silence.

"This is my war, old man—the war of my people, the peaceful and loyal Serbs of these mountains who fight for one Bosnia. We need no help from the likes of your foreigner. And your head rots, old man, if you think we fail to remember—that even you are half Croat. Yes, that is true, and we remember as yesterday the Ustashe crimes against my people during the Great War and under your Nazi puppet, Pavelic, as you herded my people to your death camps—as with your teeth you pluck the hearts from the flesh of our babies. Oh, no, we need no help from the likes of you and that pretty-faced Yankee and his sweet-smelling whore." Even lashed by the rain, his neck at the collar flushed a hot rosy red. "Mark my words. Commander Slobo takes orders from no man!"

"And you, Slobo The Great Mouth, you were not even a gleam in the eye of your father in the days of the Great War."

"That changes nothing. What is, is. Old man, you forget; it is my people, not yours, who are the victims!"

Zeljko shook his head in disgust. "You wait. That sour, lying tongue of your hate, it is that tongue that robs all our peoples the support of the West."

But now the old man paused and bit back his anger. He knew the danger of this man, so he made an attempt to patch over old differences.

"If we stay too pig-headed to learn from the past," Zeljko said, "then all is lost. You alone give orders on your mountain, as I on mine, and my Nedo on his. But this question is bigger—is a question for all of our peoples." A deep sigh of resignation erupted from his chest. "It is the fact of life; one time or other in this life, one is to hold the rag over the nose and do what is best. And you, Slobo, you must do this in this thing of the dam. Is no time for a man to live in his hate."

"Old man, I will do this thing of the dam—not for you or that filthy foreigner, but for my people. In that, you have reason." And then the actor reemerged. "But I delight in the thought of the point of my blade stuck in the swan-white gizzard of that meddling Yankee bastard." And when Slobo turned back to face him, the old man could see the curl of amusement on the wet, handsome lips, and the flame of hate that breathed from the eyes. He knew beyond question every word was an act, but more than an act, a promise born of his ancestors.

Zeljko's expression sharpened. "And this thing of the school bus?" he demanded suddenly. "How is it you stand sure both bus and children are stolen hostage?"

"Take my word," responded Slobo hotly. "As I say in the Great Hall, twenty young ones do not vanish without trace in one day. And the provocation? Hah—we both know the answer to that one."

They had reached the limestone ledges, the sheer rock face where the water spilled down, cascading onto the green rocks below painted with algae. One by one, the men lowered the red, four-wheeled metal cart and other equipment, then themselves, and kept on, wading down the streambed where the current frothed at their pant legs and babbled curious gossip at their passing. When the little group reached the point where the trail of water leveled out with the terrain and dove into the limestone, the old man held up the others and scouted ahead.

Head tucked into his shoulders, body compressed in a low moving crouch, old Zeljko stole away until he reached the abandoned railbed before the clearing beneath the power transmission lines. At the edge of the clearing, Zeljko parted the dripping pine boughs, cautiously, to assure himself the coast was clear.

He jumped back on reflex. Approaching from the left at some distance was an enemy patrol fanned out along the clearing beneath the high tension lines running away from the power station at the back of the dam. And then at that instant, there came a loud explosion like the burst of an artillery shell or a landmine. Zeljko ducked, then watched as the oncoming troopers looked up at the sky.

Zeljko used the confusion to scoot away a dozen paces, employing the line of scrub pine to shield him from view.

Reminded of the presence of land mines, he rolled and tumbled into a drainage ditch that ran beneath the ancient railbed and below the line of vision of the advancing troops. Desperate to discover a route of escape for his men, he scampered along the drainage ditch the full width of the clearing and peeked through the undergrowth at the far end. He spied what he most dreaded. His path was blocked.

Swarming up from the row of willows lining the bank of the river, he spied a second patrol—advancing straight at him. The old man wheeled and bolted back up the drainage ditch, retracing his steps. He could barely feel the pain of his injured leg.

On the bare ground beneath the transmission lines, the first patrol was closer, coming on in a broad sweep, their progress measured, relentless. He could see the rain patter down on the dark metal helmets.

Two troopers toward the rear of the patrol were talking.

"Without doubt the captain has dropped a stitch to send us on such a wild goose chase. If there is danger, it comes from the front, not the back of a dam. One attacks a dam from the front where the force of the water assists; it is a simple law of physics."

"Shush—is our duty."

"Then why must we make all the patrols while others drowse and sip beer in the barracks with nothing to do?"

"Nothing to do but wonder who is sleeping with their sweetheart back home," responded the second private. "Now you better shut up."

"Remember Comrade Miso from our first training?" asked the first private in a burst of excitement.

"The name rings a bell, but I don't place the face. Now quiet and watch the corporal."

The first private suddenly sobered. "I suppose you even forget what they made us do yesterday in the village!"

The chatter earned a sharp rebuke from the snapping eyes of the corporal up front, but the first private, now with a tremor in his voice, spoke on to keep his mind from the experience about which he had just spoken.

"No, no—you remember—the muscle man with the chest of a champion who wet his bed nightly." So intent was he in the telling, he failed to notice his corporal in the lead had halted in his tracks, cocking one ear at noises emanating from beyond a stand of stunted pine that blocked the view ahead. Yet, heedless of the action of his leader, the loquacious private went on, his voice lit with enthusiasm. "Well, before we left training, Miso received a letter from his sister in Belgrade. He says she is a diplomat."

"Yeah, yeah. Another pocket diplomat conducting her foreign relations, not between the lines, but the sheets."

"Could be." The first private paused to wipe the rain from his eyes. "Anyway, she wrote that the shore at Dubrovnik is one 'unbroken line of palm trees and topless beach girls soaking up sun.'"

The corporal in the lead suddenly dropped to his knees, motioning the others down. In one continuous motion, he then raised the long steel barrel of his rifle, slammed the butt against his shoulder, and trained the sights on the line of scrub pine ahead, the boughs swaying crazily to the queer swirl of the wind below the dam.

"And so, I have an idea about these girls...."

"Shut up!" snapped the second private, grazing his buddy's ribcage with the butt of his rifle so that the first private slumped to his knees in surprise and pain. It was only then that the gasping trooper observed the other members of the patrol suddenly crouching, motionless, while the corporal up front, aiming his rifle, still listened to the odd noises emanating from beyond the trees.

And now the first private, too, bent his ear to the queer sounds coming from beyond the trees. For only seconds did he listen. Then, the pain in his ribs forgotten, he climbed to his feet, a look of recognition and boldness illuminating his features.

Private Krautzic had been weaned on those sounds—the sharp, resounding echo of steel against wood in the dense air that compounded and intensified sound—the clear rhythmic hum that sang through the trees—the husky, almost melodic blending of voices. These were the sounds that came to him now from beyond the line of scrub pine.

He could read the fear on the faces of his comrades and sense the compressed tension of his corporal. Yet, Private Krautzic felt neither fear nor confusion, for the blend of sound coming to him was the music of his home region, and it made him feel somehow whole and important. With the calm borne of assurance, he strode past the rest of the patrol with a spring to his step. He burst through the pine boughs, ignoring the frantic gestures of his superior. He moved ahead carelessly so that the butt of his rifle nearly dragged on the ground, and once through the trees, he encountered precisely what he had expected. A crew of peasant workmen, standing in the bed of an old abandoned railway, whistling and laughing despite the rain, laboring to tear out worn ties, preparing to saw them into lengths and split them for firewood, a scene so common in the hills of his own native Bosnka Krajina.

When the corporal and the remaining members of the patrol pressed through the thicket of needles, the private was standing ahead, poised, halfway to the workers, his legs crossed, his weight leaned carelessly upon his rifle, his eyes smiling and eyeing the scene before him. The workers laughed and joked and toiled cheerfully on, ostensibly as heedless of the intrusion as they were of the rain.

The corporal gaped and gaped again, having not the foggiest notion how to greet this queer happening. Before he could compose himself, one of the workers—an old man, thick-chested and surprisingly agile for his years with large Spanish eyes—strode forward, albeit with a limp, and with a gracious, cheerful countenance, offered his hand. The corporal, now totally confused and shaken as the old man vigorously pumped his limp hand and offered a jug of plum brandy, accepted gratefully, seizing the jug in hopes of restoring his nerve. The old man, exhibiting a smile of strong square white teeth, albeit with a noticeable space in the center, nodded pleasantly, all the while speaking cheerfully and confidently in the accents of the mountain people.

The corporal still struggled for his bearings as Private Krautnic turned to his superior and spoke in a tone almost befitting teacher to pupil.

"Comrade Corporal, they come from the village as every year at this time, to dig up rail ties for the home fires and help the old ones stock up for winter. That is all; there is no mystery."

The corporal, still plainly out of sorts, paused and reflected.

"Clearly, Comrade Corporal," declared the private with assurance, recalling the village horrors of yesterday, "we cannot shoot the lot of them for nothing more than this!"

Finally the corporal recovered sufficiently to demand how they had gotten through the checkpoints.

"Corporal," explained the private, "he says they passed the checkpoint east of the river with a gift of brandy."

"A bribe, you mean. Have each man drop his pants! Then we shall see. If they are Turks, shoot them where they stand! If they have foreskins, check their papers and order them out. Now go—upon my orders!"

The corporal, having drawn down a good two inches of the jug of slivovitz, held the patrol until the last man had been examined and questioned. Then he watched the last of the work crew trudge out of sight, south to the bridge and the road that led back toward the sentry post and the village beyond—with as many rail ties as it could manage fastened onto the red, four-wheeled metal cart.

36

The rhythmic drum of the rain had ceased and the day given way to the specter of night—a night black as the old man's mood. Darkness had lessened the risk of detection, and now Zeljko groped his way up the steambed, bound for the ledge and the castle beyond. He had left the others toiling on in the shaft, and despite his sore leg he moved swiftly, for he knew the signaling must not be delayed. The shock of the icy water of the stream acted as a tonic for his wound, but his arms ached from the constant digging and each forward step shot a spasm of pain up his leg as it had ever since his flight from the patrols on the previous night.

He thought of the mission ahead and listened to the sounds of the night. Overhead the wind howled in the treetops and clawed at the long-needled branches. He raised his head to the sky, but no stars pricked through the heavens. The hoot of a distant owl carried to him on the wind, an eerie, disquieting sound; and it was that sound of the mysterious Bosnian night that brought him up short.

An omen. The thought worked at his mind, and he quickened his step. With the wind out of the north, the surface of the lake would be whipped to a frenzy. He lifted his nose and sniffed the air. Hah—air too moist and cold for this time of year—maybe a storm—and no moon to see by—and no moon to find him by if he make it back.

A battle of demons raged in his head. His duty to protect the safety of his wife, his son Nedo, and his small band of loyalists struggled against his commitment to his colonel and the welfare of the Yankee. And now weighting his conscience was this thing of the omen. Finally, through his torment, he reached a decision and immediately began rehearsing his arguments before his friends, speaking aloud and unashamedly to the wind in the trees and the darkness around him.

"I got to make him not go!" he bellowed at the wind. "With waves on the lake same as peaks of these mountains, what are the odds? To cross with safety—50/50? To go and come back, three in seven? And seven a bad number—and that only with luck. No, no; the danger, it is too big." But would he listen? And what words to warn him?

"Oh, my good friend, listen to me. This is my world here of the mountains, a small world, I admit, and I without education. But Zeljko is truly a university professor of the mountains, trust me. I know the signs; I feel it; I hear it in the wind and the hoot of the owl. Major—believe me, I know what is best!

"No, no, Major, please! If you cannot listen to me, then listen to my father and his father before him. Listen to the old man of the mountains and the signs of the earth taught me as a boy, as I in my turn teach my own Nedo. You know facts, Major, that is true. But old Zeljko, he know the signs—and the signs stand against you. And if you go this night, Major, you do not come back—so is it written.

"And what of her? And of my commander—my colonel? Of Zeljko, the hunter, then what does he think? And what of the mission?

"About the big world, I am an old and ignorant man, that I admit—I cannot lie to you. For one thing, I do not know the code you blink and the code you take from the spots of light. I do not have stuffed in my head all the facts of the world like you and the girl of the colonel.

"No!" bellowed the old man at the trees in his anguish. "Wait, Major, wait! Tomorrow is no wind, with the lake flat as a young girl. Then you go if you must. What is one day? The foolish Serb with his dogs not corner us yet. Truly, what is one day in all of the days. You see, it is simple; all right, Major? We wait one day. All right, Cil the Major— Yankee—my friend."

The old man was close to tears and close to the ledge when he heard the call of the wild bird. It startled him, and he stopped in his tracks in the silky soft spray of the waterfall. He listened. There it was again, and he could feel the spray of water soaking the heavy wool of his shirt. In less than a minute, he reached the top, throwing his good leg over the edge, dragging up the other.

The voice of the gypsy, Chipmunk, came to him almost as the squeal of a frightened animal.

"The p-patrols! All day they come—e-even up there in the castle! So I wait for you here, Gr-Great One."

"The women? They are safe?" At the answer in the affirmative, the old man lifted his bearish paw and laid it roughly upon the shoulder of the frightened gypsy. His whisper had an anxious edge to it.

"What do they find?"

"Nothing, Great One. A c-cup. Only a simple tin cup."

"Where?" The question exploded from Zeljko's mouth.

"On the wall—the high wall—by the c-cave-in." And in the darkness the gypsy could not see the old man wince as he remembered the mug he had discarded in the midst of the celebration atop the castle wall.

"And the others?" Zeljko demanded gruffly to conceal his emotion. "Where are the others?"

"The soldier with tits, she watches the horses," Chipmunk told Zeljko sober-faced as the pair moved up the slope in the teeth of the wind.

"In the castle rooms?" growled Zeljko. "What do they find?"

"N-Nothing; all was clean as my pocket the day before my Friday night pay. In the very last nick of t-time did the two womans remove all things to the slender c-cave below ground."

"Go then!"

"But there is more, Gr-Great One. One-Eye, my cousin, he watches from the ridge to the north where it f-faces the river. He gives me the call, and I go. A p-plane is down, he says."

"How so?"

"He sees the rocket of the g-godless ones. It shoots 'like a great candle s-straight up from the river,' he says. Then the boom so big it w-wash out his ears. This is how he tell me."

"Did he see a plane?"

"With the clouds like a hat down over the eyes, he sees with his ears only the b-boom."

"Hah! Your cousin—he drinks even his breakfast. Forget it and help me labor at something useful. Go now and send the Yankee woman." He patted the gypsy encouragingly on the back. "Go tend the horses and look awake—or they knife you where you sleep."

When Michelle D'Orleans arrived, Zeljko emerged from the trees, and his sudden appearance frightened her.

"Be still, Little One. So far the shovels move good," he whispered hoarsely, taking her arm to steady her; then he led her to the lower mouth of the escape tunnel.

"The gypsy tell of unexpected guests," said the old man. "You keep from their way?"

"It was nothing. All was removed to the tunnel in time."

"Not all."

"No?" Michelle was startled.

"Chipmunk, he speak of a mug that was found."

"It's nothing," she said quickly, squeezing his hand.

"I hope is nothing." He paused for breath. "But could be—is everything."

When the three of them, Cil, Michelle, and the old man had again reached the signaling position high in the turret above the castle wall, old Zeljko turned and spoke gravely to Cil.

"With the wind up and the wave, you dare not try the crossing this night!"

Cil, who had already tugged the signaling gun from his pack, joined the stock to the forward assemble; he made no response.

"But tomorrow the wind is down!" cried Zeljko. "And, too...."

"Look!" The first point of white light stabbed a pin-prick into the night. Cil squeezed the trigger twice, and then the flashes came crisp and clear in rapid succession. He dictated each letter to Michelle to record.

T.H.E...B.A.R.N...I.S...B.U.R.N.I.N.G. The prick of light went out.

"What does it mean?" asked Michelle.

"It means we go. The mission is on!" Cil's voice rang with excitement.

The old man stood by, shifting his feet. Cil raised the fat barrel of the signaling rifle, careful to measure the barrel's angle to the plane of the turret window's stone block construction. Then, with a few short bursts, he squeezed off the order for an urgent meeting at the predesignated spot. The affirmative response was slow in coming; but when it came, the signal was bright and clear.

Their task completed, the threesome packed up and began their descent.

"The barn is burning?" puzzled Michelle. "What on earth kind of code is that?"

"No code," explained Cil. "On one of the upland meadows beyond Bald Hill, there is an old shepherd's hut, the hut to be set afire if the mission is on. But now you rest. Best you go back to the tunnel and Bogey, where it is safe."

Farther down the steps, Zeljko drew Cil aside with an anxious tug.

"Quick—we go back and signal with the fat gun." his statement a plea. "Tonight is bad luck—trust me!"

For a moment Cil was taken aback by the force of the warning, but his mind was made up.

"It's all right, old man," he said, giving him a reassuring clap on the back. "Look, the rain has passed, the cloud cover is perfect. Tell me of the digging and my hot-headed friend."

Zeljko did not answer at first but at last relented.

"Good," was all he would say, the word cold as hoarfrost.

"Then we can reach the front tomorrow?"

"We?"

In a sudden burst of affection, Cil wrapped his arm about the old man's shoulder—but the old man was having none of it; he shrugged off the arm.

37

The night signaling completed, all three in the darkness, as if caught up in a children's game of blindman's bluff, had felt their way down to the courtyard. But something was wrong—Michelle could feel it. The way the old man had suddenly become separate and aloof after his hushed exchange of words with Cil on the way down the steps from the castle wall.

And now as she followed behind them at a distance, instead of veering off in the direction of the lower tunnel entrance, she pricked up her ears and listened intently. It was very queer. No sounds of laughing and joking came to her in the darkness, no good-natured flinging of barbs at one another as the two men had done this morning after the old man's brush with disaster atop the parapet. And now the tension in the air was a palpable thing.

It was not until the two men abruptly veered left, and, following at a distance, she picked up the smell of the horses, that her feeling of concern abruptly heightened to alarm. She could hear the horses' snorting and pawing restlessly at the ground around their pickets, the soft murmur of voices as the men spoke to the gypsy. Then she heard the tinkle and clank of metal against metal as the men saddled up. She could feel a twinge of foreboding prickle the nape of her neck, and her heart began to flutter in her breast as she turned to confront them.

"Why the horses?" she demanded. "Where do you go this time of night—with patrols out?"

"We won't be long." Cil ignored the question. "It's better if you rest."

"But where do you go?"

"It's best that you rest; we have to go now."

It was very dark. The shriek of the wind had all but drowned out his words, and something about his studied coolness of voice served only to fuel her emotion.

"Alone? And you won't say why—or where?" This time her voice cut the air like a knife. "Alone, hell!" She hissed. "You just try and stop me!"

The men on the horses wheeled and sprang away. Once the men were off, Michelle, disdaining the need for a saddle, clutched the reins of one of the spare horses, yanked them free from a stake, slapped the rump of the horse with a smack of her hand, then vaulted atop the bare back, Indian-style.

The men were some distance ahead, but Michelle following along, kept a safe distance behind. Since she had informed Cil of her headaches and dizzy spells, his conduct toward her had subtly altered. He had become not only protective, but somewhat remote, distant—and now this. She thought of the sensuous Muslim woman and the shameless way she had of flirting with him. But now this night she knew it was something more; her intuition told her, and she thrust forward to prod on her mount; she couldn't afford to lose them in the dark.

The men rode stirrup to stirrup through the night at a good clip, hooves pounding over the soft ground, northward, away from the dam, back through the trees toward the river, in the direction from which they had come on the first night. They were moving up the lake. When they reached a certain point, the men reined in their horses and dismounted.

Michelle had been following undetected, and now she listened hard. She sensed that they were very close to the shore of the lake, but she could not see the sheer limestone cliff where it fell away to the lake far below. She went on listening.

"Here," grunted the old man gruffly. "Use the rope from my horse."

Zeljko returned to his horse, and although she could see little in the darkness, from the commotion of men and horses, she guessed. Instantly she recalled the events of two nights past when a coil of rope had nearly cost Cil his life in the river crossing. She could tell from the old man's harsh tone that he was thinking of it, too. She dismounted and crept closer.

"Take this end," Zeljko growled at Cil. "Knot it good around your belly—if you know what is good for you. Twenty meter to rock bottom is a big way to fall."

At the starkness of his words, Michelle's terror increased. "But where...." she croaked, so overcome with emotion that she barely could speak. "Why?"

Suddenly aware of her presence, Cil whirled to face her. He dispensed with his chore and stepped to where she was standing. At first he did not speak. Instead, he gripped her narrow shoulders and drew her to him. She felt the strength of his arms and savored the moment. As if they were one, she lifted her arm, and with the surface of her hand, rubbed his long, thin Jesus' fingers where they held her so tightly.

"I must go," he told her softly, head bowed, as if to catch one last glimpse of her face in the poor murky light; yet, his tone left no doubt of his resolve. "Before," he said, "to signal from the castle was enough. But now with this thing of the school bus. Try to understand. I must go do this—tonight." He was standing very close now, looking down into her face, and she could feel the gentle firmness of his fingers gripping her shoulders. "Nedo will know," he seemed to be saying, but with the uproar of her emotions, all she could hear was the howl of the wind and the crashing of branches. "Now with the mission confirmed," he tried to assure her, "there is no time and no choice."

"But...." She lifted her face to his own in the madness of the wind.

"No but's." She wasn't sure, but she thought she sensed a smile. She could feel his firm grip. "Trust me," he said. "I'll be back soon as I can."

An impatient growl erupted from Zeljko, but Cil ignored it. Instead, he held her to him. When finally he released her, the old man checked the knots of the rope encircling Cil's waist. He yanked at them roughly, then stood back to brace himself and lower Cil down.

To the depths of her soul, Michelle could feel how she needed him. Nothing more in the world did she want than to rush forward and throw herself into his arms—to feel the warmth of his body once more—to feel his strength. She tried to run to him, but something within her forbade it. There was so much she needed to tell him, so much to say. She opened her mouth, but words failed her. And then he was gone.

She could barely see in the poor light, but she could catch the vague outline moving away toward the ledge. She watched the outline of his form and imagined the confident way he would swing his weight over the side. She was ashamed of herself and tried to be strong. It was all she could do not to fall to her knees. She just stood there alone, peering over the edge.

Now she could barely see the dark bulk of his form as it slid down the rope; and then something altered in her brain. It was someone else's form; no, the form was not even human; it looked somehow like something inert—a bundle, a dark bundle of rocks dangling below and dropping off sharply.

The noise came to her clearly even over the sound of the wind—a remote and ghostly sound rising from below in the depths of the blackness, the rhythmic lash and pounding of waves against a hard rocky shore. And from her back, the noise of the old man, grunting, grunting roundly with every slide of the hemp as he paid out the rope and let the weight down.

When it was time, the old man came to her. He said nothing of when, or how, or even if Cil would return. He only knelt with her, head bowed, holding her hand. When she had finished her prayer, he led her away.

Watching him go, Michelle D'Orleans had not merely been afraid for Cil, but observing the old man's demeanor, then hearing the pounding of the waves and the whistle of the wind, she was all but consumed with terror. But people have different ways of dealing with their thoughts and emotions, and by the time Zeljko had escorted her back to the escape tunnel, her fear had transformed to some other emotion—then to stubborn pride and a stout determination.

So he had taken one look at her and decided she was a cripple, had he? So he had felt sorry for her and delegated her this menial authority over the camp site and communications. Then, without so much as consulting her, suddenly he elects to once again risk his neck by crossing the lake in this wind.

Well, all right then. But she was not dead yet, and the enemy was closing in. The crew at the dam would need every available weapon and every ounce of spare ammunition when the time came. That was the least she could do.

But she knew, also, that he had not placed her in charge of communications simply to get writer's cramp from taking dictation. No, that was not Cil. But what was the larger reason? And if the transmitter were not to be used until the mission was completed?

Well, so be it; she could do something. She would see that the weapons and ammunition were wiped clean, packed up, and ready. And when she was done, she would see that the radio was properly set up and in position, just in case.

When she had painstakingly completed her other tasks, she took the special UHF satellite radio from its pack where he had left it, set up the flimsy wire stand, plugged in the headset, and affixed the X-shaped antenna just inside the rocks covering the lower tunnel entrance. Then, only to test it, not to transmit, she checked the receiver, activated the unit, and in the process of checking the frequencies, heard an odd sound. It sounded like a homing signal.

It was then that Bogey turned to Michelle toiling at the dimly lit entrance of the tunnel, Bogey's brow tightknit with concern.

"Michelle, please. You are a very sick woman. Come, you must rest now. They will need you at the end."

38

Cil found himself groping about in the darkness, searching the rocky lakeshore until he located the raft concealed in the undergrowth, just as the old man had said. In truth it was no raft at all, but a half dozen logs lashed together crudely, each the thickness of a fat lady's thigh. Atop the rough platform lay a hand-hewn board whittled roughly into the shape of a paddle.

For a moment Cil hung back, pondering just how seaworthy this crude raft would be in the broader reaches of the lake. And it took every ounce of his strength to launch the craft; but once aboard and in motion, she carried his weight with ease as each tiny ripple caressed his buttocks and legs where he sat, threatening to transform them to ice.

Cil made decent headway on the way across. While now and again a rolling breaker driven on the wind crashed over the stern logs, the passage proved swift and uneventful, using the distant glow of the dam lights as a marker.

But a quarter of an hour later when the bow logs scraped ashore at the appointed spot, a flit of movement caught Cil's eye. Rapidly he unslung his rifle as the silhouettes of two dark running figures broke from the trees headed straight for him.

Then the tall figure in the lead held up and spoke. "I say,

old man, not the best sort of evening for a row on the pond, is it?" The man spoke with an air of controlled nonchalance, and Cil clicked his weapon back on safety. "Baxter's the name," the big man added jauntily. "Malcolm Baxter, actually. This bloke is Ned—Nedo, I believe, in his own terms. Come."

He leaned down to extend a steadying hand as Cil struggled to rise on unwilling sea legs while the sturdy Nedo hauled in the bow logs without a word and then vanished into the tangle of undergrowth to stand watch.

Baxter led the way, guiding Cil through the blackness to a grassy nest out of the wind. Once both men had settled themselves on the sandy ground, Baxter, without ceremony, poked a bottle in Cil's direction, then lit up a smoke.

"How bad was the crossing?" he said.

"No problem."

"Well, thank God for that, old man. When you signaled for a meeting with the lake boiling like a cauldron, I nearly blinked back a refusal. Too bad to lose a good man— even an American."

"What about the patrols?" Cil pressed, ignoring the superior swagger to the voice and the smell of liquor on his breath.

"More bloody nosy Slavs than mosquitoes on a cow's ass in fly time."

"The missing children. Any word?"

"Couldn't be worse, I'm afraid," the Englishman allowed with the same practiced nonchalance. "Hostages. One of the lookouts spied the bus being escorted in. Near as we can calculate, the buggers have them cooped up in a shack at the back of the enemy compound. The Croat, Nedo, he's your man on that business." And Cil could see the offhanded gesture in Nedo's direction made by the pink end of Baxter's cigarette. "That's his department, being native and all; you best take it up with him." Cil's anger flared at the man's clear indifference and the slurring of the words, but he struggled to rein in his temper.

"The face of the dam, what do you make of it?" said Cil.

"Down last night. Concrete face of the new dam shows damned fine construction, actually—for the Slavs. No possibility there, so I've been working the face of the earthen dam with a vengeance.""

"Yes, yes—that's the stuff," said Cil, suddenly excited. "The soft underbelly. And I think we've come up with the key."

"Key?"

"A drainage pipe." Cil lowered his voice to demand the Englishman's undivided attention, but the device proved unnecessary, for even in the poor light he could sense Baxter press forward attentively. "A drainage pipe in the bed of the old spillway, just below the concrete lip at the base of the new dam. Zeljko believes it runs clear through—back to front."

"So?" The Brit's tone came across a trifle superior and condescending.

"The break in the dam," pressed Cil. "Don't you see? The source of the leaks when the new dam was built. You must have seen it in the blueprints or change orders. And the face of the dam itself; it's got to show signs of repair up front?" Cil paused to gauge the reaction, which was not long in coming.

"What's that, Chap—you've what—confirmed the source, you say?" It was suddenly dawning on Baxter like a man coming out of a daze. "I say, what a gift!" The Englishman hooted like a tree owl, slapping his knee with such gusto that Nedo on watch ducked his head through the leaves. But Cil's retort was swift and commanding.

"Dammit, Commander—you're drunk!" At the force of Cil's words, abruptly the air went out of the Englishman's sails. "And look here. Let's hold the celebration until after the mission. And let me tell you one more thing. If you think I intend to let a mission like this be scrapped on account of some lush, you better think twice, Buddy—you hear me?"

Baxter nodded his head, which Cil couldn't see, and offered a cigarette, which he could. He took one, then paused to receive the light Baxter waved under his nose. And now Cil spoke urgently.

"And it's that pipe, we're convinced, that carries away leakage from the break up front. Have you found it?"

"Can't be sure, old man; but with a bit of luck...."

"Luck, hell! Look, there's no room for luck in this operation—and that goes for those missing kids or you answer to me. I want those children out."

"Yes, Sir."

"What I'm telling you, Commander—you find that spot on the face of the dam—that's where you place your charges." Cil reached down for the bottle. He took a good slug.

"My apologies," offered Baxter. "Must be these bloody black mountains that frazzle the nerves—and the bloody awful rain that pours out your ears. And then there's the nights, silent as death, and all you can hear are light-footed elves vaulting down from the branches. Frankly, Sir, it gives me the willies."

Cil held his tongue, and Agent Baxter seemed somehow to sober with remarkable speed.

"But I think I'm on to what you have in mind. Let me explain."

In the pink glow of the cigarettes, Baxter was now perfectly cool and contained, and there was sharp precision to the clipped British words. He went on to detail his careful underwater calculations, which he had signaled Cil the previous night, and how they squared perfectly with the pilfered dam blueprints and specifications provided him through channels from Intelligence sources. When he had completed his technical briefing, he picked up the whiskey bottle and took a stiff pull.

"Damned lucky, I'll tell you, for your people to pluck those blueprints straight from under the Commie noses of those blokes in Belgrade. And if the blueprints ring true, and the mouth of the old spillway as you describe—the leaks and all—then I can tell you this—I've located a cement cap, bloody big one at that, rough as a leper's face, three meters square and about that thick." At the sudden flare of Baxter's lighter, Cil noted a gap of six to seven inches between Baxter's thumb and forefinger. "With respect, Sir, I can blow that baby without a sodding ripple on the pond."

"And if the surface is calm—as well it may be?"

"As you Yanks would put it, Sir—even if the pond is smooth as a fat baby's ass." Despite his crude flippancy, a detectable note of respect had crept into the man's voice, and the darkness concealed the thin smile now crossing Cil's lips.

"Well, I hope you can—*Old Man*," responded Cil, still amused at the sheer cheek of the man and the great vaunting pride. "Because you must—since the first blast must precede the second by twenty minutes."

"Baxter pressed forward. "When do you need it, Sir?"

"Tomorrow—2300 hours. On the dot."

"On the dot, Sir—you have my word. And the main charge?"

"X hour plus twenty?"

"Right on—2320 hours. And what about the downriver warning, Sir?

"What warning?"

"To the poor blighters down the river. Once we've unleashed the force of those waters, wouldn't do to have the local populace bobbing like a mob of drowned rats, clogging up the stream, now would it, Sir? Not when we've been dispatched to save the poor buggers."

"My orders are clear." Cil's manner was tart, testy. First Michelle, then Bogey—and now this half-drunken

Englishman. "You just leave all that to me." And Cil was compelled vividly to recall the consequences on another mission when he had strayed for humanitarian reasons from the letter of his orders. He was not about to repeat that mistake.

"No—no way!" barked Cil. "No radio transmissions of any sort until mission completion—those are the orders. I won't place the whole mission in jeopardy for the sake of an early warning—no matter the cost. And that, my friend, is final."

"It's your show, Major, but...."

"No but's. The timetable is fixed." Cil knew one thing that Baxter could not—that the big push, the combined attack, the Croat-Bosnian Government surprise offensive all up and down the whole Krajina front was to be triggered by his message once the big dam was blown.

"And one thing more, Commander," said Cil. "If there's the slightest change in plan after I speak with Nedo about the children, well—we'll work it out then. But the timetable is fixed. Now, better synchronize the watches."

Carefully they adjusted the luminous dials before Baxter moved off to relieve Zeljko's son at his post in the trees.

Here in the dark, Cil could not even see, much less study the countenance of Zeljko's son, Nedo, but he recalled the way Bogey had described the young man to him. And even now he had to grin at the mental picture.

"It is not the clean, open look of the boy that will surprise you, nor the father's large Spanish eyes," she had said, smiling. "Oh, no, something else entirely. If you have ever come across a young man like this on a back street, then you would know. Aged twenty-four—rippling muscles—that wild look in the eye and armed to the teeth. And, oh, yes— the bushy jungle hair tamed by the characteristic headband. Now do you know him?

"That's right," she went on, "the Rambo character of the American films, right down to the crossed bandoleers studded with cartridges and hanging grenades, a revolver in each holster, an AK-47 with a full clip in his hands, and so much ammunition stuffed into the sprawling chest pockets that he must move forward with the lurching strut of a gorilla out of the jungle.

"Ha, yes," she had chirped. "In this war, it is the same with the irregulars on both sides, boys really, made to grow up too soon and all the wrong way, who act out the raw, savage Rambo part every day of their short lives."

But Cil had found the young man to be keen and informed, and unlike Baxter, a quiet, attentive listener. And together they had worked out the details for altering the overall plan—with Baxter's consent, of course. Cil rose from the dewy grass; the three men crept back to the shore and the platform of logs, after which Cil turned to Nedo as they reached the water's edge.

"Thanks to the Muslim twins, your mother is safe, and I'll see that your father gets your message," Cil assured him. "And Nedo, on this other matter, just know that I'll do what I can."

Cil extended his hand in the darkness. And afterward, Nedo stooped to secure a bulky bundle to the logs of the raft.

"Careful, Sport," warned the tall Englishman, raising his head to the sky where now a few stars pricked through the curtain of low scudding cloud. "Wind's up—doesn't pay to toy with mother nature."

There was something in the Englishman's tone, an eerie, almost mystical quality, a note of premonition and warning that sent a chill up Cil's spine as he felt the Britisher's huge hand retracting and the platform of logs drift gently away.

39

It was late evening in Washington, D.C. The wisp of a man sat alone in the quiet of the exclusive downtown club, buried in the plush expanse of the sofa that dwarfed him. He sipped from his Scotch with a total of three unattended cigarettes burning in the ashtray, his eyes half closed as he listened to the hum of the traffic below the window. The whole matter had been on his mind all week, and now Secretary Of Defense Robert Levitt looked hard into his glass, swishing the cubes in a revolving motion, following their path with the movements of his eyes while his mind still mulled the question.

There is really not a great deal I can do for them now, he was thinking. The Balkans are unique, Bosnia-Herzegovina at the center of the riddle. To rule the Republic effectively, given the diversity of its peoples and the depth of their hatreds, well, it was nigh onto impossible. Yet, this is where the first of the two world wars of the century had erupted, and it nagged at him now, for history had a nasty way of repeating itself.

After WWII, President Tito had proved himself one of a kind; although a constant thorn in the Kremlin's side, he had maintained peace in the Balkans for close to half a century.

But with his death, the question arose as to how to keep the keg from exploding and drawing in the world? That was the riddle, for after the death of that wily old partisan leader, Yugoslavia had fragmented into different fighting factions, and those who hungered for power were not beneath fanning the seeds of hatred or exploiting the vacuum of power. Small wonder the brutal Serb leadership had selected this very moment to press its military advantage under the banner of a "Greater Serbia" to exploit long-standing grievances in a grab for land and power.

With a precise movement of his hand, the small man plucked one of the cigarettes from its place of repose, dragged on it mightily and snubbed it out, sighing.

Now just look at President Tudjman and the Croats, he reflected, our presumptive allies—look at what they are doing this very minute to the Muslim villages of Herzegovina—and the indigenous Muslims outnumbered and poorly armed.

He made a slow, pondering shake of the head.

What can we do for a Muslim people struggling for a patch of land when that land lies deep in the breast of Central Europe—when our principal allies, the British and French, content themselves to play out their own perilous charade as UN Peacekeepers?

He absently reached to light up another cigarette, thought better of it, and shoved it aside.

And now with these bullyboys, Karadzic, Milosevic and the young Mussolini, General Mladic, blackmailing the West by blatantly snatching UNPROFOR Peacekeepers as hostages, was constantly raising the stakes. Perhaps Eisenhower was right about Hungary back in fifty-six. Maybe as here the risk of direct Russian military intervention was simply too great. If those traditional Serb protectors did elect to come in, it could mean nuclear war.

Just then the familiar figure of Deputy Secretary James Lockwood, hulking and disheveled, appeared in the doorway.

"Good evening, Mr. Secretary," intoned Lockwood with the briskest of smiles. "I hoped I'd find you here."

"Yes, Jim. At this hour of the night, I feel quite safe holed up in this place away from the phone—and once again doing splendid battle against the nonsmokers! But the problems seem to follow wherever you go—what's on your mind?"

"Same as you, I guess, Sir—this Bosnian business."

"I must tell you," nodded the Secretary, his granite features sharpened in thought, "the whole thing's got me up a tree."

As the waiter bowed in with fresh drinks and Lockwood took the chair opposite, Secretary Levitt put the question to his junior.

"What do you make of this thing of the dam?"

"Well, Sir. As you know, we received the engineering data, and once confirming our suspicions, on your authority sent the go-ahead signal."

"Look, I know all that," said the Secretary impatiently, waving away the other's response with his hand. "That's not what I'm getting at. I've read all the reports, and we've discussed it at length; and I'm sure we're both convinced it was the right thing to do—as is the President. No, no; what I'm asking—well, how do you really assess their chances?"

Secretary Levitt took a fresh cigarette from a shiny case in his breast pocket, shook off his junior's move to light it, then tapped it insistently against the leather arm of his chair before striking a wooden match against the sole of his shoe.

"Well," Lockwood began. "Technically...."

"Jim, I don't give a tinker's damn about '*technically*.' I just want to know what you think—what you really think? Can they actually pull it off?"

Lockwood bowed his head in thought and sat very still in the chair opposite as the smallness of the room pressed in on them both. He lifted his glass, pulled hard on the double

Scotch, then started off slowly.

"To be honest, Sir—I just don't know. I, as well, listen to the technical people who sound impressive putting coefficients of force up on the board with neat white markers, along with their fancy arrangement of plusses and minuses—but, to be totally frank—no one can tell."

"What bothers you most?" The Secretary's eyes snapped with insistence.

"The variables."

"Go on."

"First off, tying their hands—who could imagine two ragtag bands on opposite hills, equipped with only small arms and the most primitive means of communication by virtue of our own orders—and all the while moving in and out under the noses of the Serbs with every chance of detection? Second, surely the Serbs, pinned in their momentary hibernation below the dam, have thought long and hard of their own vulnerability—especially under command of that old Russian fox. Most assuredly, he's taking every precaution against surprise attack—even ground-to-air missiles, Intelligence estimates say. And while our technical people swear a handful of explosives will do the job, like you, I put precious little stock in technical answers. And looking at it from a distance, as, of course, we are—so few people, so little time. And all but the principals untrained, inexperienced—and all against overpowering odds." He set down his drink and eyed the keen gaze and stoney-calm countenance of the little man facing him. "It's the crucial factor that gives me pause."

Abruptly, the Secretary pressed forward in his seat.

"Well?"

"The line of escape—unless all goes strictly as planned, there can be no escape for any of them."

"Yes. That's the crux of it," nodded the Secretary, as he now sat prodigiously erect on the cushions. "Lacking perfection, it's a suicide mission—as, frankly, it always was."

He drew on his cigarette until, in the depths of concentration, the cigarette grew a very long ash which dropped and skidded down the lapel of his immaculate suit. "And through the prism of cold reality, as we both know, there is no such thing as perfection—in large things or small."

At this moment, the old man seemed even smaller than his modest frame would suggest, Lockwood was thinking, perched like a falcon on the cushions of the couch, his eyes silent watch fires, yet the face stoney cold—and so pale.

"The interplay of forces," Secretary Levitt went on, "between the structure they seek to destroy and the monumental energies which it holds back is so like the people of the Balkans themselves—capable of such good and such gentleness when the forces are controlled and allowed to flow in an orderly fashion, yet a people not unlike the Greeks or Spaniards, who, once aroused, retain always the volatility to lash out with passion, almost madly—as the history of massacre and savagery in their lands suggest—to unleash a human fury rarely known to mankind. And for that reason, they remain such fascinating peoples."

His companion only nodded accord.

"Still—I envy our Major Cil and his people there," the Secretary went on, the little man suddenly animated. "Take the Brit, Baxter—clearly a rogue with a checkered past, and the best expertise in explosives around. Then the two loyalist leaders, Zeljko, the father, and Nedo, the son, crude, almost savage men of the mountains; they are hunters by vocation and hunters by nature, yet dedicated in the most simplistic sense to duty and to 'the right' as they see it." Now there were sparks in his eyes, and the eyes crackled with fire. "Then look at the partisans they lead—thieves, gypsies, cutthroats, a few men of conscience perhaps, a few in for the utter adventure of it, or who knows what? Then, Lockwood, there is a man and there is a woman—both educated, civilized, sensitive, not so different from you and me—yet totally different. You and I chose the smart way, the safe way; they did not." Now the light dazzled in his eyes. "They took their principles in their hands, their bare hands, man! They charted a course, a narrow, maybe hopeless course where action is the watchword—where there are no grays, only black and white, kill or be killed. And there they stand, each minute pitting their wit and cunning against a known, cunning, obvious, deadly enemy. Their very lives in the balance and no choice but to do—or to perish."

He pounded the table with such force that the sudden explosion of sound in the quiet room snapped the few remaining heads their way. "Yes," he added in almost a whisper, "a very simple equation—and we've got to help them."

The little man fell back in his chair, spent with emotion.

"And," Lockwood sighed, "there is great beauty and clarity in simplicity."

The old man once again picked up the ball. "You know, Jim, I sit each night in my office overlooking the grand monuments of our nation and people. But do I see them? The truth, man. Do I see any faces of real people, let alone do I see them clearly? Ha!" He flicked the ash from his cigarette with a sharp, precise motion of the hand. "I sit buried in a boundless torrent of papers—classified papers, unclassified papers, papers for the Secretary's eyes only—but always papers.

"Face it, Lockwood," the Secretary added with bitter irony. "The questions that get to the lofty reaches of your office and mine are colored in gray, the implementation of questionable policies in questionable ways, the retention and advancement of people for questionable reasons—or are they excuses? And it never stops. And the questions of black and white are long since diluted before they reach our level. So we are saved from them—and from true definition."

He took just enough time to light up again.

"On the other hand," he went on. "Look at them—look at

that tiny desperate band—their mission clear and well-defined. Hemmed in by the mountains, the enemy, and the constraints of time and space—and all laboring day and night to direct the colossal power they seek to release. Yes, Jim, I so envy them that."

"True, Mr. Secretary, they have no grays. They know their mission and what they must do within the confines of luck and weaponry, and as FDR used to put it—'the art of the possible.'"

"And if the faith is strong enough—beyond."

And now the little smoking man of granite allowed himself to sit back in the cushions.

"Tell me about the colonel?" he said. "How are his spirits? I understand he is very close to the D'Orleans woman."

"Yes, Sir. But he is a soldier."

"I understand—he was with you on the evaluation?"

"Completely."

Secretary Levitt nodded thoughtfully. "We must find a way to get those kids out. You say they should have received our signal by now?"

"Yes."

"Then there isn't much time."

"A day—two at the most."

"Jim." Secretary Levitt leaned close to his deputy. "Stay close to the colonel on this one, will you?"

"Of course."

"You know—any news, reports, bulletins—anything at all. He's a good man, and we owe him."

"I understand."

"And if—if it shouldn't turn out...."

"I understand."

"Thanks, Jim. I think I'll turn in now."

"Can I drive you?"

"No, it's short. And, oh, Jim?"

"Yes?"

"Thanks."

"Good night, Mr. Secretary."

40

Thirty yards out from shore, the warning words of the Englishman, Baxter, were lost and all but forgotten. Cil, encouraged by the ease and swiftness of the passage over, then the success of the meeting, felt ever more confident that if their luck held they just might pull off the impossible.

Of first importance, regardless of cost, they must—get those kids out. Then, if only they could unleash the power of the dam before the enemy breakout, they would thereby succeed in shielding the upcoming Bosnian-Croat joint offensive farther north. Yes, yes; he could see it all clearly in his mind. Then somehow—perhaps—he could clear his name.

The primitive raft of logs glided smoothly with the barest ripple on the surface of the lake. Only a breath of wind ruffled his hair, and Cil found himself lost in thought, his spirits soaring.

Earlier he had harbored fears of a night passage, especially after the old man's odd demeanor, but now he could think only of Michelle with old Zeljko waiting somewhere out there on the far shore; he had so much to tell them, so much to share. He was thinking of Michelle as he had left her; he could feel the touch of her lips and hear the purr of her voice. As his spirits soared, his mind had nearly erased the remembered fear in her voice and the desperate grip of her arms. Instead, he could feel the softness of her, the warmth, the spring of her hair, and it all somehow mingled with the distant memories of Sonya.

His lips curved into a smile. He recalled the old man's stark warning to postpone the crossing, the sharpness of his tongue, his unfamiliar distance and gruffness as he had stepped up to check the safety knots securing the lifeline. Cil's smile broadened at Michelle's and old Zelko's shared misgivings after his nearly drowning in the river on the way in; he could barely contain himself. He could not wait to see them, to playfully taunt and scoff at their unfounded fear and concern.

At the first sign that the wind seemed to be picking up, he was still smiling. In moments, the gusts grew more insistent, the wind gathering force—and now it began whistling past his ears.

The unexpected fury of the wind roused him from his lethargy. He looked back toward shore, anxious, puzzled, searching to gauge the direction and force of the wind; but the shore was lost from view in the blackness, and now it was plain that what had earlier been but a windy lake on a chill summer night had somehow transformed.

When he realized his mistake, roundly did he reprove himself. Even a novice seaman, a rank amateur, could hardly have overlooked the telltale signs. On account of the darkness, he had not realized that upon reaching the shore for the meeting, unwittingly he had paddled into a sheltered cove whose protective arms had given him false confidence that the wind had slackened. Worse, while on the passage over, the wind blowing out of the northeast had provided a cushioning hand at his back, but in his time ashore the wind had played a trick on him; the unseen hand of the wind had backed around and was blowing a gale, from due north—

the direction from which all summer squalls roared down through the folds of this steep Alpine range.

The old man had warned him of this change, and of the way a stiff wind and wave striking this crude keelless craft broadside could throw him off course, could shove him helplessly out into the broader reaches of the lake.

As if by some odd quirk of fate, within the space of a few minutes, frothing crests standing on end replaced the mild chop of the sheltered cove. The breakers rolled frothy-steep and unending, one upon the next, to hammer the logs and tug at the crude lashings that bound them. It was as if some great evil hand had swept up from the depths to suddenly whip the lake surface to madness, and he was reminded of the ancient mysterious tales of the Bosnian night.

As swiftly as his spirits had soared, now did they plummet. For only an instant did he think to turn back before dark memories of the past welled up to block him. The memories grew in his head, swirling, building, towering above him, dark as a thunderhead. They seemed to take on stark definition only to mock and remind of past failures—of that first Bosnian mission that had gone all wrong—of his loss of Sonya—of those whom he respected who had turned on him as one. His mind lingered on that old failed mission, and it required almost a superhuman act of will to thrust it from his mind.

He thought of the lost children, of all the others who had placed their faith in him....

And now the wind shrieked, and the lake surface rose like the wild open sea.

Yet—and yet—and now all of that changed. Focusing solely on the plight of the others, their images rising in his mind, it was as if a fresh breeze began blowing through his head. And now, nearly by magic, all thought of despair was swept away, replaced by an old familiar buoyancy, by a rising sense of easy confidence which had, so long ago in youth, been his constant companion.

The howl of the wind tore at the loosely bound logs and tugged at the buttons of his old Navy P-jacket, whipping the waves to a rage, each successive roller lifting the rough bow logs to rise and then hang free for a moment on the crest, only to suddenly plunge the small raft into the following trough. Cil's arms thrust deep with the paddle—his muscles screamed back. On and on into the night did he go.

He went on this way for a very long time. He forced his thoughts away from the ache in his arms and shoulders and the numbing cold that deadened his legs. He thought of Michelle waiting somewhere out there. He thought of the old man and Bogey—he thought of the school kids, and of his companions now caught in the shaft.

What he did not think of, because he could not see for the inky swirl and wrath of the waves, was just how far down the lake the north wind had swept him. South—into the broader reaches of the lake. South—toward the dam and the mouth of the spillway. South—toward the guard towers with heavily mounted machine guns and searchlights probing the wavetops.

41

Pale yellow light poured from the second floor windows behind the barbed wire. A blast of wind
shrieked past the corners of the headquarters building at the
Serb compound and clawed the stiff shingles of the roof
with icy fingers. Within, toasty warm and encased in his
tent of a robe, the general stood alone, towering over the situation map that lapped over the green table and curled
against the wall behind. Softly his riding crop tapped the
map at the point where Private Lajtner's corpse had been
found. Then it moved to the spot at the top of a ridge four
kilometers east of his present position. There, three had
been killed in the early morning.

"Boys," he muttered to himself. "Mere farm boys. And
what could possess a handful of youthful farm laborers to
ride through these mountains before dawn—to ignore the
warning to halt thrice given—boys armed with rifles?
Partisans?"

Only half an hour earlier had General Kerenofsky this
time completed his own personal interrogation of the patrol
leaders, yet something still pricked at his mind.

"Three killed, none beyond his teens, and all riding horses of inferior stock. Three or four others escape, one with

337

severe wounds, but no blood?"

His blue eyes shone huge and pale, yet shadowed now with consternation. Then, as he went on thinking, a cautious grin trifled with his lips and his pointer moved to where heavy brown topographical rings marked the peak of the mountain above the dam, site of the ancient castle ruins.

"And there they discovered this." He reached down and pushed one fat milky-white finger through the curve of the handle and raised and examined the rusted tin cup before replacing it on the billiard table.

"Of what importance? A rusted tin cup found high on the parapet with no other clue." His forehead furrowed under the weight of his thoughts and agitation.

"Probably none—but not certainly none." And the pointer then aimed at a spot below the dam.

"And here, after midday—a crew of peasant workmen surprised while cutting up ties along the abandoned railbed—all within the defense perimeter. And so close to the dam—and these men with a small cart. What could it mean?

"Again, probably nothing, a cheap source of fuel. Surely in the past, rail ties had been torn from the ground in this place. And in these mountains it will not be long before winter recommences.

"But if their purpose were simply to gather firewood, where then did they vanish?"

The gargantuan figure stood ponderously erect, jowls twitching, puzzling over the queer assortment of facts. For a moment, he turned and gazed at his reflection in the wall mirror, adjusted the height of one eyebrow, then returned to the problem.

"If they left in a group headed south as the corporal had reported, then how could it be that no guards saw them pass? Especially with a cart loaded with logs. And how could they avoid the checkpoint above the half-moon steel bridge? And their papers, all carefully examined by the patrol leader, yet found to be in order." He paused to consider. "But what is it these days to obtain false papers?"

He placed down the riding crop at the corner of the table, pulled hard upon one meaty jowl, then focused on the map more intently.

"No. Definitely not," he grunted. "Coincidence is one thing—treachery another!" Carefully, almost sensually, he wrung one smooth delicate hand with the other.

"It is true that any one of these apparently innocent happenings could occur without concern—but four in three days? Three today? Never!" A dark line joined his eyebrows where they refused to meet.

"Yet wait, my General," he said to himself half aloud. "It would not do to be hasty. Tanks and trucks and artillery pieces too numerous to count lie at your fingertips as Pavlov aptly points out. And you, oh magnificent general, are frightened as a timid March hare by a rusted tin cup and a handful of peasants." He placed his hands at the edge of the table and leaned on his long flabby arms, ducking his head beneath the green overhead lampshade, puzzling as the beam of the light played over the intricate oriental weave of his house jacket. From his pocket, he removed three bright-colored gum drops and popped them into his mouth.

"Perhaps for once Captain Pavlov has proven correct; the fact that a man's eyes are closely set and his hair grows halfway down his forehead does not necessarily permit one to exclude his conclusions."

A thought entered his mind, and for an instant a strange half-smile tugged at his lips. "If only I could consult with my old friend—I'll wager if I could, Ivan could smell out the truth. But alas, poor man with a fish pole, long since have they pilfered his brain. And what, pray tell, have they done with my own?"

The general shifted his weight and made an impatient sound. "Now think seriously, you over-ripe Georgian grape! True, no activity was found before this. But prior to the discovery of Private Lajtner, virtually no patrols had been dispatched. Since then, constant patrols were, almost by the hour. It is equally possible there existed as much innocent activity each day which simply was not discovered for lack of attention."

And now he tossed his head. "Oh, my foolish demented general—just go to bed! Have your snifter of vodka, look at your precious pictures if you must—then go straight to bed. The very idea—hah—a cable of alarm to the General Staff. To be justified how? On the basis of a handful of school-aged boys out riding the fields before dawn on their way to work? After all, they clearly were farmers. Or by accusing a gang of woodchopping peasants upon discovery of a a rusted tin cup?

"My general, go to bed quickly—before Comrade Yeltsin's boys come for you with a net—and suddenly in your place makes my poor Ivan the general, and you the mindless fisherman. A rusted tin cup?"

The old general poured from the decanter, then heavily tossed down the drink. That done, he swung his gargantuan bulk into bed. For a few minutes, his mind sifted through the images before he fell off to sleep, dreaming of fresh fish flopping in the dust at his side as he sat on the bank of the river. Deeper into the night, he tossed until his covers were shed.

42

Eighty feet below the guard towers—eight stories, in fact, below the cresting white wall of the dam—a family of moles burrowed quietly through the damp black earth, chewing away at the vital underpinnings, men stripped to the waist and racing against time for the face of the dam.

The crew of diggers was tired, dead tired, and unwell. The tall bearded Professor once again squinted down at his pocket watch. Abruptly he frowned and stared at his men. Dubiously he assessed their progress; it was already past midnight.

The old man had not told him precisely how much time was left, but it took no genius to comprehend how swiftly the enemy patrols were closing in.

All through the morning, the dirt, dry and powdery light, had leapt from the spades of his crew under the sheen of hard-muscled arms. But once past the vertical slab—one of the footings of the concrete dam overhead marking the midway point to the face of the dam—everything changed. The light dirt of the morning within easy range of the catch basin became the back breaking sodden soil of afternoon and evening, for each advancing step carried them nearer the break at the face of the dam and the leaks that sprang from it.

Now veins of trickling water poked icy black fingers through the dirt up front. They splattered and dripped, carving small rivulets to splash on the floor. Soon the floor of the shaft transformed to a brown carpet of mud that slid and sloshed underfoot, the mud making rude sucking sounds with each lifted boot.

The farther the diggers progressed, the greater the distance grew to the catch basin located by the entrance at the back of the dam, and into which every last ounce of dirt had to be dumped. And now each upturned shovel emptied into the four-wheeled conveyor cart. Dripping and oozing, slopping over the side, the cart had to be wheeled through the mire over the primitive track of rail ties stretching back through the shaft to the catch basin.

Inside the shaft, the atmosphere was dank and dimly lit, the chill penetrating straight through to raw bone. The tunnel carried a murky, otherworldly feel, the impression magnified by the eerie flicker of light from a row of low- voltage bulbs strung along one of the black earthen walls, the bulbs powered by a small generator placed at the entrance near the catch basin. Within the shaft, the air reeked of sweating bodies, the odor rancid and sour. The coppery taste of rusted metal from iron ore deposits coated the mouth. And most pronounced came the smell of exhaust fumes spewing from the gasoline engine powering the generator. The fumes hung in a haze of deadly blue smoke that eddied and swirled with the movements of the men, fumes that stung the eyes and clogged the nose, choking a man to coughing fits despite the double layer of kerchief worn over the nose, except by the little commander, of course, who considered such crude contrivances beneath him.

Far worse, however, was the latest obstacle encountered by the crew after passing the vertical slab, a condition which immediately threatened the race against time. Great blocking boulders—apparently placed there by the earlier Tito regime for strength at the time the original dam leaks were discovered and hastily repaired—seriously impeded the men's progress. Each boulder had to be carefully dug out to overcome the suction of mud, then interred beneath the floor of the shaft, one by one. To bury huge boulders beneath a dry, hard-packed floor of dirt would have been one thing, but to do so beneath this oozing sea of mud proved quite another. And it was this obstacle, coupled with the rising sense of urgency and danger, which, like a disease, had begun to infect and attack the spirit of the men.

It was upon this state of affairs that the Professor now focused his attention. As a rule, he was a soft-spoken man, given more to contemplation than precipitous action, but now he fixed his gaze on his twin, the Ox, laboring deep in a watery hole, huge muscled arms rippling as he dug a space to bury a boulder. All the while the diminutive Slobo stood high and dry on the rim of the hole, the little commander imperiously lecturing the slow-witted twin as he worked.

"Leverage, I say!" cried Slobo. "For the love of God, man, bend your back to it. You dig, not like an ox, but the crippled old woman your mother is!"

This sort of insolent drivel had spilled from the little man's tongue all through the night; while at first the ludicrous banter had served to enliven and amuse the men, long since had it become a nuisance and weight on the nerves. Yet, patiently the Professor bided his time, following the progress of his twin in the hole, out of the corner of his eye watching the three farm lads loading the conveyor cart, they also having felt the sharp edge of Slobo's tongue. The Professor stood back, still patient, keeping his own counsel as the irrepressible Slobo held forth, sniping and threatening and proffering advice.

"Faster, fool, faster!" The mountain commander exhorted. "A gorilla must learn to work with his hands!"

When the Ox reached a point deep in the hole where the

water rose to his chest, still the Professor held his tongue, waiting. In fact, he waited until his twin halted his digging, cast his spade from the hole, and followed it out to stand on the opposite rim. Only then did the Professor allow himself a slow, secret smile.

Standing inconspicuously behind the blabbering Slobo on the near side of the hole while his twin on the far rim slapped the water from his trousers, the Professor addressed his twin.

"Do you dig a man's grave—or a hole for a stone?" the bearded Professor challenged his twin with a tongue sharp with feigned invective.

"If you can do better, then jump in and show me!" Suddenly the Ox's face took on the red hue of rage, taking his brother's remark for the clear insult intended—until, that is, his small brain, upon reflection, registered the good-natured sparkle of fun.

"It will bury three stone or one badly tempered oaf!" retorted the Ox.

"Yes, but what badly tempered oaf?"

"The man is your choice, for you are the leader, but if it was left to me...." He glared across the watery hole at the small figure of the little commander, Slobo, standing with his back to the Professor.

The trio of farm lads, catching onto the fun, looked on expectantly.

Silently the Professor dropped down on his haunches behind the unsuspecting little commander and braced himself. With his huge hands, he seized the man's spindly legs down low. As if the man were a feather, he lifted and flung the little man headlong out over the hole filled with muck.

The shirtless figure of the little commander seemed to hang in the air, suspended in time. For that split second, he might well have been a swan diver caught by a camera shutter in the act of leaping from the cliffs of Acapulco—though the mouth gaping, the eyes staring and wild, the hands in a prayerful attitude pressed hard against the bare, bony chest. And then the disbelieving Slobo flopped in the water and sank like a stone.

"I can't swim! I can't swim!" blubbered the mud-coated Slobo when his head finally bobbed to the surface. "Get me out!"

As if on command, the Herculean brothers, facing each other from opposite sides of the rim, reached swiftly down to each capture a limb. Then they jerked the man skyward until his head bounced off the concrete ceiling above.

"I tell you, I can't swim!" shrieked the little commander, caught in the air. "Put me down!" And no sooner had the edict exploded from his lips, than great hands released him once more to plunge into the hole, all to the boisterous cheers of the farm lads.

"Get me out! Get me out!" gurgled the half-drowning man. "I'll do anything!"

"Anything?" The voice of the Professor was measured and patient. He stood there, with long flowing beard, arms folded casually over broad-muscled chest, eyes smiling appraisingly, contemplating the swimmer's queer aspect. He smiled down on the wild eyes staring up at him, two rolling white marbles staring up out of an ocean of muck.

"Anything!" sputtered the little commander, flailing his wings like a floundering goose. "Hurry!" The words both a plea and a stab at contrition.

"And not another word of our mother?"

"My—my lips are sealed!" The arms were still flailing. "Get me out!"

"And not another ill word of the old man?"

"N-not one!"

"Of the Yankee?"

"No, No!"

"And none of his woman?"

"Not one. I'm drowning. G-get me out—*quick!*"

When the smoke had cleared, so to speak, and the mud-coated specimen was safe on dry land, albeit whimpering and shaking like a stray dog hauled from the river, it was quite astounding the way the little man's estimation of the twins—their mother—the old man—Miss D'Orleans—and even of Cil—had improved.

Miraculously, spirits soared. The men attacked the wall of dirt before them with a vengeance, except, that is, for the little commander who hung in the shadows, licking his wounds.

Late that night, the Professor watched his twin assailing the wall of dirt and boulders up front with the passion of a crusader. Fearing if he failed to slacken his pace, he would collapse from exhaustion, he addressed him with finesse.

"Come, man of muscle, the night is still young. Come with me for a sip of spring water by the entrance. Let the children do their share."

"No time, brother. I drink when the old man gets back—not a second before."

To this point the Professor had done his best to ignore the plight of the old man, but now reminded, he was forced to confront it. He grunted to himself as if in physical pain. He is late. He should have been back! He fought the urge to peek at his pocket watch. Old Zeljko had promised to get back long before this, and the old man was not one to misjudge time. What could it mean, and what was the timing for blowing the front? What about the American major and the Englishman Baxter? Had they met? Had the old man's fears of the lake crossing been truly warranted?

The weight of apprehension felt as if a great stone had been lashed to his back. His crew was near the end of its rope. And now he gave in to temptation; he fished in his pocket, plucked out his watch, then uttered an oath. At the worst, if the American had not made it across on the logs, the old man should have been back by now. He turned his attention to the sulking Slobo, now somewhat recovered from his earlier bout.

"Come, mountain commander. We will show them how it is done." And they each grabbed a shovel, elbowed aside the Ox, and worked furiously until dirty water squeezed from the mud and spilled over the sides of the steel cart. The three farm lads muscled the load back down the mud-covered track of rail ties toward the catch basin while the Professor and his small companion loosened the wall of watery dirt up front, shoveling it onto the floor of the shaft.

The Professor looked down, and with his heavy boot kicked at the mud and slop half submerging the black python that was the drainage pipe. "See if we can break it. Come!" He seized a pick lying next to the earthen wall, then bending his knees for maximum leverage and hefting it high as the concrete ceiling, smashed the pick down on the cast iron pipe. But despite his efforts, the thick python of iron resisted all attempts at its violation.

"Give a man a try!" bellowed Slobo, grunting and straining to overcome the suction of water about a small boulder. He lifted the rock and flung it against the python with all his puny might. With an audible *crack*, the pipe ruptured, exposing but a shallow current of water moving inside it.

"Look there," cried the Professor. "The pipe inside—it's dry as a bone! Has to be clogged farther up."

"Hah! Watch out, book worm," cried Slobo, crashing forward. "This is a job for an artist!" And while the Professor and the others looked on, Slobo wielded the pick like a madman, chipping away at the cast iron pipe until the pipe was unclogged and the surface water began to flow freely into the pipe and drain back toward the catch basin.

In the early digging, the shaft had run wide and straight as a dye, but now with the bend around the obstruction of the vertical concrete footings of the dam overhead, the shaft at the bend had narrowed to a bare four feet. The professor wondered to himself whether, when the face of the dam was blown and the torrent of water released, the narrow width of the shaft at the obstruction would pinch off the stream and spoil the effect.

"Where is that old man?" the Professor growled to himself. "He would know. Where the hell is he?"

And on his mind, too, was the condition of the farm boys, one with the arm wound, and all having spent much of their time at the entrance of the shaft by the catch basin, emptying the cart next to the compressor where the fumes of the compressor engine were worst. Those boys could simply not be allowed to breath the fumes much longer, yet he was afraid to open the baffles and expose their working lights to the outside. Finally, he determined to shut off the lights and compressor for three minutes in twenty, then open the shaft entrance until the air was once again fresh; he would spare the men as much as he could.

When he had passed the order and returned to his place at the front next to Slobo, the little commander laid down his shovel with an imperious shrug and addressed him.

"How far to the front?" the man challenged, his face lined with fatigue.

"At this rate, who knows?"

"Another day will kill us!"

"There's no other way."

"We will all be dead in this foreigner's trap!" The pitch of his voice rose with his hysterical fear, and his eyes seemed to bulge out like a bullfrog's. "You will see, Mr. Professor. Soon the lake breaks through! Look, already the water spills from the soil. Like dogs, we are trapped in this hole! And the old man—the turn coat? Where is your great hunter now, Mr. Professor? And where is your Yankee?"

The soft-spoken Professor sneaked out his pocket watch. With pent-up fear and alarm, he squinted down at its face. The time was 2:17 AM—already they were into the third day.

43

It was night. The east guard tower atop the high dam teetered on stilts the way a long-legged grasshopper clings to a tree in a hailstorm. The twin towers, hastily built when the Serbs first arrived, provided a commanding vantage for surveillance, as well as a broad field of fire. Never intended as permanent architectural features, they were crudely constructed of raw timber which gave them a rickety, urine-yellow appearance. And while stable enough in good weather, the towers had a disconcerting tendency to creak and sway wildly when the wind whipped up and howled down the full sweep of the lake.

Such was the state of affairs on this raw night as Private Darko Sljivic in the east guard tower addressed his companion.

"Will you listen to that wind!" cried Darko, as the wind shrieked past the raw timbers and rocked the floor of the platform.

"Wind? Bah, this is no wind," intoned Private Slappo. "Chickens like you should come to the hills above Sarajevo where the wind is a freight train." But this bombast did little to allay the fears of Darko Sljivic, who made his reply through chattering teeth.

"I don't know if I am more cold or more scared." Darko was still looking out over the lake where the waves stood on end to crash against the face of the dam, tossing creamy billows of froth and spray into the beam of the searchlight, exciting ghostly shapes to leap from the darkness. "This floor, it roll worse than the deck of a ship—and now my stomach."

"Bah!" retorted Slappo, himself crouching low to the floor, screened for the moment from the wind by the sideboards. Just then a huge gust assailed the platform; it lurched and bucked, teetering like a stumbling drunk fighting for balance. "All you know is to complain."

"Yeah, well, some of us got all the luck. Take you, stationed before in your own hometown—in the hills above Sarajevo."

"Little you know—hell, it was a nightmare." And Slappo made that peculiar flapping of the hand with a rapid, loose-jointed motion of the wrist.

"You say—nightmare? I been posted in these dark raining hills for almost forever, while you, ha, you go slumming with your friends in Sarajevo."

"To be stationed near home in this war is no bargain," snapped Slappo testily.

"A damned piece better than stuck in this hole. At least you were close to your friends."

"Ha, friends? Once comes the war, you fool, the friends are all gone. All of a sudden, the friends are the enemy."

"No."

"Listen. Before the war," Slappo explained, "I play soccer, see—the 'Inside Team.' And all of us buddies, you know: Serb—Muslim—Jew or Gypsy—the whole bucket. But now all of that's changed, and a man better know who his enemies are."

"Yeah?"

"Sure. First, they pluck us out of reform school straight into the army. But some had the luck and they stay in the city. But for me, it's different, posted up in the hills above the Jew cemetery. Some of the rest, they were snipers; but me, I was strapped to a heavy mortar. And you know what? Every half hour, sure, we piss off a few mortar rounds down on the city for good measure."

"Down on Sarajevo itself?"

"We got to guard our families against those freaking Muslims, don't we?"

"But?"

"Well, mostly the phone lines are down in Sarajevo, right? But sometimes we hooked 'em up again, see—just to do 'em a favor. Then, from the hills, we make calls down to our buddies on the team whose families still live down there in the city."

"Everybody? Muslims and Jews and all?"

"Well, sure—at first."

"I don't get it," frowned the shivering Darko.

"Well—see, we only call down just to say hello to our friends, right, to see how they are, and how are their family? And you know what the ungrateful bastards do? They got the balls to—hang up on us!"

"But you say you're shelling them all from the hills?"

"Protection! For their own protection. Hell, man, you don't get it, either. It's not our fault; it's us who are the victims! We up there in the mud protecting those Jew and Muslim bastards. And what do we get for our trouble? Hah—a swift kick in the ass, that's all."

On that note, a silence fell over the guard tower, interrupted only by the fury of the wind. But without the idle chatter, Darko felt the cold ever more severely. He shifted his feet and tried to wiggle his toes to work out the numbness. In the reflected glow of the searchlight, he could see his companion, Slappo, braced against the heavy machine gun for balance.

Then, for an instant, far to his right, at the extreme range of the beam of the spotlight where it touched the tossing waves, Darko thought he saw something. He put aside his misery and trained his eye on the spot. In a moment, he saw it again—a raft—a small raft, or maybe a couple of logs floating in tandem, to be suddenly lost in the blackness.

"Slappo, you see that?" And when no answer came, Darko muttered to himself. "Damn—better go down and check."

Unslinging his rifle, he started off down the access ladder, still flexing his toes to get out the numbness. But before he reached the bottom rung, a crash of spray drenched his trousers below the hem of the greatcoat, and he scrambled back up.

Anyway, the fact of the sighting didn't interest him much, numbed as he was by the cold. After all, there were bound to be chunks of driftwood blown around on this wind. And now with his socks soaked, already he could feel his throat going scratchy. But just to make sure, he had his tower mate, Slappo, squeeze off a few dozen rounds—straight at the spot where he had seen those madly splashing logs.

"Nice shooting, Slappo. And, hey—did you see what they did to that yellow school bus? Yeah, they cut off the roof with a blow-torch to store the parts in the repair shop. Then they stuck them kids in a tool shed at the back of the compound."

"Hah. What I don't get is why they'd hijack a school bus," puzzled Slappo, still smelling the smoke rising from the 50 caliber machine gun. "What do we want with a bunch of school kids?"

"Interrogation," piped Darko Sljivic with a burst of newly found confidence, for the subject was the talk of the camp, something that intrigued him—and, something he knew about personally. "The Rusky general, he's interrogating each kid one by one."

"That's horse shit," scoffed Slappo. "What can a kid tell you?"

"I suppose you're smarter than the general?" responded Darko, a bit haughtily, confident in his knowledge. "And I'll lay odds you got no idea how important this interrogation is."

"Yeah, sure."

"Well, I happen to know that all interrogations (he was in love with the sound of the word) are conducted by the general himself—in private—most always at night—without even the presence of his adjutant." Darko was enjoying his moment in the sun.

"Bah, you gotta be dizzy," snapped a scornful Slappo. "For one thing, like I say, what could a kid know in the first place? Besides, if you ask one kid, you've asked 'em all."

"Dizzy or no, that's what goes. And I can tell you something else—the general's expecting a woman."

"Oh, sure—a la-dee-da lady right here in the woods."

"A lot you know. Look, this buddy of mine changes the Rusky general's sheets. Says everywhere you look up there, the general's got mirrors—I mean, fancy mirrors—and a quilt on that bed to match drapes on the windows. Yeah, with matching flowers the size of a dinner plate."

"Bah, I tell you, you're dizzy. A forward base with a woman? Anyway, I bet he's got those kids around to run errands; I saw it once in Banja Luka where they run the useless old Muslims."

"Well, I know about the woman," rejoined Darko with persistence. "And she'll be here pretty soon, too. Why, just the other day, my buddy showed me a crate packed with nightgowns and dresses—fancy ones. And the general's name stamped right on it. And you should have seen the hot satin night things."

The gusts whipped up again, the wind shrieked, and Private Slappo took the opportunity to silently curse out his comrade for raising the subject, for he, too, had heard some loose barracks talk.

There was something about this place, Slappo was thinking, that got to a guy just like Darko was saying. Like being all cooped up in a hole—and no way out—and always with that monstrous dam up there—and mountains all round. You couldn't explain it, but somehow it got to you. And the feeling a weight—even for the officers.

The other day he had overheard two of them talking, and it had scared him—something about being in a war, but they wouldn't let you fight. They were also talking about what a few well-placed bombs could do with all of them huddled up down here; and how strong was that dam? The officers were talking about some old World War II films they had seen once, of a dam higher than this one—and what a bomb or torpedo hit could do. Yeah, it was scary all right—a lot more scary than this damned teetering tower.

And what could you make of that damned general? A Rusky general over a whole Serb battalion—over even the officers. And a woman on the way! And flowered curtains with matching damned quilts? What kind of a general? And what about those school kids?

44

In the meadow below the comfortable villa in upstate New York, the sun of early August beat down on the man clad in smart riding breeches and jacket, a spanking white scarf knotted comfortably at his throat. The scarf was not a part of his regular apparel but worn to underline his prayer for the safe return of his niece.

Colonel Mavro Anastasi stood with his back ramrod straight even as his arms braced against the top rail of the corral, one foot casually hooked under the lower rail as he pondered the smooth-muscled bay horse grazing on the far side of the oval. He gazed at the horse in the way some men reserve for eyeing the sleek lines of their racing yacht. And now the young thoroughbred, spying his presence, tossed her head gaily, wheeled, then glided nimbly to her master's side, her mane ruffling auburn and gold in the noonday sun. The colonel turned at a voice from behind.

"Plenty hot day, Colonel."

"Not for us, Marko."

"Ay, not like the homeland." The servant hoisted a small bundle. "Here, Sir. Your special lunch."

Colonel Mavro Anastasi, ordinarily an even-tempered man, acknowledged it stiffly and nodded toward the fine-tooled European saddle straddling the fence. "When you have her saddled, tuck it in the saddlebag," he instructed quite formally.

"A good day for the trail, Sir," the old servant tried once more. He had loyally served the colonel ever since army days in the old country many years before, had tasted battle at his side, and also suffered the deeper scars of war that score the soul and somehow change a man below the level that meets the eye. "A hard ride to The Ledges, that's a sure cure for bad sleep."

The only response from the ramrod-straight colonel was a withering sidelong glance at being reminded. And only when Marko had finished saddling the horse did he again turn in his stoop-shouldered fashion to the colonel.

"Sir, ah, with Miss Michelle and the major, it all go good?"

"Very well," came the too hurried response. And without further amenities, the colonel mounted up. With a touch of the rein, he turned the frisky thoroughbred; then, with a curt salute and a thrust of the heels, he trotted his favorite horse up the meadow toward The Ledges and the twin peaks beyond. Normally he took a keen interest in his pet bay, but this day he paid her no heed.

Marko, the old family retainer, stood there watching him go. Marko would be seventy-three in a month, a year older than his brother, Zeljko, and ten years the colonel's senior; he had tried to serve the colonel well, but at this moment his thoughts were not of his master, but the girl he adored as he watched the austere-looking figure sitting high in the saddle diminish in size against the green fields.

Old Marko's heavy features remained impassive despite his stern expression and habitual scowl; but there was nothing stern nor scowling about his emotions this day, and for an instant he bowed his head, overcome by a sudden flood of emotion. He was too old to cry, and it hurt too much to laugh, so instead he went down on one knee and pleaded quite bitterly. "Oh, merciful God, if you say, strike me dead—but I beg you—keep her safe. For, too, she is mine."

Marko lacked the details of the mission, but he had noted the raft of incoming calls last night from official Washington, then three in addition from Michelle's father in France. And then, long after midnight, his alarm had soared at that last urgent call from the Secretary's office. While he had caught none of the conversation, from the length of the call, he had gauged its importance. And from the heavy odor of stale tobacco smoke discovered in the colonel's study this morning, he knew without doubt that all was not well.

Colonel Anastasi invariably found the need to ride in times of crisis and stress; he could think more clearly in the open air, and events of the night had convinced him that this would be a very good day for a ride.

When the colonel reached his favorite clearing in the forest, he pulled up, dismounted, and tethered his horse. Then as he looked around at the familiar surroundings—the broad leaves of the trees overhead—the cool shade of the clearing—the brook that splashed playfully by to one side, he sucked in and exhaled a deep breath in attempt to relieve the tension of the previous night.

This was his spot. He had come here a thousand times over the years, often with his niece, Michelle, and before that with his own daughter, Sonya. He crouched at the side of the stream and went down on all fours, bracing his hands in the pebbly streambed, dunking his head in the clear, icy water. The time-honored ritual seemed to refresh him, and for a moment he focused upon a small rainbow trout almost translucent, fanning its tail and raising a tiny cloud of sediment in the streambed, struggling against the pull of the current. And then for a second the colonel lowered his hand into the chill waters to break the current and permit the small fish to move on upstream.

And now the colonel moved to his favorite rock on the

stream's bank, seating himself and hauling off his riding boots. Then, with the same felt relief experienced as a boy by the green waters of the river Sava in his native Croatia, he relaxed and dangled his feet in the stream while a family of magpies chattered and scolded in the tree overhead. The sounds of the forest somehow softened his mood, and for a moment he closed his eyes. Once reopened, a glitter of sunlight caught his attention, something shiny in the grass, and he leaned to pick up an object which he recognized immediately. A crystal goblet—one from his own set! Puzzled, he turned it over and over in his hand.

Why—of course! Just think, they must have stopped right here for a rest—at this very spot on the way to The Ledges that day Michelle was thrown from the horse.

Discovery of the goblet jarred his emotions, and despite the heat of the day, he felt a dark tremor, once again focusing on the subject which had occupied his mind since that last late night call. Holding the crystal seemed somehow to bring the crisis closer, but stubbornly he refused to give in to it this time.

Hell—what did politicians know? The two of them had proved themselves able, hadn't they? And, too, they'd made it in all right? And now with his old compatriot, Zeljko, they were in good hands. Well, all right then. He snapped his finger against the rim of the crystal, bending one ear to the answering ring. Faith, man. Faith!

For a moment he dipped the goblet in the current of the stream, then watched the water shimmer and swirl in the sunlight.

And deep in the glass, there she was—Michelle—tiny with miniature arms and legs, gay ringlets of hair tumbling down her back as she turned her head to beam up at him.

It had been here at the old estate one summer day, away from the business of war. For Michelle's sixth birthday he had surprised her with a pony, a Shetland from the Isles, and she was up with the sun, galloping over the meadows, hurdling the hedges.

It was different in those modest days. In place of today's neat rows of white-railed fences, there were only bare strands of barbed wire linked by the fence posts. And he recalled how he had been out mending fences that day when he chanced to look up, now remembering how shocked he had been to spy the Shetland pony some distance away idling by a fence post—and the child thrashing about on the ground.

He recalled his alarm as he raced in her direction while the little girl climbed unsteadily to her feet, hobbling, then, balancing and using the strands of barbed wire for support, she worked her way up the fence post and flung herself crosswise over the pony's back, slapping its flank to start it in his direction.

And he still recalled his horror at the sight when at last he had reached her—the spurt of fresh blood and the length of barbed wire driven clear through the tiny white foot.

And he remembered the frantic ride to the hospital, and that brave little face. That must have been the year before the tragic death of her mother, his only sibling.

Seated atop the rock on the bank of the stream, Mavro Anastasi could hold it within him no longer and suddenly cried out *"fool!"* For the hundredth time, stoutly did he reproach himself. And now if she didn't get back safely, it would be the blood of his own favorite niece on his hands.

"And you took his word—the bastard. How in the world could he, Mavro Anastasi, have taken the word of that man—have trusted him? Hadn't Deputy Lockwood displayed his true colors from the start—at that very first meeting in Defense Secretary Levitt's Pentagon office? Even now he could picture Lockwood's brusque and arrogant manner, the way the man had displayed open contempt for him, disparaging his connection to the former Communist regime in Yugoslavia—even resisted the idea of the Secretary revealing the photos of the great dam marked,

TOP SECRET."

Never should he have trusted Lockwood's promise to shunt the girl out of harm's way at the very last moment, before the operation began.

But now he paused to reflect. Or could it have been Michelle herself, headstrong as she was, who had disregarded explicit orders as Lockwood had once again sworn only last night on the phone? Well, he sighed, it was far too late to dwell on it now. Now he must live with the consequences.

Trying to put the whole matter out of his head, his mind took a different tack, focusing on the harsh and thoughtless way in which he himself had just brushed off his servant, Marko, his dearest friend, his old compatriot in arms. And he berated himself for his own failure to share with Marko the plan of the mission, the early discussions, the latest rumblings. And most of all, he was ashamed at his inability to share his true feelings.

Of course, there were rules about sharing the plans and discussions, even the late hunches, but there were no rules about sharing the feelings, certainly not to exclude Marko—especially Marko who had spent more hours with Michelle since the death of her mother than even her own father. To exclude him now was to deny the whole bond.

Somehow though, he could not bring himself to it, man to man. For he himself was "The Colonel," ever "The Colonel." And at some place in time that title and the aura surrounding it had somehow transformed to a shield, an emotional shield so hard to put down, and yet a shield which only fended off feelings and friendship and invited isolation. And over years you watched it increase and expand, and there was nothing to do about it, and you became, like it or not, a prisoner to it. And that wasn't pleasant to realize, for it signaled a lessening mastery over oneself.

It was a phenomenon which, now that he had arrived at

the midstage of his life, he could not, he simply would not accept. And it was not to his credit that he could not, for he knew his own motive to be not altogether laudable. For when the crunch came, if the mission failed, he could not escape the guilt, not where she was concerned; and yet he knew it would be beyond his capacity to endure all alone. If it reached that point, he knew in his heart he would no longer be "The Colonel," that solid symbol of order and rectitude, but a stranger, a miserable shell of unbearable pain—a pain he could not face alone. Only was there one he could turn to, one with the depth of understanding and compassion to share it. Yes, perhaps if that day came, they could bear it together, and they neither would have to bear it alone.

And now he shook off the thought and roused himself. So they were coming down to the final day. From now on, it was a race against detection and a race against time. But the hint of disaster in Deputy Lockwood's tone still rang in his ears. He knew that in truth Lockwood was only parroting the Secretary's own misgivings.

Still his mind churned. Suppose they get caught in the shaft? Suppose the flooding isn't fast enough? Suppose they just can't reach the horses? And what if the river is swollen and they can't get across? Suppose? Suppose? Suppose?

Suddenly Colonel Anastasi sprang to his feet.

Bah! Risk is the essence of battle. The chance—the unknown—the unexpected. If you can't face the risks, be a civil servant, be a functionary, be a damned politician—be anything—but don't be a soldier!

Calmly he pulled on his boots. He had dismissed all thought of lunch or of pushing on to The Ledges; there was no need. As he patted the bay with a tender touch and led his mount protectively back down the narrow trail, he reached out one leg, and with a firm thrust of his boot, kicked a small stone from his path—much as he had as a boy in the old country.

But before he caught sight of the long rambling house, his brain was at it again. What about her concussion? If there were a relapse, how could they ever get her out?

45

It was very real, Cil was dreaming, the two of them at the top of the world, walking in crunchy grass, and the grass brown from the sun. The sky high and cloudless and the sun just coming up and warm on his back, and not a breath of wind, and no trees, only the higher peaks in the distance. And everywhere the fresh smell of the grasses as she went on running a good distance in front of him. She would turn now and again and beckon to him, and then rush on, and he couldn't catch up, and he would look only at her, for he so wanted to catch her. But he seemed to be falling farther behind. The mist was everywhere, blanketing the ground between them, pushing gauzy fingers up to the waist of the gossamer gown that fluttered like her hair as she moved. He called to her. "Wait for me. I need you!" But she didn't hear, or didn't care, or was merely taunting him, for she kept on moving away. He shouted louder. "Please, darling, help me catch up." But she was just smiling that lovely impish smile, and moving on. And now he didn't think he could catch up, and he became all desperate inside.

On instinct he reached back to touch the outline of the broken sword in his pack, but his pack was not there. He made one giant lunge. And then he was reaching her, reaching her fine. And then he was past her—she still with the flowing white gown and that wistful smile. Then he stumbled. He was falling, falling over the side—falling weightlessly.

He knew it was over. Thoughts raced through his mind and they made no sense, the thoughts mixed like a collage, but the pictures clear from when he was a boy, and the colors, the colors brilliant and sparkling in reds and yellows and warm vivid blues. And then he just let go his breathing and waited for his soul to float out of him.

Sometime later—much later—Cil could feel his senses coming back. He hungered for the heat of her body. He could still feel himself shivering, his arms and legs trembling from the cold. He could smell the fragrance of her and feel the soft warmth of her skin against his own, the moistness of full lips, the easy pressure of firm breasts pressed against his naked chest, the fleshiness of her thighs, the soft nothingness of her hair tickling his neck, the clinging, caring pressure of her arms.

But something seemed amiss. The thighs seemed more fleshy than he had guessed they would be, the breasts softer, the lips somehow more moist and welcoming, and he reveled in their warmth.

Now his eyes fluttered open. It was so black all around that he couldn't see a thing, although he could tell they were outside on the ground, wrapped in thick blankets. He didn't know how long they had been there. He could hear the horses, restless, moving at their pickets, and he could feel the cold blast of the wind.

Sometime later his shivering stopped—the numbness receding from his face and the feeling coming back in a sluggish way to fingers and toes. And now his hearing came, too, and he could whisper in the blackness; it sounded just fine.

She rolled onto her side and reached out for something, and immediately he felt the cold invading the blankets.

Then she said, "Here, Major, take this."

That voice! It struck him with the force of a balled fist, and Cil could feel his blood running as cold as the metal surface of the flask she passed into his hands. "Take a good drink," she told him. "The whiskey will warm you."

"Oh, my—god! Bogey!"

In shock and disbelief he drew back, their bodies moist and naked—still touching. Then, for want of coherent message from his brain, he lifted the flask in his hand, leaned back his head, and tasted deeply of the smooth flowing nectar. The brandy was cold, its welcoming heat penetrating his body, and he pulled on it again, absorbing its warmth. He could hear the tinkle of her laughter.

"Major Cil. Surely you are not such an adolescent schoolboy that you should be embarrassed by this?" And again the small deprecating giggle. And for a silly moment now that the shock and surprise had worn thin, he felt a small grin on his lips in the darkness.

When she had dressed, then instructed him to put on the dry clothes she had earlier fetched from the tunnel, Cil could see that the weather had turned bitter cold. He peered down at his watch. Though the band was soaked through, he could see that the luminous second hand was still moving. It was 2:37 AM of the third day.

"Where is Michelle?"

"Gone."

"Gone?"

"That's right. After the airman."

"What airman?"

"Before you left, the gypsy, One-Eye, he was posted on watch on the north side of the mountain. Claims he saw a rocket fired from the base of the mountain, then heard a loud explosion above the clouds. It was Michelle who later picked up the homing beam."

"What!—and nobody stopped her?" His mind was reeling. "And you say, what? That she used the radio?"

"Only when it was clear that a pilot was down. Then, using a map, she got a fix through some satellite relay. I don't understand about those technical things. She said she learned it from you, in the training. Anyway, she checked the map and insisted on going alone. I tried to dissuade her, or at least get her to take one of the gypsies along, but she was so sure she had—what do you call it—a fix on the pilot? She felt that with a horse she could slip through undetected. She claimed to know his exact position."

"But she's sick!" his voice sharp, tense. "How long ago did she leave?"

"Hours."

"How many?"

"Two at least."

"Which way?"

"She said east—with the funny glasses."

"You mean, night vision goggles—damn! Don't you know, there have to be hundreds of land mines out there! That's the Serb defense perimeter!" He was shaking again. "What about Zeljko?"

"He was off looking for you. Then, after he got you out, he had to get back to the shaft—to the men digging."

Cil's instant reaction was to go track her. He struggled to his feet, staggered forward a few steps, collided with a tree trunk, and, attempting to right himself, dropped ingloriously back down on the seat of his pants.

"Satisfied, Major?"

A tense silence fell between them. He was weaker than he had thought. With a two-hour start, only craziness would think he could catch up with her in the darkness.

Like a short circuit, his mind leapt in all directions at once. He was too weak; she was gone. It was just the same—just the same as when it had all happened before— with his beloved April—with Sonya. And now Michelle sick and helpless out there with the Serbs on account of he couldn't even cross a damned lake! Well, he couldn't, he wouldn't let it all happen again.

It was Bogey who broke the silence, her tone icy and indignant.

"For your information, Major Lane Cil, I was under strict orders from the old man—so don't strain your conscience. Perhaps it comes as a surprise to you, but these mountains lack the luxury accomodations of a full-blown western hospital." She drew slightly away. "Lacking heat and motion, you would have been dead in another hour." Her tone was more hurt than anger. "And do not worry your head, Your Excellency; no one's going to give away your little secret. Despite what you may think, as I told you before, we of this land are not all barbarians."

And now he could feel a cold light rain beginning out of the north. He flexed his fingers to help restore feeling.

"You say she's been gone for two hours?"

"At least."

"And Zeljko?" It was as though with the news of Michelle, his mind was not registering properly. "You say, Zeljko, he returned to the shaft?"

"He took One-Eye. He left the grinning Chipmunk over there by the horses." She must have sensed his blush in the darkness, for the smile in her voice was understanding and sympathetic, and she spoke again quickly. "Don't worry," she repeated.

"When did Zeljko go down?"

"Not long. We rubbed your body for nearly an hour."

"I've got to go."

But just as he said it, a trace of sound caught his ear.

"Shh. Listen!"

The rain was coming harder, mixing with sleet, and the wind on the rise. Then again the distant sound. Together in the cold and the wet, they strained their ears to the south, but no sound came except for the patter of sleet in the leaves overhead, and the steady light spatter of rain mixed with sleet on the ground. They listened hard. The sound came again, and though they both sensed the danger, they could not make it out because of the distance.

"What is it?" she whispered.

"Listen!"

It came again, and then there were more sounds, louder, all run together, muffled in the falling sleet and rain. Cil could not make them out. The noises came closer, still from the south. Seconds ticked past. They did not breath, only sat tense—listening.

There, again—and this time he knew. Yelping!

Cil could feel the small hairs rising on his forearms and come to attention on the nape of his neck. He fought the whole irrationality of it all, the same sense of panic he had felt when confronted by the enemy trooper back there with Michelle by the stream.

He heard her say, "Well, what?"

"Dogs!"

"What do we do?" She was sitting very close now, and he could feel the rod of her spine as it stiffened.

"Nothing—wait! Listen for the direction."

She passed him his weapon and pack. He found a fully loaded clip in the pack and jammed it home. He snapped back the bolt of the M-16 assault rifle and heard it slide forward with the familiar metallic clank. He felt in the pack for the reassurance of a second full clip, then set the selector switch on his weapon for automatic fire. He could feel new strength flowing back into his body.

There—it came again. No voices, only the distant barking and yelping of dogs hot on a trail, but closer. The freezing rain and sleet pattered down.

"Where are they now?" she said.

"On the way up the stream."

"How far?"

"Hard to say."

"Below the ledge and the waterfall?"

"Shh!"

"They're coming closer." Her voice was small.

"Yes."

"We better move."

"Shh!" She was very brave.

They listened for a lifetime. He was thinking of Michelle. Cil could tell that the dogs had reached the ledge, and he was waiting for their decision. If they were able to scale the ledge, almost certainly they would swing this way and discover the horses. And if they found the horses....His mind broke away; he refused to follow the thought. Still it was black as soot.

He and Bogana were located some distance from the horses, though able to hear them. But one fact weighed on his mind. If the patrol stumbled onto the horses, they would discover Chipmunk—and more patrols would follow.

Suddenly he shivered violently, a reaction beyond his control. He could hear the shriek of the wind, and the wind was their ally; but if the dogs made it over the ledges....

"Shouldn't we break for the tunnel?" she asked.

"We'd only lead them straight to it."

"Then what?"

"Nothing. Wait."

"Will they find us here?"

"Not now, not if a crust of sleet builds. And the dark and the wind—and later the ground fog."

"But the horses?"

"Maybe."

"We better try to move them."

"Too late," he told her.

They did not speak. They went on listening to the sounds of the night.

"Do you think me cheap?" she asked suddenly.

Gently he touched her arm. "What do you think?"

"Thank you; I'm glad."

Cil could hear the barking and yelping clearly now, yet it seemed less anxious, somehow less focused, the noise coming in a wider range.

For minutes on end the sounds had come no closer, but still they waited and listened to see if any remnants of the patrol had scaled the sheer limestone face of the rock. As the minutes passed, the noise of the dogs seemed more subdued, confused, as if losing direction. Cil released a breathful of air, and Bogey picked up the sound.

"Better now?" she asked.

"I think so, listen."

They sat wet and listening for a good twenty minutes, the sounds no closer, finally dwindling, moving off toward their right and the lake, and Cil knew there was no way a patrol could scale the rock cliffs on that side with this ice. When he was sure they were safe for the moment, he tucked the spare loaded clip in his pocket, pulled on his pack, then rose, clicking his weapon on safety. Then he took her by the hand. Together they first searched out the gypsy, Chipmunk, cowering by the horses, beside himself with fear. With the gypsy in tow, they moved off, crunching over the brittle crust of ice that now had begun to build a solid cover over the bare ground. They made their way to the lower tunnel entrance.

This rain and sleet should cover our tracks, he was thinking. God, let it cover Michelle's too.

46

He was moving at a good clip, his glance darting cautiously side to side, the large blanket-wrapped bundle held tight in his arms. Cil advanced by fits and starts. Quick running steps through the wind-lashed sleet were interrupted by silent pauses to strain eyes and ears like a cat and to sense his surroundings. In this way, he left the narrow streambed at the base of the mountain, ducked through the pine boughs caked and brittle with ice, then dashed across the clearing before the dam.

The steady hammer of sleet came heavier now, slanting in on the wind. It bit at his cheeks and stung the bridge of his nose. He moved up through the undergrowth shrouding the earthen dam, halted to give the recognition signal to the frozen figure of One-Eye on watch, passing a word with him before moving on. Then finally Cil brushed back the first blanket baffle at the entrance and stepped into the shaft.

Except for the absence of heat and flame, it was like stepping into a burning house. Smoke was everywhere. It billowed and swirled. Beyond the second baffle, Cil's eyes instantly began to smart from the acrid cloud of fumes in the shaft. At his feet, the compressor whirred, belching out a steady stream of blue smoke.

The first reaction was to gag and choke, and Cil had to stand against the side for a time to accustom his breathing. There within the smoke-filled shaft entrance, the roar of the generators from the great concrete dam overhead blended with the noise of the compressor, the clamor deafening, the vibration enough to set the teeth on edge.

Standing there in the uncertain light, blinking to adjust to the smoke and the haze, Cil could see the stocky figure of Zeljko limping toward him down the shaft. As the old man came closer, even in the poor light, Cil tensed at his expression.

The old man took Cil's arm and hauled him deeper into the shaft where the noise of the generators was less. When they reached the protruding white slab that rose from floor to ceiling, partially cutting the shaft in two, Zeljko leaned against it and spoke sharply.

"I give strict orders to Bogana to keep you the night. This air no place for you." He brought his face very close. "And here you are not so well liked!"

"Take those guns." Cil motioned back toward the shaft entrance, and the old man squinted through the haze of fumes, barely able to make out the large bundle stashed out of the wet atop the throbbing compressor.

"What? I not let you do this," snapped Zeljko. I know him. That man, he's crazy."

"If we weren't all crazy, we wouldn't be here. But we are—and so are the dogs."

"Dogs?" demanded Zeljko fiercely.

"That's right; they prowl below the ledge. Many dogs."

Even in the pale light, Cil saw a faint shadow slide somewhere in the depths of the old man's eyes. Zeljko looked to the bundle of weapons, but he did not speak.

"Before the night is out," Cil told him, "we'll need every gun we can lay our hands on. Already One-Eye is alerted!"

"You know the niece of the colonel is gone." Zeljko looked hard into Cil's face. His words held the hollow quality of a man attempting to distance himself from the truth. "And Bogana?"

"Safe in the tunnel. The rain is all sleet now, a sheet of ice that covers the ground." He knew that Zeljko's mind was not focused on Bogey, and for a second he gripped the old man's arm. "With luck, it will save her."

The old man left Cil. He moved to the mouth of the shaft, through the two blanket baffles, and stepped outside. When he returned, picking up the bundle of weapons on the way, the shoulders of his workshirt were speckled with sleet. He nodded.

At that instant, two of the strapping farm lads appeared, hauling the mud-filled cart, forcing the pitifully small wheels down the track of railway ties. When the cart had slithered past, Zeljko and Cil moved forward up the shaft.

The shaft at the entrance began wide, six or seven feet, then narrowed down to a width of no more than four at the halfway point and the vertical slab. Then it gradually began to widen again. The pebbly ceiling of concrete stood head-high above a sea of oozing mud that rose above the ankles of Cil's work boots as he slogged forward. Even this far forward, the air was a bluish fog of fumes in the pale light of faintly flickering low-wattage bulbs strung along the wall of dirt. At the front of the shaft, a kerosene lamp illuminated the figures of two men, one tall, one short, both digging furiously at the face of the shaft, their backs barely visible through the eddying haze. On the way forward, Cil and Zeljko squeezed past Agar the Ox and one of Slobo's farm hands, both seated on a pile of the rotted bits and pieces of timber that had lined the sides of the old spillway. They looked up, eyes glazed with exhaustion, faces masked with a coating of grime. The Ox gave a nod of recognition; the other squinted, expressionless. Up front, the sides of the shaft seemed plastered with remnants of the same rotted boards, and Cil could see where spades had cut through the old wall casing as if it were cardboard.

At the face of the shaft, the naked backs of the diggers glistened, painted with a coating of grime and sweat, while the points of their spades sparked and plunged as they attacked the dirt packed around jagged boulders blocking the way. As Cil and Zeljko approached, the pair of diggers paid them no heed, their attention riveted on the wall of earth before them. It was not until Cil stepped up and raised his voice that his presence registered and both whirled to face him.

The little commander, evincing small surprise, offered a sneer of welcome, the pulp of a toothpick, suddenly excited, flipping between his lips.

"Well, look here, Herr Professor! If it's not the pretty Yankee boy. Could it be breakfast time already? And look there!" He held forth theatrically. "At the customary three paces behind cowers his man servant—the bootlicker."

Cil could feel the rush of air as the old man burst past him, lunging, his hard-muscled hands grasping the throat of the squat mountain commander. But Cil clutched at the old man's arm, forcing him back.

"Wait!" Cil could hear the bite of his own command. "Now with the dogs, there's no time to waste!" He handed the bundle of weapons to the little commander. "Here!" looking down at the sneering face. "Arm your men."

Slobo, the toothpick in his mouth flicking testily, stood back, holding the bundle of weapons and eyeing Cil. He eyed him in the way a man eyes a rabid dog blocking his path. But when he smiled, the bow of his lips curved up with satisfaction.

In a sudden, unexpected movement, Slobo tossed the bundle of weapons to Zeljko, occupying Zeljko's hands at the critical moment, Zeljko attempting to catch the bundle and save it from the mud of the floor.

At once came the glint of a knife blade, the weapon handled expertly in the hand of Slobo. "Now I show the foreigner who is master!"

The reaction came swiftly. The bearded Professor, all but forgotten in the swirl of events, seized the little man. He lifted him bodily into the air with one hand. He pressed the man's face so forcefully against the coarse surface of the concrete ceiling that a thin crimson serpent of blood sprouted from a cut above the eye. The blood spilled in fat droplets onto the mud-laden floor. At the end of the little commander's arm, the knife dangled harmlessly.

"Idiot!" The giant Professor with the spade-shaped beard spat out the words through his teeth. "What earlier I warned goes double for the Yankee. Can your small mind not grasp it? As the old man told you, we are none of us in this thing for ourselves. We are in it for our people. All of our people." The Professor reached his free hand behind him. "And the only attack from that miserable arm will come at the end of this shovel!"

Slobo's mouth hung slack. The remains of the toothpick had fallen away, though the mouth still held a sneer that looked to have clung there since birth. But the eyes were watering, and a drip of the crimson liquid hovered at the end of his nose as he groped for the words.

"A joke!" The little man's voice was shaking miserably.

"At the next joke, little commander, you answer to me."

Slobo swiveled his eyes to look at the Professor, but his lips made no sound; so he nodded, then nodded again.

"Now get those weapons to your men—with my message!" And the bearded giant lowered the little man onto his feet, providing a guiding shove toward the back of the shaft.

The tempest was over as quickly as it had begun. Possessively the little commander wrestled the blanket of weapons from one of his farm lads to whom it had been passed in the scuffle. He parceled out the contents, guarding his prerogative zealously. Only when he was out of earshot did the Professor turn to the old man.

"What is this thing of the dogs?"

"They run with the patrols," Zeljko told him, kicking one

boot against the other to shed it of mud, but Cil cut in.

"How many hours before you break through to the cap?"

"Hours?" cried the bearded Professor. "To move these big rocks—no less than two days."

Cil consulted his wristwatch, then stared at the half-naked Muslim giant. "We've less than twenty hours."

The Professor turned to Zeljko. "And now with the dogs?"

Zeljko looked up from his muddy boot, casually, not speaking at first; then he squared on the others. "Now, we work—later, we fight!"

PART III

47

Malcolm Baxter, the veteran British Navy Seal, and explosives expert, outfitted in full battle dress, sat listening in the cold and the wet at the top of Bald Hill, watching the spread of thin gauzy light before dawn. He sat quite casually, wrapped in a dark rain-slicked blanket which was pulled up over his head like a hood. Setting aside the bottle of whiskey with which he had just finished rinsing his teeth for the third time, he sat tugging absently at the corner of what eight days before had been a smartly-clipped, handlebar mustache.

He went on listening. In an effort to pinpoint the location of the sound and assess its direction of movement, he listened past the sound of the sleet and the rain. He peered again at the luminous dial of his watch. The time was 5:12 AM.

From where he sat, Bald Hill looked directly across the lake at Castle Mountain. And if it had been daylight and clear, Baxter could have looked across the way and up at the green hulking expanse of mountain climbing out of the depths of the lake with the castle ruins perched on top, while below on the right lay the curved white crest of the dam.

But at this hour in the pale leaden light, he could observe nothing but the depression carved out of the earth at his feet, its floor a shadowy jumble of rocks. Once the cellar of a fine hunting lodge of the Austrian Army, the forest fire that long ago had scorched the hilltop had erased all that. What remained was a hole in the ground at the back of a clearing fringed by tall ash and oaks, and ensconced in the hole, the sleeping members of Nedo's group who were not posted on watch.

Minutes passed. Under the blanket, the driving sleet and freezing rain sent a chill through Baxter's combat jacket, and he shivered and pulled the blanket tighter about him as he heard the first stirrings from the cellar below. Then a head popped above the level of the ground.

"Morning, Old Boy!" Baxter called cheerily despite his true feelings. "Hear our new neighbors?"

Nedo's face remained impassive. He cocked one ear and listened to the sounds but made no reply.

"Well, what do you make of it?"

The young rebel leader now looked at the Englishman before him with a pensive stare. Still without speaking, in a graphic gesture, he bent his hand down from the wrist to signify that the noise was coming from far below the sheer rock face of the hill, off to their right, where River Road curved west away from the dam to duck through the narrow pass between Bald Hill and the next ridge south.

"My deduction precisely, Chum. What do you think?"

Nedo put his finger to his lips and continued to track the sounds with his ear. He had been listening to the dogs and sifting out the alternatives for a full quarter of an hour before joining the Englishman. Only now was he satisfied.

In the beginning, he had taken great pains in choosing this spot as his base of operations. Perched at the fringe of the forest at the top of the hill, the clearing before them provided a clear field of fire, and the cliff's face off to the right, a commanding view of the road from the enemy compound where it ran through the pass. Until now, the hilltop had been remote from patrols and a perfect observation point, the cellar hole well disguised, overgrown as it was with bushes and new growth of hardwoods poking out of the rock-strewn floor. And the cellar carried added advantages, too. It was screened from the curious eyes of air traffic by the stand of tall trees forming a wooded fringe at the rim of the cliff at the back and the sides. Above all, he had anticipated its proximity to the weak point of the dam and the importance of line-of-sight signaling with the castle, and this location had been perfect. But all that was before the dogs; with the dogs, everything changed. Dogs could sniff anyone out anywhere.

Baxter asked again what Nedo thought.

At length, his shoulders erect, his manner unhurried, Nedo looked the British officer straight in the eye. "The signaling. You are sure the signaling with the mountain is all through now?"

"I'm sure."

"Then we go—now."

"What, move at once? Isn't that a bit previous? Wouldn't do to rush, you know, and make a mess of things, would it?"

"The dogs rob us of choice." The young rebel leader was not accustomed to having his orders questioned. "We move now with the ice crust for cover. Then let the snow and sleet cover the trail behind."

The Englishman was inclined to be obstinate, as only Englishman can be, especially a battle-crusted British naval officer with a half pint of whiskey in his belly.

"Now hold on, old boy," he said. "No sense getting panicky over a few mongrels straying a half mile distant."

"That's not the idea. I will tell you again."

"I heard you the first time."

"Then what?" inquired Nedo with more than a hint of impatience, his ear still cocked to the sound of the dogs.

"Look—chum. We're safe here, and we've still got

almost a bloody full day to zero hour. Here, there's precious little chance of being found out—unless we go off half-cocked and give 'em a trail to follow."

Nedo said nothing.

"Well," said Baxter, "what do you say?"

"I say we go."

"I say—we are one for Rambo tactics, aren't we?" Even in the poor light, the long-nosed Englishman was eyeing his companion sardonically: the white Rambo headband in defiance of the Serbs—the crossed bandoleers with grenades strung along the line of cartridges like so many grapefruit—the twin-holstered pearl-handled pistols, Patton style—the bulging chest pouches crammed with ammunition. It was a get-up straight out of Hollywood.

"One more time, I explain," countered Nedo, resting the nose of his AK-47 assault rifle in the V of a sapling. "True, we are safe here until it melts. But look." He bent down and lifted a handful of ice-encrusted grass and weed from the ground, pointedly holding it under Baxter's large nose. "By lunchtime," Nedo said simply, "the storm passes, the sun comes strong, and it all melt away to nothing. If we stay, tonight we go down for the placing of the charges. On dry ground, a blind man could follow the trail of these horses. The godless ones come at us as we enter the water. If not, we swim up as helpless with the gear from the base of the dam."

"I still say it's too bloody many hours," responded Baxter tartly, "and a damned sight too risky down by the lake."

"See down there." Nedo pointed down into the cellar hole at their feet. "At the base of the hill by the lake, already the wind she is down and the wet makes a ground fog like that. Good cover, yes? Unless, like a pair of old women, we keep up this jabber until the wind again rises. Look, this day the wind it blow from the west—off shore of the lake all day. If we hide by the shore until night comes, the wind, it carries the scent away from the dogs."

The Englishman looked down into the ancient cellar hole where tendrils of mist were already forming a blanket of ground fog among the larger rocks of the floor as the young man had pointed out. Then he nodded.

"Dead right, old chum—it's your show. Just do me a turn and ask your lads to go easy on my equipment."

Once roused, the rest of the irregulars huddled among the glass-coated stones. With pocket knives, they sliced their breakfast of cheese, raw onions, and salami as the rain and sleet pelted down. Within twenty minutes, the horses had been packed, the ammunition stowed, all sign of habitation erased from the camp, and the tiny troop set off, cautiously picking its way down along the fringe of tall trees that bordered the clearing.

The members of the little troop did not ride single file as one might have imagined. Instead, with boots carefully wrapped in a bulky cover of rags, each man spread out, walking his mount over the brittle surface of ice down the slant of the hill.

When they had progressed into the dripping forest below the bald patch, Nedo, who was in the lead, held up. He summoned his lieutenants, then dispatched them with orders to round up the lookouts and intercept the troop farther down. No sooner had they returned, than they plunged off once again through the trees on Nedo's orders to scout the forest below, the hooves of their horses, though similiarly wrapped, crunching over the brittle, crackling pie crust of ice.

As Baxter followed along, leading his horse through the milky pre-dawn light, still the faint yelping came to his ears. Watching the shadowy outline of Nedo in the lead, he thought of the sternness of the young Rambo-like figure, of the quiet boldness of the eyes, closer to the eyes of a leopard than those of a man. He puzzled at the talks they had had in the time since his arrival—or rather the lack of them, for the boy seldom uttered a word. When he did speak, it was not frivolous banter but always brief and serious, as if using too many words somehow burned up one's equity in life, as if words were to be rationed to avoid the sin of over-use. He had spoken to the boy openly and freely, and the boy had countered in abbreviated terms—with a nod of the head, a phrase of economy, but seldom more. Yet, in spite of himself, he had come to trust the boy's instincts, his keen sense of the enemy's moves, his knowledge of every shift in conditions and weather, his familiarity with every nook and cranny of these dark and mysterious Bosnian hills.

Even so, the coming of the dogs complicated the equa-tion, especially in this crazy David and Goliath business with the Serbs, certainly when the bloodhounds were in the hands of Goliath.

The minutes slipped by; the sky in the east altered to a light eggshell gray. A soupy mist hung in the hollows, clutching at the tree trunks, the ice-glazed branches and leaf-heavy stems offering a sagging canopy with mixed sleet and rain dripping through.

Every now and again, Nedo in the lead would raise his hand to hold up the troupe, to then take stock, training his ears to the sounds. And now he looked off to his right toward the south rim of the hill. He did not go over and peer down the sheer face of the cliff, for the effort would have been useless in the pre-dawn light; but the picture was clear in his mind. Far below, at the base of the rock lay the nar-row pass between this hill and the next ridge south where River Road ran up from the enemy compound. Except for this gap, the hills combined in a solid wall, ringing the basin and the enemy compound within. Below the compound, the south ridge pushed around, sticking out one huge foot of ledge, positioning the toes flush with the river.

Nedo was thinking of the enemy fuel dump with its great underground storage tanks cut in under the face of the rock of the south ridge where the pass opened out above the near side of the dam. In the early days of the enemy build-up, when his small band had little to do but watch and remember, he had been fascinated by the laying of the tanks. Hour after hour he had sprawled on the near shoulder of the hill and watched the enemy bulldozers backing and starting, grunting and snarling as they attacked the underside of the cliff, preparing a concealed bed for the tanks. And when the job was completed, he had watched the pair of immense cylinders being moved into place, then filled.

He remembered one warm spring day lying there on the very rim of the hill, eyeing the enemy soldiers below him, hearing the shouted orders. He recalled a moment of carelessness, a quick reflex action as his carbine started to slip. He remembered, too, the handful of loose gravel spilling over the edge and beginning its long descent—and the look of horror on the face of his comrade. And later, the casual, unhurried demeanor of the enemy soldiers below who paid it no heed.

Presently Nedo veered left, down a deep ravine. At the crease of the ravine, one by one, the party entered a normally dry streambed now gushing with water. They followed the stream to the point where it merged with the lake, then moved down the shoreline, through the shallows. When he reached the spot he wanted, Nedo gave the signal and the horses waded ashore into a thicket of leafy undergrowth.

Down here at the lake, a thick ground fog shrouded the tree trunks just as he had said, but the air here was warmer and the sleet had changed back to freezing rain which coated branches and boughs, weighing them down with ice until they seemed to grow into the ground. Nedo recalled what he had told the Englishman and hoped the freezing rain would cover and conceal the trail of the horses now that the sleet had ended. He wondered, too, if the wind would be normal as he had promised, blowing out onto the lake all day or whether it might turn fickle as sometimes happened after a storm—to carry the scent of the horses onshore.

48

Captain Pavlov knew without being told that he was in for a bad day. From the moment he received the summons at dawn and rushed through a breakfast of runny eggs and undercooked sausage, he knew. When he then stepped out into the cold and the rain only to tumble and fall on a patch of newly formed ice and split his britches, he knew he was in for it. And the general's curt response to his knock confirmed his worst fears.

One look at the general was all revealing. Even at this hour, the imposing figure of the general stood tall in a crisply pressed uniform, medals and all, with a doggedly determined look on his face. He stood scrutinizing the map of the region that lay on the green billiard table, scrutinizing it with such single-minded focus that he failed to look up as Pavlov entered the room.

"What is it, my General?"

"The downed airman, has he yet been brought in?"

"Not yet, Sir, no—the weather is fierce, but patrols are out searching the hills to the east."

"Report at first word. But at this moment—come here, come here and look at this." And Pavlov moved timidly to the contour map that lay on the table.

The old general bent to his task, carefully drawing circles upon the map with a compass, which he used with great precision and skill. He began with one large circle, and Captain Pavlov could see the point of the compass making a tiny pinprick at the axis. Then, within that circle and using the same point as an axis, he drew three other circles, all within the first, each succeeding circle of lessening radius. When he had completed the four circles, he stood back and inspected his handiwork.

"Yes, yes. You see, Captain? They have certainly been knocking at our door. Not so quietly either; but we have been sleeping."

"I am afraid I do not understand, Sir."

"I am sure you don't, Pavlov—but watch."

The general bent again over the table and picked up a piece of white chalk. With a delicate hand, he placed a large D at the common axis. Then, in rapid strokes, he marked a time and date at the top of each circle. He then placed down the chalk and stood back as might a university professor admiring his work.

"Do you see it now, Captain?"

There was an embarrassed pause before Pavlov cleared his throat, then replied in a voice more shaky than he would have wished. "I'm afraid I do not quite see it, my General," and he felt miserably wedged against the table and pained with his inadequacy.

"Do not fret. I, too, failed to see it until now. Look!" The bear of a man stepped forward, picked up the white chalk and placed an X along the circumference of the largest circle, the one that swept around farthest from the common axis, the mark covering a squiggly blue line at a position of ten o'clock, if the circle had been a clock face. He labeled it "1." "That is where Private Lajtner met his fate, where he was found with a knife in the back by the stream east of the main road running south from the village. As you reported, the poor devil had clearly been taking a—ah—swim after duty."

The next X came nearly opposite the first, but on the next smaller circle, this one at four o'clock, and the bearish commander labeled it "2."

"That, Pavlov, is where the phantom farmers of yesterday were surprised in the early mist, to the east. Yet, these were no ordinary farmers. These were young, well-muscled farmers, well-equipped with ammunition and rifles stolen from the military stores of the Yugoslav National Army buried twenty years ago in these mountains by the Tito Regime for safekeeping. While three were killed, the others got cleanly away; and despite the reports of the intercepting patrol leader, no blood stains were found. Men with serious wounds do not vanish without trace."

The next X came at two o'clock, on the second to the smallest of the circles, and took the label, "3."

"The cup, Captain. The innocent rusted tin cup. On the high wall in the castle ruins, the wall overlooking the dam and the lake and the opposite hill.

"And lastly, my friend, number '4.' Here, below the dam—only two hundred meters removed from the axis point—a crew of workmen from the village, pulling up half-rotted railway ties. All the way from the village in a summer rain to dig up rotted ties ten feet long and carry them miles back to their homes—though the forests sag with splendid hardwoods within a few dozen paces of their doorsteps.

"Tell me, Pavlov. What sense does it make to you?"

There was a pause. Pavlov said nothing, though he could feel his palms moist where he clasped them behind his back as the general began his habit of pacing the room.

"No matter, Comrade. It is why I wear the markings of the general, and you of the aide. We play our parts as the cards are dealt. And Captain, I must confess, I have played this hand badly."

The general reached in the side pocket of his uniform

jacket and plopped a gum drop daintily into his mouth.

"At last we understand the movements, if not the intent. Look at the map. It may help you to know the axis of all the circles, the central point in each instance." And the huge frame of the general ducked to peer out the rain-spattered window, which was facing north in the direction of the great dam. In the early light, the spotlights made but a faint glimmer on the towering wall of the dam. "In my youth, I would have seen it instantly, but these days my brain is less supple. And that is truly a shame—for the riddle was simple.

"What do the signs tell us, Captain? After all, we are both hunters, have hunted men in back alleys most of our lives, in one way or another."

Pavlov screwed up his courage. "Could it have something to do with the dam?"

"Why, Pavlov, you surprise me. That's it. All is focused on the dam. They are after the dam."

The general now put down the white chalk and began lecturing as elder teachers are wont to do.

"Poor Lajtner. He surprised someone moving down the trail that parallels the road to the village and the dam. That someone (or someones) was anxious—so anxious not to be discovered, in fact, that they killed him on the spot. Not with a gun, but silently, stealthily, with a knife. And to avoid detection, they went to the nuisance of rigging a dramatic scene to cast away blame. Quite professional, really.

"And the phantom farmers? Also surprised while moving toward the dam—also under cover, the cover of mist and darkness.

"And the peasants surprised at the railway bed next to the dam, then vanishing into thin air? Look how close to the dam."

The general ceased his pacing and strode back to the table and the map. Dark embers burned in the depths of his eyes.

"But, my good Captain, that is only the preview; the main

show comes next. The cup—the tiny inconsequential tin cup! The cup with the rust—but not much rust, and not old rust. Found at the highest point of the region—overlooking everything."

The huge bemedaled figure stuck one great paw in the direction of Pavlov, challenging him.

"If you were the leader of a squadron of bombers, what would you ask for? I'll tell you what—flares! Flares to line up properly for a pass at the dam. Flares that would show your planes the way. Yet, one reference point for the flares would not be enough. No, there must at least be two; the first on the wall of the castle, the second poised on the top of the opposite hill!"

The commander stood inches away from his aide, and when his chest was fully expanded, straining at the polished brass buttons and threatening to burst them, it resembled the front of a great Tiger Tank to the trembling Pavlov.

"Now you must hear of the greatest surprise, the surprise of all great surprises. And I wager you this. When their man finally arrived, I mean their big man, the one in charge of the plan, he found he had wasted his time. He didn't need the flares. He didn't need men posted. And do you know why, Captain? Well, let me tell you why." Pavlov could see clearly the whites of the old war dog's eyes, but his voice was a whisper. "Because, when their best man came, he found the flares. He found the very perfect flares. And do you know who placed those flares, Captain? Do you? We, Pavlov. We, with the brains of egg yokes. We placed the flares! Look at them, Captain! Look at the flares!" The general threw the tiny white chalk against the rain-spattered window with such force that it cracked the pane. His voice could barely be heard. "*Spotlights!* Four giant spotlights, each pair shining a beam on opposite sides of the dam that a blind man could see!

"Get them out—get them out, Captain. Get them out this very minute."

"Yes, my General," said Pavlov, feeling the ring of sweat soaking through his collar. "At once, yes." And Pavlov fled to the black field phone in the room adjoining. When he returned minutes later, the sky to the north was visibly dimmer, and the big man addressed him calmly.

"Now, Captain, you and I are taking a walk. But first, you will accomplish two things."

"Anything, General."

"You will go to the radio shed and see that this wire is sent immediately." He handed a paper to Pavlov.

"Remember, it is to go on the B machine—urgent—first priority."

"Yes, Sir."

"It will take time to receive the answer. Meanwhile, dispatch patrols to the tops of those mountains," motioning toward Castle Mountain and Bald Hill opposite, "as it will take time to find our friends and liquidate them. Is that clear?"

"At once, comrade General. At once."

"Yes, Pavlov, at once!"

The aide snapped a crisp salute and clicked his heels smartly. He was headed for the door, cap in hand, when the general spoke again.

"When you are finished, we shall take that little walk in the rain that I promised."

Later, the general with Pavlov in tow was slogging through the rain over the thin crust of ice, the short man having his hands full, holding an umbrella the size of a parachute over the bobbing head of his commander.

As they plodded past row upon row of tanks and trucks, the proud moth of a mustache the Captain wore on his thin upper lip collapsed downward with the weight of the freezing rain.

"The dogs. What have they turned up through the night?"

The small man shook his head, reaching his free hand up, flicking the hairy ornament away from his mouth. "Nothing in this, General. Not in the ice."

The general nodded, though the adjutant didn't see it, for he was too short and too busy with the umbrella.

The bear-like head turned to study the nearest tank, glazed as it was in a glassy coating of ice.

"Are all tanks, armored cars, and trucks fully gassed and ready to move out?"

"Why no, comrade General."

Color leapt to the general's cheeks—he stopped in his tracks, turning to face Pavlov, then froze like a statue. The aide had to make a tricky maneuver not to rake the smooth, fleshy face with the trailing edge of the umbrella.

"Why not?" barked the commander.

"The closeness of the formations. The danger of fire."

"Asinine! Who gave that order?"

A very long pause ensued before Captain Pavlov found his tongue.

"You did, my General."

They had arrived at the edge of the air strip. Pavlov was very wet now, and the rain coming into his eyes was making it difficult to see; and it was hard for him to gauge the maneuvers of the large umbrella with the change in gait of his superior. Twice now the points of the ribs of the umbrella had pecked at the forehead of the tall man before correction could be affected. Though the aide was frantic, his companion didn't seem to notice. Presently, the general came to a halt before a high-winged monoplane.

"See that all motorized units are fueled immediately. We move out the moment confirmation arrives. Ready the troops for immediate maneuvers. Send up one plane to patrol the mountains. Prepare the other for myself and my, ah—guest."

49

Up front amidst the choking fumes, progress in the shaft was glacial. Now water bubbled in freely to carve thin troughs down the face of the shaft as the old man and Cil hauled away one blocking rock after another. Every few moments, Cil studied the rate of flow spouting through. He tried not to ponder how much longer the cap at the face of the dam could hold back the torrent.

Just then, one of the strapping farm lads rushed headlong up the shaft, splashing along, shouting and waving his arms.

"Major! Major!" His eyes sprang wide; his voice quavered openly. Come quick. The water! It leaks down the bank. She runs all over like *spilled choco-lat-ey!*"

Cil threw down his spade and sped for the mouth of the shaft, Zeljko crowding his heels, the farm lad behind. They burst through the woolen baffles and crouched in sunlight at the top of the mound, eyes blinking to adjust to the brightness. The storm had passed, the sky washed by the rain. A chocolatey mudflow swept past the catch basin and poured over the crest of the mound to veer down through the row of weeping willows, then spill into the sluiceway relieving the great dam.

All three pairs of eyes scoured the terrain on either side

for a sign of a patrol, but the only observable movement was the relentless flow of the mudslide. Tossing caution aside, they raced down the embankment to gauge the extent of exposure and risk.

The screen of willows hard by the active sluiceway blocked all view from River Road where gasoline tankers on the far side of the river were rumbling toward the fuel storage tanks tucked under the pass on the opposite side of the dam, then returning on low springs to the enemy compound. Farther down River Road, Cil spied a line of vehicles forming into a convoy. Closer in, from where the single-span, half-moon steel bridge crossed the river, view of the mudflow was only imperfectly obscured by the column of willows marching along the bank of the river.

Zeljko thrust up an excited arm at the generator room standing above them, its three square little windows peering down from the monstrous white wall of the dam. Cil nodded, his gaze following the thrust of the old man's arm as it lifted higher to point at the crest of the dam. The guard towers were positioned on the lake side, too far forward to command any view of the mound and the runaway stream. To the men's right, a solid wall of ivy shielded all view from the power station. As the three ducked back into the shaft, Cil checked the angle of the sun, calculating the remaining hours of daylight. He turned to Zeljko for confirmation.

"Two hours—three at the most," said the old man.

"Send two of the farm boys," ordered Cil. "One on either side of the mound in good cover. We'll need instant warning the minute they come—and enough firepower to hold them until we clear the shaft."

"How bad is it?" asked the Professor with the mud-spattered beard, the others crowding around.

"Quick! Back to the shovels," commanded Cil. "There's no stopping it now!"

"Then it can be seen?"

"From the generator room. Clearly from the top, from the

air, and from the bridge crossing downstream—where below, down at the enemy compound, a convoy begins to form up."

The Professor automatically turned to Cil. "Then what?" he asked urgently, as much for the others as himself.

"Two at the front! The rest—cut back the wall at the concrete slab! We'll need a free flow once it begins, so slice it back fat and smooth around the slab." He looked to the old man and motioned at two of the farm lads. "Arm the two with automatic rifles. Post them out wide with plenty of spare ammo."

"But without the cart?"

"Forget the cart! Shovel it all on the floor of the shaft."

Cil turned to the two farm lads the old man summoned forward.

"When they come, keep them away from the shaft, whatever you do. Understand?" And when the two heads nodded earnestly, Cil stepped forward, cupping his hands around their necks. "At the first sound of guns, we'll be right behind you." He watched them load up with weapons and ammo, then duck through the baffles.

Cil turned again to the Professor. "Tear down the blankets—open the shaft—then fire up the compressor again. Let's clean up this air once and for all!"

Cil and Zeljko, pick and shovel in hand, took up position at the front. Time teetered on the edge. They did not slacken the pace until they found their way blocked.

Up front, two massive limestone boulders like elephant tusks jutted out of the floor and rose flush with the ceiling, presenting an impenetrable wall as if those who had repaired the leaks in the dam long ago had intentionally created a rock buttress behind the cement cap at the front against the massive pressure of the lake water. Urgently Cil summoned the giant Muslim twins, but no amount of muscle could budge either tusk of rock from its watery roots.

Suddenly Slobo's cry sounded up the shaft. In a moment,

his bony frame lurched into view, arms flailing.

"The generators! The dam generators go *silent*—and now comes a plane. It circles like a hawk!"

50

Everything about the room rang of power. The armed keepers of the doors—the hum of conversation from the bodyguards excluded from the room by hard wooden doors—the cold marble table—the starkness of the dark paneled walls and dead faces of the portraits displayed on the wall, which matched to perfection the faces of the ministers arranged around the conference table. The only thing alive and moving within the room seemed to be the haze of blue smoke that swirled and hovered above the heads at the table, the smoke rising from the cigar shoved in the mouth of the big, imperious personage who sat at the head of the table, and who pounded it now with a firm blow of the gavel.

"Distinguished comrades." At the sound of the voice, the room took on the aura of a tomb. "All are aware why we convene." The man's hard, expressionless gaze marched down the table. "Both the request received from General Kerenofsky in the field, and the recommendation of the General Staff in response, are before you. Due to the urgency, the army has turned to me, and I, gentlemen, to you.

"Before we proceed with discussion of the issue in chief,

I first ask for review of the situation on the ground—Comrade Karkov." The speaker's gaze strayed down the lines of stiff-collared faces until it fell upon one smartly uniformed minister. Then the President at the head of the table leaned back in the cushions of his chair, though under the cloth of the black, pin-striped suit, lean muscles remained taut and restless. He inhaled deeply on the fine cigar.

"Comrade President." Minister Karkov rose with military bearing and a pinched smile for his leader. "Secret intelligence reports from UN Headquarters in Bosnia have found their way to our hands. They reveal that our strategy on behalf of our surrogates, the Bosnian Serbs, already begins to bear fruit. At this juncture, General Kerenofsky requests permission to move out of the basin. I personally agree with the move, but—ah, not prematurely."

There came the light tapping of a pencil from the head of the table. The holder of the pencil spoke with a harshness.

"The intention is to review the position, not to reach premature and senseless conclusions—go on."

"Of course, Sir." The Russian President could see from the slight sag of the speaker's shoulders that his point had struck home.

The crafty Karkov began again, this time more slowly, more carefully.

"The strategy of purification by the Bosnian Serbs goes well. Already the process has cleansed the 70% of Bosnia now in Serb hands. In the remainder of Greater Serbia, the process goes on."

The big man at the head of the table leaned forward, interrupting.

"The military picture, Karkov—if you please, man!"

"Of course, Mr. President." Karkov's pallid complexion reddened only a trifle at the slight."

"The siege of Sarajevo goes into its fourth year. Daily shelling and mortar fire rein down on the city from the surrounding hills. The airport is again closed by threat of artillery, and UN food convoys to the central and eastern enclaves are controlled and pinched off at will." The man smiled proudly. "Seizure of UN Peacekeepers in response to recent NATO air strikes has sent a chill over the West. The UN representative on the ground—our little man—jumps to our bidding to placate the Serbs. The Muslim enclaves starve on the vine while the UN continues withdrawing protection from the so-called 'safe areas.' With Zepa and Srebrenica already captured and properly cleansed, once again aircraft from Belgrade ferry in troops and supplies to the Bosnian Serbs in open contempt for the UN designated 'No Fly Zones.'"

A cloud of blue smoke erupted from the head of the table only an instant ahead of the commanding voice.

"Karkov. Do we speak of the same war? Has news not reached your ears that the Americans have been pounding critical Serb positions around Sarajevo for days? Have knocked out command and control communications in the largest air strikes since World War II."

"And the Serbs have refused to budge an inch, Mr. President. Not more than a handful of heavy weapons have been withdrawn from the Exclusion Zone."

"The second front, Karkov. The second front! Has the fact of an imminent second front slipped your mind? The way you speak, one would conclude that the western frontier of the Bosnian Republic was drawn at Sarajevo. If such is the case, then what in the name of Lenin are we doing placing our most effective field general—and enough armor and artillery to supply a division—in a remote basin within striking distance of both Sarajevo and the Croatian frontier?" A tiny wave of forced laughter crested around the table, at once timid and self-deprecating.

"Yes, Comrade President, I was just getting to that. The western ports on the Adriatic remain ungarrisoned and ripe for the plucking."

"And that by default!" the big man cut in.

"Well—er, yes, Sir. To a great extent, ah, that is true."

"In fact, Minister," intoned the President, "the Serb armies have made no progress whatever toward the west to cut off and neutralize the Dalmatian supply ports on the Adriatic. Is that not so, Minister Karkov?"

"That is true, Sir, yes. But Bihac has proved a hard nut to crack. And there is the delicate business of violating Croatian territory to properly do so."

The President ignored this last remark. "Then what have they been doing with all our weapons and 'advisors?' Tell me that!"

The other's voice had lost all confidence; it trembled now ever so slightly as Karkov continued.

"Well, as I say, the Adriatic ports are secure and ungarrisoned...."

"Which could be accomplished from a barroom!" the big man interrupted hotly. "Since, as we all know, any shred of military planning by the Croats as it relates to Dalmatia seems to occur in just such places." Again the wave of laughter from around the table, this time less restrained. Karkov's hands were trembling now, and he hid them below the level of the table and pressed the moistness of his palms against the leg of his trousers as he resumed.

"The recent seizure of the UN Peacekeepers, as I say, has dampened the resolve of the West, witness the unobstructed seizure of Zepa and Srebrenica, as I say...."

"At the price of moral condemnation in the eyes of the world," shot back the reply. "And again you seem to ignore the ongoing air strikes."

"....and nearly toppled the British Prime Minister," Karkov continued, ignoring the President's comments.

"A victory so total," the Russian President responded testily, "that the British, French and Dutch have added a Rapid Reaction Force of 12,500 cracks troops to the 20,500 so called 'peacekeeping troops' already there; and those reinforcements growing and gaining strength. Now after fifty years, the Germans have even decided to cast in their lot. I would not term that an unqualified success. After all, Karkov, it would not do to forget that at least twice already in this century has the great serpent of the West risen up to right a perceived injustice—the first, if you recall, caused by an assassin's bullet in your precious Sarajevo."

Now the other's voice shook openly.

"At this very moment, Comrade President, the provocation caused by the very air strikes you speak of supplies justification for a Serb request for our military intervention. We expect the formal diplomatic request within the week."

"Enough, Karkov, enough."

The steady gaze of the President searched down the line of frightened faces to the end of the table before resting on the frailest figure of all.

"Comrade Malik, since the military position of the NATO powers under the guise of peacekeeping operations is growing by the hour, in your diplomatic role, tell us when the Foreign Ministry considers the Serbs will jab the knife into the Croats, then come begging for our assistance?"

The frail little bespectacled man with clear eyes and pensive brow was not expected to rise in respect to his years and the state of his health. He began in his slow, deliberative manner of speech, not because his mind operated slowly, but to avoid the stuttering impediment he had fought since childhood to conquer.

"Comrade President. Fellow Ministers. Already initiatives have come f-forth from individuals in Pale. Nothing official, let's say a mere t-testing of the waters."

The commanding voice from the end of the table cut in like the blade of a knife. "Yes, yes, Malik. A fool could see that—but when? And if you speak any more slowly and vaguely, the request will come before you are finished!" The wave of laughter was louder this time, containing a slight but perceptibly vicious edge. But the small man went on, ignoring the interruption.

"The continuation of the p-present air strikes you refer to will bring the formal request."

"When, Malik, when?—not what!" boomed the voice, and the laughing came mockingly and maliciously, with a hint of mob blood lust.

"W-Within the week, I-I believe," and the President with the emotionless gaze at the head of the table saw his quarry relieved to finish the sentence.

The President rose to his feet, taut muscles rippling under the pin stripes of his suit coat where they rounded the shoulders. He bellowed, "Are you sure?"

"Y-Y-Y-Yes. I am qu-quite sure."

"You don't sound sure!" Now the laughter was more raucous, the cumulative malice resounding in waves.

The Foreign Minister said nothing, though his eyes blazed of steel as they squared off against those of his antagonist at the head of the table.

The big man made a dismissive wave of the hand; he resumed his seat and turned back to the uniformed Karkov who again popped to his feet. The President tugged the stub of the foul-smelling cigar from his mouth and began staring the man down, enjoying the show.

"All right, Karkov, you're in charge of the army. You've read the request from the line general. Should we allow him to withdraw from the basin and thereby expose our hand at this stage? You say the formal request for military assistance from the Serbs is no more than a week away."

The Minister of Defense knew what his leader wanted to hear. He also knew the wily old general who resembled a giant Panda bear. In fact, he knew General Kerenofsky well, had confidence in him. More importantly, he had confidence in the reliability of his instincts. He would, of course, honor the general's urgent request if he could, but he could see the matter was hopeless, and he himself had his family to consider with so little time left to retirement.

Field Marshall Karkov cleared his throat. "No person

doubts that the general is an able commander, a favorite of the people. But in this one instance, the General Staff has recommended the request be denied. Assuredly, all precautions must be taken to protect the safety of our weapons and equipment and to support the commander in the field; Comrade Malik himself considers the move will come within the week. What are a few days more? Also, to expose our hand at this juncture, as you wisely point out, Mr. President," and he tossed the man a conspiratorial smile, "would raise unnecessary risks and give us a second black eye in world opinion, followed so close on the heels of Srebrenica. No. Given the shortness of time, I must go with the considered opinion of the General Staff."

The man at the head of the table held his counsel. He only slouched a trifle less warily into the fine leather cushions of his chair, eyeing the speaker steadily, and waiting for the conclusion he knew would come. Karkov is not a fighter, he thought to himself. A field marshall, perhaps, but never a fighter. Foreign Minister Malik, on the other hand, is a horse of a different color. Nonetheless, if not his vote, at least I must extract an abstention from Malik—just to be safe. For if that old war dog Kerenofsky says he must evacuate that basin at once, then no doubt the facts on the ground confirm both the conclusion and urgency. Once again his gaze marched down the line of ministers until it rested upon the diminutive form of the foreign minister.

"Malik, you have heard the recommendation of Defense. And now with these American air strikes, Marshall Karkov places the timing of the Serb plea for intervention at one week. No man can doubt that the release of General Kerenofsky and his troops and weapons from that remote basin would expose our hand prematurely—and bring on the instant wrath of the West. Afghanistan tenfold! What do *you* say?"

Malik had used the intervening moments to collect himself, to bring his voice under control, and when he spoke, it was again slowly, yet with clear determination.

"We all know the general who makes this request. There is not one a-among us who fails to accord him the respect his record deserves. Of all the commanders in the field, he is the wisest, his judgment the truest; all this is w-well known." He omitted any reference to what every man at the table knew to be his personal failings.

The voice at the end lashed out. "This is not an occasion for speechmaking, Comrade. Get to the point!"

"A little b-background, Comrade President.

"Background I have in spades. The point, Malik, the point."

The feeble Malik, with a corkscrew for a spine, began again, though the moistness was leaving his throat, and he knew he would have to be brief.

"There is no way for this body to v-verify risks in the field. We must do as we a-always do in such matters—rely on the field commander."

"How dare you refer to this body as a rubber stamp!" The President leapt to his feet. "I will not sit here and listen to this body referred to in that manner."

"I did not r-refer to this body as...."

"Do not insult us by denying what we heard this very minute—with our own ears!" A buzz of excitement and anticipation sprang up around the long black table.

"I did not m-mean to i-imply...."

"Do not call me a liar, Malik! I know very well what I heard."

The President's arm and shoulder muscles bulged and rippled within the dark suit. The stub of the cigar long since dead stabbed at the air in the direction of Malik who sat, head stolidly erect. The chorus around the table transformed to a clamor.

"Do not ever label us of this body as rubber stamps and liars. Not ever! Is that clear?" The clamor of derision grew steadily louder as the big man at the head of the table drove his point home. And now the man was shouting, and the room came alive.

The armed keepers of the doors took pains to first inspect the backs of their hands, then the polish on their boots. They avoided eye contact with even their own uniformed fellows in any way they could.

"Well, speak up, Minister—speak up!"

But there was no sound from Malik for all knew he could not speak, not for reasons of courage, but of physiology. And when the immediate voice vote was taken, there was neither a nyet nor a spoken abstention. The members filed out of the room.

51

The soldier, Ivan, sat alone in his oversized greatcoat. He sat perched atop his favorite rock on the riverbank below the dam next to River Road and the Serb compound. The force of the current running out his line tugged against the crooked stick held in his hands as he sat with one booted foot resting on the gravel of the bank, the other as always tucked up against where his buttocks rested on the rock so that he could couch his elbow on his knee.

Suddenly Ivan leapt to his feet, then threw down his pole. Even his slow mind could detect the wetness soaking through his greatcoat.

"Damn!" he cried, startled. "What have they done to me this time?" He looked the perfect scarecrow in his shabby brown oversized greatcoat. Furious, he kicked at the rock where the ice cover had melted from his body heat. Then, checking his line and ignoring the dampness in his pants, he went back to the fishing, resuming his normal position.

He had reached the bank late this day due to the storm and the ice, but he was happy to be here, for there were strange things afoot in the compound, and he needed to think. He plucked a blade of grass from the bank and stuck it between his teeth; he could always think better while chewing on something, and once more he focused on the commotion behind him. The big eighteen-wheeler tankers had been on the move since dawn, an army of long, enormous camouflaged ants scurrying back and forth between the compound and the fuel dump tucked under the south ridge by the dam.

For a moment, he glanced back. With the fury born of confusion, he glared at the long rows of trucks and tanks and half-tracks behind the wire of the compound—and some lining up right here on the road at his back.

"And orders," he mumbled aloud as was his practice when his temper was up. "Everybody yelling out orders and dancing around. An outrage—is everyone deaf?" He shook his head to clear it. "Enough to drive a man crazy."

That was the reason he had especially wanted to be alone on this day—even though the river itself seemed to be acting against him today. He couldn't quite put his finger on it, but, definitely, something was wrong. For one thing, the fishing was off; this fact he knew. But there was more, much more, and it all remained a mystery to him. He did not know the why of the commotion at his back any more than he understood the why of the bad fishing; but as to the later, his small mind was working, if not at the front like normal folks, at the back where it counted.

Yesterday, the water of the river had been deep emerald green and clear as the air, but today something was wrong. This he could accept as he accepted the mad commotion around him, but the water was more than just brown; it was downright filthy with globs of dirt riding on top. "Why, it is a mess! Dirty with scum floating like the surface of overcooked soup." He watched the scum now as it rode on the current. Countless times already had he been forced to snatch out his line and squeeze its full length with his fingers to clean it.

"Can you believe that?" he muttered. "Mud!"

Anyway, it annoyed him; it took away from the fishing,

and anybody knew you couldn't catch a fish this way, not having to pull your line out every two seconds.

And now, he shrugged muttering to himself. Well, it was all too bad, but what could a man do? Already the sun about down, and not one fish for the general's plate.

He looked back and glared once again at the commotion on the roadway and beyond the wire of the compound behind; he strained his mind, trying to figure the reason for all this god-awful racket. He could see all the activity of the tanks starting up and meshing their gears, of big camouflaged trucks hitching up to artillery pieces and waves of exhaust smoke billowing over the ground. It stung his eyes and made his nose smart. "The fools," he muttered.

He shook his small melon head and tried to solve the puzzle. The fisherman had seen it all a hundred times before, but not here, never here. This was the kind of thing you saw before a battle—but everyone knew there was no battle here. He tried to think of an enemy, but it all came to nought. "And they call me—Crazy Ivan! They prepare for battle when there is no battle. Hah, it's so simple; why can't they see it? There's no battle because there is no war. And if I lack reason, show me the enemy soldiers. How can there be a war without an enemy? Anybody knows that there can't be a war without at least one enemy!"

Indignation spat out the grass stem in his mouth. Once again he yanked out his line and cleaned off the scum, and this time with great deliberation he hooked on a fresh worm. He shrugged with impatience but held his temper. He would show them; he would just settle back and concentrate on his work.

He went on with his work long after the dying orb of the sun had buried itself behind the ridge at his back; he went on fishing and scraping his line and fishing some more. In fact, he went on with his work long after the lavender twilight gave in to the shadows of night—if someone could call it night with the rumble and roar of all those damned tanks and trucks.

"It is late, true enough," he muttered under his breath. "Still, my duty lies here. Otherwise, how will the general eat? Worse, how will there be exports for mother Russia this day? And everyone knows a great nation cannot long exist without exports."

It was dark now with a biting chill and he tugged the oversized greatcoat closer about him.

All at once a wetness came to his boot planted there on the bank. With final consternation, he jerked his boot from the water.

"Damn! Damn it all to Stalin!" He lifted the boot straight up in the air and shook it. He shook it vigorously before placing it up on the rock next to its twin. "For weeks—no, for even two months do I sit here the very same way for the luck—and now look. All that noise and racket. It shakes down the ice from the mountains and into my river—and here it runs into my shoe!"

With dampness in his pants and now also his boot, he knew defeat when it faced him. He yanked out his line, jumped to his feet, and faced his tormentors without so much as furling his line about the stick, though that was his habit. As he trudged past, he squinted his eyes and glared at the tanks and trucks now lined up on the road in a great snaking convoy, the glare of the headlights making him blink. Nuisance though he knew that he was, he could not help feeling somehow betrayed—by the river—by the ice— by the whole damned Serbian Army.

Yet, in spite of it all, he had done his level best, he was thinking as he moved off toward his barracks; it was simply out of his hands now.

Still, he was saddened, for tonight there would be no fish for the general's plate and no exports for mother Russia— and there was definitely something wrong with that river!

52

At the base of Castle Mountain, a forested finger of land thrust straight out into the lake. This isthmus, a quarter of a mile above and parallel with the dam, had long been known to the teenagers of the village as "Lovers Point." Master Haris Grebo was the ardent young son of the village aristocrat and sole landowner—the boy a hopeless romantic, inclined to think with his heart like his mother, not with his head. And for that reason, the boy remained a source of unending consternation to his cunning father, a harsh taskmaster who thrived on public whippings to keep his tenant farmers in line and assure compliance with seasonal quotas.

On this moonlit night, young Haris was celebrating his sixteenth birthday, cruising down the lake in his father's small outboard motorboat with his girlfriend at his side; and now he turned to the girl snuggled up against him.

"Here, take it and throw it over your shoulders, Iva." He throttled down to reduce the rush of cold night air, then gently tucked his expensive blue woolen sport jacket around her soft shoulders. "We are almost there," he tried to assure

413

her.

"No, no, Haris, not tonight! It is too cold, and already we have violated the defense perimeter. And you know how scared I am of this place."

"Please, Iva. I love you." One of his arms extended to the levered handle that guided the boat. The other encircled her shoulders now with the warming jacket, his fingers slipping between the buttons of her blouse to discover and caress one soft, white breast. "Don't be frightened. See—the dam lights are all out. It's the safest place around."

"No, it's cold."

"No, we will be warm. You know, Iva, that I love you."

"I'm cold," she persisted in a small but stubborn voice, for she was a good girl and afraid, though she loved her man with all her heart. "And I'm not freezing again in that awful sleeping bag."

At fifteen, Iva—the wholesome daughter of the local barman, as strict a Catholic father as any in the village—did not know if she were more frightened of her father or the village priest—or the thought of an unwanted pregnancy. But she did love him so, and they were going to be married; that he had promised, and she knew that he meant it.

He cut the engine. The small boat glided for a few seconds before crunching its bow lightly on the sand of the beach. For awhile they sat there in the stern of the boat—alone in the embrace of their love. The lake was calm, the moon rising brightly. He was kissing the thrusting nipple of her breast when the sound came.

The four-man inflatable boat of the night patrol inched in toward the finger of land, two paddles working silently. With no floodlights from the dam this night and the lake cloaked in stillness, Lieutenant Bracko's hearing somehow seemed more acute.

"Quiet—listen!" he whispered. The drone of an outboard motor could be heard in the distance, the sound moving in their direction from the opposite side of the finger of land. The other members of the patrol then, too, joined in and listened until the distant sound of the outboard motor died.

"Quiet with the paddles," snarled the lieutenant, the stiff admonition of his captain at evening briefing still ringing in his ears. Lieutenant Bracko was a tense man by nature. The earlier warning, coupled with the noise of the approaching motorboat, was enough to set his teeth on edge, a grating sound, like a dog worrying a bone. If any of the enemy were here, he would find them. And this time—no one would later be able to accuse him of "half measures."

When, not five minutes later, the harsh beam of the flashlight struck the pretty young Iva full in the face, her panicky reaction had not to do with soldiers and harm, but with the shame of discovery and the image of rage on her father's stern face.

The time—9:23 PM. Cil, clinging to a rope in the light of the moon, launched himself over the side of the rock cliff, down, down over the sheer rock face guarding the southwest flank of Castle Mountain. Only once before had he studied the terrain below, and that on that first day with old Zeljko as they had peered down from a crag a few hundred yards to the south, on the occasion of inspecting the terrain and the face of the dam. It had been only last night after speaking to Nedo that Cil had altered the plan for the final phase of the operation—and now, this very minute, with his launching himself into that final phase, he was ever more anxious about the timing.

Cil grunted softly with the strain as he shimmied, hand over hand, down the endless ribbon of rope. Even through the thick gloves, his hands burned with each additional foot of descent.

Far below, soft moonlight glimmered off the treetops and out over the spine of the peaceful-looking isthmus. The rope wound round his boots to serve as a brake and slow his descent; as it ran over the rubber coating of his wet suit, it sang. He would have preferred a double line encircling the trunk of the tree at the top, so he could lower himself gently and easily with one end knotted round his waist for safety, for that was the preferred method in the field. But given the height of the cliff's face, that luxury was out of the question; he would need the full two hundred-foot rope to make the descent. His muscles screamed in protest as the tops of the trees rose up to meet him.

At an unexpected distant sound, he jerked his head, then his whole body around. As he hung twisting on the line on a whisper of wind, he managed to double up his knees enough to plant both boot soles, hard, behind him, against the vertical cliff, so that he was facing the lake, his back to the cliff.

Cil gazed out over the surface of the lake, toward the whine of what sounded like an outboard motor. In the play of the moonbeams, he could see a tiny object dancing over the placid waters—a small boat—and he could tell from its speed and direction of travel that the boat was headed for the far end of the very isthmus below him.

It had to be an enemy patrol. So far within the Serb defense perimeter, what else could it be? Damn!

Earlier he had calculated that this, being the last stage of the mission, a rope snaking down the face of the cliff stood a small chance of discovery before morning—and morning would be too late. But now as he listened to the sound of the outboard engine and gauged its course, he was not so sure—and time was short.

Cil allowed himself to slide the rest of the way down the rope in all but a free-fall—he could feel the heat and smell the hemp burning through his gloves with the friction.

Feet firmly planted on solid terra firma, he swiftly unslung his weapon, removed it from its oily-smelling neopreme wrap, slipping the wrap under the flap of the pack on his back. Then with swift efficient movements, he affixed the silencer to the snout of the barrel, carefully with his fingers readjusted the sights, then jammed a fresh clip home and cocked the weapon.

There was nothing to do but leave the telltale rope hanging as it was. With this new threat and the pressure of time, he must put all the ground he could behind him before chancing a run-in with the patrol. With a flick of his finger, he double-checked the safety mounted behind the trigger guard. Then he was off at a trot, moving down the spine of the isthmus.

The floor of the isthmus was needled and soft, like a thickly piled carpet. He was running lightly and well, the adrenaline charge at the sight of the patrol boat extinguishing all sense of fatigue after laboring with the others in the shaft throughout the long day and previous night.

He had covered two thirds the length of the point of land when he heard it—a single chilling sound in the night, almost like the shriek of a child coming from somewhere ahead. He halted in his tracks. No further sound came. He moved off again in the direction of the sound, this time slackening his pace to proceed in cover along the right-hand shore. He wondered why the dam searchlights were out— and knew if they were suddenly switched back on he would present an easy target if caught in their glow.

A new sound pulled him up short. The crack of a twig somewhere ahead. He held up, still as death, cocking his ear to the sound, listening. There was nothing. He fought to tame his sawing breath, cursing himself silently for lending his night vision scope to the gypsy on watch.

And then—a light. Not fifteen paces ahead, an instantaneous flicker of light appeared like a firefly. He held his breath, waiting, watching, adjusting his eyes to the darkness here under the trees. When no further light came, his mind raced. A firefly? The glint of the moonlight on some shiny object?

There. Again. This time clear and distinct—and he knew.

A narrow circle of light aimed with care at the ground. And yes, there, beyond the light, the faintest breath of sound—a whisper. In the pool of light against the ground—shadows of human legs.

He froze. In the beam of light, the dark silhouette of a dog—or rather a dog's head.

A dog's head, yes, but the nose? The nose too long and fat, as if somehow distorted—a muzzle.

Quick hands reached into the cast of light, though he could not see the short, stubby fingers as they worked at the muzzle.

For a second Cil went weak in the knees, the pound of his heart pulsed in his head. Once freed of restraint, the animal let out a yelp of relief.

Now the light was off. Cil crouched, raising his weapon, clicking the setting to automatic fire. He waited, not moving, controlling his breathing, feeling in his hand the cool rounded surface of the stock. There in the quiet of night his brain played with visions of a dog at his throat as a feather of breeze whispered through the trees. He prayed it would save him.

And now a trace of movement. Muted whispers drifting his way. And then, at last, at the end of all time, the sounds moving off past him not five paces distant, the dog sniffing, sniffing, always sniffing the ground as it strained on its leash.

As they passed, the stubby steel snout of the silencer affixed to Cil's weapon followed their course with a mind of its own. He trained his eyes and ears for the first hint of stray movement, but no such activity came—and then they were gone.

New questions rushed to Cil's mind. What if they picked up his scent farther on? Would they spot the hanging rope, then double back? Badly pressed for time and gambling that the full complement of the patrol was safely behind him, he hurried off.

He took to the beach to mute the sound of his racing foot-steps while sharp needled points of the overhead boughs swished at his face. But it was those same boughs that also blocked out the moonlight, concealing his form as he dashed down the endless river of sand.

He never saw the boat. Where it was pulled up on the beach, he struck the wooden gunwale head-on with a sick-ening thud, the blow taken by his knees, his upper body pro-pelled forward over the side while his free hand darted for-ward to protect his fall.

His hand braced against something warm and soft—and wet. He reeled from the unexpected touch. A sticky residue coated his palm.

Slowly, ever so slowly, he righted himself, crouching, checking his weapon for damage, all the while glancing cautiously about him.

He discovered but the one body in the boat, that of a girl or a woman, the body slumped down in the stern. A wider search revealed the bodies of two other corpses, two men sprawled flat down in the dry, fluffy sand. The way the pair of bodies lay intertwined bore silent witness to the violence of the encounter.

Cil backed away, struggling to compose himself in the ankle-deep sand. He swiveled about, but there was no movement or sound except for the gentle nodding of the evergreen boughs overhead. He was not thinking so much of his safety now, but of the meeting last night and how he had arranged to meet Nedo on the far shore at 10:15 sharp.

He checked his watch—and winced. He was tempted by the boat with its outboard motor. But who's boat—and the noise the motor would make?

Cil stood wholly unaware of the figure creeping through the shadows, closing in from behind. The discovery of the knife brought Cil to his senses, that and the stark admoni-tion it carried, plunged as it was clear to the handle in the woman's left breast. The next warning sign was less a response to sight or sound than to a sixth sense developed in this brutal business over years.

Cil, in a single, continuous motion, turned in his tracks and dropped to one knee, at once raising the barrel of his weapon. As the assailant lunged, Cil fired. The sudden burst of fire caught the assailant in the center of the chest, the force of impact at this close range first lifting the man clear off the ground like a straw man, then flinging him down in a fog of smoke onto the fluffy white sand.

Cil, when he fired, found that the shots propelled from the M-16 with silencer affixed made no more noise than might the faint rustling of leaves on a soft summer breeze. And now with the assailant writhing in the sand at his feet, twitching in his death throes, Cil crouched in the damp night air, his senses keen and alert. He glanced about him, eyes squeezed nearly shut to cut through the gloom of night.

Cil had fired on instinct alone, but not before the assailant's blood spattered—and not before the assailant's knife-hand shot down and the nine inch dagger-like blade found its target, slicing across his arm.

He had been foolish, and it had cost him. He had been as wrong about the identity and intent of the occupants of the outboard motor boat as he had been ignorant of the presence of—and in error about the size and deployment of—the enemy patrol. Already two strikes stood against him; he was not anxious to try for strike three.

And then he realized with a start that except for the cliff face, the isthmus was accessible only by water. There had to be a second boat!

53

Outside, the night was cool, clear, with the soft sound of the wind; but inside, Bogey knelt alone in the moldy dampness of the escape tunnel below the castle, unnerved by the silence. Struggling to ignore a feeling of impending doom, she stuffed the last of the clean rounds into cartridge belts as Michelle had instructed last night before leaving to attempt rescue of the downed airman. But in truth, Bogey was silently pondering the meaning and likely impact of the recent unexpected visit from Major Cil.

Earlier, Cil had strictly forbidden use of the radio transmitter pending completion of the mission. But not half an hour ago, he had burst in—after removing the covering stones—and without explanation, transmitted two coded messages: one to an aircraft carrier off the Dalmatian coast; the other, a swift radioed warning to his contact in Mostar with orders to relay the alert to other posts downriver.

A woolen army blanket, frayed at the corners and discolored with use, was spread on the dirt floor of the tunnel before her. Upon the blanket, like so many round, scalloped fruit, lay the spare hand grenades left behind by the men, along with two submachine guns that had never been fired. While her mind struggled against the implications, Bogey reflected upon the look on Cil's face the moment he discovered that Michelle had not returned. And then he had announced his intention—to again attempt a lake crossing.

To divert her attention, she replayed in her mind the strange conversation she had had with Michelle the previous night—before Michelle had caught the homing signal on the special satellite radio and made her hasty departure.

In the cramped escape tunnel last evening, the worry and anxiety had been building with each passing hour, and Michelle had spoken to lessen the tension.

"When it is over, where will you go?" Michelle had asked her in a quiet, innocent tone.

"Oh, it will not be over for me," answered Bogey offhandedly. "Anyway, I expect I shall go right on cooking and caring for Zeljko and the men. And you?"

Michelle suddenly beamed. Her even white teeth sparkled to the light of the single candle flame. "Why, it is all decided," she began, suddenly breathless with excitement. "We will be married, at Papa's place in Bordeaux—at the little chapel on the hill above the vineyards, with our good friends and all the relations. Oh, Bogey, you must be there." Her voice, childlike and lilting, carried the heartfelt joy so eager to blossom within her, the kind of hopes of which, in this war-torn land, Bogey had not even let herself dare dream. "Oh, *Cherie*, please. Say you will come."

Bogey, taken aback, carefully eyed the glowing countenance of her opposite number. When finally she spoke, her voice held a certain reserve.

"Did he say that you were to be married?" she asked slowly.

There was a pause. "Well—not exactly."

For a moment a silence fell between them, like a cold, damp fog rolling in from the sea.

"Michelle, please; you must listen to me. Sometimes, well, sometimes the world cannot always be joyful—even for the fortunate of us." She hesitated, searching out just the right words. "You know, there is but the slimmest chance we shall ever come through this." Her words were measured, yet gentle. "Perhaps not in your heart, but in your head, you know it is true."

Gradually Michelle's head dropped to her chest. When she spoke, the excitement was gone and an inner control gripped every word. "Yes—I know," she said slowly, bravely, and her eyes stared down at her ringless hand. "I have known from the start," she said. "But still in my heart, I carry the hope." She raised her chin to face Bogana squarely, and there was unmistakable strength in the reach of her jawline. "In the quiet moments, in spite of it all, I pray it will all come out. That he will...."

It was the sudden sound of a voice just outside the stones of the cave entrance that now shocked Bogey out of her reverie.

"Bogey—hurry!" The firm woman's voice was unmistakable. "Help me with the rocks here at the entrance."

Swiftly Bogey crawled to the escape tunnel entrance and helped tug aside the covering stones. As soon as the entrance was clear and the fresh air of the night poured in, Bogey could smell the pungent odor of a horse lathered with sweat.

"Quick!" exclaimed Michelle. "Help me get him off the horse."

Only after they had lowered the wounded airman from the horse, then made a bed for him in the safety of the tunnel, had Michelle returned the horse to the gypsy who was guarding the others at their pickets. By the time she returned, Bogey was already swiftly and silently working over the semiconscious airman. The man's flight suit was badly torn, his face streaked with mud and fresh perspiration, his body trembling with fever. After brief examination, it was clear to Bogana that the airman had suffered a severe blow to the head resulting in a concussion as well as a leg wound from which he had lost considerable blood; and even in the poor light, Bogey could tell from the man's shallow breathing, deathly pallor, and feeble pulse, that he was close to death from exposure and lack of proper medical care.

Michelle watched Bogana as she worked over the man. She could not help but marvel at the deftness and speed of each movement of the hands with which the Muslim woman went about her task. Bogana had already carefully laid out the needed items from Michelle's first aid supplies, and now she was arranging an IV with glucose on a portable stand, and another to administer a transfusion of plasma. Michelle, also on her knees beside the moaning airman, began rubbing his limbs to improve circulation.

"No, no," reproved Bogana sharply. "Instead, go find another warm blanket. When a patient has lost this much blood, rubbing the limbs only draws blood away from the vital organs."

Michelle moved back in the tunnel in search of an additional blanket, pondering the obvious medical expertise of her companion. Who was this woman?

54

Back in the shaft, Zeljko, together with the giant Muslim twins, Slobo, and the last farm lad, had all labored feverishly since Cil's departure. With a vengeance, they assaulted the limestone tusks rising out of the floor at the front. Yet, despite their labors, the obstacles remained, blocking the slightest forward progress. While the little commander and the farm lad toiled with pick and shovel to widen the shaft where the walls of black earth curved around the huge concrete slab at the midpoint, Zeljko and the giant Muslims occupied a hole at the front, the hole brimming with brackish water as cold as an ice flow.

They knew they were close; they could all taste the end. Yet, both at the ceiling and watery base, the two blocking columns of rock wedged together and held fast. With a fury born of desperation, the men struggled to get at the stubborn roots of the boulders. Already the hole had grown to a width of six feet and a depth of eight in places. As he hauled himself out of the hole, Zeljko could feel the numbing cold in his limbs and a deep weariness penetrating to the bone, his exhaustion magnified by the pain in his leg.

The Ox remained in the hole, stooping to dig in water that swirled around his great naked shoulders while his twin, the Professor, climbed out and worked from the rim, laboring at the ceiling, prying one rocky tusk back and forth ever so slightly.

"Come out, little brother," warned the Professor from above. "We are almost there."

"No, the answer is here!" bellowed the Ox stubbornly from below, and old Zeljko turned to observe the water sloshing at the huge hairy chest of the Ox deep in the hole, the man shivering with cold as he groped with his pick.

"Come out—damn it. Come out!" the Professor shouted. A note of desperation sounded in his voice as he eyed the great quaking tusks. But his twin, gasping for breath, barely glanced at the columns of rock looming above him.

"Big brother, stop playing the sick cow and hand me a crowbar," he demanded. "And do not order me! Do you forget who in this family is the real man of action?"

The other crew members turned at the angry words, their attention fixed on the man in the hole.

"I tell you, the answer is here at my feet. For one time in your life—you will listen to me!" And as he attacked the great tusks of rock, his features took on the savage tension of a man possessed by his mission.

With reluctant hands, the Professor handed down the crowbar.

"Just push—not shout orders!" growled the Ox from below. "We are near out of time! Now—when I say—shove with all your puny might."

The shaggy head deep in the hole looked up at Zeljko and shouted a caution.

"Retire! Retire!"

The old man stepped away as the Ox turned up his face to look at his brother.

"On my signal," he shouted—"Now!"

With every ounce of his strength displayed in the cords of

his neck, with every muscle and sinew of his great body taut with the strain, the Ox thrust his full weight against the shaft of the crowbar. The muddy stew at his shoulders churned to a tempest as the arms of the Professor above pried against the stubborn stone tusks at the ceiling.

The first began to fall. Only at the last second was the Ox, struggling against the resistance of the water, able to leap clear as the first vertical tusk plunged down and struck the water scant inches from his back as he lurched from harm's way, the huge rock splashing down with such force that a tidal wave swept the walls of the shaft.

The shouted warning of the Professor came late. The second tusk, wedged into position by the first, fell now and stabbed down like a spear. The body of the Ox sank out of sight. No sign of him showed, only angry air bubbles that burst to the surface.

For what seemed forever, the men gathered on the lip of the hole just stood there—silent—staring—stunned. They stood there on the lip of the hole, not comprehending, staring down at the dark brackish water and blinking at the air bubbles exploding to the surface, first large, then ever smaller, the men with naked expressions drawn on their features.

Then all plunged in as one. Yet, despite their efforts, the bubbles ceased.

At last, the men regained the rim of the hole. All stared without staring at the Professor in the poor light. He stood tall, facing the East. In a soft voice, he began his chant. Rhythmically his arms stretched up in aspiration, there to shudder for an instant before smacking down until his whole body bowed so low that his large hands slapped down on the muddy floor. Again he rose. He seemed relaxed, his arms reaching up once again to pause, then beat down at the floor. The process went on and on, slow and graceful and rhythmic, and except for the chanting, no sound but the periodic slapping invaded the silence of the tomb. The tremble of the man's shoulders as he bowed in the direction of Mecca told the whole story.

Now with the two granite tusks cleared away, the crew threw themselves into their task. Picks and spades flew. The Professor with Zeljko at his side launched the attack upon the last layer of hardpan up front, the final shield of red clay, chipping it away with the picks as slivers of clay flew and arrowed and bit at their faces.

A commotion sounded at their backs, but the pair at the front paid it no heed.

"Shooting! There is god-awful shooting! On the far side of the river, at the front of the dam!"

The men at the front did not budge. They knew their job. They went right on waging their own private war on the stubborn clay foe at the front.

55

Cil had been paddling, he sensed, for too long already. And now once again he lifted the paddle free, rocking forth, digging deep, then hauling back on the shaft in a controlled even stroke. The inflatable dinghy drove through the water at a rippling pace. With the point of the isthmus fading behind, he stared ahead, his gaze glued on the opposite shore, his eyes scouring the features of the shore at the base of Bald Hill to make out the prearranged rendezvous point. He was paddling well despite the flesh wound to his arm bound up with the lining of a sport jacket found in the sand next to the dead girl.

The rhythmic motion of the paddle freed his mind, and with a pang of guilt his thoughts returned to those left behind whom he had abandoned. What of Michelle? Had he really run off and deserted her, also? He reeled at the play of his conscience.

Confirmation of the whereabouts of the missing village children at last night's meeting with Baxter and Nedo had forced a last minute change in plan. He had determined to act alone, had withheld from the others word of the change of plan, for now, with the enemy closing in, the capture of a single one of them could have compromised the lives of all, that and his fear that the old man might have tried to forestall him.

But never in his wildest dreams had he suspected the force of the reaction. And even now he blinked in disbelief as a wave of pent-up emotion and guilt swept over him. And just look at him now—he, here, free in the fresh air and moonlight—safe. And the others left stranded deep in the shaft with the lake pouring in. And Bogey trapped in the escape tunnel without protection—and Michelle....

Cil could still see in his mind the image of the old man's face, the fire of shock in his eyes and the fierce reproach. He could also see those finely parted lips of Slobo, his face oddly handsome, yet wearing a mixed mask of contempt and amusement at Cil's open retreat from the shaft.

And then he had entered the base of the escape tunnel to retrieve the bundle containing the wet suit provided by Baxter the previous night. The tunnel was dank and dark and stinking. Bogey was huddled there alone in the light of a flickering candle, with that wild and frenzied look of a caged animal facing death in the dark and the cold. But when she had spied him entering the tunnel, her expression had instantly changed. With not a single word of complaint, only the sudden composure and that taunting voice in league with the mysterious smile, she had scrambled to the back and brought it to him, had thrust in his hand two cold legs of rabbit and ordered him to eat. He wondered if he would ever see Michelle again.

Cil sighted along the line of the shore until he spied the taller outline of the marker tree. It was standing alone at the base of Bald Hill, just as Nedo had said.

He was no more than fifty yards out when the clamor erupted. That unmistakable crack-cracking sound of small arms fire—then the instant shouting of frightened men. Cil could feel a tremble in his arms, from the knife wound or the fright or exhaustion, he could not tell. And now the firing all up and down the shore sharpened over the water, ever more insistent with the screams of wounded horses echoing through the trees. And now there on the shore, the marker tree was standing lone silent sentry with the world exploding all round.

Pausing only long enough to locate the focus of fire and check his watch, Cil plunged the clumsy inflatable raft straight in for the shore.

The firing was just up the shore—at Nedo's launching site. Time was short. They would be bolting any second now. The hammer of the guns came louder. He plunged the paddle deep. He felt the pain in the depths of his shoulder as he hauled back the blade of the paddle. He pulled with all his might.

56

Captain Pavlov was sweaty, anxious, his temper short. For most of the evening the Russian general's adjutant had been listening to the steady pacing of the general next door and thinking about the coded cable he had sent off on the special machine. The moment he had first read the answering cable from Moscow, the muscles in his right thigh had begun to twitch, and now with the shrill ringing of the field phone on the table before him, he came right out of his chair.

"What is it?" he barked into the phone to the sergeant downstairs.

"Captain, my apologies; there is a slight problem. The crazy one. He demands to see the general—at once."

"Sergeant, you know better than to bother me now. Send him away. Stand alert at your post for further orders."

"I understand, Sir, but...."

"Wait." Captain Pavlov caught himself. "I will be right down."

As he rose and moved to the stairs, Captain Pavlov paused to listen, but the pacing next door in the general's office continued unabated. Pavlov resented the intrusion, doubly so now in his nervousness when the commander's temper could flare at any moment. But where "Crazy Ivan" was concerned, he was left with no choice. He did not understand the bond between the old general and this lunatic, but sad experience had taught him that any matter involving the general's favorite called for sensitive handling.

The second he reached the waiting room below, he knew it spelled trouble. One look into those wild and staring eyes told him Crazy Ivan was in "one of his states." And judging by the military set of Ivan's shoulders under the tattered greatcoat that dwarfed him, the captain could see that Ivan considered himself present on important business.

"What is it, Sergeant? Quickly."

"Ivan here demands to see the general."

"I come to see the commander," Ivan echoed, holding his position of attention, his lower lip protruding stubbornly as a child's might. "The commander only."

"I can surely understand, Comrade," said Pavlov easily, summoning a solicitous smile. "Take my word, I surely do. But just now, the general is occupied with serious business. You can understand that, Ivan."

"Only the commander."

"Perhaps in this instance, I could be of help."

"I speak to no peon." The little man, standing there with floppy ears, a miniature head, and a crew cut that looked like a badly mown lawn, placed his fishing pole against the wall with soldierly care as if it were a rifle and returned to his former position. Then, his face lit with purpose like an obstinate child, he planted his feet before the general's adjutant.

Captain Pavlov, seeing that he was getting nowhere and concerned that the Serb desk sergeant not witness his failure, abruptly altered his tack.

"Very well, Ivan, as you wish. If you will tell me what

burdens your mind, I will take it up with the general the moment he's free—you have my word."

Ivan the fisherman, his eyes rimmed with suspicion, cocked his head with doubt as water seeped from the seams of his boot to puddle on the floor. He did not answer at once but looked down at the floor, examining gravely the widening puddle. Then finally he spoke.

"Only if I have your word as a Russian officer and gentleman," he declared.

"You have it."

"And your mother, Comrade Captain. She is living?"

Captain Pavlov looked perplexed. "No, Ivan, my mother is dead."

"Very well. Then I shall expect your promise on the grave of your dead mother."

Pavlov blinked in wonder. "I promise—now out with it!"

"Put your hand on your heart and bend down on one knee."

Under his breath, Captain Pavlov issued an oath. A furtive glance at the Serb sergeant revealed the suspected sneer of contempt, but before Pavlov could decide whether to comply, the words blurted from Ivan's lips.

"It is the water!"

"What water?"

"I tell you, the water is dirty—the river rises!"

"I understand," responded the adjutant solicitously. "But how do you know this?"

"The floor, you fool—look!" The fisherman shook his muddy boot in the puddle that darkened the floor.

"Ivan—I must caution you to watch how you address an officer of the forces of the Motherland."

"I must speak to the commander at once."

"Concern yourself no longer," spoke Pavlov softly. "I personally will take the matter up with the general. As I said, you have my word."

"And the children?" demanded Ivan. "Why are the children penned up like cattle in that shed at the back of the compound?"

"What children?" retorted the captain.

Ivan stood there. A querulous frown grew on his face as if puzzling the business out for himself was too much for him.

Then, without so much as another word, he snatched up his fishing pole, turned on his heel, smartly, as he had long ago learned to do as a young soldier, and stalked from the room. Abruptly as he had appeared, now did he vanish from sight.

Captain Pavlov issued a sigh of relief and remounted the stairs. The Serb sergeant resumed his seat and went back to his comic book.

Only when he found himself clear of the building did Ivan raise his face to the night sky, then his voice.

"Well," he declared with solemnity, "I try to do my duty to the exports, but the river won't let me. I try to do my duty to the general, but the lunkheads won't hear me. Now I do my duty to myself—before the time is past."

Upstairs, General Kerenofsky finished his pacing. He stood gazing down at the incoming cable lying flat on the billiard table. He had received the cable one hour previously, had read it three times, and now he read it again.

COMMANDER
BALKAN FORCES

REQUEST FOR INSTANT WITHDRAWAL DENIED.

SUPREME COMMANDER
GENERAL STAFF

The general scrutinized the few simple words with the

same disbelieving eyes as when first he had read them.

It was at that moment that he heard that old familiar sound, a crisp, crackling noise, like a string of Chinese firecrackers going off in the distance. He summoned his adjutant.

"Yes, my General."

"Raise someone on the field phone. Get a report on that gunfire."

"Yes, General."

"And before, what was all that commotion?"

"Nothing, Sir. Nothing at all."

"Captain?"

A pause. "Only the fisherman, Sir."

"What did he want?"

"To see you, my General. A minor matter, which I took care of directly."

"Captain." Pavlov could see that he had made an important miscalculation. "You know the standing order."

Words of grave apology were forming on the adjutant's lips when the distant cracking of small arms fire came louder.

"Enough," commanded the general, peering down from the window to where the convoy stood motionless, ready to move, snaking out onto River Road and forming a silent parade of headlights. "Take a cable."

SUPREME COMMANDER, GENERAL STAFF

HAVE RECEIVED NO REPLY TO URGENT REQUEST—STOP—URGENT REQUEST RENEWED FOR IMMEDIATE REPLY—STOP—LACKING REPLY BY 2200 HOURS LOCAL TIME, WILL PROCEED ON BASIS OF "CUSTOMARY FIELD COMMANDER DIS-CRETION"—STOP.

COMMANDER,
HEADQUARTERS, BALKAN FORCES

"Send it, Captain—this instant."

"But, ah, my General. Already we have received...."

"I have received nothing," General Kerenofsky said simply.

"Yes, Sir." It took a supreme effort of will for Pavlov to tear his gaze from the earlier cable from the General Staff in Moscow—the cable lying flat on the green billiard table in plain sight of the general. Then another thought entered his mind.

"But, my General. There is not sufficient time for this new cable to be received in Moscow and a reply transmitted by 2200 hours."

"Send it, Captain—at once."

57

Bogey was still treating the downed pilot within the confines of the escape tunnel, watching the effects of the blood transfusion, the warm blankets, and the dose of powerful antibiotics she had administered as the color began to return to his face. It was as she glanced over at Michelle that she noted with a start the sudden alteration in Michelle's demeanor—Michelle raised her finger to her lips in the dim light of a single candle.

"Shh!" As soon as she mouthed the warning, Michelle moved to the rocks at the tunnel entrance. "Listen!"

There was nothing—then a faint cracking sound—and all at once more, like fireworks at the annual fiesta day in the village, Bogey was thinking, but set off at intervals in some faraway place. Then silence—and now, there it was again, a whole string of them set off at once.

Now both women knelt together inside the tunnel, ears pressed hard against the flat rocks blocking the entrance. They waited. It came again. Abruptly, Michelle began to shove one covering boulder aside.

"No," insisted Bogey. "We mustn't—he said to wait. Not to go out for any reason."

"The lamp, quickly!" ordered Michelle. "Blow it out.

Then come help with these rocks." Michelle was once again the quintessential operative, cool and controlled and efficient, her voice firm, uncompromising. She spoke now with such sudden command that Bogey was startled. It was the unmistakable assurance of one accustomed to wielding authority, and Bogey, with neither resistance nor hesitation, found herself moving to carry out the order.

Once in the open, Michelle stood silent and composed as a statue, her ear cocked to the source of the sounds. Here in the open, the mountain air was brisk and clean, the moon high and softly bright, the sky a speckled dome of stars that shimmered above the silent forest. The sounds of the gunshots were clearer here, more distinct. Michelle listened in an effort to gauge the precise direction.

The shots came in rapid succession, the noise of the gunfire echoing off the surrounding hills, confusing the direction of sound. For only an instant did Michelle ponder her course of action.

"Back in the tunnel. *Allez!* We must gather the weapons."

Bogey could scarcely believe that this woman of stout purpose and fierce determination was one and the same as the star-struck girl of the remembered conversation, idly dreaming aloud of her wedding plans. Within minutes they had ducked back within the tunnel, hastily filled their packs, slung loaded cartridge belts over their shoulders, grabbed the spare weapons, and moved toward the entrance when Michelle paused, looking down on the moaning airman. "Will he be all right?" And only upon Bogey's firm assurance did Michelle, without further hesitation, duck out through the entrance, Bogey in tow.

"This way and stay low," whispered Michelle.

With Michelle in the lead, the two women set off through the trees to where the gypsy, Chipmunk, lay low near the horses, shivering quite openly with fear.

"It's all right, Chipmunk," Michelle told him soothingly, her voice soft and low. "We'll be back as soon as we can.

But wait—the horses! I count only six. Where are the rest?" She stooped and grasped his hand, a compassionate gesture.

"T-There," he stammered, lifting his arm and pointed down through the trees. "I tied t-three down there in the trees in case these were f-f-found. B-But the guns...."

"Be calm. The guns are far off; they won't hurt you." Her voice remained calm, reassuring, but he lifted one hand to his ear, like an old man attempting to amplify the noise of the gunfire.

"Look, Chipmunk," she said softly. "Listen carefully to my orders—for all our lives depend on you." She looked at him squarely and spoke slowly, yet with unmistakable assurance and authority. "You know where the old man's ledges are, down by the stream and the waterfall. You are to round up all the horses and lead them down to the ledges. Those are my orders, understand?"

"Y-Yes, my flower, I know," he nodded. "I-I will do it for you." He was attempting to compose himself. "Do not worry your p-pretty head," he said, nodding, and the moon made deep pools of his eyes. "Ch-Ch-Chipmunk is here."

"When you reach the very top of the ledges," Michelle instructed, still holding his hand, "tie the horses securely, using always the knot that I taught you before. Then you wait. Is that clear?" Again the nod. "You must wait all night if need be. Until we come, do you hear?"

"Until h-h-hell freezes over," he assured her earnestly, and for a second, on impulse, she tightened the grip on his hand.

Seconds later, the two women were gone, their flitting shadows tracking down the mountain in the direction of the ledges and the waterfall.

"Stay low. Try to keep up," Michelle whispered to Bogey who soon could make out but the pale shadow of the lithe, gliding figure moving swiftly before her. Bogey in her fear marveled at the woman's poise, the head keenly erect and watchful, the long doe-like legs covering the ground in long, graceful, effortless bounds. The shots came to them with grim insistence now, and Bogey rushed to keep pace with the dark fleeting shadow flying before her.

They had rushed on this way for some minutes when Bogey, a dozen paces behind and struggling to keep up with her heavy pack slapping uncomfortably against her back, noticed something odd.

She observed the tall silhouette up ahead all at once falter, seem to lose balance or footing and stumble blindly. And by the time Bogey caught up, gasping to capture air in her lungs, Michelle was leaning helplessly, clinging to a tree trunk as if an awkward fawn braced against it for support.

"What is it?" Bogey panted.

"Nothing. One minute—I—I...."

"The spells again!"

"A moment. It—it will pass," murmured Michelle.

"Sit down. Put your head down as before."

"No time," whispered Michelle. "A minute—that's all."

The two women stood gasping for breath, their clothes now perspiration stained in the cool night air. Close in, there came no sound beyond the occasional hooting of an owl somewhere off in the trees, and the soft whisper of the wind. But in the distance, the noise of gunfire was a cacophony of sound.

Presently the voice of Michelle was again sharp and clear. "Come—we're almost to the waterfall. We must reach them in time." Then Bogey watched her spring out ahead, head held high, her slim shadow gliding over the uneven ground.

58

Upon breaking the surface, he heard it. Before shedding his mouthpiece, it came to him as if out of a nightmare—the shattering noise of it everywhere and no place to hide. It came to him where he treaded water, chin deep in the frigid waters at the face of the dam on the far side of the lake from the castle.

Nedo felt a cold ball of fear clench in the pit of his stomach. He tried not to stir, not to make a ripple, not draw attention for fear of discovery and death. He had been submerged in the dark icy waters before the face of the dam for many minutes, and now he hovered on the surface, thanking the good Lord for the darkness, for the fact that somehow the searchlights on the crest of the dam were not beaming down on this night.

In spite of the insulating properties of his wet suit, he shivered as he waited. Seconds passed. He was watching the pattern of fire on the shore where he had left his people, where he had considered them safe in the undergrowth couched at the base of Bald Hill. He was gauging the telltale points of the muzzle flashes bursting against the night—a zigzag line some distance back from the shore.

From where he hovered, sculling with his hands, the dark

water lapping at his rubber neck sheathing, Nedo listened to the countering stutter of twin Russian AK-47s firing from the thicket by the shore, the firing steady and insistent in desperate attempt to keep the superior enemy force at bay. In between, punctuating the breaks in the firing, the screams of wounded horses coursed through the night.

The water churned at his side. Baxter surfaced. Nedo lifted one arm until a single warning finger broke the surface. He placed it to his lips while his mind worked to capture the drama playing out on the shore. He counted five or more guns firing down from the high ground back from the shore, and two of his own men firing up at them from water's edge.

The two were not only his men, but buddies he had known all his life. Even in his fear, he longed to stand with them. He and Baxter had been submerged for too long, and he wondered how long his men had been holding off the attackers. With this concentration of fire, how long could they last? His brow furrowed as he calculated. He wondered just how many horses were down—and which carried in its saddlebags the crucial cargo.

"I have to get in there!" he whispered tensely. "To now, they are not outflanked—but soon." The sound of Baxter's voice broke the spell.

"A real party, eh, sport? What do you recommend?"

"Shhh. Be still; do not stir up the surface—see there." Nedo gestured with his head toward a clump of bushes projecting out from the shore. "First I go. Stay close."

Once they had reached the shallow water, Baxter whispered again, this time a trifle hoarsely.

"Now what?"

Nedo scanned the scene cast in pale moonlight, his brain placing where the weapons were stashed hard by a grainy flat rock, and from there, the location of the horses. He studied the lay of the terrain running back from the shore. He waited for a break in the firing. Surprise was their only weapon. He turned to Baxter.

"There. To the right. On my signal."

Beneath the screen of covering leaves, with only their heads poking above the licking wavelets, soundlessly they discarded tanks and fins. Then, as racers at the starting blocks, with legs drawn up beneath their chests, with bare toes digging into the sandy lake bottom for purchase, Nedo cried: "Now!"

For a moment, both men struggled against the restraining force of the water. Then they were upright, sprinting, bolting through the shallows, over the bank and up the shore, side by side, contestants caught in a bizarre otherworldly competition.

The zigzag line from higher up retrained its fire. Hastened by fear as the noise of bullets were slapping off rocks and ripping at the undergrowth in their wake, they reached the trees and the cluster of horses. Nedo, deafened by the noise of the guns, swept past the shrieks of the horses, past wild thrashing hooves flailing up from the ground. He groped toward a pair of horses still standing, one with bulging saddlebags as Baxter lunged for another spooked by the clamor.

Nedo ripped the reins from their tie in the leaves. Hearing a cry, he whirled to see the Englishman stagger and fall. Grasping the reins of the pack horse, Nedo hoisted the motionless Baxter while bullets hissed and sliced at the bark of the trees. He draped the limp body over the back of the pack horse, lashing it down with a pack rope. Ducking low against the gunfire, he mounted the forward horse, thrusting his weight forward, setting off at a gallop, the rein of the following pack horse gripped tightly in his hand. At that moment, he felt a searing hot burn in the calf of his leg. His mount bounded on through the trees.

Within fifty yards, Nedo spotted it looming before him. A solid, dark shadow obstructing his path. A fit of cold panic seized him. On instinct, he reined in the horse.

Directly before him, not three horse lengths ahead, loomed a lone gunman crouched in his path, blocking the way. The intruder's automatic weapon sprayed a deadly chain of fire through the trees. And it was only at that moment that Nedo snapped to the realization that he himself was not only barefoot—but unarmed. In the confusion and haste to aid Baxter, he had neglected to arm himself from the cache of weapons stashed by the rock.

Inexplicably the man looming before him broke off his fire. Nedo, wide-eyed, heard the intruder yell out— "Nedo!"

They were galloping north over the forest floor at a furious pace, Nedo in the lead, the lake shore on their right. Bright patches of moonlight spilled through the high branches to paint splotches of light beneath the quick flashing hooves. On the pack horse behind the draped and swaying body of Baxter, Cil clutched his own wounded arm close into his body to lessen the shock of the hoofbeats.

Finally Nedo in the lead struck off up the slope of the hill, leaving the shore behind. They were moving well, north, circling wide, maneuvering counterclockwise up and around the fat waist of Bald Hill. It was only when they had safely reached the back of the hill that Nedo pulled up. Working swiftly, the two men lowered Baxter onto the forest floor in a patch of moonlight. The woods lay soundless except for the distant echo of the guns.

The horses stood lathered and stinking with sweat as Nedo, limping slightly, checked them for wounds while Cil bent over the prone Baxter, running his hand over the Englishman's chest and abdomen. Then Cil turned to Nedo.

"It's no use." Cil could feel the blood oozing like heated crankcase oil from the gaping hole in Baxter's wet suit, the escaping liquid spilling out, dark and warm and sticky to the touch. "With a gut wound like that, there isn't a chance."

"But in the village...."

"He'd never make it to the village." Cil pressed his index finger up under the Englishman's jawline, but he could detect no sign of a pulse.

"You can't just leave him!" cried Nedo. "Besides, without him we're lost. Only he knows how to take care of the tanks."

"You're right about one thing," snapped Cil. "We cannot leave him—he knows too much."

"What?" When Nedo observed Cil drawing his knife, he fell back, appalled.

Cil's voice was fierce and low. "I told you. He knows too much." He was glancing back over his shoulder at the dark woods from whence they had come. "They'll be on us soon. I won't put the others at risk."

Cil had already raised his knife when the tiniest flicker of movement caught his eye. Startled, he halted his arm in the middle of the stroke. The eyelids of the "dead man" fluttered open.

When Baxter's arm moved, Nedo, standing nearby, bolted as if confronted by a ghost as a faraway voice seemed to rise from the ground.

"I say, s-sport—aren't you j-just a bloody bit previous?" Then the voice broke off and Cil, dumbfounded, quickly bent down and placed an ear to the struggling lips. "No time now—lis-listen...." In a few halting phrases, Baxter murmured instructions; but when he was done, he had one last question, and with his last strength he strained to lift his head couched in Cil's hand.

"The w-warning down the river?"

"Easy, chum. Already gone out," Cil assured him. A last responsive smile played on the Englishman's lips as he sank in the soundless way of a great ship slipping below the waves. In a moment, he was gone.

Nedo, shaken, stood over Cil in the haughty, superior Slavic fashion which it must have taken centuries to perfect. He glared down with a contemptuous leer at the knife still gripped in Cil's hand. "Are you not going to knife him now?" he hissed.

Cil eyed him swiftly. "If you don't get busy and bind up that leg, you won't make it either."

"We've got to move now," cried Nedo as he ripped off his belt to bind up his own leg wound, himself glancing furtively back down the slope. But Cil, now seated, worked calmly to unlace his boots.

"Put these on," he ordered.

"But then you...."

"I said, put them on!" Cil got to his feet and squared off with the young warrior. "Now you listen to me—I want those children out. And your men?" Cil demanded. "What about your men?"

"You saw my men on the shore," Nedo retorted bitterly, not looking at Cil, but seating himself to lace on the boots Cil had left on the ground.

"Think, man, think!" snapped Cil. "I mean your men on the south ridge. How many?"

"Four. Already positioned and waiting."

Cil consulted his watch, then looked back down the slope. When he spoke this time, his voice held the bite of blue-tempered steel.

"Look, fella. This is war! In war, soldiers carry out orders." His voice gentled only a fraction. "And about your men back there—you had to leave them because those are the orders." And then as an afterthought as he watched the young Rambo mount up, "War allows for heroes, you know, only in the movies. And take this—you'll need it before you're through."

Cil handed up his own assault rifle, silencer and all, then hooked his ammunition pouch containing two extra clips over the pommel of Nedo's saddle.

"Besides," added Cil, and Nedo may have glimpsed the shadow of a grin in the moonlight. "I've got a knife, remember?" For the briefest instant, their eyes met. "I'll follow you in as far as the South Road—according to plan. Then you're on your own—just bring out those kids."

59

Zeljko and his crew of burrowing moles did not linger at the mouth of the shaft, wringing their hands while listening to the cracking of gunfire from the opposite side of the damn. These were men accustomed to danger and death. In their way, the elder among them were seasoned veterans, and these sounds were their warning.

Instead of fretting, each man bent to his task with heightened resolve. Each knew they were close to the end. It was a race to the finish, and not one man intended to squander the lives already lost—or forfeit the prize for which they had paid such a high price.

The Professor and Zeljko returned to their posts at the front. They faced the stubborn layer of red clay braced firmly against them. Slobo and the remaining farm boy still toiled to slice back and widen the dirt walls past the concrete slab in order to open the shaft and assure a free flow. Outside, One-Eye maintained his position with the two farm boys flanked out wide on the mound in the cover of young growth, guarding the south and easterly approaches.

Up front, as he chipped away at the circle of red clay, Zeljko was keeping a weather eye on the Professor working beside him since the sudden untimely demise of his twin. But he had no cause for concern on that score, for the giant

Muslim, though his face remained pale and impassive above the muddy beard, swung his pick with the single-minded fury and passion of a man flailing against the red face of Satan himself.

"It cannot stand against us now," the old man muttered almost to himself. The face of clay concealing the thin concrete cap had to cave in. With each new thrust of the pick, clear lake water sprouted forth to spurt in miniature geysers.

"Narrow the hole," instructed Zeljko, but the bearded giant never turned his head, never acknowledged the command, but merely narrowed his aim at Satan's red face.

There was a sudden splashing from behind. As if practicing wind sprints, the little commander launched himself up the current of mud.

"Here they come! The whole damned army of them— coming fast up the bank of the river!"

The old man wheeled and looked to the Professor.

"Go!" growled the Professor. "Everyone out!" At the crisis, the man's demeanor was hard, even glacial. "Fan out in cover—top of the mound. Hold fire until they reach the base of the mound."

Zeljko held back. He stared at the Professor, then at the red wall of clay remaining up front.

"You go!" commanded the tall Muslim, placing his hand on the old man's shoulder for only an instant. "If I'm not out—take your men out. And stay wide of the opening!"

"But the first blast?" The old man glanced down at his wristwatch. The watch read 10:52 PM.

"Go!"

60

At the first sound of gunfire, Crazy Ivan knew exactly what to do. Lying fully clothed in his cot in the barracks at the Serb compound, wrapped in his oversized greatcoat the way he always slept, he hopped out of bed and ran to the auto repair shop where he picked up a crowbar, a prodigious length of rope, and one other small implement. Not a man to waste time, he then promptly wove his way through the noise and confusion of barking orders and armor on the move. For only a moment did he pause, looking up, outside the general's headquarters before making directly for the very rear of the compound where it butted against the slant of the south ridge. If others were losing their heads, he would just have to take matters into his own hands.

When he reached the back of the compound, the clamor at the opposite end of the military encampment was less, the noise of the gunfire muted. Ivan dropped to his knees and, after considerable toil, managed to complete the first phase of his plan. Once the job was done, he moved to the shed positioned next to the high wire fence. He tried turning the knob of the door, but the door would not budge. Quite deliberately, he tried the knob three more times just to make sure.

He listened with his ear flat up against the door. Soft sobbing sounds came from within—and that made him mad.

Wielding the crowbar, he smashed open the door to find himself surrounded by a flock of sobbing, cowering children. Though frightened himself, Ivan stooped to comfort each child in turn. Then on trembling legs, he led his flock to the site of his first piece of handiwork, helping the children gently as a mother, passing them through the narrow square hole he had cut in the wire fence.

At first, Ivan did not hear it. Only after he had knotted the rope around each child, the smallest of the children first and paying out a generous interval between each child, then taking the lead child by the hand, did the thrashing noise in the bushes come to him clearly.

61

The pair of riders, having circled the base of Bald Hill, pulled up on a small rise and dismounted. The rise upon which they found themselves looked down upon the South Road where it ran through the gap between Bald Hill and the next ridge south.

On silent feet, they led their mounts down into cover at the side of the road, the horses streaked and pungent with sweat. For some time they had heard no sound of gunfire, the night still and silent—except for a *puzzling new sound,* a sound hard to place.

The road leading through the pass appeared peaceful, even serene—a river of moonlight as it flowed through the trees. Now, even over the low snorting of the horses, Cil could hear that same strange sound, a bare rumble in the distance, and he could see the soft glow of the guard hut's lights farther down the road toward the pass before the dam.

It took only seconds for Cil to remove the vital equipment from the saddlebags of the pack horse, though he winced from pain as he slung the black python of cable around his neck so that a cluster of two small brick-like parcels hung from one shoulder, a tiny metal box from the other. The hammering pace of the ride had opened up the wound in his arm, and he could feel the wetness where it oozed down his wet suit. The time was 10:44 PM.

Nedo, once again mounted, hung back, rifle in hand, prepared to provide covering fire as Cil slipped off through the trees down the near side of the road toward the faint, distant lights of the guard hut. Stealing barefoot through the undergrowth with the road to his right, Cil in his wet suit, his pack on his back, moved swiftly, concealed from the road by a screen of foliage. Dry twigs nipped at his feet as he brushed through the leaves, and now and again he stumbled, clutching the cable to his hip to dampen the sound.

He was approaching the guard hut at the pass where the overhanging cliffs squeezed in on the road. As Cil moved closer, he could see a shaft of light slanting out of the open door of the guard hut situated on the far side of the road, the swath of light extending across the road. It was as if a bar of pure shining light had been deliberately erected across his path to bar his passage.

Cil worked his way through the trees until his hand touched the wet hardness of the stone face of the cliff which was Bald Hill. With the pack on his back hugging the base of the cliff, he crept along slowly, in a crab-footed gait. Through the open door of the guard hut on the far side of the road, he could hear the muted sounds of voices, could see bloated human shadows projected against the pine boards at the back of the hut.

He waited—then advanced, waited—then advanced—all the while training his senses ahead to pick up that first hint of sound, that first flick of telltale movement in the shadows that would signal disaster. But no sound came, no out-of-the-way movement—so on he crept.

He was close, very close to the road, and the hut on the opposite side of the road squeezed ever closer by the cliffs. He crept along, sideways, advancing, hearing the sound of his canvas pack sliding along the wall of the cliff at his back. He was feeling his way, holding his breath and his thoughts, clutching the box and bundles at the ends of the cable in close to his body to still them, creeping along, but moving, always moving, sideways, back to the cliff-face.

Now his full frame stood illuminated by the beam of golden light, the light emanating from the guard hut across the road not twenty feet distant.

The sudden jangle of a field phone in the guard hut brought him up short. The silhouette of a soldier, tall in a visored cap, pushed out through the lighted doorway of the guard hut, carbine in hand, advancing straight toward him.

Cil froze, shoulders hunched in an attempt to make himself smaller. So close was he now to the enemy soldier that he caught the smell of stale beer and the aroma of tobacco smoke in the air. Like the grasp of a mighty hand, the rigid beam of light seemed to reach out and hold him.

Nedo, back at the side of the road, was faring little better. A scampering squirrel spooked his horse; and as his mount shied, mincing hooves, then bucking, Nedo, weakened by the loss of blood, found himself ingloriously tossed from the saddle to clatter to the ground. Stroking the horse to steady her, his gaze was searching hastily about to assure he had not been discovered; he found the stirrup and cautiously regained his mount.

Nedo knew this place. With his compatriots in the early spring he had spent days spying from the cliffs above, but the thought reminded him of his friends, and for the third time in the space of a minute he listened for the sound of gunfire; but no sound came. He recalled Cil's words, but they gave him no comfort. His heart sank.

He thought back to those carefree, hell-raising schoolboy days he had shared with his pals, and in the rays of the moon his eyes searched out the opening in the trees on the far side of the road down by the guard hut. He could see in his mind the way the old trail snaked up the south ridge on the far side of the road.

It had been one of those hot spring days when the whole

gang, skipping school, had galloped out to the dam on a frolic. In high spirits they had stolen a jug of clear native plum brandy from the barn of the old sheepherder who farmed the basin. Nedo recalled how they had all tied their horses just down the road from here, next to the pass, before stripping to their waists and swigging down the thick, sweet liquid. On the fourth passing of the jug, someone had thrown down a challenge as to which of them could first scale the sheer face of the pass.

It was shortly after that the old man had caught them, caught them red-handedly, and Nedo vividly recalled how the whole gang had bolted for their horses, piling on in the way often seen in American westerns on TV from Belgrade, to gallop away wildly for that opening in the trees. He recalled the way the old man had waved his shotgun and how Nedo himself had whipped the flanks of his mount, storming up the south ridge, weaving and winding up the rough trail until he reached the very crest. And then when the others had reached him, they held up, waving and showering raucous insults and taunts down upon the old shepherd who by that time was firing wildly in their direction.

The images brought him back with a start—for now the old shepherd was gone, along with his crops, his fields, his sheep, and his home—which had now been converted to the headquarters building in the enemy compound. And now gone, too, were his lifelong companions.

Closing off his lament, the sturdy Nedo surveyed his situation. That day long ago had been innocent fun. They had ridden away in broad daylight—not dark. He had been strong—not riding a spent horse and burdened with a leg wound. And on that day, too, he had confronted an arthritic old shepherd—not crack enemy troops, ready and waiting and aching for combat.

Cil found himself still frozen to the spot in that rigid beam of golden light. And now the tall sentry, who had come striding out of the door of the guard hut towards him, suddenly turned and moved off into the woods. Cil could see the outline of the man, the way the sentry turned his back, hunching his shoulders. And then Cil heard one of the most common sounds in life—a soft tinkling sound which left no doubt of the man's mission.

Seizing the moment, Cil stole away, freeing himself from the accursed grasp of that golden beam of light.

And then he was out, through, away from the light, leaving the voices behind, scurrying through the narrow pass. On the far side where the terrain widened out, he held up in the underbrush, checking his bearings.

Here on the lakeside of the pass, that strange deep-throated rumble like far-off thunder was louder now—more distinct. But what could it be? For a moment, he threw a glance to where the great dam slumbered in darkness. To the left of the dam lay the surface of the lake, peaceful, shimmering, silvery in the moonlight; and he could see the finger of land, the narrow isthmus jutting out from the far shore and from whence he had come; he shivered at the thought. Beyond that point of land rose the black bulk of Castle Mountain and still higher the skyline cresting above it. In the flood of moonlight, the castle stood silhouetted in stark relief against the night sky, eerie and quaint in its medieval grandeur.

Returning to business, Cil looked to his right—toward the far side of the road. He wondered how a narrow mountain road could look so wide. He started across. He was out onto the coarse gravel, crawling, crawling with the black python of cable looped over his shoulders. He was near the center of the road when it came.

Firing! A new cracking of gunfire, this time from the far side of the river; and in seconds Cil isolated the point of origin as the back of the dam.

The sentries must have heard it, too, for Cil could see lengthening human shadows on the road running toward him, the shadows cast by the reflected light of the guard hut funneling through the pass. Cil braced his hands against the rough gravel of the roadway. Then he raised up and dashed across, barefoot, feeling the course pebbles of the road dig into his feet, all the while intent upon the shallow ditch on the far side of the road, intent upon the safety offered by its grassy hollow. And when he arrived, he sprawled headlong, flat—hard down on his bad arm.

The pain came in waves—deep—penetrating—jagged. Beads of oily sweat popped out on his forehead. For a moment his mind went white from the pain; he was needing to cry out and scream, and only a supreme act of will held back the sound. With the sentries so close, he lay there on the arm, unable to move.

When his senses returned, both sentries were standing close by, conversing excitedly, one soldier's shadow nearly blanketing the spot where he lay. The men just standing there, not moving, one lifting his rifle, motioning in the direction of sound.

The firing from across the river came louder now, heavier, and Cil could detect the fitful bursts of automatic weapons fire mixed with the cracking of rifles, then the unmistakable staccatto beat of a heavy machine gun—a filthy, deadly sound—a fifty caliber, he guessed.

Cil thought of the old man and the crew in the shaft, wondering if they were caught in the bowels of the shaft, or out on the exposed mound. He thought of Bogey huddled alone in the escape tunnel. He thought of Michelle.

Nedo, still sitting his horse on the far side of the pass, first heard the noise of the gunfire, then saw the guards run. He fought his first impulse; it would be useless; he could do nothing for his father now. And the Yankee major? Though unable to see from this vantage, it required no insight to reckon his position of peril.

Nedo stared across the road at that small opening in the trees down by the guard hut. Then, with a quick slap of the reins to the horse's flank, he was off, the big animal's hoof-beats pounding over the hard gravel of the road. Racing for the opening in the trees, Nedo fired into the air to create a diversion, then suddenly comprehended with a shock what a small noise the automatic rifle with a silencer made. So he reacted on impulse, letting out an Indian war whoop as wild and bloodcurdling as ever he had heard explode from the throat of his favorite film star.

The last thing Nedo observed before swerving up the trail onto the south ridge was the sight of two other sentries spilling out of the guard hut.

At the sound of the war whoop, even over his pain, Cil's lips swept up in a grin. When the clatter of hoofbeats subsided, the sentries fled back through the pass toward their post. Cil, abandoning all caution, broke for the cleft in the south ridge thirty paces distant and slightly above him.

The enemy fuel storage tanks sat up on a small rise on the inner elbow of the road across from the dam, the tanks tucked into a cleft blasted into the ridge for the express purpose of concealing them from enemy aircraft. It was as if the base of the cliff had been chopped away by a woodsman's ax, although at this hour the site was unlit and deserted, the sole foreign presence being a moonlit half-track, tilted on its broken carriage, resting on the dirt apron before the giant tanks.

Cil scrambled up the apron of dirt, each crunching step seeming to echo in the night. He crawled the last yards, up under the nozzled steel pipes extending out from the base of the storage tanks.

Under the outlet pipes, the stench of raw gasoline was a palpable thing. At the top of the rise, the mysterious sound he had heard in the distance resounded off the high metal cylinders as if they were a pair of giant amplifiers.

"*Tanks!*" Cil raised himself, squeezing between the outlet pipes to his full gathered height. On tiptoe from this vantage, he could peer over the crest of the gravel apron, looking south.

Far down the pencil line of the south road, a parade of lights glimmered up at him from the direction of the enemy compound—the snaking white headlights of a convoy, and they seemed to be moving. The clanking sound came louder; the impulse to run was a powerful thing.

Steadily, methodically, he began digging with his hands in the moist, oily gravel, straining to recall Baxter's exact words. The firing from across the river came in short angry bursts.

Cil's hands increased the pace of their digging.

62

Back of the dam, at the mouth of the shaft, the old earthen dam formed a high sloping mound dotted with scrub oak and poplar. With the floodlights extinguished, the crew of exhausted moles lay in darkness, clear of the tunnel entrance. The light of the moon threw a silvery sheen over the leaves of young growth to flutter and glimmer in the eddying breeze.

Zeljko and his men—Slobo, the little commander, the three farm lads, and One-Eye—lay flat on their bellies on the damp earth, fanned out along the crest of the mound, concealed by the undergrowth. At nearly point-blank range, they fired down on the enemy positions.

Rapid hostile fire erupted from the base of the mound all up and down the line, the fire evenly spaced. This the old man could see by the muzzle flashes, vicious red tongues of fire lashing out of the night. The staccato beat of a heavy machine gun hidden at the bank of the river to his far right hammered the mound and raked across it at will, pinning Zeljko's men to the ground where they lay.

Zeljko, his nose raised from the dirt, lay still as death while he studied the front. Vainly his eyes searched for the first sign of weakness, the smallest ticket out. Without a path of escape....

He bided his time, waiting, probing the darkness with old hunter's eyes. Minutes passed, and with the passage of time the enemy guns seemed to multiply, boring in, concentrating their fire. Any attempt at escape in this hail of fire....

In his state of helplessness, Zeljko found himself very lucid and clear in his mind; he was thinking not of escape, but of his boy on the far shore of this unlucky lake—he was thinking of his woman. What would become of them now? And what of the others of the village who depended on him? And what of his colonel? He had failed on missions before, but....

And what of Cil the major—the Yankee? The man he had first set out to serve only out of obligation, but now at the last he had been tricked to come to think of as his own? Yet, lying here belly down in this graveyard of dirt, his agitation grew as he thought of the cock-sure Yankee officer; he could feel the boil of his temper. Maybe the sneering Slobo was right—for hadn't it been he, Zeljko of the mountains and a fine soldier, too, who had time and again gone out on a limb for this young Yankee upstart? And how had the man repaid him? Had not the thankless bastard insulted and defied him? Why, the man was a fool—yet again flinging away his life in another lake crossing? And all against his advice and the fates of the gods.

And the sick niece of the colonel he had tried so hard to save. No, no. He himself, Zeljko, had been right in the first place. The both of them—totally lacking in discipline, reckless. A pair of fools adrift from some foreign soil. Bah! And the niece of the colonel in these last vital hours? Off chasing phantom aer-o-plane drivers.

Now the muzzle flashes from below the mound came even more rapid and insistent. But old Zeljko had already stopped firing his rifle. He was preparing himself. He was thinking this one last time of his two great achievements in life. Thinking of his woman, now, of all the years—and he was thinking of his boy.

Of course, he knew his son's fate, but he would not give him up at this last hour no matter what. Calmly he released his right hand from his rifle and crossed himself. Yes, he himself would go, but the honor was that his son would live on. No! At this late hour he would not permit his faith in the boy to run off and desert him.

63

Colonel Mavro Anastasi sat alone, holed up as he was
in the small office of his mountain retreat, feeling the
walls of the room closing in on him. He had been waiting
for the call, but now the snapping sparks of the fire in the
hearth seemed only to mock him. He felt isolated, abandoned, imprisoned in this world of his own making. Still the
black phone lay silent before him on the top of the desk. As
he sat there, he fought the empty feeling rising like a serpent
in his gut.

On the desk stood two gold-framed pictures carefully
dusted, one large, one small. Momentarily his gaze wondered to the larger of the two, the photograph of a tall, stately figure elegantly dressed, a delicate creature captured in
the flower of womanhood, eyes so gentle and smiling, and
yet the air somehow aloof, as if in effort to veil a sadness of
the spirit behind, as if to conceal an almost funereal sense
of loss and remoteness. And while the collective image
aroused his pride and deep devotion, so too the image
aroused his compassion.

But now his eye moved to the smaller picture, but a snapshot, really. At the sight of it, despite his agitation, he was
startled to feel the memory curl up the corners of his mouth.
Staring up at him was the likeness of a child. Not a serene

likeness as the photograph of his daughter, Sonya, but the image of a cheeky little tike of six or seven years, clinging to the back of a small pony, teeth clenched and eyes flashing, ramrod back stretched forward boldly, the pony's mane ruffled and flowing, the child's long braids trailing in the wind.

He sat back in his chair and thought of them both. Without conscious thought, he reached out and raised the smaller picture and pressed it to his cheek. His beloved Sonya lived in another world. Would this child, too, be lost to him now?

A fresh sense of foreboding gripped him. His glance darted to the face of the wall clock. His hand reached out and snatched up the receiver while the other punched the redial button. Waiting, the fingers of his free hand drummed in agitation against the desktop.

As if to mock the very violence of his pent-up emotion, a small thrush lit on the sill of the open window and warbled gaily beneath a calm and warming sun; the fragrance of lilac flirted with the breeze.

On the second ring, a woman's voice with a soft Southern drawl sounded in his ear.

"Office of the Depidy Secretary. May I hep you?"

"Lockwood, please—and urgent!"

"Who may I say is callin'?" the voice still unhurried.

"Anastasi."

A notable pause. "Is thet Mr. Anastasi or...."

"Colonel—and hurry!"

"One minutes, Sah."

A maddening pause fell over the line—then the brisk, no-nonsense voice as clear as if its owner were striding into the room.

"Colonel, excuse the delay. I have Communications right here on the line."

"Is there news?"

"Sorry; nothing—oh, wait—just a minute, Colonel."

This time the pause was interminable, so long in fact the phone seemed to go dead in his hand. The colonel's gaze shifted involuntarily to the snapshot on the desk, but the shock of the reminder came at him with such violence that his eyes turned away. For a moment his mind went blank. Only in echo did his ear catch the clipped words.

"Colonel, I'd better ring you back. The only word from the off-shore aircraft carrier is that the final stage has begun. And, oh yes—a pilot is down."

"What pilot?"

"One of our NATO carrier pilots—Serb surface to air missile close by the dam."

"Nothing else?"

"Look, Colonel. Secretary Levitt is doing all he can. As I say, I'd better get back to you—yes, yes, at the very first news—yes, Colonel, you have my word."

The line went dead. Replacing the receiver, the colonel battled the urge to slump in his chair. He fetched his pipe from the stand on his desk and clamped down hard on the pipestem. His gaze strayed out over the sun-bathed fields that stretched beyond the window. It would be the middle of the night over there.

The thrush had vanished—but Mavro Anastasi was not thinking of thrushes.

64

Zeljko lay there on his belly, flat down in the dirt of the mound and clear of the shaft entrance with the other men flanked out on either side. He was firing again as fast and furiously as he knew how. If this slimy gang of Serb bastards had a mind to take him, then, by god—they'd better be ready to fight.

Eyes darting, he rechecked his watch. 10:58. Two minutes to go—that damned Professor—where is he? He cursed every individual Muslim on the face of this earth as his elbows dug deeper into the earth where he lay. Spent cartridges, searing hot, winged past his ear.

Where was that overgrown, yellow-bearded stubborn, Muslim son-of-a-bitch? He could see the enemy field of fire below, could see it advancing. Bullets raked and savaged the dirt of the mound.

What he could not see were the two gray shadows close overhead, feminine shadows moving in a crouch low atop the shelf formed by the concrete lip of the dam.

Nor could he see them fan out along the shelf, silent, diverging, until one hovered directly above the spot where the enemy 50 caliber machine gun was positioned. Nor could he see the faint stirring of delicate, experienced hands as they reached into fat canvas satchels to pluck out

one metallic, scalloped fruit after another, lining them neatly and carefully against the back of the shelf where it met
the high white wall of the dam.

65

Cil knelt in the darkness. He knelt at the base of the enemy fuel storage tanks on the far side of the river with the pungency of raw gasoline fumes weaving a tapestry around him. He dug into the loose gravel with the claws of his hands. He could hear the staccato beat of the machine gun fire from across the river. He could hear the hard metallic clanking of the tank treads announcing their approach.

As Baxter had instructed, Cil ripped off the protective coatings and packed a single bundle of plastic explosives closeup against the steel skin at the base of each storage tank where the tanks converged, wedging them in, tamping the loose dirt with the palms of his hands to support them in place, taking care not to sever the small wires leading back to the cable. Then, slowly, methodically, he filled in over the python of cable; and with the face of the detonator turned toward the moon, he paused.

He listened to the sound of the gunfire, picturing in his mind the scene at the dam, calculating the effect on Zeljko and his men. In his mind's eye, he measured his own route back through the pass and the time it would take him. If he allowed for a three-minute interval? No. He set the timer on thirty seconds flat. He looked at his watch. It was 11:04.

But Cil did not press the activator button at that moment.

Instead, he listened to the rattle of the machine gun and the crack-cracking of answering rifle fire from the back of the dam. He listened as the rumble of enemy tanks crept closer. Cil thought of the flash of light the explosion would cause and he waited, listening with care to the noise of the guns.

66

From where Zeljko lay on the mound with heavy fire erupting up and down the line before him, he neither heard nor saw the pair of crouching figures moving into position not six feet above his head on the concrete shelf or lip of the dam. And if he were told that those silent figures were none other than Michelle and Bogana, he would have denied it down to his last living breath.

Nor did Zeljko hear the pulling of the pin—nor observe the high arcing parabola of the throw as the first hand grenade hurtled into the clear starlit sky. But his whole body jounced and lifted off the ground at the force of the explosion, followed by a sudden jewel of light out before him, the blast jarring his teeth and, a second later, showering his back with dirt and debris.

What?—and then another burst—and another—and still another until his voice cried out in the din and his ears shrieked for relief. As he lay there stunned, he could still hear the ringing in his ears, and in his confusion it seemed so like the sound of the bells on the night of his wedding so long ago as he hung on the rope in the belfry of that old village chapel.

But now the old man was suddenly assailed by a different sensation, totally beyond his experience—a stillness. It was a stillness so full and serene it seemed that a velvety curtain of silence had descended over the earth. He felt the slide of his guts and the bite of the chill mountain air. Yes, yes; his eardrums, they must be burst from the near blast of that first grenade.

He lay there, blinking his eyes to clear up his brain, shaking his head to rid it of that confounded ringing.

Instinct alone brought him to his feet. He rose and his mind worked. With a burst of speed, he galloped away—wildly, pumping his rifle straight up over his head, bawling out orders to the others to follow as he dashed off over the mound—across the small clearing—past the power station on his right—racing for the railbed and the pines and the stream that lay beyond.

As he dashed on, he could hear the hammer of his heart as well as the pounding of booted feet close behind him; but he did not look back. He did not look back even when he heard the splashing of his boots or when the icy water of the stream acted as a tonic to his injured leg or when the bulk of his frame crashed through brush overhanging the streambed as he moved in a head-long rush upstream for the ledges, for the waterfall, for the waiting horses and safety.

67

Cil knelt next to the detonator timer. With the rumble and metallic clanking of approaching enemy tanks shaking the ground beneath him, he cocked his ear—still waiting, attempting to gauge the sound of the gunfire from back of the dam. He went on waiting—he waited three lifetimes.

At last the sounds changed. A sharp yet unmistakable noise swept in on the breeze. "*Grenades!*"

Quickly he nodded. He rechecked the timer, pressed down the red activator button, and started to run. The time was 11:08.

68

As for the explosion, the old man saw the flash before he heard the sound. A fireball so high and magnificently bright in the sky that it transformed night into day. But Zeljko did not slacken his pace.

With the ringing still in his ears, and now the terrific blast that colored the sky, he did not hear the first hollow *whooooosh* and surge of the break-out, nor the way it transformed over time to a vast, roving thing, though by the time he reached the ledges and the first spatter of spray from the waterfall, he felt the earth lurch and tremble under the soles of his boots—and he had trouble keeping his footing.

69

The detonator timer, half buried in the sand between the great cylindrical walls of the fuel storage tanks, lay ticking off its final seconds. Cil raced past the abandoned half-track, sped off the gravel apron, ducked back through the pass, and crashed into the woods behind the guard hut, bracing himself behind a broad tree trunk.

When the explosion came, the concussion erupted with such force that the guard hut, though shielded from the blast by the mountain pass, exploded to kindling as if struck by a cyclone. Three sentries, caught inside, suffered the fate of the flimsy wooden structure. The other, having heard the commotion made by Cil crashing through the underbrush, had concealed himself behind a tree in wait—and it was that commotion that had saved him.

When the first wave of heat and concussion had passed, Cil found himself face to face with the remaining enemy sentry. Except for his knife, Cil was unarmed. The sentry, not staring at Cil, but at the wave of flame rolling toward him and towering over the trees above where Cil stood, dropped his weapon and fled down the road. Watching the man flee, Cil, with his last energy, followed behind down the road in search of his horse.

Once mounted up, so depleted did Cil find himself for

loss of blood, he had no choice but to place his fate in the animal he rode. The old nag had long served as a pack horse for Nedo's band. The horse gravitated back, circling the hill the way it had come at a leisurely pace, though climbing, ever upward, eventually arriving at its home on the top of Bald Hill where the horses had formerly been picketed next to Nedo's now abandoned cellar camp.

Wavering atop his mount, Cil now sat quite dumbly, unafraid. Across the narrow cut, he could see the forest on the south ridge engulfed in flame, the heat of the fire lofting sparks and plumes of fire into the night sky like fireworks on the fourth of July.

As if nerveless, Cil looked down upon the pass and the dam and the river beyond, the whole macabre scene noon-day bright. Clad in the protection of his wet suit, he was insulated from the scorching heat, though his face livened to a shocking pink as if overexposed to the sun while sparks from the south ridge showered down all around. Yet, despite the increasing heat, as before, the old horse refused to shy away but went on grazing, nonchalant, content to be home.

Cil urged his mount closer to the rim. Below, at intervals, he could see through the rising plumes of coal-black smoke, could see the way the gasoline spilled from the remains of the ruptured storage tanks to flood and pour down the South Road, converting the curve of the roadway to a flowing river of flame. The lead Serb tank, firing blindly and itself afire in the pass, stood blocking the column behind.

To Cil in his present condition, it all seemed quite com-mon, if surreal. He watched a soldier pop open the hatch on the lead tank. In the roar and hiss of the flames, Cil could not hear the man's screams but watched quietly as the Serb soldier tumbled to the ground, arms flailing, clothes engulfed in flame.

It was the odd sound that drew Cil's attention to the dam. Not exactly a rumble. More like the first sounds and sensa-tions of an earthquake writhing up from the bowels of the earth. Through the flanks of his horse, he could feel the tremors.

On the lake side of the dam, Cil could discern no change in the placid surface of the lake except that the shimmer of moonlight had been replaced by reflections of fiery yellows and reds amid deep scorching orange.

The back of the dam was a different story. In the gorge where the river had been, a witch's cauldron frothed and boiled, spilling forth in quest for the sea.

Cil watched with no sense of time. Below the dam, a line of trucks sat stranded on the single-span bridge, the hand of the current reaching pluming white fingers up through the steel latticework of the bridge, knocking about the loaded troop carriers like so many Christmas toys.

In a moment the bridge was gone, yet Cil remained oddly impassive and serene, viewing the scene that stretched out before him.

70

At the time that it occurred, Cil had been too intent upon the final stage of the mission to concern himself with the slash wound to his arm. But now with the loss of blood, he lolled astride the pack horse at the crest of Bald Hill as if in a sleepwalker's trance, blinking his eyes in the orangy brightness of the fuel dump fire. It was as if he were caught up in a dream, staring down the slope of the hill, oblivious to the lick and crackle of the flames, his attention trained in rapt fascination upon the witch's caldron of the river below the dam. At the mercy of that mountain of water, no human could survive, and it was the force of that thought that pricked the goad of his conscience.

"Michelle! Bogey!"

Shaking his head to clear it, he thrust forward on his mount and swung over the reins; but before the horse could respond, there came a new commotion—odd—dissembled—blowing on the wind. Earlier, the snapping of faraway gunshots had come to him over the noise of the flames and the roar of the river, but now a different sound—and the new sound was building.

Human sounds. *Voices*—and the voices rapidly *closing* in. Again he prodded his mount. And then he saw.

At first they came on in two's and three's—men advancing at him out of the forest. Not soldiers, no, but cautious, ragged men tramping out of the shadows as if weary, as if they had come a long way. Some were tall, others fat with weapons in their hands, a few limping and supported by canes, even a handful of women dragging tired small ones behind—and all flocking toward him out from amidst the trees.

Cil, unperturbed atop his grazing horse, blinked his eyes and watched them come. All walking, none on horseback like himself, but coming out of the woods, now a solid wall of humanity moving his way. A sea of bobbing heads, their approach becoming louder with each second. And now he could see them clearly.

Mountain people, folks of all ages—some angry and grim-faced, others with faces oddly red and contorted in the glare of the firelight, and still others laughing and joking and waving their arms. The shadows of the flames from the fire at his back seemed to brighten and lend stark definition to their faces.

As they approached, Cil could see that most bore arms. Not rifles and grenades and machine guns as he had feared, but simple farm tools of crude manufacture: rakes and clubs, scythes and sickles and pitchforks.

They were almost upon him, yet the old pack horse was still refusing to budge. And now in the midst of the crowd came a single rider on horseback, a young man, trim, well-sculpted, clad in a dark, form-fitting wet suit like himself, the young man seated boldly and erectly like some ancient, valiant warrior, his smile at once shy and proud and holding a certain deep satisfaction and peace, shining even through the grime that coated his face.

All about the young man's horse were townspeople of all ages, swarming, shouting, pressing in on their champion and singing his praises, reaching up an ocean of hands just to touch him.

Behind, coming on more slowly was a second procession

as Cil sat staring dumbfoundedly at the whole queer sight.

Out front strode a different figure—a man—a slim twig of a man, neither tall nor terribly short, a scarecrow really, an odd, stick figure clad in a greatcoat so long that his feet kicked at its hem with each forward step. Yet the man came striding over the uneven ground with a superior, almost swaggering air. And Cil could see the small head adorned with a fedora right out of the twenties and the exaggerated brim tugged down upon huge dumbo ears. And beneath the brim of the hat—the gleeful grin like that of a newborn. And at the man's back, like a great waving tail, paraded a line of school children, each child in line clad in soiled, tattered clothing, and yet laughing and singing quite boisterously. And though the strange man was not seen to be playing a pipe, he appeared for all the world the Pied Piper of Hamelin.

The throng of townspeople, once taking Cil in tow upon command of their leader, had proceeded but a short distance when a sudden new presence lifted the crowd's gaze above the tall trees.

In contrast to the multitude of bewildered faces crowded around, instantly did Cil recognize the steady whomp—whomping—whomping beat of heavy rotors slashing at the rarefied air of the mountains. And when the flotilla of choppers thundered in, they swooped in nose down, hot and low over the crest of the hill. The four Black Hawk attack helicopters in diamond formation emerged not from the lake side, but from the west, past the spiral of smoke and flame from the back of Bald Hill; and judging by the timing, Cil guessed they approached on a direct line from the US carrier under NATO command that he had radioed earlier and which lay ready off the Croatian coast in support of the great Croat-Bosnian offensive coming farther north.

At the clamor of the incoming choppers, the mob of townspeople surged back towards the trees in fright, shrinking from the sudden invaders. But the gunships neither

opened fire nor touched down, but instead deployed themselves, still in diamond formation, hovering at the fringes of
the forest, spaced out at tree level, protectively, just above
the shower of sparks drifting in over the clearing.

Cil, by now so faint and unsteady that he feared at any
moment he might topple from his horse, failed at first to
observe a new arrival. Shielded by the tumult of the gunships, an additional lone chopper skimmed in over the trees,
and now Cil recognized the old familiar shape of the Viet
Nam vintage Huey chopper advancing on the clearing to
finally hang suspended only feet above the ground, itself
now shrouded in the drifting smoke and persistent shower
of sparks.

It came to Cil now that he could barely focus his eyes.
When he spied the opened side door in the belly of the
chopper, his sight somehow clouded. Nor over the roar of
the chopper engines could he hear the shouted command or
observe the phalanx of dark-suited marines leaping from the
chopper, the men fanning out in combat formation.

"Cil?"—Major Cil?—oh, thank God. This way, Major—
quickly. No, no, we'll see to the kids. Here, Sir—let me give
you a hand."

Nor in the tumult did Cil hear the hollow *thud* of the flare
fired, nor see the flash suddenly streaking skyward above
the castle on the mountain opposite, almost as if the hand of
a heavenly child were dragging a white crayon across the
night sky. Nor did Cil spy the tall, slim figure standing there
in the ramparts, a flare gun in her hands, expectantly awaiting an answer. Neither did he see the tears of joy and heartfelt thanks glistening in her eyes at sight of the return signal.

EPILOGUE

Five full years had elapsed since the night the military rescue helicopters had plucked the surviving members of the troupe from the mountains of Bosnia. And on this fine autumn day, Cil sat idling on a rock in the glade at the rustic upstate New York estate, watching the small boy skipping pebbles into the stream.

"Daddy, is Aunty really really coming today? *Will she* bring me that puppy she promised? Will she, huh—will she?"

The look of delicious expectation on the little boy's face evoked a smile from his father, and the question took Cil back.

A few months after the mission—when Michelle had recovered from emergency surgery and the tumor (benign, thank God) successfully been removed from her brain—Colonel Anastasi, true to form, had assembled the survivors at a plush hotel in Monte Carlo on the French Rivera for an epic reunion, a location suitable to the colonel's impeccable taste.

Cil, having received a warm yet noncommittal personal note of thanks and congratulations from Sonya, had gone to meet her where she had arranged to attend a discreet reception of dignitaries at the casino preceding her usual evening at the tables.

Cil found himself inside the entrance door of the elegant old casino, waiting among a small group of well-heeled regulars talking and smoking before a night at the tables. Any moment now she would appear.

Suddenly the sleek, long black limousine pulled into view beyond the entrance door. At once, a brass band struck up a lively tune; photographers bustled in through the entrance to take up their positions. And then, after all the years....

There—there she was, coming through the grand entrance. She was tall, exquisitely poised before the flash of the cameras, dressed in ermine and pearls and looking even younger and more radiant than he had remembered. And immediately he noticed the way she picked him out of the crowd, the old twinkle of recognition in her eyes.

And now here she came, striding straight toward him, almost as if they were alone, as if it were yesterday. She came on with that familiar, slightly regal toss of the head, her eyes trained only on him, and the sight of her white even teeth breaking into a widening smile.

But then something strange happened, something amiss that caught him off guard. As she approached, she was suddenly not looking at him, but at a stranger, an older man on the stairway behind, the man distinguished looking, short, with pink cherubic cheeks and a singularly regal appearance. And then Cil realized with a start that she had not been looking at him at all, had not even noticed him, but was walking right by and on up the steps as if somehow he had never existed.

For a second, as she greeted the older man on the stairs, Cil heard that voice, soft yet vibrant, holding just that form of intimacy he had known so long ago. "Good evening, Prince. So kind of you to come down."

Undaunted, Cil mounted the steps and approached her.

Taking her lightly but firmly by the elbow, he guided her into a small private room above. And when they found themselves alone, she turned to him.

"Oh, Laney!" She paused, and for an instant one delicate hand reached up and hovered indecisively at her throat as a confused expression of love and compassion mixed with guilt flitted across her fine noble features. "It has been so long. I—I'm so sorry. I meant...."

"I saw you downstairs."

"Yes," she said. I, too, saw...." Then swiftly her composure returned, her voice calm and distant, almost formal. "You must join us upstairs—at the private tables. You must meet my husband."

Cil stood silent for a moment. And then he passed her a kind, yet knowing smile. "No," he said firmly. "I've had my fill of roulette for a lifetime. Actually, I came only to tell you the news."

"News?"

"You remember—how was it you once put it?" he said. "Well, anyway, I finally decided 'to marry above' myself." He then reached swiftly under his suitcoat, withdrew a solid, shiny object from the band at his waist and handed Sonya the stubby broken sword he had carried so long and so far.

For a moment, Cil watched his son stuggle to throw a stone too large and too thick to skip on the surface of the stream, the boy's head of soft curls jostling with the effort. And Cil recalled the events that had followed on the heels of that one last mission.

Secretary Levitt had seen to it that both Cil and his co-operative on the first mission were quietly exonerated on the public record. Further, Cil and Michelle were officially recognized for their contribution to the success of the recent Bosnian mission, both accepting their Presidential citations in an official, if private, ceremony in the East Room of the White House (not the more public Rose Garden).

In their own good time, Michelle and Cil were quietly married in a simple ceremony at the chapel above her father's vineyards outside Bordeaux, France, just as Michelle had planned, the wedding attended by both families and the other survivors of the mission. Even Bogey made a special trip away from her busy medical practice in a Sarajevo at last free of panic and shelling.

The joint Bosnian-Croat military offensive to recapture those portions of the Croatian and northwest Bosnian Krajina, overrun early in the war by the Bosnian Serbs, had amounted to a blitzkrieg. With the southern flank of the Croat military thrust protected by the flooding of the Neretva River, vital Serb reinforcements were prevented from moving up from the south at the critical moment. Within the space of three weeks, the lion's share of the Krajina was reconquered and placed under the protection of the Croat-Bosnian Muslim Confederation, thus paving the way for a peace agreement.

In the years that followed, once the dam had been reconstructed by friendly hands, Zeljko, Ari, the Professor, and Nedo, rewarded by the townspeople for ridding their land of hostile forces, were appointed to operate the great dam and extended the personal use of all that land west and south of the lake, including Bald Hill, the south ridge, and the land which the enemy encampment had formerly occupied, such right granted in perpetuity. But in truth, while the Professor and Nedo had joined forces to see after the dam and raise sheep and goats and cultivate the land, old Zelko had spurned all attempts at taming his spirit. Instead, any day could he be seen contentedly roaming his hills and mountains, gun in hand, hard on the heels of a wild boar or bear or thickly antlered buck—or, on occasion, the resentful Serb who ventured too close to his land. And on the odd day, lest he lose his edge, the old man could be found chasing down one of the wayward gypsies, Chipmunk or One-Eye, or haggling with the belligerent Slobo over one disputed pasture or another, the mountain commander, once hostilities ceased, having resumed control over his domain in the hills to the east.

Ari, the Professor, stranded within the shaft when the first blast and breakthrough came, had been propelled out of the shaft by the torrent of water as if shot from the mouth of a cannon. Only by the grace of God and the limb of a friendly tree overhanging the river had he survived, albeit with a left leg badly mangled in the process. And for the remainder of his days would he suffer from rheumatism of the knee joint as a constant reminder of the gift conveyed from on high.

Crazy Ivan, never fully able to master the English language, lived comfortably with Cil and Michelle, tending the domestic animals about the grounds of their home, instructing their young son in the art of fishing and military drill, and generally doting upon the boy in whom he took a boastful pride. In his spare moments, which were few, he would help out as well in small tasks about the growing ski area the couple had purchased with the colonel's insistent backing, and later scrupulous oversight, the ski mountain situated only a few miles up the hill from the rambling New York estate.

Yet, at no time did Ivan's countenance reflect greater pride than one day when Colonel Anastasi, reading the paper, broke into a sudden rage. The colonel, slapping the table with his open hand, announced the name of the newly appointed Russian Minister of Defense—none other than that revered old general, Nikolai Kerenofsky.

"Come on now, Little Marko," declared Cil, climbing to his feet and taking his pint-sized son by the hand. "Get a move on. You don't want to be late the minute mamma pulls in with Aunty Sonya."

"Daddy, remember that town you grew up in, where Grandma and Grandpa used to live. You know, where you used to take me to your old sugaring-off house in the woods with those old buckets and all the neat cool tools for making maple syrup, and all like you see in a museum. Well—can we go back there sometime? Can we—can we?"

Cil abruptly looked away. "It's a long way, Marko."

"Not so far—really."

Cil was looking off as if his gaze were trying to penetrate to some far distant point.

"You know, son," he said, his words flat and measured, "it seems more and more to me like the other side of the world."